"A delightfully tricky tale of **M**
A **page-turner** that's also grea
M. G. LEON

"*The Great Fox Illusion* is a **glittering tale** of magic and mystery, trust and tricks, friendship and family. Let Justyn Edwards take you behind the scenes of a world of magic and illusion, on a **mind-bending adventure** to find the truth. Reading this brilliant book is like opening a **magician's box of tricks** and discovering their secrets for yourself."

THOMAS TAYLOR

"*The Great Fox Illusion* is **magic**! A page-turning mystery about family, friendship and magic tricks, told with real **panache** and **pizzazz**."

CHRISTOPHER EDGE

"This book did a **vanishing trick** on me – I didn't reappear until I'd read the very last page! A **spectacular, page-turning mystery** that will have you guessing until the very end. I can't wait to see what other stories Justyn Edwards has up his (magician's) sleeve!"

CLARE POVEY

The Great Fox Illusion

JUSTYN EDWARDS

WALKER
BOOKS

First published 2022 by Walker Books Ltd
87 Vauxhall Walk, London SE11 5HJ

2 4 6 8 10 9 7 5 3 1

This book has been typeset in Stempel Schneidler

Printed and bound by CPI Group (UK) Ltd, Croydon CR0 4YY

British Library Cataloguing in Publication Data:
a catalogue record for this book is available from the British Library

ISBN 978-1-5295-0194-0

www.walker.co.uk

For Rachel and Josh

This book is a trick. Please don't trust it or sit back and enjoy it. In fact, don't take your eyes off it for a second, because by the end of the story I'll have vanished from a room hidden deep underground, surrounded by security guards and dozens of cameras, beneath a burning house, with a very valuable secret. A lot of extremely clever people will have tried to stop me and they will all have failed.

The question is, will you be able to work out how I did it?

There will be plenty of clues throughout this book to help you. Be assured that, like all tricks, there's a perfectly logical explanation. If you get it right and you're good at solving these kinds of problems, we'll probably ask you to join us. We will need your help for what's coming next.

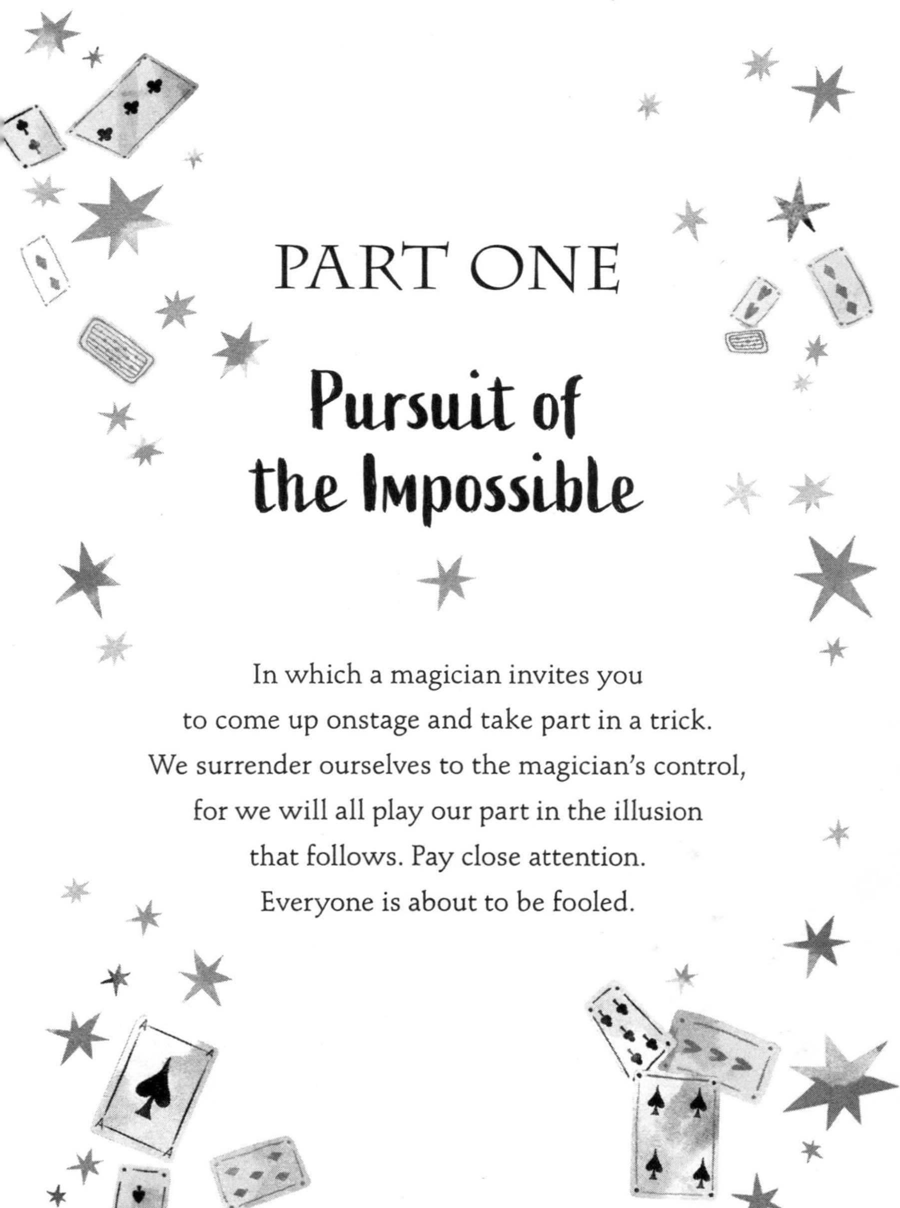

PART ONE

Pursuit of the Impossible

In which a magician invites you
to come up onstage and take part in a trick.
We surrender ourselves to the magician's control,
for we will all play our part in the illusion
that follows. Pay close attention.
Everyone is about to be fooled.

1

The Robbery

Few robberies are advertised. Thieves don't broadcast their crimes on TV or put up huge signs telling everyone what they're about to do. Some might occasionally wave banners at music festivals, but as a rule, criminals don't normally like to attract attention.

And yet.

Flick was looking at a sign. Advertising a robbery. That would happen on live TV.

Admittedly, it didn't use the word *robbery*. You had to read between the lines, but it was obvious where this was going.

The banner draped over the gates said:

WELCOME TO THE GREAT FOX HUNT

ENTER THE FOX'S DEN AND UNCOVER ITS SECRETS

The Great Fox Hunt was a new TV show about solving the hidden tricks in a dead magician's house. It was hosted by another magician who clearly just wanted to get his hands on his rival's illusions. It was a robbery.

Flick stood with her mum in a long queue of people hoping to be part of the show. Now and then, they would edge forward with Flick wheeling her suitcase behind her. When she eventually arrived at the front, there was a makeshift table and behind it sat a man with a beard, a lot of tattoos and a heavy dose of boredom.

He shoved a form at Flick. "Fill this out."

Was that a Daffy Duck tattoo on his arm? Unless Daffy was a big part of his life, that might be one to regret.

He chucked a pen at Flick and stifled a yawn.

She carefully put her details in the right boxes. All the important facts: Felicity Lions, female, thirteen years old, address, not a huge Daffy Duck fan. Not even his early watercolour work.

And now was the moment where this could all go wrong. To be honest, this was one of many moments that could end in disaster, but these next few seconds would be crucial. Would they recognize her name? Flick could feel her heart beating in her chest and her hands shook as she passed the sheet of paper back.

The man looked at it.

Flick waited, half expecting him to reach under the table and set off some sort of alarm. Maybe a warning light would flash or a distant klaxon would sound.

But nothing happened.

Instead he examined the form as if he'd never seen words before. Which was possible. Then he stamped it, tossed Flick a numbered badge and used the same empty smile he'd tried on everyone else.

Glancing down, he added, "Will you be requiring special—"

Flick shook her head. "Nah. I'll be fine."

He put the sheet in the out tray, collected and labelled her suitcase and waved her through.

Welcome to *The Great Fox Hunt.*

Her mum gave her a big hug. "A final goodbye," she said.

Flick smiled. "Haven't we had at least six of these?"

"Just remember," her mum said, disengaging from the hug. "Be careful."

"I will."

"Andar com um amigo no escuro é melhor que caminhar sozinho na luz. 'Walking with a friend in the dark is better than walking alone in the light.' That's what my mother always said to me."

Flick laughed. "Because all the best wisdom comes in Portuguese."

"I'm being serious." She fussed over Flick's badge. "Ask for help if you need it. You don't have to do everything alone."

"I will."

"This is better." Her mum reattached the pin and stepped back. "And promise you'll have fun."

"Now that my badge is straight, how can I fail?"

"I want you to make the promise."

Flick nodded. "I promise."

"Good."

Flick hugged her mum one last time. "Love you," she said.

"You too."

Flick let go. "Now, I've got a competition to win." She blew her mum a kiss and turned, heading towards the entrance. She passed through the impressive gates and followed the path that wound its way towards a large tent. On either side of her were gardens filled with dozens of flower beds and several lawns framed by tall trees. It was a damp day and the trees had a mist hanging over them. Here and there a few remaining leaves clung to the branches. Soon they would all have to let go as autumn became winter.

Arriving at the tent, Flick found it full with a couple of hundred hopefuls, all chatting away. At the front, there was a large screen and a stage with a podium. Flick chose a seat towards the back and sat down, relieved to take the weight off her leg.

She tuned into the conversations going on around her. Everyone was excited. Some were worried about how difficult the competition would be; others were hoping to become TV stars. Flick was probably the only person in the tent who knew what was really going on. Like all good tricks, the people behind this one had created a brilliant distraction.

They were it.

2

The Last Trick

The lights in the tent dimmed and a film of the Great Fox onstage started playing on the screen. A voice-over said: "Famous man of mystery the Great Fox performed his final trick six weeks ago at his Las Vegas show. After revealing to the rapt audience that he was terminally ill with only a few weeks left, he stepped into a wooden cabinet and vanished into thin air. Was this just another publicity stunt from the master of the headline-grabbing illusion? Or was he being straight with his audience for once? The only thing we know for certain is that after the performance, his show, which has run for six years, was immediately cancelled and no one has seen him since."

The footage cut to shots of the Fox's website.

"The Great Fox has always had a knack for publicity and it seems that being dead hasn't slowed him down. Last weekend, a mysterious video appeared announcing a competition. He died leaving no heirs, but it seems he was keen to pass on his secrets."

Flick leant forward as they started showing pictures of the house.

"For the past five years the Great Fox lived as a recluse in this three hundred acre estate located outside the seaside town of Weymouth in Dorset. He always had an affinity with the town, having performed his very first magic show here, as a teenager, as part of an end of pier act. Early in his career, he vowed that if he ever made it big he would return to Weymouth and buy the derelict old mansion near by. Decades later, he realized his dream. He is rumoured to have spent millions on the property, employing teams of builders to restore its features and carry out vast highly secret alterations. What exactly went on in the house has since been the subject of much speculation, especially after the Great Fox surrounded it with a twenty-foot military fence and made anyone involved sign a gag order."

There were more shots of the Fox at awards

ceremonies. The voice-over continued: "Such secrecy was typical of the Fox. No one ever saw his face. Some claimed he was heavily disfigured in an accident when he was a child, others that he had a large facial scar. There are no known photos of him because his real name remains a mystery even today. Those who met him said his piercing blue eyes could be seen through the mask he always wore."

Shots of the Fox ducking into a car were shown, seemingly taken through a blurry zoom lens.

"He hadn't been interviewed in years and, apart from his appearances onstage, the only time he'd been seen in public recently was in court. In June of this year the magician Dominic Drake filed a suit against the Great Fox over the rights to a new trick. Drake claimed that the Fox had stolen the concept of the illusion from him and was suing him for intellectual property theft. The Great Fox strongly denied such claims.

"The court case was conducted behind closed doors because of the sensitive nature of the hearing, with both magicians concerned about their secrets becoming public. As a result, very little is known about the trick at the heart of the dispute, except that it was described by Drake as the 'ultimate illusion', and by the Great

Fox as 'probably the greatest magic that has ever been performed'. The only piece of information that has been leaked to the media is that it is known as the Bell System."

And there it was. Flick's reason for being there. She could vividly remember the moment her father told her he'd invented the Bell System. He'd said it was an illusion that would change the history of magic. And then, because life can be cruel, it had ended up in the hands of the Great Fox. But Flick would put that right. She would get it back. Somehow.

3
The Last Message

The film ended and a blonde woman in a dark business suit stepped onto the stage. As she addressed the audience, she looked down on them, in every way.

"We've run out of space so you're the lucky ones." She beamed into the microphone and laughed like this was the funniest thing in the world. "My name is Christina Morgan. You probably recognize me from my summer glove slash mitten modelling campaign, and extensive radio adverts."

At the front, there were some cheers. Flick decided to keep her joy in check.

Christina held up her hands as if afraid a riot might break out, and the audience quietened. She put on her best serious face. It was an incredible thing to watch – slight scowl, pursed lips, head slightly forward. Ideal for local radio.

"So, here we are in the grounds of the Fox's Den, where four lucky contestants will compete in pairs over the next few days." She pointed dramatically at the audience, towards the expectant faces. "Just think, two teams will race each other to solve a series of fiendishly difficult puzzles and uncover the amazing secrets of this mysterious house."

Yes, shock news. Someone entering the competition would win it.

Christina's expression transitioned from serious to earnest – raised eyebrows, head tilted to one side, lips turned slightly down. "Finishing first will give you an opportunity to change your life for ever."

Well, that was probably true. What was about to happen would certainly make a huge difference to Flick's life.

"So let's get started. What I'm about to play you are the last known words of the Great Fox. Pay close attention. From now on, everything should be treated as a clue to unlocking the Fox's Den and all the extraordinary secrets it contains."

The Great Fox appeared on the screen wearing his trademark fox mask and standing in what looked like a library with rows and rows of books behind him. He spoke directly into the lens.

"If you're watching this, it means I've performed my last vanishing trick. I won't be reappearing. Don't be sad; don't mourn me. I've had an amazing life and been very fortunate to perform illusions all over the world. I leave behind me six series of *The Great Fox Presents* and two series of *Fox Night* – and let's not forget my *Fantastic Fox* show in Vegas that ran for six years. It's been a blast."

He paused as if remembering some special moments. "Nothing lasts for ever. But let's get down to business. The big problem I have is that I've no one to inherit my legacy. I have no children, and most of my more distant family don't like me. And yet I have a lot of very valuable secrets. I want these to go to someone worthy. Hence *The Great Fox Hunt.*

"For the last five years, I've had teams of builders in my house following my designs. What I've constructed is a series of tests to find someone who deserves my legacy. Think of it as a giant treasure hunt! The most important rule of the hunt is this: no one over fourteen can take part. This is the age I was when I first got into magic. It's a very special age. I want the person who wins my treasures to still have the imagination to introduce my magic to a new generation. I want someone young enough to dream big and not be constrained by commercial concerns or limited by an adult perspective."

He hesitated, choosing his next words carefully. "Magic is about dreaming the impossible and making it possible. It's the innocent young mind in all of us that loves it. We want to be filled with wonder; we want to believe. I want the winners of this competition and the recipients of my legacy to dare to dream big. So, let *The Great Fox Hunt* begin. I wish everyone who takes part the very best."

The film ended and the screen faded to black.

Christina faced the audience. "We're very pleased at Channel Seven to have won the rights to make *The Great Fox Hunt* into a TV show. We hope that the winners will go on to become stars of the future. With all the Fox's tricks, they'll certainly have everything they need. The Great Fox listed his career highlights in that video, but maybe his best show will be the one he'll never get to see. And you could be the star!"

There was some more cheering from the first few rows. Flick rolled her eyes. Where had they found these people?

"Let's start the selection process. It's a very simple concept, but very hard to crack. This will test you, so I hope you're all ready!" Christina flashed her blindingly white teeth like she'd once seen a photograph of someone smiling and now thought she'd have a go. "But you'd better get used to being tested because this competition will only get harder."

She paused again to laugh.

Just get on with it, Flick thought.

"You're about to see a magic trick. After you've watched it, we'll interview each of you and ask how you think it was done. From those who get it right, four of you will be chosen to enter the Fox's Den."

This statement was not met by manic cheering, just a lot of muttering. Someone near by threw up his arms and shouted, "What? No way! Too hard."

Flick, on the other hand, didn't think it sounded very hard at all. Her dad was a highly skilled magician and he'd taught her all his secrets. He was a better performer than the Great Fox had ever been, and she was certain she could easily work out how any trick was done. Not that she cared about winning the stupid competition. She wasn't interested in the Fox's legacy. The Great Fox had destroyed her family, and a man who'd done such a thing didn't deserve a successor. She was going to search that house and find the Bell System, the trick her father had invented, something that was rightfully hers, something that the Fox had stolen from her family, denying her a legacy and taking away a piece of her father. She was going to get it back. Because the Bell System was her only hope of saving him.

The Great Fox and Flick's father had been rivals, performing similar magic acts on the same tour circuits. Years ago, her dad had had a big show on Blackpool Pier and the Fox had been performing in London. Channel Seven visited both shows but chose the Fox to front their new TV project. Her dad's contract at Blackpool expired at the end of the season and he was replaced by a punk magic act. The Great Fox went on to receive rave reviews for his TV show.

Flick knew her dad had been just as good a magician as the Great Fox, but the chief executive at Channel Seven had disagreed. Later she found out that the chief executive's sister had been dating the Fox at the time, which surely wasn't a coincidence. After that everyone wanted to book the Fox and her dad's career took a nosedive. As the years went by, her father struggled to find work, and recently it seemed as if no one had wanted to book him at all. Finally after one very poorly supported small-scale show three months ago, he had disappeared. He'd packed his bag and walked out of their lives.

The Great Fox had destroyed her family as surely as if he had pulled a trigger.

A couple of months before he walked out, her dad had told her he'd invented the Bell System. He was so excited to have created something that he believed was a game changer. He'd said it was his last chance. But he had no show, nowhere to perform his vision and no means of making it a reality. So he'd sent it to the Great Fox and begged for his help in promoting it. And it had to still be here, inside the Fox's house. It would end up being bundled up with all the other tricks and given to whoever won the competition. Flick had to stop that happening. She was determined to find the Bell System, for her father. If he knew she had it, he might come home.

Her mission wouldn't be easy. There weren't many female magicians, and there were even fewer one-legged female magicians. In order to win this she didn't just need to be better than her male, two-legged colleagues. She needed to be a hundred times better. But the Bell System was her chance to save her family and no one was going stop her.

The lights in the tent dimmed and hundreds of intense faces became transfixed by the big screen.

Flick sat forward. She didn't want to miss a single detail of what was about to unfold.

4

The Blended Phone

The screen showed a magician on a chat show. In front of him were three stools. On two of them rested black bags; the other held a pile of envelopes. The magician borrowed a phone from another guest, then handed a knife to the show's host and told her to have it ready for later.

The magician took the borrowed phone and placed it inside one of the small brown envelopes from the pile and sealed the flap. He explained to the guest that it was very important he remembered which envelope his phone was in, because the three other envelopes held decoys – a bit of aluminium and plastic – the same size and weight as the phone. He produced a spare decoy from his pocket and threw it onto the floor to demonstrate its weight. The dummy phone skidded across the studio.

The magician explained that to prevent the envelopes from being mixed up, he was going to put a clear mark on the one that contained the guest's phone. As he said this, he drew a big black cross on the envelope with a marker pen. Unfortunately, he revealed, the other envelopes also had a cross on them.

The audience laughed as he held up the envelopes, all with identical black crosses drawn on them.

Having shuffled the envelopes so that no one knew which one contained the real phone, the magician asked the guest to select one. The other three he placed back on the stool.

The guest looked doubtfully at his envelope, clearly hoping it contained his phone.

The magician announced that they were now going to play a game of "find the phone". He produced a hammer and held it over the remaining three envelopes. There were murmurs and laughs in the audience as the magician viciously smashed the hammer down on them. Next, he lifted up the black bag on the first stool to reveal a blender, and he threw the envelopes into it. There was a terrible crunching noise as he pressed the start button. Within seconds the contents were reduced to pulp.

The guest now looked close to panic, but the magician reassured him that he had every confidence the guest had picked the right envelope. He called for a round of applause and asked the guest to open his envelope and hold up his phone in triumph.

The audience clapped as the guest opened his envelope. Inside was a decoy. He did not look happy.

The magician glanced nervously at the blender. Then he had an idea. He grabbed the other black bag from the second stool and pulled out a large honeydew melon.

The guest looked confused.

Seeing where this was going, the chat show host brandished the knife she was still holding, and the magician took it and sliced open the melon. Pulling the fruit apart, he revealed a phone in the centre, nestled inside a clear plastic bag.

People started to clap but the magician held up his hands, interrupting the applause. After all, he said, it could be anyone's phone in the melon. He invited the guest to check the phone was his. The guest examined it carefully and sounded very relieved to confirm it was indeed his phone. The magician breathed a theatrical sigh of relief and the studio erupted into thunderous applause.

5

The Rules of a Good Trick

The screen faded and the lights in the tent returned.

Christina reappeared at the podium. "That's the trick." She laughed. "Pretty easy to work out how it's done? I don't think so. Next, we'll call you one at a time for your solutions. Remember to make them as detailed as possible."

She sauntered off the stage, pausing briefly to acknowledge the crowd. No one even looked in her direction because the tent had erupted into excited chatter.

The two boys in the seats next to Flick immediately started complaining. The one wearing a black hoodie turned to his friend in a stripy jumper and said, "This is impossible."

"Contestant number one," a voice boomed, "make your way to door one, please. Contestant number two to door two, please. Number three to door three, and four to door four. Thank you."

They were only seeing four people at a time. Flick folded her arms and made herself comfortable. This was going to take ages.

Stripy Jumper nodded in agreement and said to Hoodie, "The whole point of a trick is that you can't tell how it's done. Otherwise there would be no point in doing it."

Hoodie sat back and folded his arms. "This is pointless."

At the front of the tent, two of the contestants had climbed up onto the stage and were performing a little magic show of their own to the first few rows. They looked like brother and sister. The boy was tall and pale and had a mass of curly light blond hair, almost white. His sister was shorter but with the same curly hair and colouring. The boy had just performed a string of card tricks which had earned him a lot of cheering, and now he was making some solid metal rings interlock and then break apart.

Flick was squinting to see if she could spot the gaps

in the rings when another announcement boomed, "Contestant five to door one, please."

"You see," said Hoodie. "They've made it too hard. That guy was only in there for a couple of seconds. Just long enough to say he didn't have a clue, and then they kicked him out. No one is going to get this."

"Someone might," Flick muttered, and then realized she might have said it a little too loudly.

Hoodie turned to her. "Yeah? If you're so smart, how's it done, then?"

Flick didn't really want to get into a conversation.

He glared. "Go on then."

"Well," said Flick. "Just think about the parts of the trick that stand out."

"What, like the phone magically teleporting inside a melon?"

"No, I mean things that don't seem necessary."

He looked blank.

"Why does the melon need to be in a bag?"

Hoodie shrugged. "So he can reveal each part as he goes along? Because he felt like putting it in one?"

"Nothing in a good trick is done just because someone feels like it. The bag was there for a reason."

"So that's it? That's the clue to how it was done?"

“Part of it. The other stand-out moment is that he throws a dummy phone on the floor.”

Hoodie frowned. “He does. But that doesn’t tell me much.” He turned back to his friend. “She thinks she’s worked it out. Bet she hasn’t.”

Flick settled back into her chair. She would find out soon enough.

6

The First Door

Flick was called about an hour later and exited the tent through door one. She followed a roped path to a Portakabin. As she arrived, the door opened and a bald man from the production crew asked, "Felicity Lions?"

She nodded.

He beckoned her inside. "Come in."

He held the door as she slowly climbed the steps. The cabin was a tiny space after the huge tent, and the large spotlights in each corner and the two men with cameras made it feel even more crowded. One pointed his lens at Flick as she walked in, while the other was busy filming Christina, who was sat behind a table.

"Welcome, Felicity," she said, with all the enthusiasm

of someone very aware they were on TV. "Please take a seat." She gestured with a long, elegant hand to a seat opposite her. "This is *The Great Fox Hunt*: interviews."

She actually said, "*The Great Fox Hunt* colon interviews." As if they were going to ask Flick's large intestine some questions.

"Were you a fan of the Great Fox?"

Flick resisted the urge to pretend she'd never heard of him. It would have been fun to watch Christina's overly zealous face drop. Instead she nodded.

"And did you enjoy the trick?"

"Yeah."

Truth was, Flick had felt quite emotional watching it. It was brilliant. The sort of trick she'd adored since she could remember. When she was younger, she'd spent months learning how to palm the top card off the deck – trying again and again and again until she got cramp. She'd always wanted to follow in her dad's footsteps. To pursue the impossible and try somehow to make it real.

It was that fire that had carried Flick through the loss of her leg. She'd been getting a lift back from a friend's house when a car had ploughed into the passenger side at a junction. Her injuries had been so extensive that her right leg had needed to be amputated below the knee. Over the following year, Flick had struggled to keep going. It was her love of magic that kept her moving forward – taking each step. If she could make the impossible real then maybe she could learn to walk again. Maybe she could even live a normal life.

Christina picked up on her expression. "It was a great trick, wasn't it?" She examined Flick's registration form. "No dad?" she probed.

"Haven't seen him in months."

"Oh. I'm so sorry." Christina's face instantly switched to extreme empathy.

Flick shrugged. "Saved money on Father's Day."

Christina started to laugh but hastily checked herself. It wasn't good to be seen laughing at such misfortune on TV. Instead she furiously concentrated on the form as if examining every atom.

"Why did you decide to enter the competition, Felicity?"

Flick paused. She wanted to say that her father was greater than the Great Fox and he had been cruelly denied the recognition he deserved. And that he was brilliant, and in the months before he left he had designed the most amazing trick that had ever been created. That only out of desperation had he shared it with the Great Fox, who'd promptly stolen it. That she was here to get it back.

But she didn't. "I've loved magic since I was six." Which was also true. And probably more like the answer they wanted.

Christina put the form down. "Well, I think we're OK to film your solution. So when you're ready, you can begin."

"Well..."

Christina nodded in encouragement.

Flick took a deep breath. "The magician takes the guest's phone and places it inside an envelope. But this envelope is different from the others, as it has a clear plastic bag inside it. So, when he puts the phone in, he also slides it into the bag – it's now ready for the end of the trick. The envelope also has a slit cut into the bottom. That's why he has to hold it so upright. This means that even though he seals the envelope, the phone easily slides out. When he talks about the dummy phones he drops his right hand, with the phone in it, to his side.

"At this point, he does a lot of distracting. While his hand is hidden behind his body he lets the phone drop out the bottom of the envelope and into a special pocket in the right side of his jacket. Now the envelope is empty.

Next he throws a dummy phone across the floor. This is also a great distraction. While everyone is looking away he drops his hand to his right side again and switches the empty envelope for one containing a dummy. This was stored in another hidden pocket in his jacket. All the envelopes now have dummy phones in them.

"Most of the trick is now done. He goes through the show of smashing and blending the envelopes, safe in the knowledge that the real phone is tucked away inside the bottom right flap of his jacket.

"At the end of the trick, he picks up the melon. Two questions to ask are why does the melon need to be in a bag and why do you only ever see the melon end on? The black bag is very important because it has a slit in it. When he picks it up he holds it in front of him. And as he does this, he removes the phone from the special pocket in his jacket and places it inside the black bag. The melon is hollowed out and has a slot cut into the bottom. He pushes the phone, in its clear plastic bag, up into the melon. This all happens inside the bag. He's very careful to always keep his hand over the end of the melon so we never see the slot. In fact, at the very end of the trick, he even puts the bottom half of the melon back into the bag so we never catch sight of it."

Christina opened her mouth.

Flick shrugged. "That's pretty much it."

After a couple of seconds, Christina said, "I watched that trick twenty-three times and... One moment."

She stood up and walked out of a door at the back of the cabin, returning about a minute later with a man who Flick recognized immediately as Dominic Drake. His grey hair, grey beard and bright green eyes had made him a hit with mums the world over. Flick had read articles that claimed he'd made magic sexy again. That was a matter of opinion. He was carrying his trademark silver cane and wearing a green shirt that made the colour of his eyes stand out even more.

"Leave us." Drake dismissed Christina and the cameramen.

"What do we have here then?" he asked.

Flick said nothing.

"Did you think you could fool me?"

Flick sat very still.

"Did you think you could just walk in here and no one would work out who you are?"

"I've not done anything wrong," Flick said. But her voice sounded like someone else was using it. And that person was very small. And a long way away.

"You're Samuel Lions's daughter, aren't you?"

Flick cleared her throat, hoping to get her voice back from the scared child who'd borrowed it.

"Yes," she managed.

"Your solution to the trick was perfect. That's exactly how it was done. And that wasn't one of your dad's, was it?"

"No."

He hesitated, working something out. Considering his options.

"We have several problems." He sighed. "Firstly, I don't think girls should even do magic. Girls make good assistants, but not showmen. The clue is in the name. It goes against the natural order. But beyond that, we can't have the daughter of a magician – not even if he's a failed magician – winning this competition. That wouldn't look good. So in theory I should throw you out. However..." He paused. "I'm going to cut you a deal. I'll let you stay in this competition if you do something for me."

He was smiling now, but there was no warmth. Gesturing to the back of the Portakabin, he said, "Follow me."

Flick stood up and followed him as he opened the door.

"After you," he said.

What Flick should have done at that point was run in the opposite direction. She should have turned and run and run and run as fast as her leg would carry her. But she didn't. Instead, like the fool she was, she stepped through the door.

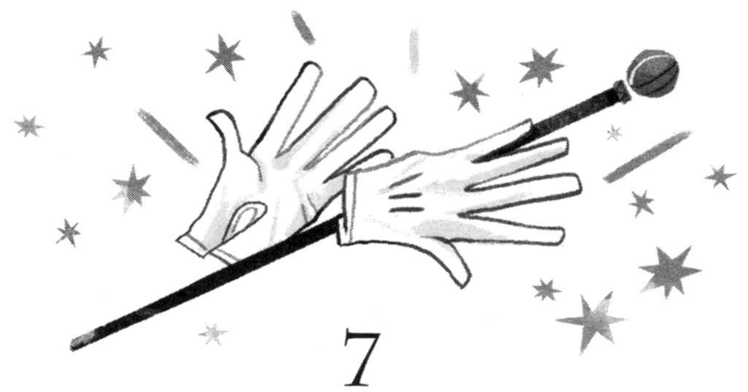

7

The Second Door

Flick found herself in a TV control room full of film crew with headsets and focused faces. In front of her was a wall of screens.

"You see there?" Drake pointed, in case she hadn't noticed the entire wall of TVs. The top row had close-ups of four contestants. She immediately recognized a shot of herself, sat in the tent with her arms folded. She had a bit of a double chin. Not her strongest look.

"Those are the contestants so far who've worked out the solution to the trick and will likely go through to the main competition."

Flick looked at the three other faces. Two girls and two boys. Nice and balanced. Very convenient.

"You're up there at the moment but whether you stay or not depends on the next few seconds." He fixed her with his lizard-green eyes, weighing her up, before he continued. "You see those two on the left, the fair-haired boy and girl?"

Flick studied their photos. Masses of curly almost-white hair and pale skin – the brother and sister who had been performing in the tent.

"They are both..." Drake trailed off as an engineer walked by. He waited until she was out of earshot before he continued in a quieter voice. "I have reason to believe they are working for Synergy. You've heard of them?"

Flick nodded thoughtfully to show she was paying attention.

"What do you know about them?"

"Synergy? Well, they're a group of street magicians. They've had three series now on PDEN. They do some pretty cool stuff. Looks very improvised, although of course it isn't. They did that famous flying over the Houses of Parliament trick as a climax to their last series."

"Very good." Drake smiled at her. "Now, I have no doubt that Synergy would be very interested in getting their hands on the secrets hidden in the Fox's Den."

Flick could just make out the children's names in small text at the bottom of the screen – Harry and Ruby Townsend.

"The plan is clearly that these two will win the competition and hand over the Fox's secrets to Synergy."

"Isn't that against the rules?" Flick asked.

He laughed. "It is against the rules," he said, in a tone you would use for a small child. "But once someone has won, it's very hard legally to control what they do with their winnings. They will be able to do whatever they want with it. And my bet is they'll give it all to Synergy."

A couple of the camera crew had strayed a little too close, so Drake put his hand on Flick's shoulder and ushered her into a corner where no one would overhear them.

"Now," he whispered into her ear. "I would like you to do something similar for me. I'll let you be in this competition if, when you win it, you give me one of the secrets you find."

Flick opened her mouth to say something and then thought better of it.

"You need to remember that once you're in that house, everything you do will be filmed and recorded, so you can't talk to anyone about this. No one. If you do, there will be consequences."

"What if I say no?"

"Then you don't make it through and you go home today. Is that what you want?"

"And I give you all the tricks?"

"No. Listen to what I say. You can keep all of them apart from one. What you win will set you up as a magician for life. You'll have all his secrets, all his illusions, everything. Except the Great Fox's last trick: one suitcase-sized wooden box. The Bell System. You need to give that to me."

Flick felt like she'd been punched in the stomach.

8

The Art of a Good Trick

The secret of a good trick is to claim you'll do something so outrageous that people can't help but watch, even if only to see you fail. If you tell the right story, your audience will be hooked, and the rest is all about the performance – controlling their attention, directing where they look and what they feel. Making the impossible possible.

That was what Flick needed to do now. The only way she could get the Bell System was to promise to give it to Dominic Drake. If she could pull this off it would make sawing a woman in half look easy. It would require the mother of all tricks.

Flick was escorted back to the tent by a member of the production crew, where she found a seat at the back and flopped down. What was she going to tell her mum? She would be thrilled that Flick was one of only four contestants to be selected. Flick couldn't explain to her that the only way she could compete was to agree to cheat. To agree to help Drake steal her father's last trick.

Flick waited in the tent for the final few contestants to be called, guilt gnawing away inside her. There were a couple of camera crews circling, filming the contestants as they waited. Two cameramen were lapping up the Harry and Ruby show on the stage, which now seemed to be on its fifth encore. Flick hoped they'd saved some material for their future TV careers. One of the crew had clearly been ordered to get plenty of material on her. They were trying to be subtle but the lens spent a lot of time panning in her direction. She suddenly realized her mum would see this, and she had an amazing skill at knowing when something was wrong. So Flick swallowed down the guilt, pushing the lie deeper so not even a chink of it would show.

She hoped she didn't look too sick.

When she didn't think she could wait any longer, Christina finally reappeared on the stage, and Flick breathed a sigh of relief.

Christina whooped into the microphone. "I'd like you all to put your hands together, please, to welcome someone very special. Ladies and gentlemen … boys and girls … I give you … my co-host … MR … DOMINIC … DRAKE!"

Drake strode onto the stage waving his cane triumphantly and grabbed the microphone from Christina, nearly knocking her over.

He pointed at her as he said, "Thank you. Give her a big round of applause. My assistant, the lovely Christina Morgan. Didn't she do well?"

Christina's face was full plastic smile, but her eyes gave her away.

Drake continued, "I'm going to reveal to you all, right now, who worked out the trick correctly and will be entering the Fox's Den."

A member of the production crew walked on and handed him a golden envelope, which he opened with an exaggerated flourish.

"We have a couple of hundred of you here today. But out of all of you, only the following four have been successful." He paused for effect, staring deadpan into the camera. Music with a rhythm like a heartbeat played as the tension built and built. Drake continued to stand there for what felt like a lifetime.

Finally he announced, "In no particular order, the winners are..."

The music changed key and the rhythm got stronger. Some children were on their feet now, shouting, but still Drake paused.

Eventually he said, "Harry Townsend, Ruby Townsend, Charlie Riley and Felicity Lions."

The audience erupted into yells and groans of disappointment as people realized their names were not on the list. This was punctuated with pockets of joy as others gathered around the winners.

Flick sat very still and felt a bit sick.

Drake had to shout to be heard over the noise. "Can those four please come on up to the stage?"

Without warning, Flick was gently pulled to her feet by a member of the film crew and then propelled forward through the crowd towards the front. She passed one or two in the audience who were crying while their friends tried to console them – telling them the test was too difficult and it was pure luck the winners had got it right.

As Flick neared the front, Drake said, "I'll leave you in the capable hands of my assistant while I get this show started."

He disappeared off the stage, leaving Flick to wonder

how much he'd been paid for his five minutes' work.

She reached the steps to the stage and stopped. Stairs were not her thing, and she didn't want to fall over on TV, so she took them slowly, one at a time, holding on to the handrail and making sure both feet were on each step before she attempted the next one. The others were on the stage already and Christina awkwardly fiddled with the microphone while they all waited. Eventually Flick stepped up and joined them. All four contestants now stood in a line.

Christina advanced towards them. "The rules of the competition mean you will be split into two teams. That won't be a problem for you two, though, will it, as you're brother and sister, right?"

She shoved the microphone into the face of Harry Townsend. Up close, Flick could see how pale and skinny he was – like someone who'd spent a lot of time practising magic in his bedroom but never actually left it to perform. Or find sunlight.

Harry nodded. "That's right. Ruby and I are used to working together. We do all our magic shows as a double act."

Ruby nodded enthusiastically, gazing up at her brother.

Christina smiled. "Are you confident you can win this?"

Ruby grabbed the microphone and pulled it towards her. "Of course we're going to win."

Someone in the audience cheered. Clearly a fan.

Christina firmly eased the microphone back, keen to maintain control. "Well, we love a confident contestant, don't we?"

Sensing that Ruby could be a nightmare to interview, she quickly moved on to Charlie, asking, "Do you think you can win?"

Charlie had curly brown hair and was wearing blue denim dungarees. He planted his feet apart confidently and said, "I'm going to win because I'm teaming up with Flick, and she's quite a good magician. I've seen some of her stuff on YouTube and it's actually almost professional. I have every confidence that together we have the skills to win this and go on to have a career where she is the magician and I can be her assistant, and we can have our own TV show, and spin-off movies, and an action figure franchise, and those little toys they put in Happy Meals, and a Las Vegas show, and the show will have lasers and perhaps a disappearing tiger or two. And after the interval, we will—"

Christina pulled the microphone away. "Whoa. Thanks for letting us know your plans."

Finally she came to Flick.

"Charlie here is obviously quite a fan," she said. "Are you as excited to work with him as he is with you?"

Flick looked at Charlie's idiotic smile. "Not really."

"Fabulous," Christina continued. "Let's hear it again for our four contestants." She turned towards the audience with a sweeping gesture. "So now it's time for you to enter the Fox's Den. Let the competition begin."

Fireworks exploded from either side of the stage and the back of the tent dropped away to reveal a brightly lit path leading towards the house.

9

The Den

"Follow me," Christina said with an exaggerated wave.

Flick turned to Charlie and spoke quietly, barely moving her mouth. "You've seen my stuff on YouTube?"

"Your juggling chainsaws was good, although I could tell it was a fake arm. But most people probably wouldn't notice that, so, on balance, I would say it was a success, as was your close-up magic card trick and your—"

"You talk too much."

"You're not the first person to tell me that. Anyway, in my opinion, it was obviously a fake arm, and the trick could have been done better."

"The number of likes the video got says differently," Flick replied.

They were guided onto the path by a couple of production staff and started walking towards the house, Christina leading the way. A woman with a camera walked backwards ahead of them, filming from in front, while another two camera crew followed behind.

Christina suddenly stopped and turned. "Harry, be a gentleman and let Flick go first, so we all keep together."

Flick started to say, "It's not a prob—" but a cameraman gently pushed her to the front, and they all set off again at a slower pace, in single file, with Flick on the heels of Christina and Harry pressing in behind her. He nudged up close and shielded his mouth from the cameras as he whispered, "I'm glad you're not in my team. You'd just slow me down."

Flick bristled. "I'm quicker than you think."

He laughed. "Who're you kidding?"

The path veered left and flowed along the side of a moat that ringed the house, eventually coming to a pair of towers, complete with battlements. There were white flags with black fox head silhouettes flying from them.

The path passed between the two towers and up to the bank. On the far side of the water, it continued to the front entrance of the house. Christina led them down to the water's edge and they all lined up along the bank, staring across the gap. The water looked cold and sludgy.

"Here we are at your first test." Christina gave an elegant gesture towards the moat. "At this point, I'm to read you a message from the Great Fox."

There were now four cameras filming them from all angles. The wind tugged at Christina's hair and she kept having to tuck it behind her ear. It must be exhausting having to maintain perfection, Flick thought.

Christina cleared her throat. "The Great Fox's message to you is this: *To do well in this contest you will need belief. Are you brave enough to step across the void?*"

And then Flick realized there had to be a bridge across the moat, right in front of them. It was probably made of very clear Perspex – used a lot by magicians to "float" through the air or across water. She tilted her head, trying to get the light to catch it. It must be very good quality.

"Who's going to go first?" Christina asked.

Immediately Harry stepped forward. He puffed out his chest, but Flick could see his hands shaking as he stepped out into empty space. He even flinched a little as he lowered his foot and first made contact with the bridge, but once he was on it he quickly recovered and strode confidently to the other side.

Ruby went next, keen to keep up with her big brother.

Then it was the turn of Charlie and Flick.

"Do you want me to go with you?" Charlie whispered. "Just behind, in case you have a problem?"

Flick scowled. "I can walk." Although it was kind of him to ask. And he had asked in a very nice way.

She stepped onto the bridge. The effect was utterly disconcerting; even when she was on the Perspex she could barely see it. She tried not to look down or think about how much it would hurt her pride to fall. Instead Flick focused on the entrance of the house ahead of her. Just one foot in front of the other. Like when she was learning to walk again. She had spent months looking straight ahead and concentrating on keeping her balance, moving forward, pushing through the pain.

She was relieved when she finally got to the other side.

Charlie came next. "You OK?" he asked.

"Of course. Why wouldn't I be?" Flick hissed.

Christina brought up the rear and then bounded up to the large wooden doors and made a big show for the cameras of getting a massive ancient-looking key out, inserting it into the lock and throwing the doors open.

"Welcome to the Fox's Den!" she said, giving every one of her facial muscles a thorough workout.

Flick took a deep breath and stepped inside.

PART TWO

Vanishing a Lady

In which a magician shows you a house. The walls are solid, there is nothing out of the ordinary and everything is exactly as expected. Except, of course, we know none of that is true.

10
The Library

Christina, the four contestants and several members of the crew all filed through the front doors into a grand entrance hall. The floor was polished marble and there were deer antlers and large gold-framed portraits on the walls. In the middle of this vast space was an ornate wooden staircase.

A crew member with pink hair and a nose ring approached Flick and pinned a small microphone to her top. “You need to wear this all the time,” she ordered. “Remember to put it on every morning.”

The other contestants received the same instructions, and when everyone was ready, Christina stepped into the centre.

“This is the hallway,” she explained, beaming into the lens while a camerawoman panned around so fast that the sound guy struggled to keep his cables out of the way. “The Great Fox himself restored this magnificent staircase to its full glory. It is rumoured that some of the panels contain hidden spaces, although we’ve not found any yet. Feel free to press on them as we walk past. You might be the first to discover one.”

Harry, of course, wasted no time in running his hands over the staircase, pushing against various panels. Not that anything moved.

Ruby started up the stairs towards some of the hundreds of little panels further up.

“Not yet, little lady,” Christina called. “Our first stop is the library.”

“You’re not my mum; you don’t get to tell me what to do,” muttered Ruby as she clomped back down the stairs. “This is *our* puzzle to solve. How am I supposed to do that if I can’t go anywhere?”

Christina raised her eyebrows. “Hold your horses there. The library is where we’ll find your first clue. Once you’ve got that and I’ve shown you some of the basics of the house, you’ll be on your own, and then you can do as much exploring as you like.”

They turned right out of the entrance hall into a long corridor. Here the walls were covered in framed pictures of famous magicians. At first, there were old paintings and black and white photos, and then as they passed down the corridor, more colour shots began to appear. At the very end were faces Flick recognized.

"This corridor is the Fox's tribute to the history of magic. You'll find pictures of all the greats here."

On the left side of the passageway were several alcoves and it was at one of these that they stopped.

"The Fox has dedicated the alcoves to some of his favourite artists from history. This one, for example, is full of pictures of Houdini."

The alcove was big enough for them all to step into. Flick ran her eyes over the walls, taking it all in. There was a photo of Houdini about to jump into the Charles River in handcuffs and shackles; another of him being locked into a giant milk can; and, of course, one of him suspended upside down in his famous water torture cell.

Flick felt excited to see so many photos of famous individuals that she looked up to.

Harry just yawned and sighed.

Christina led them out of the alcove and on down the corridor. They passed a few other recesses filled with pictures, each lit up with spotlights, dedicated to David Devant, Lance Burton, James Randi, Penn and Teller, Apollo Robbins, David Blaine, Criss Angel and many others. Flick was thinking about the fact that almost every single one of these was a man – and a privileged white man at that – and wondering if she'd ever be worthy of an alcove as a one-legged girl, when she arrived at the end of the corridor and entered a grand library.

It was a huge room with every wall covered floor to ceiling in books. Here and there, ladders were attached to shelves to allow access to the higher areas. Flick's eyes were immediately drawn to some metallic semi-circular pods dotted around the room. They looked very modern and alien in such an ancient space.

It was to one of these pods that Christina led them. They gathered round.

"Although you will have access to every book in this library to help you to solve the puzzles, you'll find these pods invaluable. Each one has a set of virtual reality goggles and gloves. You'll also find the floor moves, so, although you sit down in them, you can move your feet to walk around the VR environment. And what these pods do is give you access to the Fox Files – a digital library that the Great Fox compiled of every trick and magic act ever known. If film footage of a magician exists, you'll find it on here, along with biographical information, schematics and diagrams of their creations and also plenty of 3D renderings of their tricks. Why don't you pick a pod and try it out?"

There were seven pods and only four of them, so they each picked one, climbed in and sat down. Flick put on the gloves and pulled the goggles down over her eyes. They had earphones for a fully immersive experience.

She was immediately presented with a screen that said:

WELCOME TO THE FOX FILES

Anything you've ever wanted to know about magicians and their tricks, and plenty of other stuff that no one cares about but me.

Study the greats and you'll learn to be great...

The voice of the Great Fox announced, "Welcome to the Fox Files. To get you used to using this equipment, why not try out the search facility."

A magnifying glass icon flashed in the top right-hand corner of the screen, so Flick reached up with her gloved hand and a cursor moved to the top of her vision. She tapped the icon.

The Great Fox said, "Very good. Now type in *Fox's Den* to see some information about this house."

A keyboard appeared and Flick moved her right hand around to type in *Fox's Den*. Information started to flash up in front of her.

Photos of the house through the ages scrolled across the screen, while a voice-over said: "Fox's Den is one of the last privately owned grand homes in Dorset. It was originally built by businessman Sir Edward Vaughan, who was sent to Fleet Prison in London in the 1770s for failing to pay his debts. The family managed to keep hold of the property and it was his grandson Charles who extended it by adding the east tower, billiard room and gallery, which housed his very extensive art collection. These expensive additions inevitably proved a stretch too far and the house was eventually abandoned, until it was bought by the Great Fox. It is said that when he took it over there was no glass in the windows, but there were still paintings on the walls and a tiger skin rug in front of the main fireplace. It seems the squatters who had been living there had even enjoyed eating off the fine bone china on the banquet dining table."

Footage of the hallway played as the voice-over continued. "The entrance hall at Fox's Den. Notice the fully restored staircase. The Great Fox is rumoured to have spent fifty thousand pounds renovating the woodwork."

And then the film moved on to the library. The camera swept over the many shelves and books.

"The library at Fox's Den is widely regarded as the largest collection of books on magical illusions in the world. It contains rare signed first editions of works by Houdini, and the diary and notebooks of Harry Blackstone Senior, an American magician famous during World War Two. He was best known for his floating light bulb trick. In a darkened theatre Blackstone would remove a light bulb from a lamp and float it above his hand. He would make it pass through a hoop and even out over the heads of the audience. It is thought that his notebooks contain many of his methods and secrets, some of which are still unknown today."

The film cut back to the hallway and ascended the stairs.

"The landing gallery has also been restored to its former glory. It contains a large quantity of Victorian art, as well as many other eclectic pieces. Probably the most valuable painting in the gallery is this picture by

Hieronymus Bosch called *The Conjurer.* The magician on the right of the painting captures his audience's attention with a game of cup and ball. The focus of the picture, however, is the man of rank in the centre who leans in and concentrates on the actions of the magician, unaware that his wallet is being stolen by the man behind him.

"Animals are used in the picture to depict human traits. The owl in the basket on the conjurer's belt symbolizes his intelligence; frogs jumping out of the mouth of the wealthy man signify his loss of reason and giving in to bestial impulses. Bosch was fond of using proverbs as the basis of his paintings. This one is thought to exemplify the Flemish proverb, 'He who lets himself be fooled by conjuring tricks loses his money and becomes the laughing stock of children.' It probably sounded snappier in the original language.

"The Great Fox declared in an interview when he purchased this artwork at Sotheby's that it was his favourite painting. 'It shows the true democracy of magic,' he explained. 'Both rich and poor are equally entertained.'"

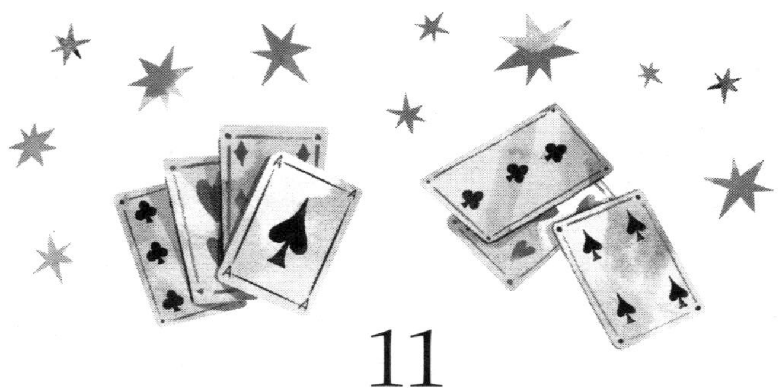

11
The Lady Disappears

Flick's vision went black and she was brought back to reality by Christina's voice.

"So, now you've all got an idea of how to use the Fox Files, it's time for the first clue."

Flick ripped her goggles off and blinked. The others were doing the same, and Harry was already on his feet by the time she'd removed her gloves.

Christina laughed. "That got your attention pretty quickly."

She walked towards the far end of the library and everyone followed. There was a small section with a TV screen on a stand between some shelves. They all gathered around and a clip started to play.

The Statue of Liberty was being filmed from a circling helicopter. The magician David Copperfield was narrating. "The statue is over three hundred feet tall, weighs two hundred and twenty-five tonnes, and tonight I'm going to make it disappear. I've constructed two scaffolding towers on Liberty Island and there will be a helicopter to give an aerial view of the illusion. There is a circle of spotlights at the base of the statue which will be shining on it at all times. A curtain will then be raised between the scaffolding towers. When it is lowered the statue will have disappeared. Searchlights will be shone through the space where the statue was just moments before. There will even be radar to show the location and disappearance of the statue. But most importantly, there will be a live audience watching the moment unfold."

The film cut to a view of the statue from the perspective of the audience. At Copperfield's command, the curtain was raised. He then walked over to the radar screen and passed his hands over the dot marking the statue's position. It vanished from the screen and the magician returned to stand in front of the curtain. The curtain was lowered and, as promised, the Statue of Liberty had disappeared.

Searchlights played over the empty space as the helicopter circled. The audience cheered wildly. The film cut back to the view from the helicopter – the ring of searchlights was still there, but in the centre was an empty space. The audience gave him a standing ovation. Copperfield took in the moment and then asked for the curtain to be raised once again. When it was lowered, the statue had returned.

The screen faded to black and the following words appeared:

THE LADY VANISHES,
BUT HOW IS IT DONE?

UNDERSTAND THE METHOD
AND YOU'LL FIND DOOR ONE.

Ruby turned up her nose. "We're supposed to work it out from that?"

"I'm afraid that's all you'll be getting," said Christina. "The Great Fox is looking for someone smart to inherit his legacy. Which brings me to one other vital bit of information. Everything relating to this specific trick has been removed from the Fox Files. So it's no good you plugging yourself into one of those pods and searching the database for this particular trick. What you'll need to do is look at other similar tricks and work out what method could have been used."

Harry tutted.

"And if you follow me over here," Christina continued, "we have our scoreboard."

They crossed to the far wall, where there was a large stone fireplace. Several logs were burning away and there was a good heat coming from the glowing embers. In front of the hearth was a collection of red leather wingback armchairs and above the mantelpiece, surrounded by a gold picture frame as if it were a painting, was a flat-screen TV. On this were the words:

SCOREBOARD

Harry and Ruby: 0

Felicity and Charlie: 0

Christina pointed at it with one beautifully manicured finger. "And there are our two teams. You'll be awarded points for solving each puzzle and there'll be bonus points for finding extra clues along the way. If both teams have the same number of points at the end of the competition, the winners will be the team who solved the most clues first."

The fire crackled as sparks disappeared up the chimney.

"You'll be called back to the library for filming whenever a team solves a puzzle and enters a new level," Christina added. "But in the meantime, while you start thinking about the first clue, I'll show you where you'll be sleeping for the next few days."

They all turned to leave except Harry. He glared at the scoreboard and the zero next to his name as if, just by staring at it, he could will it to change.

12

The Dining Room

As they followed Christina out of the library and back down the long corridor, Flick's brain was spinning with the first clue. Making a lady vanish was one of the oldest tricks in the book. Right from the start, men had been putting their glamorous assistants into boxes and making them disappear. It was always the man in charge while the lady had to look beautiful and be controlled, Flick mused. The problem with this long history was that there were hundreds if not thousands of versions of the trick, which meant there were hundreds or thousands of methods.

To make matters worse, her leg was starting to hurt. She had to wear two socks on her residual limb to help the prosthetic fit, because the top of it was a bit too big.

This was because her limb had shrunk. The two socks were temporary until she could get a new prosthetic that would fit better. And hurt less. Meanwhile, when she put the socks on that morning, she must have missed a wrinkle and now she was paying for it. She winced as it rubbed with each step.

"Can't you walk any faster?" hissed Ruby. She shoved Flick from behind. "Some of us have a competition to win."

Flick was relieved when they finally arrived back in the entrance hall and Christina stopped in front of a wooden door. She paused while the camerawoman repositioned herself to capture the whole group.

"Of course," Christina said, "you won't have our camera crew following you around during the competition, as there are remote cameras installed throughout the house. So when I leave in a minute they'll be coming with me."

The camerawoman gave a little wave from behind the lens.

Turning to the wooden door, Christina said, "Inside here is a lift." She twisted the handle to reveal a set of modern chrome doors. She hit a button and they swished open.

"As you solve each clue, you'll gain access to a new level in the house. The lift is a quick way back to the entrance hall. Also, if we announce your name at any point, you'll need to return to the library immediately. This is in case there's an emergency. Failure to return to the library will result in instant disqualification."

"What's to stop us just taking the lift to the secret levels?" asked Harry.

"Smart question." Christina smiled.

Flick scowled. It *was* a smart question. An annoyingly good one. In fact, Harry was starting to be irritatingly clever at everything.

"But this is a smart lift," Christina went on. "If we all get in, I'll show you."

They piled in. Flick found herself right in the corner. The doors closed and a slightly metallic chirpy voice greeted them. "Welcome, everyone. Where would you like to go?"

"Take us to the first secret level," Harry said.

"Nice try," said the lift. "But I know you haven't solved the puzzle yet. Once you've found the secret door to that level, I'll be able to take you there."

Harry narrowed his eyes. "Where is the secret door to that level?"

"Like I'm going to tell you that."

Harry scowled.

"As you can see," said Christina with a smirk, "this is no ordinary lift."

She pressed a button and the doors opened again.

"Oh, come on," complained the lift. "We were just getting started. We haven't gone anywhere yet, not even up to the first floor."

"We'll come back," promised Christina as they all filed out. "Our guests need to see one more area before we go upstairs."

"Stairs! Who wants to use those old things," muttered the lift as the doors closed behind them.

Flick couldn't have agreed more.

"Next, I'm going to show you where you'll be eating," Christina said.

Harry and Ruby led the way as they followed her out of the hallway, this time turning left and heading down another passageway. This one was lined with traditional artwork, the type you'd expect to see in an old house: men posing with the animals they'd killed and their wives – neither of which looked like they wanted to be there. Flick was just reflecting on the fact that a man was at the centre of each painting when they came to the end of the corridor and entered a grand dining room. The walls here were covered in oak panelling and there was a vast marble fireplace on one side. Down the middle ran a long wooden banqueting table. A door by the fireplace opened and a man entered dressed in a black jacket with tails, white shirt and black bow tie. He had a pale face and brown hair greying at the temples.

"This," Christina gestured, "is the butler, who'll be staying in the house to look after you."

They all stared at him as he gave a slight bow. Flick noticed he had a long, dark red birthmark down his left cheek.

"Good day to you all. My name is David. I was manservant to the Great Fox, so I sort of come with the house." He smiled. "I'll be here twenty-four hours a day, in my small apartment through this door, which will be locked and out of bounds to you at all times. But if you want something to eat, just pull on this bell rope here and I'll come and take your order. Or if you need anything at all, again just ring and I'll try to assist you. The only thing I can't help you with, of course, is solving the clues."

"Is there a menu we can order from?" asked Charlie.

David shook his head. "A gong will go three times

a day for breakfast, lunch and dinner. The rules of the competition state that you have to come here and eat something at those times. You can order anything you like, and there is nothing to stop you ordering food at any other time of the day or night."

"So if I want fried chicken for breakfast, that's OK?" Ruby asked. Now they were on the subject of food, she seemed very interested.

"You can order whatever you want."

"Sick," she said.

"So, now you've met David," said Christina, "the last thing I need to do is show you to your rooms. Then you're on your own."

They filed out, this time with Charlie taking the lead behind Christina, who said over her shoulder, "We could use the lift to go up to the first floor, but let's take the stairs."

Flick let herself fall to the rear of the group as they arrived back at the main staircase. She took the steps one at a time, getting her left leg up first and then pulling her right one up next to it.

When Flick was halfway, Christina looked back and said, "I'm so sorry. I didn't think. Felicity – you can, of course, take the lift if you like."

Flick glanced back down the stairs. It would take her just as long now to retrace her steps so she decided to keep going. The others were already at the top and she could hear Harry laughing and saying, "How is she expecting to explore this house?" He and Ruby came to the landing rail and looked down.

Ruby giggled. "Better hope there's no stairs on the other levels."

Flick felt herself go red.

13
The Fading Image

"While we let Felicity get up here," Christina said from the landing, "the rest of you can choose your rooms."

Harry and Ruby disappeared. When Flick reached the landing a few minutes later, she found them making themselves comfortable in two huge bedrooms. Each had a large four-poster bed. That left a choice between the two rooms at the end of the corridor. Charlie was patiently waiting by the door to the first of these.

"Which one do you fancy?" he asked.

"I don't mind."

So he took the next bedroom and Flick got the one right at the very end. She walked through the door and took it all in. Not that there was much to take in. It was small but comfy, with a window overlooking the front of the house and a small red tiled fireplace on one wall. Above the fireplace were a mantelpiece and a plain mirror. On the right side of the room was a black metal-framed single bed. The walls were white and clean and on the floor was an old blue carpet. A door led into an en suite bathroom with a shower, toilet and basin.

"So, that's it," called Christina from the landing. "I'm leaving now with the camera crew, but I just need to remind you that all the time you're in this house you are, of course, being filmed. And you must keep your microphones on at all times. The only exceptions to this are when you're in the dining room, your bedrooms and the bathrooms. There will also be additional filming at certain times each day – you'll be called to the library for this. I'll be informing your families that you've been selected, but for now I'm going to leave you to get on with it. It just remains for me to say, may the best team win. Let the hunt begin!"

Flick could hear her heels tapping back down the stairs as Charlie came into her bedroom.

"How do you like your room?" he asked. "Mine is pretty cool and it's nice that we have our own bathrooms, and we don't even have to bring our luggage up as they do that for us, and how amazing is it that we can order whatever food we like, whenever we like, so we could have ice cream at midnight if we wanted to, not that I'm saying that's what I'll do, but it might be—"

Flick held up her hands. "You can tell me all about when you're going to eat ice cream later. Right now, I'm going back to the library to take a look in the Fox Files. I have an idea."

"I can help if you like."

"Nah. I'll be fine, thanks."

Flick walked past Charlie, out of her room and along the landing towards the lift.

Since her dad had left, she'd found she preferred to be alone. And at that moment, she needed some quiet to think. She couldn't afford to get distracted – there was too much at stake.

What advice would her dad have given her? In the months since he'd left, she'd found that he'd started to blur in her mind. She could picture him less and less clearly, his features becoming a bit hazy, leaving her not really sure if he did look like that or if she'd exaggerated him. His voice was fading too. She had to keep trying to imagine what he might say to her. He'd always been such a big support, particularly after she'd lost her leg. He'd always known how to make things right.

About six months before he went missing, she'd got in trouble at school. It was the end of the day and everyone was waiting to be picked up from the car park. Poppy Stevens was being an idiot. She'd already put glue in Flick's hair that afternoon and now she was mouthing off. So Flick pushed her. But Poppy's school things were on the floor behind her, and she tripped over them and went down pretty hard. That made her really mad so she picked up Flick's bag and threw it under a parked car.

The car, it turned out, belonged to Mrs Ashcroft, the school deputy head and one of the scariest people Flick had ever met. She never smiled. Her face was so wrinkled it looked like it had been left in the bath. For years. Her hands always shook. Flick guessed she had a medical problem, but it made her appear permanently angry, as if she was on the brink of losing control and lashing out. She always wore rubber-soled flat shoes so she could move about the school silently. Hunting the corridors like a shark. She just knew when trouble was going down and would materialize behind you. In contrast, the head, Miss Weston, was lovely. They had a classic good cop, bad cop thing going on.

As Flick pulled her bag out from under the front of the car, it caught on the number plate and ripped it off. Flick couldn't believe it. She tried to push the plate back on but it snapped. Another teacher spotted her and she was hauled off to Mrs Ashcroft's office, given a detention for the next day and told to wait for her dad to come and fetch her.

When he arrived, it was explained to him what had happened. He asked if Mrs Ashcroft knew who had thrown Flick's bag under her car. She replied that Flick was the one who had done the damage; Flick was the one who had carelessly pulled her bag out and broken the number plate. But Flick's dad just kept going, kept asking questions and defending Flick. They argued back and forth but her father would not give up. He paid for the number plate and got her off the detention and bought her ice cream on the way home. And most importantly, he got Flick to laugh about what had happened.

He'd rescued Flick so many times, but now he needed her help. The least she could do was return the favour. He hadn't given up with Mrs Ashcroft. Now she had to do the same for him.

14
The Mystery Stop

Flick made her way to the lift and pressed the call button. The doors swished open and she stepped inside.

"How are you?" the lift asked.

Flick shrugged. "Not bad."

"And where can I take you today?"

"Hmm, let me see. Where are you offering to take me?"

"Well, today I'm doing a special offer on up or down. I can try for a bit of left and right, but I'm rather limited in that department. Or I can offer you a mystery stop."

"Ooooh. I choose the mystery stop." Flick smiled.

"Very well. Close your eyes then."

Flick shut her eyes. The doors closed and the lift descended.

"By the way," the lift whispered, "you don't actually need to close your eyes. It doesn't make any difference."

Flick opened them. "I was peeking anyway."

"Thought you might be. You seem like a pretty switched-on sort of a girl."

"Thanks."

Flick felt the lift stop and then go back up again.

"Have you just…?"

"You asked for mystery, but I have only a limited set of tools for creating it. Work with me."

"OK."

The lift stopped and the doors opened on the landing, back where they'd started.

"Ta-dah!"

"Really?"

"I know. I've even disappointed myself. Shall I just take you to where you want to go?"

"Yes, please."

"Is that down?"

"Yes."

The doors closed again and the lift started to drop.

It felt like Flick had hurt its feelings, so she said, "Well done for trying, though. Good effort on the mystery."

"Thanks. Do you think it would have helped if I'd played some dramatic music?"

"Possibly."

"And maybe some mist. There's always mist around mystery, don't you think?"

Flick nodded.

"You know, I've spent all these years in this house, living with a great magician, but I've never actually seen a trick."

"Really?"

"Don't you think that's sad? Could you show me one?"

"OK. Not right now. But later. I'll do you a deal. I'll show you one if you take me to the first secret level."

"Sure," said the lift. "I'll do that right now."

A few seconds later, the lift stopped and the doors opened on to the entrance hall on the ground floor.

"This isn't a secret level," Flick said, disappointed.

"Of course it isn't. I'm not allowed to show you as it is against the rules of the competition. I wasn't born yesterday. In fact, I was installed over two years ago."

Flick stepped through the doors. "Thank you anyway."

"It's a pleasure. But if you could show me a trick one day, that would be greatly appreciated."

"Deal."

"See you around."

With that, the doors closed.

Flick crossed the entrance hall and turned right, towards the library. Once there she picked the same Fox Files pod as before, plonked herself down and put on the gloves and goggles.

She noticed that the initial screen had changed. The user was now taken straight to a search box, and there was also an alphabetical list of every trick in the database. She browsed through it and found that there were thousands, perhaps tens of thousands, of magic tricks and illusions in the system. They were listed by both the magician's name and the type of trick. Flick was looking for something that involved a lady vanishing. The problem was knowing where to begin.

She ran over what she already knew. She was sure the trick had originated with a Spanish magician. Maybe that would be a good place to start.

15
The Secret Compartment

Harry stood in his bedroom and scanned the ceiling. It was painted white, with a light fitting and what looked like a smoke alarm in the centre. But nothing else. He ran his eyes around the white coving that edged it. No strange boxes or suspicious lumps could be seen.

This was a good thing.

"What you looking for?" asked Ruby.

"Shh," Harry hissed, holding his finger to his lips.

The rest of the room consisted of the massive four-poster bed, a fireplace, a small desk with a chair, a large bay window overlooking the front of the house and a door leading to the en suite. Harry squatted down in front of the fireplace and ran his hands over the tiles around it. Then he stood and checked the mantelpiece. It was clear of anything that looked out of place. Finally he got down on his knees and looked under the bed.

"But what are you actually looking for?" Ruby repeated in a whisper.

"I'm checking." Satisfied there was nothing under the bed, Harry stood and walked to the bathroom door. He gave it a cursory once-over. It was unlikely they would put anything in the bathroom but he wanted to be absolutely certain. He couldn't mess this up. He could hear his mother's voice and what she would say if he did – he couldn't let her down again. This time she would be proud.

"Checking for?" Ruby had followed him to the bathroom door.

"They're not supposed to put cameras in our bedrooms and bathrooms. But I'm just making sure."

Harry walked back past Ruby and crossed the room to his suitcase. Opening it, he ran his fingers along the inside bottom edge. He found the small concealed button and pressed it. There was a popping sound and the whole bottom panel of the suitcase came away, revealing a row of items zip-tied into the hidden space. Harry removed the one on the far right – a rectangular item about the size of a phone. Then he walked over to the window and peered out. He had a great view of the gardens and the path leading to the front door below; there was no sign of anyone out there. All was quiet. He looked up at the ceiling above the window. This was where they had told him to do it because of the pitch of the roof.

He moved the chair underneath and stood on it to attach the rectangular object to the ceiling. Suckers in each corner held it fast. He checked it was in the right spot before pressing a button. There was a whirring sound and then slowly the device started to creep along the ceiling above him in a wide arc.

16
The Virtual Magician

It took some searching, but eventually Flick found the trick she was looking for: a vanishing act performed by a Spanish magician called Marquez in the nineteenth century. She tapped on the details, selecting the virtual version of the trick. The screen went dark and next thing, she found herself standing on a stage in an old theatre. It had been beautifully rendered and by moving her feet on the pad she could walk about.

Flick took in her surroundings. The wooden stage was lit by powerful spotlights from a gantry above her and framed by red velvet curtains. The details were quite beautiful. When she looked down, she could even see the grain in the planks of wood. And looking out into the auditorium, Flick could see a packed virtual audience, silently waiting for the action to begin.

She walked across the stage towards a wooden platform that was raised on four legs. It had a ceiling supported by four thin uprights, one in each corner, and a set of steps leading up to it. As she approached the platform, a play button appeared, so she tapped it.

A voice announced, "Ladies and gentleman, please welcome virtual Valentino."

The audience cheered and clapped as Valentino came on from the wings and walked around the platform, showing that all the sides were open and you could see underneath it. He climbed up the steps onto the platform to show it was a solid, empty structure.

Next, a beautiful assistant with long dark hair and a fancy hooped dress from the 1800s walked on from the other side of the stage. Valentino, like the gentleman he was, helped her up the steps and onto the platform. She stood in the centre and smiled sweetly at the audience. Valentino climbed back down and then reached up to the platform ceiling and pulled down some blinds. He lowered them on the front, left and right – the three sides facing the audience. But he only lowered them halfway, so the assistant's dress could still be seen. She gave a shimmy to show she was still there. Then he quickly lowered the blinds completely and in the blink of an eye pinged them fully up again.

The woman had vanished.

The virtual audience gasped.

The assistant reappeared from the side of the stage.

The audience burst into applause. Valentino took a bow and his assistant gave a curtsy before exiting the stage.

With the trick over, the virtual audience returned to their silent, expectant state and Flick was presented with a *How it works* button. When she pressed it, a set of technical notes popped up, which she scanned through.

When the assistant climbed up onto the platform and the blinds were lowered halfway, she reached up to the top of the frame and grabbed four ropes with hooks on the ends. She attached these to four eyelets in her flouncy dress. Then she undid the back of the dress, ducked down and climbed out the rear. At the same time, Valentino was walking around the platform, and he hit a button on the side which dropped a mirror down underneath it. From the front, it looked as if you could still see beneath the platform, but in reality the mirror now reflected the floor. Thus the audience couldn't see the assistant drop down off the back of the platform and onto the floor. Using the stairs as a cover, she then crawled over to the side of the stage. When the blinds were dropped fully, a false ceiling above the platform also dropped to the floor, concealing the dress beneath it. Meanwhile, the assistant was frantically pulling on an identical dress at the side of the stage. All that remained was for the great magician to raise the blinds and show the empty platform, ping the mirror back into place and have his assistant reappear.

Flick sat and thought through the trick. Although it involved obscuring the audience's view, this method couldn't have been used to make the Statue of Liberty disappear. She wondered if there was an easier way of finding the correct method. She was looking for a clue that would give her a location in this house. Something she'd walked past on their tour. She ran over the house's layout again in her mind, remembering its library, corridors, dining room, entrance hall, stairs, landing and bedrooms, trying to think of a detail she had missed. Then she once again browsed through the tricks. There had to be a connection somewhere.

This time she looked for a trick that involved making a large object disappear. Maybe that was a better approach. Before long she found one involving a vanishing motorbike.

Pressing the button for the virtual version, she watched Valentino do his stuff. This time he arrived onstage on a motorbike, which he parked in front of the curtains. He dismounted and opened the curtains to reveal a stainless-steel cage about the height of the motorbike. Returning to the bike, he rode it into the cage, which was then locked and raised above the stage. From high up, Valentino gave a wave, before fireworks flashed and the cage floor and walls dropped, springing it open. But the motorbike and magician had vanished. The audience gasped as Valentino appeared at the back of the auditorium, still on his motorbike, waving to the crowds.

Flick pressed the *How it works* button.

The first part of the trick happened before the magician even rode the motorbike into the cage. When he opened the curtains, he stepped behind one for a fraction of a second and was replaced by a double. At this point, the magician could begin making his way to the back of the auditorium for the big reveal.

Meanwhile, the double started the motorbike and rode it into the cage. Inside were black roller blinds held in place by a simple release system. At the start of the illusion, the blinds were up to allow the audience to see into the cage. However, when the double pulled a cord, the blinds dropped. From the front, it looked as if the audience could still see straight through an empty cage to the black backdrop. But really, the black shades were all they could see. The cage floor and walls also seemed to drop away at this moment. In reality, the walls and floor were fake – the magician's double and motorbike were still safely in the real cage behind the black roller blinds. All the double had to do was make sure to duck down behind the blinds, and he did this at the same moment the fireworks temporarily blinded the audience.

All that remained was for the real magician to reveal himself at the back of the auditorium.

So, here was a technique for making a large object vanish. Could something similar have been used to make the Statue of Liberty disappear? Well, maybe. It was strange that the statue had been vanished at night. Why could the trick not have been done in the daytime? The use of spotlights and scaffolding with bright lights on it was perhaps a similar technique to the fireworks, blinding the audience at key moments.

And then Flick's goggles blurred and the database vanished as the screen faded.

"Can I have a little word?" said the voice of Dominic Drake in her ear.

17
The Unpainted Fence

Harry and Ruby walked into the dining room, where a laptop had been placed on the table. Each competitor was allowed to make a video call home once a day and a member of the TV crew had already set up the call. Harry sat in front of the laptop and adjusted the screen. He could see his mum sitting at the kitchen table.

"Oh, there you are," his mum said. "So you've finally decided to call me, have you? I hope you realize the mess you've made of things here. There's a man talking to your father, been here all morning, says his name is Mr Synergy or something. He doesn't seem very happy with you."

"Synergy are in our house?" Harry asked.

"Yes, I've had to cancel my Pilates class because he insisted on talking to your father."

"What are they talking about?"

"Your father was supposed to be repainting the fence this morning and now he's just been sat in the living room for hours getting nothing useful done at all. All because you insist on pursuing your silly hobby. I wish you'd just learn to play the cello or do something useful with your time instead of causing us all this trouble."

"We're through to the main competition, Mum! If we win—" Harry started.

"Oh, if the sky turns green all sorts of things might happen. I knew that no good at all would come of this. It gave me indigestion all day yesterday and I've not been able to start my new diet."

"But—"

"All right, tell me about what you've been up to. I'm all ears. Have you performed any magic tricks yet?"

Harry sighed. "No, Mum, I told you. We're not doing tricks. We have to work out how they're done."

"Oh, that sounds hard."

"It is."

"Why have you got to work them out? Don't they know how they're done?"

"It's a competition. They're like puzzles we have to solve."

"So it's all made up then."

"What do you mean? They're real tricks."

"You can't have a real trick. That's a silly thing to say."

"Well, they're tricks that have been performed by real magicians."

"If you say so. Now, why don't you put Ruby on the line? See if I can get any sense out of her."

"Hi, Mummy," said Ruby, shuffling her chair in front of the laptop.

"Ah, that's better. Now I can see you properly. How are you, sweetie pie?"

Harry clenched his fists and walked away.

18
The Reminder

A kaleidoscope of colours whirled around Flick as she was transported to a modern apartment with sliding glass doors leading onto a balcony. The skyline looked familiar, and as she squinted at it, Flick recognized the Weymouth seafront. In front of the doors was a pair of black leather armchairs facing each other across a glass coffee table, and beyond these she could make out a breakfast bar and a kitchen.

A wide and muscular dark-suited man leant against a granite worktop and watched her. He didn't look like he was there to do the cooking. In fact, judging by the overly clean and shiny stainless steel saucepans that hung from a rack, no one did any cooking in this kitchen.

Dominic Drake walked through a door. He'd dressed up for the occasion and was sporting a navy blue suit, white shirt open at the collar and no tie. He was leaning on his silver cane.

He gave Flick a cold smile. "How nice to see you."

The wide man turned and left. Presumably to choose a recipe.

"I just wanted to remind you of our little deal, Felicity," Drake said. "I wouldn't want you to forget your priorities, so I'm going to be checking in on you from time to time."

Her name was Flick. Only her mother called her Felicity.

He walked closer to Flick, his cold green eyes moving over her face as if calculating odds and possibilities.

"You're probably wondering how you're here. You just need to know that you can see a virtual me and I can see a virtual you. And in that house, I can see the real you all the time. Day and night, I'm watching."

Flick said nothing. Not because she thought it was a good idea or clever tactic, but simply because she didn't have a clue what to say.

"You're no doubt keen to win the competition. But I want you to remember why I've let you be part of this."

Flick felt a bit sick.

"Do we understand each other?"

Her voice didn't seem to want to work.

"You know what the most important skill in magic is? Misdirection. You don't want the audience looking where all the important things are actually happening. So you move your hands around. You have a beautiful female assistant. Some bright lights. Well, the TV show is my assistant. In fact, this whole competition is just a lot of noise and light to distract people's attention from the real action. Do you understand?"

Not really. She was struggling, to be honest. A glass of water might help.

"And you, my friend, are the trick." He laughed like this was the funniest thing he'd ever heard. Those quick eyes had ceased their movement and landed on her as if they had homed in on their prey.

Flick tried to swallow. Her throat was so dry.

"Come. Walk with me," he ordered. He turned and strode towards the glass doors, tapping his cane with each step. He pulled one of the doors open and stepped out onto the balcony.

Flick shuffled her feet on the virtual pod floor and followed, blinking as her eyes adjusted to the outside light. They stood side by side and watched the busy seafront below. Traffic was stacking up at the lights, and Flick could make out people doing some afternoon shopping or heading to the various bars.

"Look at those people down there, Felicity."

It was *Flick*. Flick Lions. She'd wanted to be called that because it was something you wouldn't dare do. Flick a lion. Make it angry. She wanted people to take her seriously. But who was she kidding?

"Why do they enjoy magic? Because they like to be fooled. It entertains and amuses them. And people like to be fooled in their real lives too. They like to believe that their pathetic lives have meaning. They like to think they matter. They love democracy because they believe their vote can change the world. They like to work to earn money so they can buy things, because they believe this will make them happy. And then they throw those things away and buy more things. And more and more, because they love to be fooled. As long as their wages go up and there are more things to buy, more holidays to go on, everyone is happy."

Flick nodded to show she'd heard of people going on holiday and being happy.

"The real power in this life comes from controlling

how people are fooled. Making them think they need what you have. That is the secret to being rich. You and I understand that power. We both know that people love, maybe even need, to be fooled."

They faced each other. Drake stared at her like a lion might look at a zebra.

"Find me the Bell System, Felicity."

She gulped. She needed to get her voice working, say something to fend him off.

"I will," she managed.

"I hope so. To help you concentrate, I want you to know that I have your mum's address. You saw Angelo inside? The big guy in the kitchen? Well, Angelo has a lot of friends and we wouldn't want them to visit your mother, would we?"

"No," she croaked.

"I didn't quite catch that."

She heard her mouth say, "No, I wouldn't want that to happen."

"And of course there's your mum's job... You know what happened to your father when things weren't going very well for him in that area. Do I make myself clear?"

"Yes."

"Good. Get me the Bell System and she will be safe. But make sure you do. Don't be fooled, Felicity. Understand?"

And in an instant, her goggles blurred and went black. She was breathing hard as she pushed them up onto her head, relieved to be back in the library. She could feel the panic rising from within. She needed to get herself under control.

Breathe in.

Breathe out.

Breathe in.

Breathe out.

She fought back the tears.

When she was younger, they had a garden with a big tree. Flick used to enjoy climbing it. But one time she lost her grip and fell. It was a long drop. When she hit the ground, she was totally winded, every ounce of breath knocked out of her lungs. She had that same feeling now.

She couldn't have her mum ripped from her as well. She needed to find the Bell System and give it to Drake. Absolutely had to. Or die trying. Because she would not be responsible for more loss.

19
The Dinner

When the evening gong sounded for dinner, they all assembled in the dining room. David solemnly took everyone's order as they arrived. Then he disappeared back through his door and returned about twenty minutes later with the food.

Ruby and Harry had got there first and so started eating before the others. They sat at one end of the huge table, as far away from Flick and Charlie as possible, and whispered as they chomped their way through fish and chips followed by sticky toffee pudding.

Charlie and Flick sat at the other end. Flick was enjoying a very tasty burger and fries. Charlie had been the last to arrive and was still waiting for his food.

"What if we can't solve the puzzle?" they heard Ruby ask Harry through a mouthful of sticky toffee pudding, which she appeared to be eating at the same time as her chips.

Charlie smiled. "Giving up already?"

"No!" Ruby scowled, realizing she'd been overheard. "I'm just wondering if there's, like, a time limit or something. Anyway, I'm not talking to you."

Charlie shrugged. "I don't think there's a time limit."

David appeared with Charlie's order – beans, egg and toast – which he placed in front of him. Charlie thanked him and then immediately started to separate the items, making sure that the beans didn't touch his egg or toast.

Flick watched him, fascinated.

Harry and Ruby finished their meals and got up from the table. As they passed behind Charlie on their way to the door, Harry deliberately knocked Charlie's arm so his beans crashed into his egg.

Charlie looked down at his food.

"See you all around, losers," Harry said, walking through the door. "We don't have time to sit around chatting; we've got a competition to win."

Charlie picked at his toast for a bit but didn't eat any of it.

"Why don't you just order some more food?" Flick asked.

"I don't think..." Charlie poked the white of his egg. "I don't think I can."

Flick sighed. "What's up, Charlie?"

"It's complicated."

"Most things are."

Charlie looked as if he might be about to cry.

"Whatever it is," said Flick, "I'm sorry it's happened."

Charlie nodded. "Thank you." He put down his knife and fork. "It's about my brother."

"You have a brother. Is he in trouble?"

"Yes. A lot. And I need to win this competition. It could save his life."

Flick nodded. "Well, we're going to give it all we have, right?"

"Right."

"Andar com um amigo no escuro é melhor que caminhar sozinho na luz."

"What?"

"It's what my mum says. 'Walking with a friend in the dark is better than walking alone in the light.' We're a team."

"Yes." Charlie smiled. "Thank you."

Flick put her hand on Charlie's shoulder.

"That's very nice of you to say that," he added. "Does this mean after we've won this, we can become a proper team and work together?"

Flick laughed. "I'll think about it."

20
The Circle

Harry had set his alarm for two in the morning. He'd heard it was the time when people's sleep cycles were at their deepest. Weren't the SAS supposed to always attack then for that reason? He sat up in bed and groggily rubbed his eyes, trying to wake up. One of the more awake parts of his mind pointed out that if they always attacked at the same time, surely people would be ready for them, so maybe he'd got that wrong.

Harry swung his legs out of bed and listened. One thing was for sure, he couldn't hear any sounds in the house.

"What's going on?" asked Ruby, appearing at his door.

"Shh," hissed Harry. "Just go back to sleep."

"Is it morning?"

"No, not yet. Well, yes, technically it is morning, but—"

"It's very dark."

"Yes, that's the idea."

Harry tiptoed across the floor to his suitcase. He opened it and ran his fingers along the inside bottom edge, feeling for the button. There was a popping sound and the bottom panel dropped away. He felt along the row of zip-tied items and removed the one on the far right – a torch. He turned it on.

"What are you doing?"

Harry was sure the SAS didn't have to put up with this sort of thing.

"There's something I need to do," he whispered. "I don't want anyone to know about it so we both need to be very quiet, OK?"

With the torch on, he removed the phone-sized object from the suitcase. Then, with the torch off so he wouldn't be seen, he silently moved the chair over to the window again and stood on it, attaching the object to the ceiling in the same place as earlier. He checked it was correctly positioned to complete the cut he'd already started, and was about to press the button when he paused.

What would his mum say? She would tell him to stop and think, make sure of all the details. He tried not to imagine how she would be if he got this wrong. And what had Synergy been doing in their house? It had all seemed so straightforward when the company had approached him before the competition. They only wanted one small item from the house – something the size of a suitcase. If he found it for them, they promised to use Harry and Ruby in their next TV series. It had seemed like a price worth paying. Now he wasn't so sure.

He got down off the chair and grabbed a pillow from the bed, placing it on the floor in the right position. This would muffle the sounds of falling plaster. Then he got back up on the chair and checked everything one more time. When he was certain the pillow was lined up correctly, he pressed the button and the phone-like object whirred in a slow arc, completing its circle. With a crack, a section of the ceiling about a metre in width fell away.

Harry reached up and turned the phone-shaped cutter off. He removed it from the ceiling and carried it over to his suitcase, placing it back in its compartment. Then he took another item out – a harness and some wires, which he unfurled. He carried these over to the hole, stepping over the pillow and plaster on the floor.

"Help me clear this up," he whispered to Ruby. "We can hide the bits under the bed."

21
The Suits

The next morning, Flick woke up early and hopped into the shower. When she'd washed, she sat on the end of the bed and got her leg ready. First she took a liner. She turned it inside out to expose the silicone cup at the bottom, then placed it against her residual limb and rolled the liner up her leg, being careful to avoid any air bubbles. Next she took her two over socks, which she needed to pad her leg because it was getting smaller. She rolled these over her limb and up to her thigh. Then she slid her limb into the prosthetic. The liner had a pin on the end, and as she stood, putting her full weight on the prosthetic, she heard the pin click into the socket.

She pulled on some shorts, finished getting dressed

and then headed for the library. They had to film some pieces to the camera about their thoughts on the competition so far and how they were getting on with the first clue. Not that they had much progress to report. Harry went first, followed by Ruby, both of them boasting about how many ideas they had and how they were certain to win. Charlie went next and managed to take for ever. Even the camerawoman looked bored. Flick was up last. She mumbled a few things about being excited to be part of the competition – things she thought the producers would want to hear.

When they were all finished, the others dashed off to explore the house, but Flick stayed in the library. She watched the camera team pack up and then she started to explore the shelves. She had never seen so many old books. Lots were covered in dust and didn't look as if they had been read in years. She pulled several off a shelf and carried them over to a desk, where she opened them and started to browse. The dust made her sneeze.

She was flicking through a particularly heavy leather-bound volume – written by a magician in the nineteenth century who she'd never heard of and whose main magical qualification seemed to be a large twirly moustache – when she heard Harry shouting.

He sounded very excited, so she left the book on the desk and headed out of the library and down the corridor towards the entrance hall, following the noise.

Beyond the dining room was another corridor with several doors leading off it. She'd not considered exploring the house as important as working out the solution to the clue, but Harry and Ruby had clearly thought differently. They had been trying doors, looking behind pictures and generally poking the house in every way possible, hoping to find something that moved.

And it sounded like they might have been successful.

At the end of the corridor, Flick could see Ruby standing in a doorway, pointing and saying something she couldn't make out. To her right was a walk-in wardrobe, all lit up. There were several rails with what looked like white spacesuits hanging off them. As Flick drew closer, she could see Harry putting on one of the suits. Beyond the open door where Ruby stood was some sort of metal chute that led off in four different directions, and above it a sign that read:

SEARCH THE MAZE
TO FIND THE KEY...

Harry appeared from the wardrobe with the suit on and a black joystick controller in his hands.

"Out of the way, losers." He shoved Flick aside and stepped towards the chute. As he did so, he gently rose into the air. For a moment he seemed freaked out by the sensation, but it didn't last long.

"Awesome!" he declared as he effortlessly floated off down one of the metal tubes and disappeared around a corner.

"What are we all waiting for?" asked Ruby. "I'm getting me one of those suits!"

22
The Maze

Flick stepped into a suit and struggled to pull it up over her leg. Charlie had finally turned up and kept offering to help. It was embarrassing, so Flick ignored him. It wasn't like she couldn't get it on; it was just going to take her a bit longer.

The suits were made from nylon but were very heavy. And they were also really warm inside, so by the time Flick had pulled it up over her shoulders she was sweating. There was a zip on the front which she tried to do up, but it got caught on her microphone. She reached down and unclipped it, cradling the tiny black object in her hand.

"Aren't we supposed to keep these on at all times?" asked Charlie, removing his for the same reason.

Flick shrugged and finished zipping up her suit.

On a rack near by were white helmets, like cycle helmets. She removed one and laid her microphone carefully in its place. Then she put the helmet on and fastened the strap under her chin. The final bit of equipment was the little black box with a joystick on top, which Flick held in her left hand so she could move the stick with her right.

They joined Ruby at the entrance, ready to explore the maze. Ruby went first, stepping into the chute and pulling back on the joystick so she rose a metre into the air. But then she yanked on the stick too hard and flew straight upwards, crashing into the ceiling, before plummeting straight down and landing in a crumpled heap on the floor. She burst into tears.

Flick and Charlie pulled her back into the corridor, where she was able to sort herself out before having another go. This time she was gentler with the controls and successfully set off after her brother. Charlie went next and in no time he was hot on her heels. And then it was Flick's turn. She tried to be as gentle as possible with the joystick. She had just risen a little way off the ground when Harry reappeared from one of the side chutes.

"How far do these tunnels go?" Flick asked him as he flew past, knocking her into the wall.

"It's massive. There are tubes heading off at all different angles."

"See anything interesting?"

"Like I'd tell you."

He floated off down another stretch of chute and Flick followed. It was like flying along inside a giant air-conditioning duct. The walls, floor and ceiling were all uniform and smooth, made of shiny silver metal. They rounded a corner and crashed into Ruby coming out of another tunnel.

"How do you think they work?" asked Ruby.

"Dunno," said Flick. "The Great Fox had more money than sense."

Ruby shook her head. "Really? This is awesome. When we win this competition, I'm going to have one installed in my house."

23
The Find

Harry had got the hang of flying. That was the easy part. The real challenge was keeping tabs on where you were and where you'd been. All of the chutes were identical. He might have been down this one a dozen times before. Except … what was this? He hovered and looked up. Either it was a new chute, or he'd previously missed this vertical junction by flying straight underneath it.

He pulled back on the joystick and rose upwards, climbing several metres. At the top was a square room, made of the same uniform silver metal, and suspended in the middle, floating in the air, was a large golden key.

Harry smiled to himself as he reached out and grabbed the key. It was about ten centimetres long and heavy, possibly made of brass or maybe even gold. He turned it over in his hands. The handle was an intricate lattice pattern and it glinted in the light.

Harry wanted to look at it some more and enjoy the moment, but he could hear the voices of Flick and Charlie echoing down the chute below, so he quickly unzipped his suit and shoved the key inside. Using the joystick, he slowly turned himself around and went back down the way he'd come. He watched from the junction as Flick and Charlie passed below him without even looking up; and then, when he was sure they were out of sight, he lowered himself and set off in what he hoped was the direction of the exit. He took the next left turn and then a right. Was this the way out? No, maybe the last turn should have been a left again. He retraced his path and this time went left. At the next junction, he was relieved to bump into Ruby.

"We need to go," he said.

"What's happened?"

"I have the key; we need to get out of here fast so we can use it."

She threw her arms around her brother, nearly making them both crash. "Well done!" she said. "The exit's this way."

Harry followed her back the way he had come, taking a right, two lefts and then a turn downwards to get back to the entrance. As they passed out of the chute, they dropped gently to the floor, where Harry unzipped his suit and removed the large golden key.

Ruby took it from him and examined it. "We must be looking for a very big lock."

Harry had already removed his helmet. "Yeah – it's huge, isn't it? But I think I know which door it's for." He tugged his suit down. "We need to hurry, though, before the others realize we've gone. Give me your suit."

Ruby struggled out of hers and Harry carried them back into the wardrobe. He was just about to chuck them into the corner rather than hang them back up, when a thought struck him. At the rear of the wardrobe was an electrical panel. He knelt down and examined it. There were six big switches that looked like circuit breakers, and a dial with a needle on it that hovered at the end of a scale labelled *volts*. The whole thing hummed with energy.

"I thought we were in a hurry," said Ruby from the doorway.

"Just give me a—"

"Found something?" Ruby peered past him eagerly.

“Oh, yes.”

Harry flicked each of the switches to off and watched as the needle dropped to zero. The humming stopped.

He smirked. “Let’s see if that slows them down.”

24
The Power Cut

Flick was just rounding a corner when suddenly she plummeted to the chute floor. She lay there for a few seconds, trying to understand what had just happened. At first she thought she'd made a mistake with her controller, so she stood up and pulled and pushed on the stick a few times, but it did nothing. Something was clearly broken. She walked slowly down the chute, trying not to slip on the polished metal, and turned right into the next section, nearly tripping over Charlie, who was sprawled across the floor going through a similar routine with his own controller.

"Not just me then," he said.

Flick offered him a hand and pulled him to his feet.

Harry's voice echoed down the metal walls. "Fun's over, kids."

"What have you done?" Charlie shouted, but there was no answer.

"How are we going to get out?" Flick asked.

"This way, I think," Charlie said, pointing.

They walked as far as they could in that direction until they reached a vertical shaft. Charlie tried a few times to pull himself up the smooth metal walls, but got nowhere.

Then Flick had a go.

Charlie took off his helmet and sat down, while Flick continued trying to pull herself up. She could manage to get a few feet off the ground, but then slipped back to where she started. Frustrated, she threw her helmet at the wall. It clattered along the metal floor.

"We've just got to wait," Charlie said.

Flick nodded. "But for what? And how long?"

"Well, I'm pretty sure Channel Seven can see everything that happens in this house, so they'll soon know we're trapped. They won't let us starve to death."

He was right. They would come and get them out at some point.

"But," she said, "meanwhile, Harry gets to keep looking for the first door."

Charlie shrugged. "Why do you want to win this so bad?"

Flick sat down next to him so they were side by side with their backs to the chute wall.

"It's kind of a long story," she said.

"I've not got much in my diary right now."

"When people say 'it's a long story', it's a polite way of saying 'I don't want to tell you'."

"Well, I could guess. I've got lots of good ideas."

"Have you?"

"Yep. I'm good at being creative. It's my thing."

"If you're so great at ideas, how come you haven't worked out the trick yet?"

"Well, I've got hundreds of ideas about how it might be done, but I'm just not sure which of them is—"

"Let's hear them then."

"What, now?"

"I've not got much in my diary either."

He nodded. "OK. The Statue of Liberty can't really vanish, so it must still be there. It could be that when the curtain comes down we are looking at a big TV screen instead, showing an empty space. But it would be hard to make that look realistic. Or it could be that it wasn't the Statue of Liberty they were looking at in the first place; but these were people who lived in New York, so you would think they could spot a cardboard cut-out. Or it could be that it is the real one at the start, but it's replaced by a fake. But again, you would think they would notice. Or it could be that they are all hypnotized and think they can't see it when they still can. But that doesn't explain what we see on camera. Or maybe what they're looking at moves, so they're looking at the statue at the start and then looking somewhere else. Or it could be that their angle of view is shifted up above the statue. Or it could be that—"

"What did you say?"

"Erm … which bit?"

"The last bit."

"The angle the audience is looking from is shifted up."

"Before that."

"Well, a similar idea, but the angle the audience is looking from is shifted to the side."

In Flick's brain, things were crashing together. Big things. She grabbed Charlie by the shoulders. "Of course! That's why the trick needed to be done at night with lots of spotlights. And that means I know exactly where to look for the door."

She examined his face close up. He held her gaze. He was open and content. Comfortable. He had faint freckles all over his nose and cheeks, like a sprinkling of chocolate.

And then something odd happened. She was pretty excited and all fired up because of working out the trick, and maybe it helped that they were alone and without microphones so no one could listen in. She opened her mouth to say something, not really sure what, and you know how sometimes when you get excited you don't think for very long about what you're saying, or bother to check that the words are coming out in the right order? Well, lots of surprising words came out of Flick.

She told Charlie her story.

All of it.

She told him who her father was, about the trick he'd invented called the Bell System, about Dominic Drake wanting to get his hands on it. She told him that the only reason she hadn't been kicked off the show was because she'd said she would steal it, and she told him what Drake was going to do to her family if she didn't. She said all these things and Charlie listened and absorbed it all.

Maybe some of what she said wasn't in the right

order, but when she was finished, she felt a tremendous rush of relief.

Charlie sat in silence for a bit and then said, "There might be ways we can use this to our advantage."

His reaction surprised her. She looked at his face again. Maybe there was an edge to him she hadn't noticed before.

"How?" she asked.

"Well, I'm not sure yet. Leave it with me. I'm good at ideas."

25
The Locked Door

Harry and Ruby sprinted back to the hall and then down the corridor that led to the library. Beyond the library's entrance was a small wooden door, tucked around the corner out of sight. Harry had found it earlier but the door had been locked. And he remembered it had a large keyhole. He tried the key. The lock gave a satisfyingly well-oiled click.

Once inside, Harry quickly locked the door behind them so they wouldn't be discovered, and then turned and surveyed the room. They were clearly in the Fox's private study. There were floor to ceiling bookcases on two of the walls, while a third was covered in large posters of the Fox's shows, including one of his *Fantastic Fox* show in

Vegas, and one of his *The Great Fox Presents* TV series. The latter looked as if it had been signed by everyone involved.

Ruby walked over to the far wall where there was a large desk, and sat down behind it in the Fox's leather chair.

"What's that?" she asked, pointing near the door they'd just come through.

Harry turned and saw that the wall opposite the desk had a huge screen on it showing a camera feed from the hallway. Suddenly it flickered and changed to footage of the upstairs landing.

"This works," said Ruby. She had a remote control in her hand.

"Where was that?" he asked.

"On the desk."

She pressed the button again and now the screen showed the dining room.

"Let me have a go," he said.

Ruby passed it to him and he scrolled through footage of all the rooms. He could see corridors, and the library, and members of the TV crew coming into the house to rescue Flick and Charlie, and then sections of the maze, and eventually he found Flick and Charlie.

"Interesting," he said. "Let's watch and see what they do when they get out."

26
The Descent

Flick and Charlie had to sit on the floor of the metal maze for an hour before some of the crew managed to turn it back on again. As soon as they could float, they sped back to the entrance, stepped out and quickly shed their suits. Then they made their way back towards the hall.

Charlie was in overdrive. "We should totally do a deal, right now, team up as a double act. I can see this working long-term, you know. I can probably draw up a contract, although I don't have anything to type it up on in here or any way of—"

Flick held up her hand. "Charlie," she said. "Enough."

He nodded and mimed zipping his mouth.

"There is one place in this house where I've seen round floors and lots of spotlights," Flick said.

They entered the corridor with all the famous magicians on the wall. Each alcove had a round floor. And in one of them, the spotlights seemed brighter. A little too bright. At the back of the alcove, Flick even found a picture of David Copperfield, his arm around the Great Fox.

"Now what?" asked Charlie.

"Well..." Flick said. "I'm not sure."

"Let's think about the trick," he said. "So the magician gets a load of people to sit in some chairs on Liberty Island looking across at the statue. It's night-time and there are spotlights and a helicopter flying around filming the statue. The audience are sat on a platform which has towers on either side of it to support a curtain. David announces that he's going to make the statue, which is three hundred feet tall and—"

"Just the important bits, Charlie."

"Sorry. So there are two scaffolding towers. He raises the curtain, and then after he's looked all mystical for a bit, the curtain is lowered and the statue has gone. The helicopter shines its searchlight across the empty space."

"And the secret must be in the floor the audience are sitting on," Flick said.

"Yes, why else does he need to do it at night? Also, when you watch the footage, the curtain goes up and down, not across, and there is always a certain amount of curtain already up, blocking the audience's view of the ground. The platform they're on also has screens limiting the audience's view to the right and left."

"You're right," Flick said. "The platform the audience is on pivots around very slowly and gently, so no one can feel it, like a turntable. When the curtain goes up, the statue is right between the scaffolding towers, but as the platform moves, the statue is hidden behind one of them. Then the helicopter shines its light on a different bit of sky."

"Bingo!" Charlie nodded. "*The lady vanishes, but how is it done? Understand the method and you'll find door one*. So..."

"So the secret to the trick is a moving floor."

"The floor in this alcove must move."

"That's my guess."

They both glanced down. The boards looked solid enough. Charlie put his hands against the wall and pushed with his feet. There was a faint squeaking noise and the floor began to move away from the wall. Flick stood alongside him and joined in with the pushing. The floor disappeared under the opposite wall to reveal an opening, with a set of stairs disappearing into the gloom.

"I gotta get me some paperwork printed," muttered Charlie. "We are pure awesome."

They high-fived.

Flick stepped onto the stairs. And stopped.

"Erm," she said. "I'm not very good at these."

"What would you like me to do?"

"Could you go first, and I'll hold your hand?"

"Sure."

They swapped places.

"And could we go really slowly?" she asked.

"No problem."

And so, very slowly, they descended into the blackness.

PART THREE

Walls Have Ears

In which the magician makes the ordinary house do something impossible. Now there's no going back. We're inside the trick, trapped in a world of the magician's making, fully under their control. Only they know where this is going and how things will end.

27
The Assistant

It was a metal spiral staircase. Cramped and twisty. As Flick and Charlie gingerly descended, automatic lights hummed into life so they could see each step. Above them, there was a grinding noise as the floor shifted back into place, concealing the way they had entered. Flick hoped that would stop Harry and Ruby from stumbling upon their victory. She was sure they were the first to find this level, and she allowed herself a little smile at the thought of being in the lead. Although this was quickly wiped off her face by the next jarring downward step.

"So David Copperfield's most famous magic act wasn't actually performed by him at all." Charlie hadn't stopped talking. "If you think about it, while the trick was being performed, he didn't do anything. He just spoke to the camera and looked all mystical, with that stupid fake radar screen. The secret was in the moving floor and that was done by his assistants."

"What's your point?" Flick asked, wincing at each step.

"That no magician ever works alone. Probably something you should bear in mind."

As they arrived at the bottom, more lights flickered on to reveal a huge corridor that disappeared into the distance in both directions. The floor, walls and ceiling were all painted white, and at regular intervals, as far as the eye could see, were black doors. Directly in front of them, so they couldn't miss it, was a TV. It detected their presence and started playing.

Charlie and Flick stood there, eyes glued to the screen.

A magician stood on the stage of a talent show. In front of him sat a huge audience and four judges. He approached the judges and asked them to be part of his trick. Then he took out a box of crayons and opened it to show that the crayons were all different colours. Clear plastic windows on both sides of the box revealed a good mix of crayons inside. He gave the box a shake and asked the first judge to pull out a crayon. He did so, removing a red one.

Next, the magician asked the second judge to take a Rubik's cube out of its box and mix it up. She twisted the sides around so the coloured squares were thoroughly muddled. The magician then asked her to put it back into the box. He approached the third judge with a pack of kid's animal playing cards. These had different cute cartoon creatures on them. He riffled through a few cards to show they were all different and then fanned out the pack, face down, asking the third judge to pick one. The card she chose was a penguin.

Finally the magician gave a pen to the fourth judge. He opened a book on a random page and asked the judge to draw a circle on that page. Then the magician walked back to the stage and began to tell the audience a story.

A few years ago his wife had been diagnosed with cancer while pregnant. They were terrified about the baby surviving through the chemotherapy. But they were given a miracle. Their baby daughter was born healthy. The screen at the back of the stage showed a home video of the magician's beautiful daughter. His wife was there too, fully recovered. The camera cut to her waving and smiling from the audience.

The magician explained that all the elements of the trick were to do with his daughter. The screen behind the stage showed his daughter scribbling with a crayon, as the magician explained that she would only draw in one colour – red. The screen then cut to shots of his daughter in her cot with a cuddly toy. The magician explained that she would not go to sleep without her favourite toy, a penguin. And he told them that she liked playing with her daddy's things and mixing up his Rubik's cube. The screen showed a jumbled Rubik's cube and the magician invited the second judge to open the box to reveal the cube she had muddled up. It was in exactly the same pattern.

There was one thing left to do. The magician asked the fourth judge what word he had circled in the book. The judge turned over the book and announced the word to be *hat*. The magician played another video of his daughter. In the film he asked her what word the judge would say. She said, "Hat."

The audience burst into applause and the judges awarded the magician with a place in the talent show final.

Charlie and Flick stood in silence for a beat.

"There are a lot of bits to that trick," Charlie eventually said.

"Sure are," Flick agreed, looking around. "And I have no idea where to start so let's explore."

They set off down the corridor and Charlie opened the first door on the right. As the lights in the room flickered on, they could see it was perfectly square, painted all white, and in the middle were the props for an illusion – a wooden frame with a red curtain draped over it and a metal box of some sort. As they stepped out of the room and the lights went off, the door automatically closed behind them.

They opened the next door and found an identical room, but this one contained a huge metal table with a circular saw suspended over it. The third door revealed a series of metal rings hanging from a massive gantry, the next a wooden coffin, and the one after that three large packing cases. The following room contained two huge wooden wardrobes, and the next had five steel drums. When they exited each room the lights turned off and the door shut automatically.

"What are we supposed to do?" muttered Charlie.

"Maybe this time we're just supposed to find the tricks in the video."

"Could be. But I thought the point of this contest was to test our skills. That would just test how quickly we can look in every room."

"That's a skill," Flick said.

"Not for a magician. No, the Great Fox must want

us to work out how the tricks in the video are done. And somewhere on this level there must be a way of performing them."

They walked all the way to the end of the corridor, passing maybe fifty doors, and found another corridor leading off at a right angle. The lights pinged on in this one too, revealing it to be identical to the last corridor, with black doors on either side disappearing into the distance.

Charlie shook his head. "There could be thousands of tricks down here and no—"

A grinding noise made them spin around. A wall was moving across the corridor behind them, blocking the way they had come.

Charlie ran towards it and Flick stumbled after him. When she arrived at the new wall, she found it had opened up an entrance to another corridor, also identical to the last one. She opened the first door on the right and found yet another trick. There was a grinding noise again and the walls moved once more, closing off one corridor and opening up yet another.

"How are we ever going to find our way out?" Flick asked.

Charlie shook his head. "Maybe that's the skill."

28
The Silhouette

Harry and Ruby were sitting in front of the laptop in the dining room again, having been summoned for another call home. Harry peered at the screen. He could barely see his living room as it was so dark.

"Where's Mum?" asked Ruby, leaning forward.

Harry fiddled with the settings and tried to improve the screen brightness, but it made no difference.

"Hi, Mum. Are you there?" he called.

A blinding light filled the screen as if a spotlight had been switched on, and a figure appeared in silhouette.

Harry squinted. "Is that you, Mum?"

"Of course it's me," said a familiar voice. "Who were you expecting? The Queen?"

Harry breathed a sigh of relief. "I just thought something might have happened to you."

"Don't be ridiculous. We're perfectly fine. Although your father still hasn't finished the fence."

"What's with the lamp?" Harry asked. "We can't see you."

"It imitates sunlight and is doing wonders for my itchy scalp. Although most of that is probably to do with the stress you two cause me. How are you getting on?"

"OK."

"And how's my Ruby doing?"

"We're OK, Mum," said Ruby.

"Haven't you got any more to say than that? You must have some news. Have you performed any magic tricks yet?"

"We're not really performing tricks here. Just solving clues in a big house."

"I thought it was all about magic?"

"It is, but—"

"It's a competition," interrupted Harry.

"Yes, yes. I know that," snapped their mother. "You've told me all about it before." She adjusted the lamp. "When does it finish?"

"When we solve all the clues," answered Harry.

"Well, how long is that going to take?"

"We don't know. But it's a really important competition. If we win it, we'll be famous and have our own TV show."

"I'm sure. But in the meantime, your father was hoping to have some help with painting the fence."

Harry sighed and nodded. "We'll be home soon, Mum."

29
The Vanishing Coin

Charlie and Flick spent hours looking in room after room. Flick was feeling more and more despondent, and wondering what the point of it all was, when the voice of Christina suddenly boomed down the corridor from unseen speakers: "All contestants must report to the library immediately."

Charlie stopped in his tracks and looked at Flick. "How are we supposed to find the lift?"

As if on cue, there was a grinding noise and a wall began to shift in front of them. Beyond it they could see another wall doing the same. And then another and another. The noise was deafening and the floor shook under their feet as wall after wall moved aside to reveal one very long corridor. The lights around them dimmed, while in the distance they became brighter, encouraging them to walk forward. At the far end, they could see the lift doors glinting.

"That's impressive," said Charlie.

"How does the house know we need to find the lift?" Flick wondered.

"Well, there's a question." Charlie was unusually lost for an explanation as they hurried to the lift.

"Hi, Flick and Charlie," the lift said in its chirpy electronic voice.

"Hello. Ground floor, please," requested Flick.

"We have a deal," said the lift, not going anywhere.

"What's it going on about?" asked Charlie.

"We're in a bit of a rush," Flick said to the lift.

"A promise is a promise," replied the lift stubbornly.

Flick sighed. "OK. I'll show you one trick."

She had a fifty pence coin in her pocket and she dug it out.

"Charlie, will you be a willing volunteer to help me show the lift a trick? It's never actually seen one."

He smiled. "Of course."

She reached out and shook his hand. As she did so, she applied the lightest pressure to his wrist with her index and middle fingers, guiding him across her body to the left. This was actually a move from salsa, but it was a great way of finding out what kind of partner he was going to be. Flick knew that if people followed her lead, they were more likely to do whatever she asked. She increased the pressure and Charlie moved a little bit further to her left.

They were on.

In order to perform this trick, she needed to get close to him without setting off any alarm bells. If you move head-on into someone's bubble of personal space, they tend to feel uncomfortable. So what you do is give them a point of focus.

Flick said, "OK, I'm going to give you this fifty pence piece and I want you to hold on to it and we'll see if I can steal it back."

She gave Charlie the coin. As she did so, she broke eye contact and looked down at the fifty pence, then pivoted around until she was standing alongside him. She took his hand with the coin in it and lifted it up to shoulder height, palm facing upwards.

Flick had closed the gap. She was now right in his personal space.

"OK, close your hand. Would you be impressed if I could take the coin back now?"

"Maybe," said Charlie.

She smiled. "OK, open your hand."

He opened his hand and she snatched the coin from his palm, saying, "Thank you very much."

"That's lame."

It was a silly joke but she had achieved her goal. She was controlling where he focused his attention, she had him used to being touched and she was in his personal space. Under his radar.

"I'm not impressed," he said, laughing.

"Well, let's try it again," she said. "You try and steal the coin off me."

This time she put the coin in her left hand and got him to hold her wrist with his right.

She said, "Ask me to open my hand."

"Open your hand."

Flick did and the coin wasn't there.

It had actually never been in her left hand. She'd palmed it into her right hand while pretending to place it in her left, and when she took Charlie's arm to get him to grip her wrist, she'd balanced the coin on his left shoulder.

Flick pointed to the coin.

"Now I'm more impressed," he admitted.

Flick put her left arm behind him to take the coin off

his shoulder, giving him a tiny push forward as she did so. In the same moment, she reached down with her right hand and placed another coin into his back right pocket, using the momentum of his movement to conceal the action. When we move, we expect our clothes to alter shape, so Charlie didn't register this extra touch.

"You'll find some payment for your time in your back right trouser pocket," Flick told him.

He reached into his pocket and brought out a pound coin.

"To do the trick properly that should be another fifty pence piece, and I make this one" – she opened her hand – "disappear and pretend that I've made it reappear in your back pocket. But I've only got one fifty pence on me."

"Well, it's still a great trick," said Charlie, smiling from ear to ear.

"I agree," said the lift. "Very impressive. I'm now happy to take you anywhere you want to go."

"We just really need to get to the ground floor," Charlie said.

The doors shut and they started to go up. When they arrived in the hallway, they stepped out.

"Thanks for that," said the lift. "Greatly appreciated."

"A pleasure." Flick headed off across the entrance hall and down the corridor, unable to resist checking the David Copperfield alcove on the way past. She was relieved to see there was no sign of the secret opening.

Harry and Ruby were already in the library, sat by the fireplace, and a cameraman and woman and their associated sound teams were fussing about them.

"Come on, you two," said Christina. "Come and join us."

Charlie and Flick plonked themselves into the two remaining chairs.

"So, Charlie and Flick, and Harry and Ruby, you have all made it to level two."

Flick gulped. When did Harry and Ruby find the hidden door? She exchanged glances with Charlie, who shrugged.

"This means," continued Christina, using her most extreme shock face, "that Flick and Charlie are in the lead, having solved the puzzle and arrived on the second level in the shortest combined time. This gives them ten points, but Harry and Ruby have picked up five bonus points for finding the key in the maze, so the competition is still wide open and either team could easily win."

The scoreboard above the fireplace changed.

SCOREBOARD

Harry and Ruby: 5

Felicity and Charlie: 10

Christina stared dramatically into the camera lens until someone shouted, "Cut!" Then she gave one last flash of her sparkly white teeth and walked out without another word. Maybe she'd pulled a facial muscle.

The cameras had been set up so they could all be filmed in their chairs around the fireplace. They were supposed to record their feelings on the competition so far so the viewers could feel connected to them. Flick hated these bits. Thankfully it was soon over. The camera and sound people packed up their kit and rushed out of the door, and the four of them were back to being on their own.

Flick turned to Harry and asked, "How did you find the door to the second level?"

He glared at her. "We worked it out right after you did."

"Bit of a coincidence," said Charlie.

"Not really," snapped Ruby. "We're just surprised you were ahead of us. Although not very far ahead, after you took a week to get down the stairs."

Harry stood. "Don't worry," he said. "You won't be the first to find the next door."

He and Ruby walked out.

When they'd gone, Charlie groaned. "I can't believe it."

"Don't dwell on it," Flick said. "Let's split up for a bit. It's nearly time for me to call my mum, and then I want to come back here and research a hunch."

"OK," agreed Charlie. "I've got lots of ideas on how the different parts of the tricks were done, so I'm going to go back down to level two and watch the film over and over until I've worked it all out."

"Sounds like a plan."

Charlie grinned. "We're in the lead. We can win this."

30
The Melted Cookies

It was Flick's turn to call home, and the crew had set the laptop up in the dining room as usual. Her mum had answered the video call on her phone and was struggling to keep it pointing in the right direction. Flick had to wait for the camera to stop wildly spinning around before it settled on her mum's face. She was in the kitchen. Something looked different.

"I've only been gone a day and you're already repainting?" Flick cried.

"Yes, I fancied a change." Her mum laughed with a playful, dismissive wave.

"Didn't Dad choose the green?"

"He did."

"So why would you change it?"

Her mum glanced down and fiddled with something on the kitchen table.

"Because..." She trailed off. "Let's not do this now."

"He loves that kitchen," Flick persisted.

"He never did any cooking in it!"

"He said the green was like being out in the fields."

"Well, I never liked the green. And he doesn't want to be here to look at it."

Flick sighed. "Please don't give up."

"I'm not. But I'm stuck here with the green I never liked, and for what? He doesn't want to look at it but I have to sit here with it?"

"He'll come back."

"Well, when he does, he can paint it green again if he wants."

"I liked the green too."

Her mum rolled her eyes. "Oh, suddenly everyone loved the green!"

"I'm sorry. I like the blue too. I just don't want us to ... lose him."

"We won't. I promise. It's just paint, it doesn't mean anything. It's easily changed. I just—"

"I know."

"I needed to do it for me."

Flick paused. "I understand," she said. "How was work?"

"Really busy. I'm doing extra shifts again over the weekend."

Flick remembered Dominic Drake's threats. "Has there been any talk of cutbacks?"

"No. They are so busy."

"So no one has said you might lose your job?"

"No, not at all. I don't think there's any chance of that. Where is this coming from?"

"If anyone mentions it at work, you will let me know, won't you?"

"There's no problem at work. Why do you keep asking about it?"

"I was just wondering. Just promise you'll let me know if there's any talk of redundancies."

"Work is fine. Stop worrying. Look, I will distract you with my wonderful baking." Her mum tilted her phone so Flick could see.

"Cookies?" Flick laughed.

"Yes, but look at them! They look like they melted."

"It's because you didn't preheat the oven. Again."

"I know. But it made you stop asking questions about

work. So now we can talk about important things – how is the competition going?"

"Really good," said Flick, sitting back in her chair. "Right now we're in the lead."

"And tell me about this Charlie."

"Charlie? Where do I begin..."

31
The Phone Conversation

Flick climbed into her usual pod in the library and was just about to reach for her goggles when she realized she could hear Christina talking on her phone out in the corridor, and she didn't sound very happy.

"Well, I can assure you that I had no idea," she was saying.

She paused while the person on the other end spoke.

"Who did you say she was again? The daughter of Samuel Lions. And who's that? Right. Well, I don't know. This really isn't my area, you know; I'm in the fashion industry. Yes, she's still in the competition. Yes, that's right. It will be difficult to remove her now as she's been in for a while and is a key part of all the footage. Yes, I see. Yes, I understand. I'll see what we can do. We'll sort this out. Yes, I understand."

There was a pause as she hung up.

Shortly afterwards she spoke again.

"Hi, Dominic. It's Christina. We have a problem. The network rang me about Felicity. Yes, they don't sound very happy. I think that— Yes, I understand. Yes, of course. We just might need to speed things up a bit. Why have *I* got to do that? Why can't you? I'm not your assistant; I'm your co-host – we're equal. Well, that's a matter of opinion. You know, one day I'm going to make sure I don't have to put up with this. I'm sick and tired of being treated like— Don't you hang up on me!"

Flick listened to the sound of Christina walking away. She sat motionless for a bit, worrying about what she had just overheard. She wasn't sure what to make of it, so in the meantime she decided the only thing to do was press on.

She put on the gloves and grabbed the goggles. A couple of things had occurred to her. Firstly, there were hundreds of tricks stored on level two, so there was a good chance the Bell System was behind one of those doors. And secondly, she hadn't yet searched the Fox Files for information on it.

It was time to take a look. She pulled the goggles down over her eyes and her vision blurred. She typed *Bell System* into the search box. A film popped up and she pressed play.

The caption *Greatest Magic Trick Ever* flashed up below pictures of the High Court. A reporter stood outside the entrance, microphone in hand.

"We've been hearing arguments from the defence this week in the ongoing trial between magician Dominic Drake and master illusionist the Great Fox over the rights to a new trick. Drake claims that the Great Fox stole the concept of the illusion from him and is suing the Fox for intellectual property theft.

"The Great Fox has strongly denied Drake's accusation, and this week his legal team presented evidence that the trick was invented as the result of a collaboration between himself and a Mr Samuel Lions. The court case is being conducted behind closed doors because of the sensitive nature of the hearing so we can't bring you any details of the trick, except that it has been described by the Great Fox as 'probably the greatest magic that will ever be performed'."

The film cut to a shot of the same reporter outside the court building but wearing a different tie. He was holding an umbrella to shield himself from the rain.

"The world of magic is awash tonight with rumours of a new partnership between the Great Fox and lesser-known magician Samuel Lions. This follows revelations brought to light during the ongoing court case between the Fox and Dominic Drake over the rights to a trick known as the Bell System. Part of the Great Fox's defence is that the trick was the result of a collaboration between himself and Mr Lions and nothing to do with Drake. As evidence, he presented correspondence from the last couple of months between himself and Mr Lions in which they discussed the trick. Lions himself is due to give evidence tomorrow."

The scene changed again. Same reporter, but this time he was standing on the steps of the building at nighttime.

"Today in the High Court it was the turn of Samuel Lions in the witness box. His testimony supported the Great Fox's defence that the two of them were collaborating on a new trick called the Bell System and that this illusion could not, therefore, be the intellectual property of Dominic Drake. Lions stated that he and the Great Fox had previously been bitter rivals, but over the last couple of months they had struck up a close friendship. Lions invented the concept of the trick and together they worked out how to make it a reality. The evidence from this key witness brings to an end the Great Fox's defence in this trial, and we now await the judge's decision."

The final segment of the film was a single black and white shot of a box.

"This is the only known picture of the trick that everyone is talking about. What does it do? Well, rumours are rife but verifiable information is scarce. Apart from all the superlatives used by both Drake and the Great Fox about how good a trick it is, all we actually know is that the box is made of wood. Doesn't sound very impressive, does it? I guess we'll just have to wait for someone to perform it so we can be the judge of how good it really is."

At the end of the film were links to photos taken during the court case. Flick scrolled slowly through them. There were dozens of shots of the Fox arriving at the courthouse and some of her father too, including one with his arm around the Fox, both of them smiling away. How had she missed this? It seemed as if their relationship had completely changed. Were they friends? Had her dad actually saved the Fox from Dominic Drake? Why hadn't her dad told her the whole story?

She ripped her goggles off and sat back in the chair, staring at the fireplace. A log crackled as smoke gently disappeared up the chimney. She remembered her dad talking about the court case but she didn't remember him saying anything about testifying. And yet there it was in the archives. So she guessed their relationship wasn't so bad after all. It certainly didn't look as if the Fox was responsible for destroying her family.

So why did her dad walk out on them?

32
The Brother

Charlie sat in the dining room in front of the laptop. He could see his mum and dad sitting on the sofa.

"How are you, Charlie?" asked his dad.

Charlie leant closer to the screen. "How's James?"

"Tell us about you first," Charlie's mum responded.

"It's this amazing old house, and in it are these secret passages to different levels and we have to find them and get to the final level to win."

"Sounds amazing," said his dad.

"How is he?"

"He's not been too good," his mum replied after a pause.

Charlie sighed.

"You need to forget about us for a bit," she said. "Concentrate on what you are doing."

"That's not so easy."

"I know, but you have to. You need all your energy and focus to be on winning this competition."

"Has the funding stopped?" Charlie asked.

"Well…" His dad searched for the right words. "It just means that the new treatment won't happen. But the NHS are going to come and make an assessment, and we'll take things from there."

"Will they turn the machine off?" Charlie leant forward even further and gripped the laptop.

His mum tried to soothe him. "We don't know. We just don't know anything yet. James is OK for now."

"We're doing everything we can," added his dad. "We're not giving up. A Riley never quits, remember that."

"I'll win it for James," said Charlie.

"No," his dad said sternly. "You need to try and win it for yourself, Charlie."

"But if I don't win…" Charlie slumped in his chair.

"You're a good boy, love." His mum tried to smile. "But you need to focus on the puzzles."

"I understand." He nodded. "I miss you all."

"We miss you too, Charlie," said his mum.

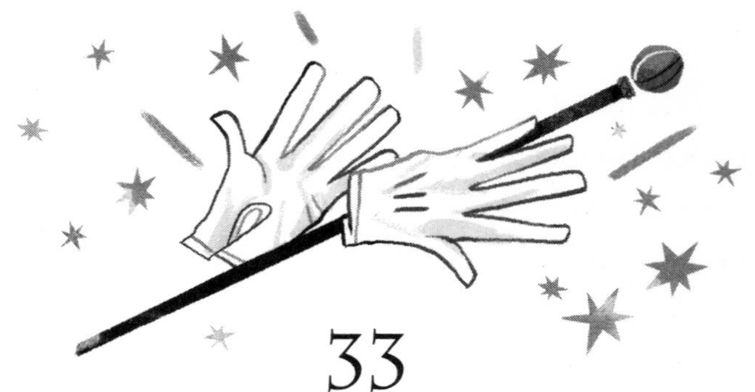

33
The Control Room

Dominic Drake was standing in the control room, watching the wall of TV screens.

"How many cameras do we have access to on the new level?" he asked.

"We aren't sure, sir. Still counting," replied one of the operators.

Drake shook his head. "How can you not know?"

This was typical. Why did he always end up working with idiots? Why couldn't he get some decent help for once? He'd never got his show in Vegas, never been able to take his career to the next level. Because he'd never got a lucky break. That was all it came down to – being in the right place at the right time. He had the skills to be a thousand times better than old Fox had been. He just needed the universe to hand him an opportunity to showcase them. And this was it. The Bell System was his ticket to the next level.

The operator said, “Well, we only get footage from each level as they discover it, and then we have to keep scrolling through the feeds to work out what we have.”

“Well, work it out faster,” Drake growled. “And someone get me my coffee.”

A few moments later, a young member of the production crew ran into the control room and handed Drake a cup. Her hands trembled a little as she passed it to him.

He took a long sip, closed his eyes and breathed in deeply.

“What type of milk did you put in this?” he demanded.

The girl looked blank.

“What type of milk?” he asked again. Slowly, so she could understand.

“Erm,” mumbled the girl. “White milk?”

“I said I wanted filtered oat milk,” he said, handing her back the cup. “And get here faster with it. I don’t want to drink it cold.”

The girl took the cup and ran.

Drake closed his eyes again and tried to focus on the problem. When he opened them, he said to the operator, "Level two is just lots of corridors, is that right?"

"It seems to be a bit more than that, sir," said the operator. "It's some kind of constantly shifting maze. All the walls move and so the corridors keep changing."

"How does it work?"

The operator shrugged. "We've no idea, sir."

At that moment, Drake's phone rang. He stepped out of the control room. Putting the phone to his ear, he said, "Yes, this is Dominic Drake. I see. Right. So, you're saying this person is the daughter of Samuel Lions? Yes, I can see the problem. Yes, I can see how it would look if the winner of *The Great Fox Hunt* was the daughter of another magician. No, that would not be fair at all. I see. No, I had no idea who she was. I will do that. What? Are you threatening to kick me off my own TV show? You listen here, young lady. This is my show and I won't let you do that. Don't you worry about Felicity Lions. I will have her removed at once."

34
The Walls

Flick roamed the corridors on level two looking for Charlie. There was no sign of him as she trudged past a line of identical doors. And then another. On and on. Turning handle after handle, opening door after door. Each room the same size and shape. Each containing a single trick – wooden frames, giant playing cards, curtains, mirrors, hoops, tables. A room with brightly coloured boxes. Then another with more brightly coloured boxes. Then another.

But no Charlie.

And the walking was playing havoc with her residual limb. She could feel a ruck developing in the socks, rubbing with each step. Walking and walking. Rubbing and rubbing and rubbing. Literally wearing her down. Maybe she would never find Charlie. Never find her dad. Never work out what happened to him. Never solve the puzzle. Never find the Bell System.

She stopped and leant against the wall. Then she slid down it until she was sitting on the floor. She stretched her legs out in front of her and massaged her limb, fighting back tears.

There was a low rumbling as the walls reconfigured themselves again. The corridor was suddenly a lot shorter. And then the door opposite was flung open, making her jump, and Charlie burst out.

"The way I see it," he immediately started saying, "it comes down to only a few possible methods for each part of the trick. But what I don't get is what each of those methods has got to do with this level."

He reached down and helped Flick to her feet.

She was so pleased to see him she wanted to hug him. She couldn't stop smiling. Wiping a tear from the corner of her eye, she distracted him by saying, "Tell me what your solutions are and maybe together we can work it out." Her voice was a little shaky but he didn't seem to notice.

"OK. Well, as I said, there are several possible options for each trick, and the one I'm about to tell you is only my best guess out of all the possibilities, and may not be correct, but it seems the most likely given a weighing up of all the most likely methods that I have—"

"CHARLIE!"

"OK. Sorry. Here we go then. So, in the first part of the trick, the judge picks a red crayon. Now given that the video of the magician's child must have been recorded in advance – it's unlikely that it's being played live – the magician must be controlling what colour crayon the judge chooses. There are several ways of doing this, but, having watched it over and over, I think it was done like this. The box of crayons is divided into two compartments. When the magician first shows the box to the judge, he opens the top. The compartment that is revealed genuinely contains crayons of all colours. So there are red ones, and blue ones, and green ones, and—"

"I understand what colours there might be."

"Of course. So the judge looks at those crayons in the box. Then the magician takes the box back and shakes it. Why does he need to do this? I suspect that at this point he flips the box over. He then presents the box back to the judge and asks him, without looking, to reach in and take out a crayon. He even keeps the flap half shut at this point, so that the judge doesn't see what crayon he is choosing. That's because with the box this way up, all the crayons in that section are red."

"But what about the fact that there are windows in both sides of the box and you can see different coloured crayons through them at all times?"

"That could easily be faked by sticking some different coloured crayons onto the sides, so they show in the window."

"OK." She nodded. "So far so good."

There was a low rumbling and the corridor was suddenly twice as long.

"What about the next part of the trick?" she asked.

"The second judge is given a Rubik's cube to shuffle. She does this and puts the cube back into the box. I think the solution here can be found in the answer to this question: why does the cube need to go back in the box? When it's put in the box and the lid is shut, a magnetic face then clips onto the cube so that it looks as if the judge has muddled up the cube in exactly the same way as on the video."

Flick nodded. "Again, makes sense."

There was a deep grinding noise and the corridor became even longer. The lights flickered and dimmed. Then the far end of the corridor got much brighter.

"Do you think the walls are listening to us?" asked Charlie.

"Something weird is going on, that's for sure," Flick agreed. "Tell me the next bit."

"The magician offers the playing cards to the third judge. He shows her that all the cards are different by flicking through the first few. Then he fans the deck out. Now, this part could be done very easily in a couple of different ways. Firstly, it could be that all of the cards after the first few are penguins. The magician could fan out the rest of the deck and pull the first few cards away from the judge so she won't pick one of those. Or it might be that he has a penguin card palmed, which he drops on the top of the deck and gives to her. I suspect it's as simple as the first method. All the cards after the first few are penguins."

"Sounds good to me."

The floor shook as the corridor lengthened even further. The lighting also shifted again; now they were practically in the dark. The far end of the corridor was very brightly lit.

"I think the walls want us to go this way," Flick said.

They started walking down the corridor. Charlie was wide-eyed.

"Tell me the last bit," Flick whispered.

"Well, finally the magician offers the last judge an upside-down book and asks him to draw a circle on the randomly opened page. This part can only be done one way and again is very simple. All the pages in the book are the same, that's why the magician opens it upside down. And the pen doesn't work. It makes no mark at all. All the pages already have a circle around the word *hat.*"

Flick nodded. "That's what I'd worked out for that part too."

The wall ahead of them retracted and the lights strobed wildly. At the end of the corridor, a TV screen rose out of the floor.

Charlie started to run. Flick did her best to keep up, wincing with every stride.

"Sorry," said Charlie, slowing down to a jog and waiting for Flick to catch up.

She bumped along beside him, her leg killing her with each step. But she didn't really care. They'd solved the puzzle.

35
The Notebook

Harry stood in front of the screen in the study and watched Flick and Charlie. As soon as they'd discovered the entrance to level two, footage from that part of the house had started appearing on the screen, and he was able to follow everything they did.

"This is interesting," said Ruby.

Harry tore his eyes away and walked over to the desk, where Ruby was reading through the Fox's notebooks.

"Look at this page," she said, pointing. "He's written *A moving maze of walls,* which seems to be a description of level two. And then this looks like some kind of shopping list for the TV screen, including stuff about the cables and the stand; and look, here is the motor for making it come out of the floor. But look at what this says here."

Harry followed her finger to some words that the Fox had underlined and drawn a box around.

Work out the pattern of how they're done,
And the winner you surely will become.

"What could that mean?" asked Ruby. *"The pattern of how they're done*. How what is done? The tricks?"

Harry read it again and thought it through. "That would make sense," he said. "But what *is* the pattern? What do all the tricks have in common?"

36
The Epic Tweet

Down on the second level, Flick and Charlie watched the screen as a film started to play. A magician was a guest on a talk show. Before beginning his trick, he pointed out a padlocked box suspended high above the audience from the studio lighting gantry, and explained that it had been there since the start of the show. He would get it down in a minute, but in the meantime, he wanted the audience to raise their hands if they followed the show on Twitter. Plenty raised their hands. The magician wondered if they could try to write a tweet with three members of the audience. It would be an epic tweet, he promised.

To start the process off, he produced a beach ball and asked the host to choose someone in the audience. The host picked a woman in a coral-coloured top sitting next to the aisle. The magician took the ball and gave it to the woman, asking her to stand up and state her name.

"Rachel," she said.

He explained that he was going to get three people from the audience to help him write this tweet, but unfortunately Rachel couldn't be one of them because the host had chosen her, and she could be in on the trick. He thanked her very much and told her that sadly she was just going to have to shut her eyes and throw the ball over her shoulder. This was exactly what she did and a man sat a few rows behind her caught it. The magician instructed the man to stand up and throw the ball again. This time the ball was caught by a woman in a blue dress. She stood and chucked the ball again to another woman on the far side of the audience.

The magician then asked the man to choose an activity, the more random or obscure the better.

"Singing," said the man.

Next, the magician needed a place. Anywhere in the world.

"Tahiti," said the woman in the blue dress.

Lastly, the magician needed a celebrity. Who were they hanging out with in this tweet?

"George Clooney," said the woman on the far side.

So they were singing in Tahiti with George Clooney, and the ball had started with the brilliant Rachel. The magician gave Rachel a thumbs up and then went on to relate a dream he'd had the night before. In the dream he had been singing in Tahiti with George Clooney. When he woke up, he'd tried to tweet about the dream, but because he had no phone service, he'd written this tweet on a big sheet of paper instead. And this was now in the box suspended above the stage.

The box was lowered and the magician unhooked it. An assistant wheeled a table onto the stage and the magician put the box onto it. He reached into his pocket and got out a key, which he used to unlock the padlock and open the box. From inside, he took out a clear plastic tube. He removed the cap from the tube and pulled out a large folded sheet of paper. He unravelled this one line at a time to reveal the words:

I'm singing
In Tahiti
With George Clooney

#luvURachel

The clip ended with the audience cheering and giving him a standing ovation.

Charlie frowned. "I guess all we need to do is work out how that was done and say it out loud for the walls to hear."

"Hmm," Flick said. "Not easy. Do you think the walls will help us find our way back?"

Before she'd even finished speaking, there was the familiar rumbling noise and all the walls started moving. When they finally stopped, there was a dead straight corridor ahead of Flick and Charlie, and at the end of it were the shiny doors of the lift.

"This house is starting to freak me out," Charlie muttered. "Hey, do you know what time it is?" he asked, looking at his watch.

Flick shook her head.

"Just after midnight." He was staring at her as if this was vital news.

"And?"

"And that means it's officially ice cream time."

"It does?"

"Sure," he said. "I did this last night. You wanna join me tonight?"

37
The Midnight Snack

David brought Charlie a bowl of chocolate cookie ice cream with white chocolate sauce. Flick had plumped for vanilla ice cream with caramel crunch and hot fudge sauce, so it melted into gloopy heaven. Well, if you're going to do ice cream at midnight, you may as well go big.

The large bowls were made of white bone china with a posh blue swirly pattern, and the spoons were heavy and old. Flick checked the back of hers and could see some type of hallmark on it. It was probably silver. She wondered if this was the most expensive bowl and spoon combination she'd ever eaten ice cream from. That seemed likely. Then she wondered if it was the most expensive combination she would ever use in her whole life. Also likely.

As Charlie shovelled heaped spoonfuls into his mouth, it occurred to her that this was the quietest she'd known him, so she decided to make the most of it by getting in a question.

"Tell me about your family, Charlie?"

She waited for him to swallow.

"Frommm Croygggon," he said.

"From Croydon?" she deciphered.

Charlie nodded.

"My mum's from Brazil," she said. "And there's just me. How about you? You said you have a brother?"

"That's a long story."

"I told you my story."

He thought about this for a bit before saying, "I can't talk about it."

"For you not to talk about something, it must be very serious."

There was something in his expression but Flick couldn't work out what it was.

They ate on in silence for a minute or two, but she could see Charlie was desperate to say more. Eventually he muttered, "Fell off his bike and banged his head and he's been in a coma ever since."

"I'm sorry, Charlie."

But Charlie was shaking his head. "That's not it."

He carefully placed his spoon back in the bowl.

"We have to win this competition or..." He trailed off and stared down at his melting ice cream.

Flick reached out and put her arms around him.

"A Riley never quits," he muttered.

"Then we'd better win," said Flick. "We'd better win."

38
The Roof

"You stay here," Harry ordered Ruby as he put the harness on and pulled the cord. There was a sound like a zip and he was propelled up through the hole he'd cut in the ceiling, into the gap he'd created by removing the roof tiles. At the top he undid the harness and pulled himself up the final couple of feet onto the roof, where he lay on his back gazing at the stars. It was a beautiful clear night. Carefully he rolled onto his stomach and took his first look across the roof. The pitch was shallow and he could see a large block of chimney pots ahead of him. Just where they'd said they would be.

He pushed himself up onto his knees and crawled his way over to them. As he rounded the red-brick chimney pots, he could see a large section of flat roof stretching between various other groups of chimneys. Once on the flat area, he stood and reached into his pocket, pulling out the phone they'd given him. It wouldn't work in the house because the producers had done something to jam the signal, but up here it should. The screen lit up and showed three bars, more than enough. A text message was waiting for him. He opened it.

DON'T CALL. YOU NEED TO TALK TO THE WALLS. YOU'RE NEARLY THERE. REMEMBER, SYNERGY WILL ALWAYS KEEP ITS PROMISES.

Harry stared at the message. *You need to talk to the walls?*

He turned the phone off to preserve the battery and looked at the view. Although it was dark, he could see out across the gardens to the far wall and then the lights of Weymouth and the sea beyond.

He started to make his way back down again. *Talk to the walls?* What on earth was that supposed to mean?

39

The Stupid Table

The next morning, they all assembled for breakfast again. David took everyone's order as they arrived and disappeared back through his door. Twenty minutes later, he started returning with food.

Ruby and Harry had booked out their private end of the table, as far away from Flick and Charlie as they could get. Flick tucked in while Charlie methodically separated the items on his plate, particularly making sure that his beans didn't touch his egg or toast.

Harry watched from the other end of the table. "Do you ever eat anything else?"

Charlie ignored him and carried on spooning beans into his mouth, careful not to allow them to fall on his egg.

"What happens if the beans touch the egg?" Ruby laughed.

Harry smirked. "Maybe the world will end."

"Leave him alone," Flick said.

"Or what?" asked Harry. "You gonna hop after me?"

Ruby giggled.

"Leave him alone," Flick repeated, standing up, "or when we win this competition, we'll spend the first episode of our TV show talking about how stupid you are."

"You'll have to win first," Harry retorted.

"Duh. Of course."

Harry scowled and stood up too, walking around the table towards Flick. For a moment, she thought he might try to hit her, but he seemed to think better of it and instead stormed past her and out of the door. His sister followed obediently on his heels.

"See you later, losers," Ruby said. "We don't have time to sit around this stupid table with you all day."

Flick watched them go. Relieved, she sat back down.

"Actually, this table isn't stupid," said Charlie. "It was originally David Copperfield's and kept in his house on the Caribbean island he owns. He gave it to the Great

Fox as a gift after a dinner party where the Fox expressed a liking for it. And the Fox had it transported…" Charlie stopped. "Sorry. I'm going on again, aren't I?"

"It's OK."

"And I'm sorry I wasn't able to tell you more about my brother."

Flick shrugged. "It's fine. I know you'll talk about it when you can."

Charlie thought about this for a beat and then said, "I'm just really worried about him. He's not getting any better, and we were hoping he would qualify for some deep brain stimulation treatment, but he hasn't, and the NHS are saying they can't keep him there for ever if he isn't going to get any better."

"Well, thank you for telling me that."

Charlie smiled. "I'm trying."

"And you're doing really well."

"A hug might help."

Flick laughed. "Come on, then."

They both stood and hugged until Charlie pulled away awkwardly, banging his leg against the table. He laughed. "Maybe Ruby was right. It is a stupid table."

And then it hit Flick. The stupid table. That was the answer.

She grabbed Charlie by the shoulders. "Charlie, once again you're a genius."

"Well," he said. "Naturally, of course. Except I have absolutely no idea what you're—"

"Charlie," Flick said, very slowly, raising her hands. "Shut up and follow me."

40
The Promise

Dominic Drake was standing in the control room watching the camera feeds. It seemed as if no one who worked for Channel Seven was capable of making a decent cup of anything. Earlier on he had asked for a simple iced Ristretto venti breve with five pumps of vanilla, seven pumps of caramel and four Splenda, poured not shaken, and they had looked at him like he was insane. He felt tired. What was wrong with these people?

His phone rang. What now?

Placing the phone to his ear, he said, "Hello? Yes. We are in the process of removing her, but it's not straightforward. She is fully integrated into the competition at the moment and… Well, there's no need – what? You can't replace me. I have a contract with Channel Seven to present this show. You want to get Electro in? Well, he's a very different type of artist, if you know what I mean. He won't give your show the professional image I bring. The whole thing will be poorer for his involvement. And I can assure you that contractually you can't do this."

There was a long pause. Then Drake said, "What if I promise to get this girl out in the next few hours?"

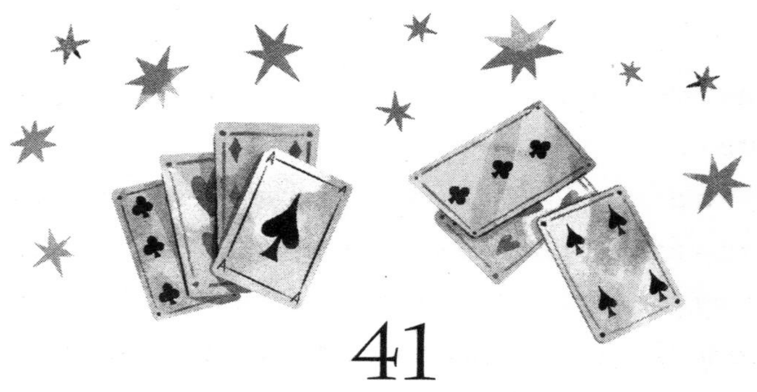

41
The Summons

Back on level two, Flick and Charlie stepped out of the lift and into the long corridor.

"OK," Flick said. "I think we need to say each solution again. The first is the box of crayons had a false bottom and was turned over while being shaken by the magician. This forced the selection of a red crayon."

The corridor lengthened ahead of them.

"Next," she continued, "the magician – no, wait. Charlie, you say this one. I think we need to work together."

"OK," said Charlie. "Next the magician gives the second judge a Rubik's cube, which she shuffles and puts back into the box. The box has magnetic sides that snap onto it so it looks like the judge made a particular pattern."

"And next," Flick said, "the magician forces the third judge to take a penguin card. He does this by only showing that the first few cards are different and then getting the judge to pick a card from the rest of the fanned-out deck. All of these cards were penguins."

"And after that, the fourth judge makes a mark on a page. Except the marker doesn't work and all the pages have the word *hat* circled on them."

By now the corridor had fully extended and they could see the TV in the distance. They headed towards it.

"What about the next trick, then?" asked Charlie. "The tweet one. The problem with this trick is that there is no way the magician could know what those people would say. Unless they were all fake audience members?" He looked hopefully at the walls.

Flick shook her head. "No. They weren't fake audience members. He didn't know what they were going to say."

"So how could he have written it down in advance?"

"He didn't."

"So how was the answer in the box?"

"It wasn't."

Charlie frowned. "I don't understand."

"The audience members give their answers and while they are doing this, an assistant behind the scenes writes down the combination on a piece of paper. They then put this piece of paper into a special compartment in the table. The table is wheeled onto the stage and the box is lowered onto it. There are secret flaps in the table and in the bottom of the box, and at this point a mechanism pushes the bit of paper up into the box. The magician then opens the box and pushes the paper through another flap, into the plastic tube, before lifting it up so the audience can see it."

They arrived at the TV screen. There was a grinding sound and it retracted into the floor. The lights flickered as the walls ahead of them opened up to reveal a set of stairs descending to the next level.

Christina's voice suddenly boomed down the corridor from unseen speakers: "Felicity Lions must report to the library immediately."

Flick looked at Charlie.

"That's very suspicious timing," he said. "They just happen to need you at this exact moment?"

"If you don't report to the library straight away," Christina's voice continued, "your team will be disqualified."

“Don’t leave me to go down there on my own,” said Charlie.

Flick shrugged regretfully. “I don’t have much choice,” she replied.

At the other end of the corridor, the walls moved to reveal the lift doors.

“Please get back as fast as you can.”

“I will,” Flick promised.

42
The Confession

Christina was in the library, standing in front of the fireplace. “Felicity, please be seated,” she said. “You need to use a VR chair.”

“Let me guess,” Flick said, trying to sound brave, “Dominic has really missed me?”

“Just do as you’re asked.” Christina gestured to the nearest pod.

Flick sat and placed the goggles over her eyes. Her vision blurred as she was sucked back into Dominic Drake’s apartment. She could see the seafront through the glass doors.

The suited man was there again, leaning against the granite worktop. He still hadn’t done any cooking.

Dominic Drake entered the room through the doors behind the kitchen. Today he was wearing a grey shirt and jeans. He hadn't even bothered with his cane.

"Time is up, Felicity," he said. "You will be removed from the competition tomorrow. It's all over. You only have today."

"You can't just kick me out for no reason."

"It's not up to me. The network know who you are and have insisted that you be removed. They can't have the daughter of a magician who was friendly with the Great Fox winning this competition. It would not look fair. So they have said that in the morning, you'll be replaced."

"What if I refuse to go? What will the viewers think if I suddenly get thrown off?"

"They're going to say that you had a family emergency and so you and Charlie were replaced."

"You're not going to kick Charlie out too?"

"You're a team. You come and go as a pair."

Flick felt sick.

"I don't care about you winning this competition," Drake said. "I just want you to find me the Bell System."

He paused.

The goggles went black and Flick could suddenly see camera footage from inside the house. Harry and Ruby were running down the long corridor, shouting out the solutions to the tricks. They got to the end and Ruby recited the final method, with the table, and the TV retracted into the floor and the stairs appeared. Excitedly they ran down them and disappeared.

The screen went black for a second and then Flick was back in Drake's apartment.

He said, "My money is on the Townsends winning. Especially since I don't want you getting distracted by the competition from now on. You only look for the Bell System or your family will suffer. Do I make myself clear?"

"Yes," she mumbled.

"You don't want your mum to lose her job, do you?"

She shook her head.

"I also want to show you this."

The screen changed and she was suddenly looking at a film of her father. He was sitting in an interview chair, talking straight at her.

From behind the camera, the interviewer asked, "What is this secret that you have kept your whole career?"

Flick's father looked uncomfortable. He shuffled in his seat and Flick could see beads of sweat on his brow.

"Go on," said the interviewer.

"My whole career I've been a fraud. Every trick I ever performed I stole from Dominic Drake."

Flick gasped.

Her father had a tear in his eye as he said, "Everything, all of it, was stolen from Drake."

The screen blurred and Flick was once again in Drake's apartment. She felt suddenly cold.

"Where did you get that?" she managed. "When was it filmed?"

"It never was." Drake smiled. "It is, of course, a trick. Pure illusion. I've spent a lot of money having some very clever people collect footage of your father from over the years. They made that film."

Flick's stomach cramped.

"And when I post it online, your father's reputation will be ruined. The makers have assured me it's impossible to tell it's a fake. Whatever was left of your father's pathetic career will be over."

He walked up very close to Flick so she could see right into his piercing green eyes.

"Find me the Bell System, Felicity. You have until tomorrow."

Flick nodded.

"Don't make me come in that house and get you."

43
The Theatre

Flick took the lift all the way down to level three this time. As she stepped out, Charlie was waiting for her.

"You'll never guess what just happened," he said.

"Harry and Ruby," Flick replied. "They've solved level two and they're now here on level three."

"How—"

"Drake showed me."

"This level is very different," said Charlie. "If we want to beat them, we're both going to have to bring our A game."

They entered a large theatre. There was a stage to their right, lit up and framed by red curtains. On the left was an auditorium full of empty seats. It looked just like the VR theatre in the Fox Files.

Right in front of them was an easel with a sign that read:

THE ASSISTANT IS WHAT
THE MAGICIAN MUST BE.

UNDERSTAND WHY AND YOU'LL
FIND DOOR THREE.

Looking around the theatre, Flick calculated that there had to be a thousand seats across three different levels. It was a vast space.

Harry and Ruby were already up onstage exploring. Flick could see them moving about behind the curtain.

"There's loads of props in the wings," Ruby was saying. "Is that a fireman's helmet? And look, a workshop out the back. Maybe we're supposed to make a trick and perform it."

Harry walked back onto the stage and spotted the others.

"Shh," he hissed.

Ruby appeared round the curtain and scowled at Charlie.

Flick ignored them. "I reckon Ruby might be right,"

she said to Charlie. "Let's split up. You're the genius at making tricks, so get in that workshop and see what tools there are. I'll search this level and see what other clues I can find."

"OK," agreed Charlie, bounding up onto the stage.

Flick turned and headed down the rows of seats towards the back of the theatre, the words of the clue running through her mind. It was common for the magician and assistant to swap places. It was a useful way to get the magician from one part of the stage to another in plain sight without arousing suspicion. But like the other clues, this one could potentially describe hundreds of tricks. Maybe thousands.

She arrived at the back of the auditorium and found a set of doors. Pushing them open, she entered a lobby area complete with a ticket office and snack counter down one wall. Behind the counter, she could see ice cream and popcorn and a selection of fizzy drinks. In front of the ticket office was another easel and sign, which read:

WORK OUT THE PATTERN
OF HOW THEY'RE DONE,

AND THE WINNER YOU
SURELY WILL BECOME.

There was a large set of doors that was clearly the main entrance to the theatre. Flick tried to open them but they were locked. She explored a few side doors and found a set of toilets and a store cupboard full of supplies for the snack counter. She helped herself to a packet of sweets and munched on them while she thought. *The assistant is what the magician must be*. It made sense to head to the library and do some more research to remind herself of how this type of trick might work.

As Flick searched through the tricks in the Fox Files database, she was struck by how often assistants and magicians swapped places. It was especially common in teleportation tricks, where the magician would be tied up in a box and then magically appear on the other side of the stage. She watched Valentino perform several of these types of trick while her brain spun. She needed answers fast. For all she knew, Harry and Ruby might have already found the next door.

Think, Flick.

Think.

She removed her goggles, stood up and slowly walked around the library. It seemed logical that they needed to perform a trick on the stage. But what did the riddle mean? They were in pairs, so was one of them supposed to be the magician and the other the assistant? But how were they supposed to swap? And what good would that do?

And then a thought hit her. It was perfect. And like all tricks, the solution was actually very simple. It was quite brilliant.

44

The Greatest Trick Ever Invented

Harry stood in the theatre and looked up at the stage. *Work out the pattern of how they're done, and the winner you surely will become.* What was the pattern that all the tricks shared? It had to be something obvious, staring him in the face. He ran through them all again in his mind. And then he wondered – even if he found a pattern, what was he supposed to do with it?

"You're not being much help, Harry," shouted Ruby from the stage.

She was right – he wasn't helping. He'd make a terrible assistant. Of course! Harry slapped his forehead. That was it! He sprinted to the lift.

"In a hurry?" the lift asked.

"Level two," he said. "And fast."

When he arrived on the second level, he ran into the corridor.

"I know how it's done," he announced in a very loud voice.

Nothing happened. The walls remained unmoved.

"I know we have to perform a trick on the stage on level three."

Ahead of him the walls moved and the corridor lengthened. He sprinted to the end.

"I know the secret of this house."

The walls didn't budge.

"I know the Great Fox's secret."

Still the walls refused to move.

Harry thought about the wording. *Work out the pattern of how they're done, and the winner you surely will become.*

He chose his next words carefully.

"I know the pattern of how all the tricks are done," he said. "The magician and the assistant, they—"

The walls in front of him slid to the left, revealing another long corridor. Harry was plunged into gloom as the lights dimmed, while ahead of him they brightened, encouraging him forward.

He moved down the corridor as the lights flickered and pulsed, trying to see what had been revealed at the far end. It wasn't a TV and he couldn't see a door. In fact, he couldn't see anything. Just a spotlight on the floor. A pool of light in the dark.

Harry edged closer and closer until he could make out a wooden box about the size of a small suitcase sitting on the floor. It had two words written on it:

BELL SYSTEM

He picked it up and weighed it in his hands. It wasn't very heavy. It didn't rattle. But he knew that inside was the greatest trick ever invented.

PART FOUR

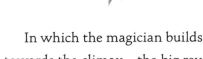

In which the magician builds
towards the climax – the big reveal.
Of course, it's just a trick. All an illusion.
But the question is: how is it done?

45

The Shortest Chase Ever

Flick arrived on level two and stepped into the long corridor. At the far end, she could see Harry picking up a wooden box like a little suitcase. That was how Drake had described the Bell System. Her heart lurched. Harry turned and gave her a wave before disappearing round a corner.

"Wait!" Flick shouted, breaking into a run. She bumped along, pushing as hard as she could, but the walls were already moving. She lengthened her stride, flinching with the pain of each jarring step. But it wasn't enough. With a slow, inevitable grinding noise, the corridor shortened, cutting her off from Harry. She stopped running and doubled over, panting.

"The pattern," she managed. "I know the pattern."

She looked up at the walls. They didn't move an inch.

She stood up straight and said more loudly, "I understand how the tricks are done."

Nothing.

"I know the pattern behind all the tricks."

The walls refused to budge. Harry had beaten her to it. Defeated, Flick hobbled back down the corridor towards the lift, each step causing bright, yelping shocks of pain to course up her leg.

46

The Destruction of a TV Show

Dominic Drake flung open the front door to the house and stormed into the hallway, flanked by two security guards and with Christina trotting in his wake.

"The network will go crazy," she wailed. "We'll be all over the footage. They'll have to declare the whole competition void. They'll scrap the show and we won't get paid."

Drake turned on her. "If you're just going to follow me around complaining, you can go back to the Portakabins."

Christina opened her mouth but then seemed to think better of it.

Drake's phone rang. He pulled it from his pocket. "Speak."

"We've lost all the camera feeds," said a very worried-sounding voice.

"What do you mean?"

"It's like the power has been pulled. We've got nothing."

"How has that happened?"

"We don't know, sir."

"Where is the Bell System?"

"We don't know. We can't see anything."

Drake hung up and turned to the two security guards. "I know who'll have it. Let's end this. Follow me."

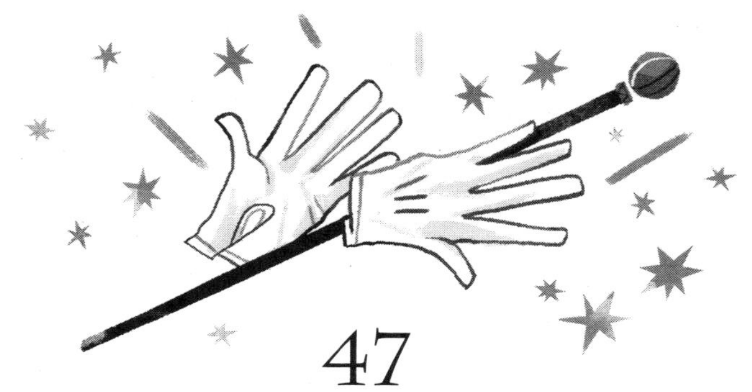

47
The Trap

Flick stepped out of the lift and headed back into the theatre. “Charlie?” she called. She hurried towards the stage. “Are you there?”

Charlie appeared from the wings. “How’s it going?” he asked.

“Harry and Ruby have the Bell System.”

“How? When did that happen? Hang on, I’ll come down.” Charlie jogged to the far end of the stage and started to walk down the steps.

At that moment, they heard a swish as the lift doors opened again. Charlie paused halfway down the steps, open-mouthed, as Dominic Drake entered, followed by two large Channel Seven security guards and Christina.

“There you are,” Drake called across the auditorium. He started to head down the right-hand side of the seats, towards the front, so Flick motioned Charlie to come down and the two of them began to edge along the front and up the other side.

Drake nodded to one of the guards, a bald stocky man who doubled back towards the rear of the theatre to head them off.

“Let’s not waste time,” Drake called across the chair-filled space. Which was rich coming from a man who’d clearly taken the time to pick out a pocket handkerchief that matched his eye colour.

“We don’t have it,” Flick yelled back. She and Charlie edged along the rows towards the back of the theatre.

“Interesting. But I bet you know where it is.”

“Harry has it,” Flick said. She glanced down. They were at row D.

“And you’re going to tell me where Harry is.”

“We don’t know.”

“You expect me to believe that? A clever girl like you?”

The bald security guard had now reached the back of the theatre and was heading down the side aisle towards them.

"We don't have it and we don't know where it is," shouted Charlie, panic in his voice.

The other security guard had followed them along the front, between the first row of seats and the stage. They were now surrounded. Flick glanced down again. Row K. Their only option was to change direction and head into the middle aisle. But then they would be really exposed. Trapped with nowhere to hide.

They edged past rows L and M. The guard following them was now only a few rows away and the bald guard was closing in.

Flick suddenly noticed the outline of a door beside them. It was painted the same colour as the theatre wall and was hard to spot, but there was definitely a handle. As they drew level with it, she spotted a small sign.

A toilet.

Flick made a dart for the handle, yanking the door open and pulling Charlie inside. It was a single cubicle. Very cramped. She slammed the door shut behind them and quickly slid the bolt across. There was barely enough room for them both.

The handle turned as someone tried the door. And then, when it didn't open, they pulled on it harder and harder. The door creaked under the pressure.

On the back wall above the toilet was a slim frosted window. Flick tried to peer through it but all she could see was blackness.

"Where are you going to go?" Drake called through the door, laughing.

He had a point.

Flick looked around the tiny space again.

One toilet. One basin. One hand towel dispenser.

They couldn't escape down the toilet or through the plughole in the basin.

One window.

It was only a small window, a couple of feet across.

One window.

It had no catch. It was not designed to open. There was just darkness beyond it.

One window.

Could they fit through it?

Flick grabbed the lid of the cistern and hurled it. There was a huge crash as the glass shattered. She quickly unfurled a large wad of hand towels and wrapped the soft paper around her hands as protection, and then she started punching out the remaining shards of glass. Next she climbed onto the toilet seat and pulled herself up to the empty frame. As she wriggled through the opening, she could hear the security guards really going for it with the door. It would surely break soon.

It was a difficult squeeze and she had a moment of panic when she couldn't get her prosthetic leg through, but Charlie gave her a helpful push and finally she dropped down into a corridor. She landed awkwardly on her shoulder and lay there for a couple of seconds, trying to catch her breath.

"Pull my arms," called Charlie.

Flick rolled over and got to her feet to yank Charlie through. He came out like a cork from a bottle and they both ended up in a heap on the floor.

"Where do you think this passage goes?" Charlie asked, helping Flick to her feet again.

The corridor was in darkness, the only source of light coming from the smashed toilet window, but as their eyes adjusted they could see a spiral staircase in one direction.

"I think we should go up," said Flick.

48

The Out-of-Body Experience

Charlie started to run towards the stairs, then slowed when he realized Flick was struggling. She bumped along, doing her best, wincing with every step.

"Hold on to my arm," he urged.

"I managed to hurt my shoulder when I fell out of the window," Flick muttered. "And my leg feels like it's on fire."

They reached the spiral staircase and Flick looked it up and down. So steep. So tight. So twisty. Why did it always have to be this way?

"You go first," said Charlie.

So she did. One step after another, slowly climbing

and climbing, around and around, higher and higher into the darkness. At the top, there was a metal gantry and some sort of soft emergency lighting coming from above a door. Flick stumbled forward and felt for the handle. It turned and she pulled the door open.

At which point someone grabbed her and shoved something over her head. Some sort of hood.

Which was a surprise.

She struggled, trying to reach up and pull it off. But she couldn't. She tried to turn but someone was holding her. The only things she knew for certain were that the hood was itchy, smelt faintly of lemons and made her feel very tired. Not because she was having a relaxing time under it, but because something was making her body feel heavy. Like lead.

Sounds became muffled and distant. They seemed to echo and bounce around her mind, knocking and crashing into things. As if someone near by had taken up playing the cymbals.

Her head slumped forward.

Her legs buckled.

She dropped to her hands and knees. As if she wanted to crawl through the door. Which she didn't.

And then she slowly tipped forward as her arms

collapsed. As if she wanted to examine the floor very closely. Which she definitely didn't.

Somehow she was floating above herself now. Looking down. As if she wanted to fly away. Which she did. She *really* did. She wanted to fly a long, long way away.

But she couldn't.

So instead she looked down and watched as the bald security guard grabbed her arms and dragged her across the floor. Charlie, very wisely, put his hands up and followed.

49
The Instructions

Harry placed the Bell System on his bed and walked over to the hole in the ceiling.

"You go first," he said to Ruby. "Put the harness on."

Ruby examined it. "It's just like the one we use for the levitation trick."

"It's identical. Except the wires are more heavy duty, because they don't need to be invisible."

Ruby wrapped the harness around herself and did up the fastenings.

"Now," Harry said, "you just pull on this cord and it will take you up. Be careful because it's quite fast, so keep your arms in or you'll hit the ceiling."

Ruby nodded.

"When you get up there," Harry continued, "you need to pull yourself up onto the roof. It's not a big stretch so you should be fine. Then take the harness off and let it drop back down through the hole for me. Once you've done that, you can crawl up to the chimneys. Behind them is a massive flat area where you'll be safe. Have you got all of that?"

Ruby nodded again.

"OK," Harry said. "Pull the cord."

Ruby pulled, there was a zipping noise and in a flash she had disappeared through the hole.

Harry walked back over to his bed and picked up the Bell System. He examined the lock and then tried to get his fingers under the lid to prise it open. No chance. Without the key, it was going to be impossible to get into it.

He smiled to himself. *Work out the pattern of how they're done, and the winner you surely will become.* There was a pattern to all the tricks, and he'd found it. On his own. And then he'd talked to the walls and it had worked. Synergy were going to use him in their next show. He would be famous. And his mum would be proud.

Behind him, there was a clunk as Ruby dropped the harness back down through the hole. He took the Bell

System and placed it at his feet while he strapped on the harness. Then he picked it up and pulled the cord.

Harry shot through the hole. He pushed the Bell System up onto the roof and pulled himself up after it. Then he removed the harness and wedged it at the top of the hole.

Pushing the Bell System ahead of him, he crawled across the tiles to the chimney pots, where he found Ruby admiring the view.

"You can see for miles up here," she said.

He reached into his pocket and pulled out the phone: I HAVE IT.

A couple of seconds later, the phone vibrated with a response: WE'RE COMING TO GET IT NOW.

Harry thought about this for a second and then replied: I'M ON THE ROOF.

The response was almost instant: YES. STAY THERE.

50
The Worst Carpet Ever

Flick opened her eyes. She was sitting on a chair, slumped over a desk. Her mouth felt like a badger had been sleeping in it. She tried to lift her head a little, but pain shot through it. She squinted. It was a square room, the magnolia walls were scuffed with use and there was a hideous brown swirly carpet on the floor, like some kind of seventies nightmare.

In the corner were boxes of crisps and popcorn. Maybe this was another storeroom for the snack counter at the back of the theatre? The carpet was making her headache worse, so she rested her forehead back on the table, and when that didn't help, she tried massaging her temples.

Breathe in.

Breathe out.

She ran her tongue around the inside of her mouth. It might have been more than one badger.

Someone had left a couple of bottles of mineral water on the table, and she grabbed one and gulped it down. It tasted so good that she picked up the second one and drained that too.

The adrenalin rushing through her body slowly subsided and she became aware of how much her leg hurt. She pushed the chair back and stretched it out. It was badly bruised. Every time she touched it, even for a fraction of a second, she could feel hot waves of boiling pain. Extending it fully, she unclipped the pin from the socket and pulled off the prosthetic.

Flick winced as a whole new wave of pain, in its many bright and jangly colours, hit her. Taking a deep breath, she very gently rolled down the liner and pulled the silicone cup away from the bottom of the limb. The skin was now free to communicate its anger fully. She looked at the damage. Well, she wiped the tears away from her eyes first, and then she looked.

Her limb looked like it had been burnt. The skin was an amazing collection of raw reds and purples, weeping and bleeding too. And then she couldn't see any more as she started to cry.

She let the tears come. It was a relief to finally let it all out, so she kept them flowing by allowing thoughts of her dad to run through her mind. She would never find him. Never understand what had happened. He would never again make her laugh, or fly her kite, or play his dreadful Oasis songs too loud, or make up stories with her teddies, or have water fights with her in the garden, or buy her Lego she didn't want and then spend hours making it himself.

She didn't understand why he had left without any explanation. Why he hadn't been in touch since. What he'd been doing with the Great Fox and why he'd lied about the court case.

She didn't know, and she always seemed to be one impossible, painful step away from answers. They were always out of reach. A step too high. Around a corner.

It hurt too much.

She shuddered with each wave, each line of thought, watching the tears fall off the end of her nose into her lap.

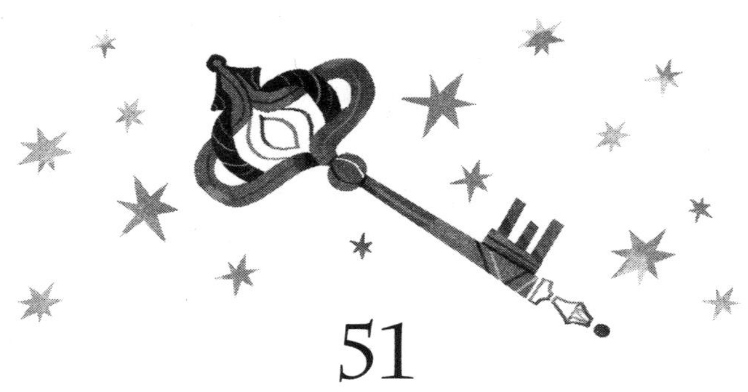

51
The Cat and the String

Someone was coming into the storeroom. Flick heard a key slide into the lock and turn. The door opened and the bald security guard stepped inside.

Flick quickly tried to compose herself. She dried her eyes and sat up, attempting to control her breathing. She wiped a final tear from her nose.

Christina followed the guard into the room and took the key from him. She placed it in her pocket and walked towards Flick.

"How are you feeling?" she asked, giving Flick her best fake concern. Full-width smile, plenty of teeth, slightly raised eyebrows.

The bald guard stayed by the door and eyed Flick suspiciously.

"Awful," Flick said. "Can I have some more water?" She held up the empty bottles.

"Of course you can, darling." Slight roll of the eyes, straight mouth.

Christina stepped forward to collect the empties and as she did so, she glanced down and noticed Flick had removed her leg. People tended to react in one of two ways to this. There were those who could not look at it. Their eyes would dance around, looking anywhere else in the room, as if they were following an invisible fly. And then there were those who had to look. Their eyes became glued to it.

Christina was a had-to-look type of person. Her eyes locked on Flick's limb and that was it. She was hooked.

Flick let her limb work its magic and then knocked one of the bottles onto the floor. Christina moved closer to help, eyes still glued to Flick's leg as Flick bent to pick up the bottle.

Flick's dad had taught her that if you move your hand in a straight line, sometimes people will follow it with their eyes, and sometimes they won't, as their brain predicts the movement and they look to the end point.

But if you move your hand in an arc, people are much more likely to follow it. So Flick grabbed the bottle from the floor with her left hand and, as she straightened up, she looped it in a high arc in front of Christina, before placing it back on the table next to the other bottle. At the same time, she reached out with her right hand and, in a split second, slipped the key from Christina's pocket.

Christina picked up the bottles from the table. As she did so, Flick dropped her right hand down, away from her right leg – which once again had Christina's full attention. Flick moved her hand under the table and out of sight.

"I'll be back with a couple more," Christina said, tearing her eyes away from Flick's limb.

The guard opened the door for Christina and then slammed it shut behind them.

Flick listened.

She could hear the guard whisper, "I thought I gave it to you."

As the muttering continued, Flick started to feel a whole lot better about her situation. A plan was beginning to form in her mind, and she decided it was time to get her leg back on. Call her old-fashioned, but she liked to go to war with as many limbs attached as possible.

Once her prosthetic was back in place, she paused before attempting to stand. Summoning her courage, she slowly manoeuvred herself upright and pushed down hard. The pain hit her like a tsunami, but she kept pushing until she heard the pin click into the socket.

She stood for a moment, supporting herself on the chair. She noted that it had been quiet outside the door for a good minute or so, and while she felt sick with the pain and had a splitting headache, she knew she had to take this chance. She stumbled towards the door.

She tried the handle.

It turned and she slowly edged the door open. She could see the snack counter and the lobby area and ticket office beyond. There was no one there. She gave the storeroom and the horror of the brown carpet a final glance before stepping out, closing the door silently behind her.

She could hear Drake's voice echoing inside the theatre: "Forget her." Christina responded, but Flick couldn't make out what she was saying. Then Drake said, "I know where he'll be. All of you, come with me."

There was another door right next to the storeroom. Flick tried the handle. It was locked, so she put her mouth close to the crack and whispered, "Charlie, are you in there?"

There was no response.

She gently knocked on the door. "Charlie?" she hissed more loudly.

Nothing.

She stepped away from the door and around the snack bar, slowly and silently approaching the doors to the theatre. She edged forward and took a peek. The auditorium was empty; Drake and the others had gone. She stepped into the theatre and looked around, just to be sure, and then she walked back to the snack bar and shouted, "Charlie? Are you here?"

She listened. Nothing.

"CHARLIE!"

There was a noise from the ticket office. As she drew closer, she could see the door handle jiggling up and down and hear a muffled voice coming from inside.

She put her mouth next to the keyhole. "Charlie, you in there?"

"It's locked," came the response.

"You OK?" she asked, trying the door herself. It wouldn't budge.

"Yes, I'm fine. You OK?"

"All good here," she said.

She put her shoulder to the door and tried forcing it. It didn't even move a fraction, so she knelt and examined the lock. "If you pull on the door, I'll push at the same time," she said.

Still it wouldn't move.

Flick stood there panting from the effort, uncertain what to do next.

"Look," she said. "I need to go and find Drake and Christina. If I can get the Bell System, I can force them to open this door."

"OK," came the muffled response.

"I know it's not much of a plan, but it's all I have. Unless you have a better idea?"

There was silence for a moment and then Charlie said, "I haven't got a better idea. I'm sorry, I can't think of anything else to try. I don't know what to do."

"Don't apologize, Charlie. I'll be back for you, I promise."

Flick let go of the handle and stepped away from the door. Truth was, it was a terrible plan. How likely was it really that she could somehow get the Bell System from Harry and use it to force Drake to release Charlie? Not very. But it was the only plan she had.

52
The Plan

Flick took the lift to the entrance hall. It didn't say hello this time. When she arrived, she stood and listened carefully, trying to work out where Drake and Christina might be. She could hear voices on the landing above, followed by a zipping sound. And then silence.

Creeping to the bottom of the stairs, she listened again.

Nothing.

She was going to have to walk up the stairs. She couldn't risk the noise of the lift and having the doors swish open in front of them. So, slowly and quietly, she began to make her way upstairs. As she neared the top, the landing came into view. There was no sign of Drake.

And she hadn't heard anything since the zipping noise earlier.

Stepping onto the landing, she peeked into Ruby's bedroom. Nobody there. She tried Harry's room. No one was in there either, and she was just about to move on when she spotted something hanging from the ceiling. Creeping closer, she could see what looked like some sort of harness dangling from a hole.

The harness was out of reach so she dragged a chair over. Standing on this and stretching as high as possible, she was able to dislodge it.

Without stopping to think about what she was doing, Flick put it on and pulled the cord. She heard the zipping sound from earlier as she was catapulted up through the hole and into a loft space filled with rafters. It was cramped, but there was a small gap where some roof tiles had been removed. Poking her head through the gap, Flick could see that the pitch of the roof was shallow. There was a large collection of chimneys above her, so she hauled herself up and started crawling towards them. As she got closer, she could see that in the centre of the chimneys was a large open section of flat roof where Drake, Christina and the two security guards were standing. Harry and Ruby were at the far end, Harry clutching the Bell System as he backed away from the adults.

Then Flick became aware of a sound. A *whump-whump-whumping,* coming from the sea. She rolled onto her side and saw a helicopter coming in, low and fast. It banked around the house and hovered above them, its wash beating down. Flick put her hands over her ears and watched as Drake, Christina and the two security guards dropped to their knees, trying to shield themselves from the downdraught.

The helicopter pitched and rolled, edging in closer and closer, until it was right above Harry and Ruby. And then the door was opening and a man was reaching down for them. Flick could only see the side of his face, but he looked like the guy in Synergy. Harry dragged himself forward, bent over and shielding his eyes from the wind, the Bell System still in his hands. Ruby was already up on the helicopter skid, being pulled inside.

And then Flick saw the bald security guard get to his feet and run at Harry. He moved surprisingly fast for a big man, pushing forward against the downdraught, running in a crouch. Ruby was now safely inside the helicopter and Harry had almost reached the man leaning out of the door. He was just stretching out a hand when the security guard hit him with the full force of his body. They both fell onto the tiles in a heap.

The Bell System was flung out of Harry's hand and sent skidding across the roof, propelled by the force of the helicopter's downdraught. Flick watched the box slide. It came to rest right on the edge of the roof, nearer her than the others. She got to her feet and, battling against the pitch of the roof and the blast from the helicopter, she ran towards it.

53
The Edge

Flick staggered forward, desperately trying to keep her balance as the wash of the helicopter and the pitch of the roof threatened to send her flying. She could see the Bell System box teetering right on the edge of the roof, caught on the black iron guttering. She allowed herself a glance to her right and saw the two security guards on their feet, their jackets billowing in the wind as they ran towards her. They were shouting something. Not that Flick could hear it over the helicopter.

She turned back towards the box just as she ran across a patch of moss. Her prosthetic leg slipped, skidding out from under her, and before she knew it she was sliding across the tiles towards the Bell System.

And the edge.

She couldn't stop herself as she clipped the Bell System with her good leg and sent it flying. And then she was following it. Falling. Until, at the last second, she managed to reach out with her left hand and grab the rim of the guttering. It bowed and shuddered under her weight as she dangled over the front of the house. Looking down, she saw the Bell System tumbling through the air in slow motion. As she watched, open-mouthed, it flipped end over end, getting smaller and smaller. Then it hit the concrete path below her and shattered into a thousand pieces.

The security guards arrived and leant over her. She could hear Drake shouting, "Leave her. We need to get down there and salvage whatever's left."

The bald guard gave her a little smile and a wink and then they were both gone.

Flick's left arm felt like it was going to rip off with the strain. She managed to hook her right hand over the lip of the guttering too. Then she made the mistake of looking down again. It was a long drop. Onto concrete.

Her mind was racing. She needed to move fast, while she still had some strength in her arms, because as they became weaker things would only get harder. She lifted her left hand and managed to clasp the far side of the guttering, closer to the roof. Then she did the same with her right, pulling herself a little higher. Next she began to swing her legs back and forth, trying to build enough momentum, until finally she managed to reach beyond the guttering with her right hand and grab hold of the edge of a tile. She did the same thing with her left hand, and finally, finally, she was able to haul herself slowly up onto the roof.

She closed her eyes and lay there, exhausted, massaging her arms, which felt like they'd been pulled out of their sockets. After a minute or two she opened her eyes and stared groggily up at the helicopter, which was now hovering over the front of the house. She could see Harry mouthing something at her through the helicopter window. She tried to focus. What was he saying?

It was the same word over and over. A short word that looked like it began with an *f*. Far? He was pointing down. She could barely move, but she turned her head to the side and looked down. All she could see was the path below and some bits of the Bell System. She squinted back at Harry, who was urgently gesturing for her to get up.

“Far, far,” he was mouthing.

Well, yes, it was far. The ground was a long way down. What was he getting at? And then the helicopter banked and slowly rose into the sky.

She closed her eyes once more and listened to the sound of it recede, trying to catch her breath. After a while, she opened her eyes again, but all she could see was mist. She rolled onto her side and lifted her head. Rubbing her eyes, she strained to see the way back to the hole in the roof. And then she realized it wasn’t her eyes that were the problem. The mist was really there. In the air. And it wasn’t mist.

It was smoke.

The word Harry had been mouthing was *fire*.

54
The Rescue

Flick needed to get to Charlie fast. Images of him trapped in the ticket office as flames ripped through the theatre filled her mind. She stumbled to her feet and towards the hole in the tiles. Dropping down into the loft space, she hastily put the harness on again and was zipped back into Harry's room. She took the harness off as fast as she could and rushed out onto the landing, hitting the lift call button.

Nothing. The button didn't even light up. So she turned and hustled to the top of the stairs, where she started to bump her way down. Each jarring step sent shock waves through her limb, but she didn't care. She'd let Charlie down; she'd let her dad down. She'd failed to get the Bell System. How would she get Charlie out of the ticket office? If they couldn't budge the door before, how would they manage it now? And even if she did get him out, what would they do then? They would have made a great team; they could have taken the Great Fox's tricks to a new level, just like he wanted. They would have been worthy winners. What would happen to Charlie's brother now? How could the family pay for his treatment? And what about Charlie? Whose assistant would he become?

And then it hit her.

The solution to the final puzzle. The answer to the riddle.

Work out the pattern of how they're done, and the winner you surely will become.

She thought she had worked it out already. But what if, like all good tricks, there was more than one layer to the solution?

As Flick descended the stairs, the stench of smoke grew stronger, and by the time she arrived in the hallway her eyes were stinging. Thick black plumes were pouring from the corridor that led to the library. She was just feeling grateful she didn't need to go that way when she noticed things weren't much better in the other direction. As she entered the corridor to the dining room, she could see that several of the paintings down the left side were on fire and flames were starting to creep along the wall. She slipped her right hand up her sleeve and put it over her mouth to stop herself choking on the smoke. The heat stung her face as she moved as fast as she could down the corridor.

She pressed onwards, trying to shield herself from the sparks, until she came to the door of the dining room. She ducked inside, relieved to step out of the heat, and knocked urgently on the butler's door. There was no answer, so she knocked again, harder this time, and rang the bell.

Outside in the corridor there was a loud crack, followed by the sound of something heavy falling.

Eventually she heard a voice from beyond the door. "OK, OK. I'm coming."

The door opened.

"Do you require an emergency omelette? Or a cup of tea, madam?" David asked.

"The house is on fire, do you know that?"

"Oh yes. We're perfectly safe."

"We are?"

"Yes, quite safe."

Flick regarded him for a moment and then took a deep breath. She said, "I know you're the Great Fox. You're the answer to the final clue. *The assistant is what the magician must be.* That's you. You're the assistant, but really you're the magician in disguise. Or rather, without your disguise. Because you've always worn a fox mask, no one has ever known what you look like, so you could just pretend to be dead and be your own butler."

He grinned at her. "Well done."

"I'm right?"

"I am the Great Fox."

"So you're not dead?"

"Not currently."

"*Work out the pattern of how they're done* – all the tricks were done by an assistant. The turntable in the Statue of Liberty trick was controlled by an assistant, the tricks involving the magician's daughter and the video were prepared in advance by an assistant, and the answers in the tweet trick were written down and placed in the table by an assistant. That's the pattern – all the hard work was done not by the magician, but by the assistant. And you are the assistant. So that means you were also the voice in the lift, and you controlled the walls on the second level. You were listening in, and when we got the clues right, you changed the walls so we could find the next level."

"Very good, Flick." The Fox reached out and shook her by the hand.

"In which case, I really need your help. Charlie is trapped in the ticket office. And, obviously, the house is on fire."

"Then the moment has arrived. I've been waiting a long time for this. Better get my things."

He disappeared for a moment and when he returned he was wearing his trademark fox mask. "Now I'm ready for action."

"What are we going to do?"

"Firstly, don't worry about the house being on fire; it's designed to burn only in certain areas. Until I tell it to do otherwise." He waved some kind of remote control in his hand.

"You actually started the fire?" asked Flick.

"Of course," he said.

"You're burning your own house down?"

"We've reached that stage in the trick. Don't worry, it's all under control. Now, to win this competition you need to stand on the stage on level three and perform a trick yourself. You know that. So that's what we're going to do. But first we'll get Charlie out, and then I'm going to perform it with you."

"What trick are we going to do?" Flick asked.

"One that will put everything right. Just follow me. I've got this covered. This old house still has a few surprises up its sleeve."

55
The Last Trick

Flick and the Great Fox stepped out of the dining room into the burning corridor, where the Fox stopped. Flick nearly crashed into the back of him.

"That's interesting," he murmured.

"Interesting?"

"Yes, it's not supposed to be doing that."

"Doing what?" Flick asked, squinting at the flames.

"Burning."

Flick coughed on the smoke.

"After the Bell System was discovered," the Fox said, "I programmed a device to set off a couple of smoke machines in the upstairs bedrooms. I thought it would be a good distraction while I performed the next part of the trick. But this…" He trailed off and waved his hand at the fire.

And then he seemed to reach a decision. "We need to go," he said, grabbing Flick by the arm and starting to run. "Things seem to have got a little out of hand."

"Do ya think?" Flick muttered, jolting along behind him.

The Fox led her down the corridor. The walls were on fire in places and several more old paintings were now ablaze. They rushed past, Flick using her arm to shield her face from the heat. They reached the entrance hall and the Fox led her towards the lift. He pressed the button on his remote.

Nothing happened.

He pressed it again and stared at the lift.

Flick looked at him. "Doesn't it stop working in a fire? I thought you weren't supposed to use the lift wh—"

"Shh." The Fox glared at her, putting the remote control to his ear and shaking it. He paused. "Perhaps it has a safety cut-off." He scowled at the remote as if it would supply him with some answers.

"Do you have any fire extinguishers or sprinklers installed?" Flick asked, looking nervously at the smoke coming from the corridor leading to the library.

"What?"

"Fire extinguishers?"

The Fox looked blankly at Flick.

"So," said Flick. "You spent years building all the puzzles in this house, even fitting it with a three-dimensional maze and smoke machines, but you never thought to buy a fire extinguisher?"

He looked confused. "We need to get to the theatre. How can we get there?"

"You're asking me?"

"I'm thinking out loud," the Fox snapped. "We have to get in there" – he pointed to the burning corridor – "and open the floor in the David Copperfield alcove."

"Which is on fire."

"I..." The Fox looked down at the remote control in his hands and appeared to reach a decision. He threw it across the hallway, where it skidded across the polished marble floor before crashing into the stairs and breaking apart.

"We need... Erm. Do you want my jacket?" the Fox asked. "To cover your mouth?"

"I can use my sleeve."

"Take a deep breath before we go in there and move as fast as you can."

"I'm not the quickest."

"We've got to do this. Ready?"

Flick took a deep breath and nodded. Then together they ran into the smoke. It stung Flick's eyes so badly that she had to shut them, but the Fox kept pulling her forward. Maybe his mask helped protect his eyes. She tried again to open her eyes, hoping to get her bearings. Bright orange flames licked the walls on either side of her. She could hear the roar of the blaze now, as if the air itself was boiling. Still they kept moving. She would need to breathe soon.

And then the Fox was pointing.

Flick tried to see what he was gesturing at. There was an arch of fire, which had to be the alcove. She stepped in that direction. A burning beam had fallen from the ceiling and was blocking their path. The Fox leapt over it and beckoned urgently for her to follow. Flick stared in terror at the flames licking along the beam. She was going to have to jump as high as she could to pass through the gap.

She looked behind her. This would require a run-up.

She took several steps back. She heaved in a breath, which made her cough, so she clamped her sleeve over her mouth even more tightly and slowly took another.

Then she held her breath again and ran. As she reached the beam she launched herself into the air and flew through the gap, landing on her prosthetic, which buckled under her. She went down hard.

And then the Fox was above her, reaching down to help her to her feet. She didn't have time to think about the pain. They were completely surrounded by huge flames. The sound was deafening; the heat was unbearable. It felt as if her skin were peeling off.

The Fox somehow found a section of the wall where there were no flames and put his hands against it, pushing with all his might. Flick joined him, and slowly they began to move the floor away to reveal the opening. Flick ran to the gap and started down the stairs. She almost fell several times but she didn't care. All that mattered, as she stumbled downwards, was that she could feel the air getting cooler. She landed at the bottom, gulping in huge suitcase-sized chunks of the cool fresh breeze.

The Fox appeared behind her. She could hear him breathing heavily, but he seemed to be OK.

"Need to keep moving," he spluttered from under his mask.

Flick's eyes were watering and a coughing fit wracked her body, but she nodded, and they trudged forward in silence down the long corridor past all the doors. All the way to the opening in the floor and the next set of stairs. Flick went first again as they descended to the next level, where they stepped out into the theatre.

There was some faint smoke coming from the stage, but Flick was relieved to see no flames here yet.

"By the way," she said. "You should also know that Drake is going to release a fake video of my father that will destroy his reputation unless I take him the Bell System, which has been smashed to tiny bits on your front path."

She felt her face. It stung to touch it.

"Don't worry about Drake," the Fox said. "He's finished. And don't worry about the Bell System. That was just an empty box."

"What? An empty box?"

"It was a decoy, of course."

"I don't understand."

"You will. Now, where is your friend again?"

"In the ticket office."

"Ah, yes."

They hurried out through the doors at the back of the theatre and into the lobby, where the Fox rummaged through a big set of keys he'd produced from his pocket.

"Now, let me see. It should be one of these," he muttered, trying one of the keys and failing to open the door.

"Hi, Charlie," Flick called. "You OK?"

There was a sound from behind the door and she heard Charlie say, "I've not gone anywhere."

The Fox eventually found the right key and the door swung open. Charlie's face was a picture as he took in Flick's singed and ash-covered appearance.

"What on earth happened to you?" he asked.

"I'm fine," Flick said. "There's no time to explain."

Charlie turned to the Fox. "Are you…?"

"The house is on fire," the Fox said. "Which is OK, because it won't come in here yet. Although it will eventually."

"Charlie, may I introduce the Great Fox," said Flick.

"Pleased to meet you," said the Fox. "Any friend of Flick's is a friend of mine. But maybe we can all have a cup of tea and get to know each other another time."

Charlie looked confused. "Just to be clear," he said. "You're the Great Fox?"

"That's me," the Fox said, reaching out and shaking Charlie's hand. "This is my house. My stage. My show. And now I'd like you all to join me in a trick."

"Ooooh, yes please," said Charlie. "I've always wanted to join you in a magic trick. In fact, I would say that you're in my top twenty magicians of all time who I would most like to join in an illusion, so it would be a great honour. You could say that this is a dream come true, or at least it will be when we do whatever we are about to do. I can't wait to—"

The Fox held up his hands. "We'll discuss my disappointment at only being in the top twenty another time; for now, can we just get on with it?"

Flick thought she caught a glimpse of the magician rolling his eyes behind the mask.

"He's always like this," she said. "Especially when he's excited."

"Sorry," said Charlie.

The Great Fox grabbed Charlie by the hand and they made their way out of the lobby and into the theatre. Flames were now visible in the wings and part of one curtain was smouldering.

"A very important lesson for you both," said the Fox, "is that the show must always go on. Even when things go a bit wrong." He led them down to the front, where they climbed the steps up onto the stage.

"Even when we might burn to death?" asked Charlie.

The Fox positioned Charlie beside him and then they waited for Flick to join them.

"Flick, you go on the end," the Fox said. "Everyone in a line."

As Flick took the final step onto the stage, she looked up into the top tier of the theatre and saw that many of the chairs were now ablaze. Behind them, more flames were licking at the sides of the stage and the curtain was now very much on fire.

The three of them stood next to one another looking out into the empty auditorium.

"I always imagined," said Charlie, "that my role would be the ideas man. The guy that designed the tricks and then stayed safely in the wings. How did I get here?"

The Fox pointed out into the thickening smoke. "The camera is at the back, on the balcony."

Flick couldn't see anything now past the front row.

"Right," said the Fox. "Ready?"

Charlie and Flick looked at him.

"Erm, what do we need to do?" she asked.

"Well," he said. "The alarm has just gone off." He reached into his jacket pocket and pulled out another remote control which was buzzing.

Charlie stared at it. "What does that mean?"

"This tells me the fire service have now entered the house which means we can make our escape." He pressed a series of buttons on the remote to turn it off. "All that's left for us to do is raise our arms and wave."

And so that is exactly what they did.

56
The Fox Files: Final Entry

The reporter was standing outside the Channel Seven offices at night. "*The Great Fox Hunt* ended in disaster this week," he said, "when the house used as the setting for the show caught fire. The resulting blaze raced through the building and left parts of it a smouldering wreck.

"According to the fire service, it took them four hours to put out the blaze. The fire itself was described by the emergency crews as 'catastrophic'. It gutted the library and the dining room, and swept through the entrance hall with its valuable wooden staircase. What wasn't burnt received extensive smoke damage. It seems as if the house had a complex series of underground levels and these were also very badly damaged by the blaze.

"Rumours have been circulating that following the fire, magician and co-host Dominic Drake was in a great hurry to re-enter the house and search these lower levels. Sources close to the show have told us that Drake has insisted the Great Fox is still alive and somehow responsible for the blaze. He has hired ground-penetrating radar and infrared equipment to look for any trace of secret passages, convinced that the Fox and two of the contestants escaped the fire together. So far nothing has been found."

The film cut to pictures of graphs as the voice-over went on: "The share prices at Channel Seven took a dip yesterday after the network officially admitted it had lost two of its contestants during filming for the show *The Great Fox Hunt*. It is not believed that the participants were killed in the fire; rather it is thought that they somehow left the house without detection and deliberately disappeared. Channel Seven said it had launched an inquiry into what went wrong. Plans for a second series have been shelved."

Next came footage of Harry and Ruby getting out of a car onto a pavement crowded with reporters.

"However, as a result of this decision, two other

contestants from *The Great Fox Hunt* are suing Channel Seven for breach of contract. Harry and Ruby Townsend, who were declared the winners of the competition, have initiated legal action against the network after it was announced that a TV show featuring them would not be going ahead. As competition winners, they had been promised their own series and stage show. However, in light of the fire and the disappearance of the two remaining contestants, Channel Seven has said it will not be developing any spin-off shows. A spokesperson for the Townsend family said they were bitterly disappointed."

Finally the film cut to the reporter outside the gates to the Fox's Den.

"Is the Great Fox still alive? Sources close to *The Great Fox Hunt* said they thought they saw the Fox inside the house just before it caught fire. Could Dominic Drake be correct in his allegations that the Fox was involved in the blaze and subsequent disappearance of Charlie Riley and Felicity Lions? Is this all a prelude to an incredible reappearance from the great magician? We'll have more on this story as it unfolds. Back to the studio."

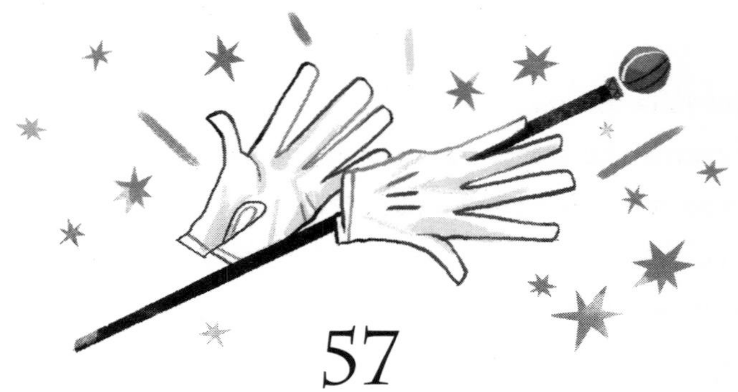

57
The End

Dominic Drake collected up all the pieces of the Bell System and tried to reassemble it. He checked every last splinter for clues or hidden parts but found nothing.

In the end he had to conclude that it was just a box. An empty wooden box. He has watched the footage of Flick, Charlie and the Fox standing on the stage and waving again and again but hasn't yet worked out how they got out. Or even if they did.

He hasn't released the video of Flick's father. The Fox thinks he's holding on to it, hoping still to do a deal for the real Bell System. Plus there's the problem that no one will believe him at the moment.

In fact, Christina and Drake are both being sued

by Channel Seven for their reckless behaviour while hosting the programme. No one knows where Drake is right now. He's gone into hiding.

58
The Perfect Cookies

As for Flick, she went home to her mum accompanied by Charlie and the Fox. Charlie's parents drove down to join them and they all sat in her front room drinking tea, transfixed as Flick and Charlie told them everything that had happened. The clues, the secret levels, the Bell System, Dominic Drake and Christina Morgan, nearly falling off the roof, unmasking the unmasked Fox, getting locked in a burning house and escaping under everyone's noses.

At times Flick thought her mum was going to explode, but she let them get to the end. They told the complete story. Every detail.

"So the whole thing was a trick?" giggled Charlie's dad. "Even your own death."

"Yes," said the Fox. "The whole thing. What I really wanted was to find someone worthy of being the new Great Fox to carry on my legacy. And Flick worked it all out, proving she's perfect for the job."

"But," Flick's mum said, "you nearly killed her in the fire!"

"I'm very sorry about that. Things did get a bit out of hand," he admitted.

"A bit?" Flick's mum shook her head and stormed off into the kitchen.

The Fox turned to Flick. "I didn't mean for it to get so dangerous in the end."

"At least we're all OK now," she replied.

"It was very dangerous," Flick's mum said, re-appearing with a large plate of cookies. "And I also don't understand why the Townsend kids have been declared winners of the competition. They might still get a TV show and they've got all your tricks."

"You made cookies again!" Flick exclaimed. "And they actually look like cookies!"

Her mum looked proud. "I've been practising."

"They've got *some* of my old stuff," the Fox continued. "Tricks that have been done to death. When the time is right, I'll reveal that I didn't die and that Flick has inherited my real legacy. No one will care what they do then. People will laugh at them for being fooled."

"What will you do now?" Charlie's mum asked.

"Protect the real Bell System."

"And what's that?"

"Something a lot bigger and more important than a suitcase." The Great Fox smiled. "The box that Harry found was a fake prize. He thought he'd solved the final clue, but in fact he was a long way away from the real answer. Flick was the one who worked out the pattern and discovered my real identity. She is a very worthy winner, and will be perfect for what needs to happen next."

"Where will you go?" asked Flick's mum. "You don't even have a house now. Or do you plan to live in the ashes?"

"Well, I do own six more houses. And I would love to fly you all to my home in the Bahamas. That's where we will start planning what happens next with the Bell System."

"Well, I…" said Flick's mum.

"You want to fly us all out to the Bahamas?" asked Charlie's dad.

"Yes," said the Fox, making it sound like the most natural thing in the world. "I'd love you to come." He opened his hands wide. "I'll cover everything. And I'll pay everyone five thousand a month to work for me. Although actually doing any work is optional."

Charlie's mum shook her head.

The Fox tried to reassure them. "I can make it more if that helps?"

"I'm sorry," said Charlie's mum. "But my husband and I couldn't leave James."

"Of course," said the Fox. "I understand. Absolutely." He turned to Charlie. "But I hope you will come?" Then he looked at Flick's mum. "What do you think?"

"Well," she said, "I don't know. For me, it's up to Flick."

"I want this like nothing else in the world!" Flick beamed.

"That's decided then," her mum said.

"That's good," said the Fox. "Except..." He turned back to Charlie's mum. "If you don't mind my asking, how long has James been in hospital?"

"Three years," she revealed. "Some of the additional experimental treatment has been funded by a charity but..." She looked down at her hands.

"I want to help," he said. "I'm going to be paying for all of James's care from now on."

Charlie opened his mouth but nothing came out.

"Whatever the cost is to get the help for this young man, I will pay it," the Fox insisted.

"That's amazing," said Charlie's dad. "Now we just have to find funding for the deep brain stimulation clinic."

"I'll pay for that too. Whatever you need, I will sort it. It's the least I can do after everything I've put Flick and Charlie through."

Charlie opened his mouth again and then closed it. He said in a very quiet voice, "You will?"

"Of course. Whatever it takes."

"Fantastic." Charlie's mum wiped away a tear. "In that case, I'll contact the clinic and tell them we're back on."

Charlie said, "I – I'm really, really…" He closed his mouth again. "I can't speak."

"It's OK," said the Fox. "Sometimes we don't need words."

59

The Blue Paint

Flick sat at the kitchen table and removed her prosthetic. One of the first things the Fox had done after they escaped the house was to arrange for a doctor to check them all over. The left side of her face still stung from the heat, but it wasn't badly burnt. The doctor had also examined her leg after all the punishment it had been through. She now had an impressive array of ointments and creams that she was supposed to apply every few hours. She rolled off her socks and surveyed the damage. Her limb was still a red and purple mess, but at least now she would have time to rest it. As she gingerly applied some lotion, she could hear the Fox in the other room laughing about Synergy hiring a helicopter for their failed attempt to steal an empty box.

Her mum bustled into the kitchen.

"I've decided I prefer the blue," Flick said.

Her mum smiled. "Good, so do I." She looked at Flick's leg. "You're going to need to do a lot of resting for a few weeks."

"I will." Flick winced as she touched a particularly sore area.

"Promise?"

"Promise."

Her mum smiled and put her arms around her. "Thank goodness you're back safe."

"I never told you why I really entered the competition. It wasn't to be like Dad. It was to try and get him back."

Her mum nodded and sat down next to Flick.

"Before he left," Flick continued, "he said the Fox had stolen the Bell System. Or rather, that's what I thought he said. But I think he might have meant the Fox had stolen his chance with the Bell System. Which is quite different."

"Your father has always been a mystery. That's partly why I love him, but also why I find him so frustrating. You have done something amazing by winning this competition. He would be very proud of you."

Flick nodded.

"But your dad needs to want to come back into our lives. We can't be for ever chasing a shadow. It has to come from him."

"Yes," said Flick. That was certainly true.

60
The Plane

Flick and Charlie were on the Great Fox's private plane. It was a black Gulfstream with a cream leather interior, and they had plonked themselves in the super comfy seats at the back, while the Fox, who was so relaxed he had removed his mask, gave the pilot some last-minute instructions. Flick's mum was sitting at the front and looked to have already fallen asleep.

Flick had removed her prosthetic leg to give her limb a rest during the flight.

The Fox returned from the cockpit and sat down next to Charlie. "How does it feel to be the real winners?" he asked.

"Great," said Charlie. "But what exactly is the prize?"

"Not to have all my old tricks. They've been done. They're in the past, spent. What we're going to do is something that has never been done."

"What's that?" Flick asked.

"All will be revealed in time," said the Fox. "So, Flick, will you become the new Great Fox?"

She frowned. "I'm not sure."

"Why would you say that? You worked out the puzzles and won the competition, and you beat Drake."

"You know I've only got one leg, don't you?"

"And?"

"Well, it..." Flick trailed off, searching for the right words. "It limits me."

"Take a look at my face," said the Fox. "What do you see?"

"I can see you have a birthmark. If that's what you mean."

"For much of my childhood, I was bullied because of it. People told me I would never have a career onstage where people were expected to look at me. I would certainly never have a TV show. And yet look what I've achieved."

Flick nodded.

"But I did it by wearing a mask. And I wish I hadn't.

Because I hid what makes me unique. Your leg makes you one of a kind; it gives you a different perspective. It makes you beyond ordinary."

"That's a nice way of looking at it." Flick smiled.

"Plus it's a great place for hiding things in a trick. I'm sure we can put it to good use."

Flick laughed. "OK," she agreed. "I'll take you up on your offer. But I have two conditions."

"Which are?"

"I don't want to be a Fox. That was you. I want to be the Great Lion. Carry my father's name."

Fox smiled. "Absolutely. The Great Lion it is."

"And second, I want Charlie to be my assistant. We come as a pair. In fact, we only work together."

Charlie opened his mouth. "Yet again. No words."

"I prefer the new Charlie," Flick said.

The Fox laughed. "Of course Charlie can be your assistant. The Great Lion and her assistant will take the world by storm."

"So, what are we going to do?" asked Charlie.

"Well," said the Fox. "A lot of people want to get hold of the Bell System, but it's a very dangerous trick. Thankfully, it's now in a safe place."

"Where's that?" asked Charlie.

"We are on our way there now. And perhaps when we get there, we'll find Flick's dad."

Flick nearly fell off her chair. "My dad?"

"Yes. Do you want to see him?"

"Is this for real?" Flick asked.

"Very much so."

"You've spoken to him?" Flick glanced at her mum and saw she was still asleep.

"Of course. Your dad and I have been working on this for months. Trying to keep the Bell System from getting into the wrong hands. He's very excited you're now part of the team, and he can't wait to see you."

It was Flick's turn to run out of words.

61
The Question

In case you're wondering, we got out of the burning house, surrounded by guards, while buried deep underground, very easily. We did it by— Well, see if you can work it out. Like all good tricks, the method was simple but effective. I'm sure it won't take you long to figure it out, and when you do, send me a message, because you might be able to help us on our next assignment. What comes next is a very tricky puzzle indeed and we'll definitely need someone with your skills to help us solve it.

THE FOX FILES

A step-by-step guide to learning a new card trick

This is a great card trick to try if you want to improve your magic skills – and impress your friends! Your audience member is going to pick a card at random from a pile of nine, and after seeming to thoroughly mix up the pile, you will reveal their card to them at the end of the trick. Remember to practise it a few times before trying it on someone else. The Great Fox always says that preparation is the key to a good trick!

1. Ask an audience member to shuffle the cards, then fan out the deck and have them select nine cards. Get them to deal the cards face down into three piles of three. They should pick up one of these piles, shuffle it, then look at the card on the bottom.

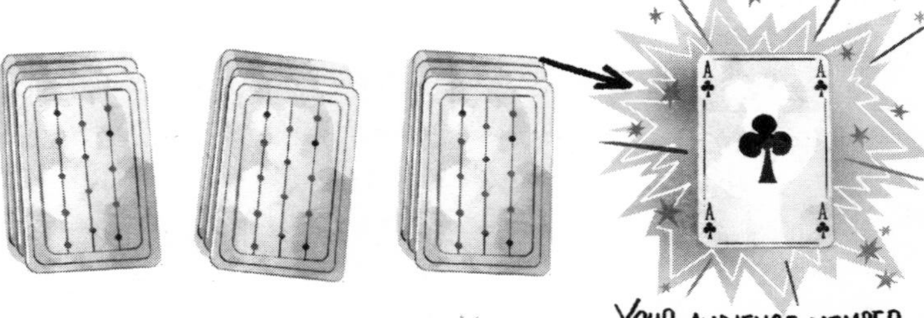

THE third CARD IN the PILE WILL BE THE ONE that YOUR AUDIENCE MEMBER LOOKED AT

2. Gather up the three piles of three cards so that they are one pile of nine again. **As you do this, ensure you place the group of three cards that your audience member chose on the top of the pile.**

3. Take the remainder of the pack and ask your audience member to choose another card. They should place it face up where you can both see it.

4. Now you return to your pile of nine cards. Explain that to randomize things further, you are going to use this pile to spell out the number and suit of the card your audience member just chose.

For example, let's imagine you are spelling out the ten of hearts. You should put three cards into a pile, saying the letters T, E and N as you lay each card face down. You then place the six cards that remain from your pile on top. **It's very important that you place the remaining cards from the pile of nine on top of the cards you used to spell out the word.**

5. Do the same for the words OF and HEARTS. **By continuing to place the remaining cards from your pile of nine back on top each time you spell out a word, you will end up with your audience member's original card as the fifth in the pile.**

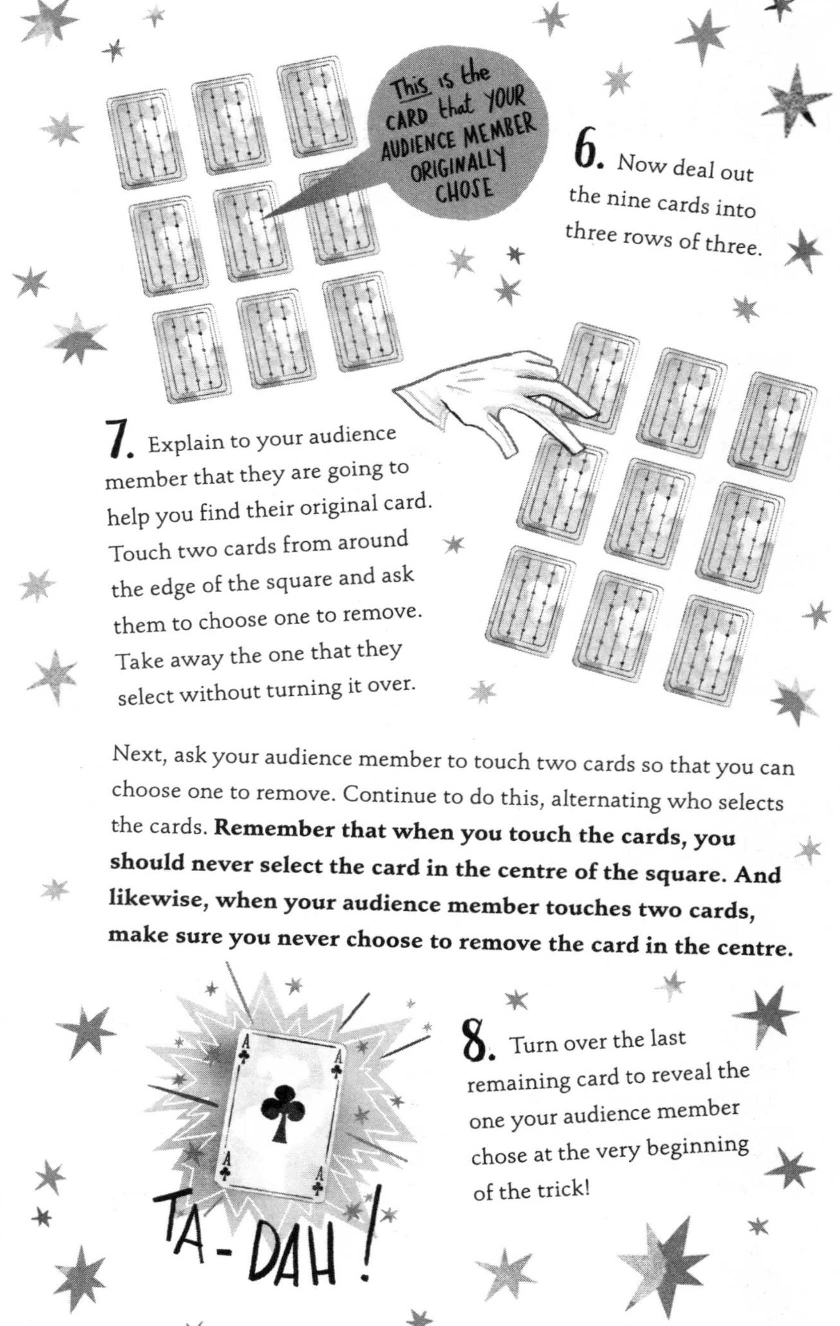
This is the CARD that YOUR AUDIENCE MEMBER ORIGINALLY CHOSE
TA-DAH!

6. Now deal out the nine cards into three rows of three.

7. Explain to your audience member that they are going to help you find their original card. Touch two cards from around the edge of the square and ask them to choose one to remove. Take away the one that they select without turning it over.

Next, ask your audience member to touch two cards so that you can choose one to remove. Continue to do this, alternating who selects the cards. **Remember that when you touch the cards, you should never select the card in the centre of the square. And likewise, when your audience member touches two cards, make sure you never choose to remove the card in the centre.**

8. Turn over the last remaining card to reveal the one your audience member chose at the very beginning of the trick!

Acknowledgements

I'd like to thank my wife, Rachel, and good friend Josh for wading into some very early drafts of this book without any thought for their own safety; my editor, Emily, for her amazing diligence and patience in polishing up my efforts; and my agent, Kirsty, for believing I could do this when I didn't. I'd also like to thank LimbPower, a charity doing fantastic things to help amputees and individuals with limb difference, for their help in accurately portraying Flick. Thank you all for your support, kindness and help in making this book happen.

The Answer: We got out of the burning house, surrounded by guards, while buried deep underground by dressing up as members of the fire service. The Fox had planned our escape and left a pile of kit behind the stage in preparation. So, we all put on fireproof safety clothing, boots, gloves, helmets (the Fox actually had to take his mask off) and breathing apparatus. Then we simply made our way to the ground floor, walked out of the door and slipped away into the night. No one gave us a second glance.

JUSTYN EDWARDS graduated from the University of Southampton with a degree in archaeology. Since then he has worked as a caravan park attendant, a paperboy and a software engineer, but never as an archaeologist. He has always wanted to be a writer, and his inspiration for *The Great Fox Illusion* came from watching magic shows. He realized that what elevates the tricks magicians perform are the stories they tell their audience. And in turn, stories themselves are a kind of magic trick, with authors choosing when to reveal their secrets to the reader. And so his debut novel was born. Justyn lives in Cornwall with his wife and two cats. Visit his website at www.justynedwards.com

We hope you enjoyed

We'd love to hear from you!

#TheGreatFox
@WalkerBooksUK
@JustynEdwards

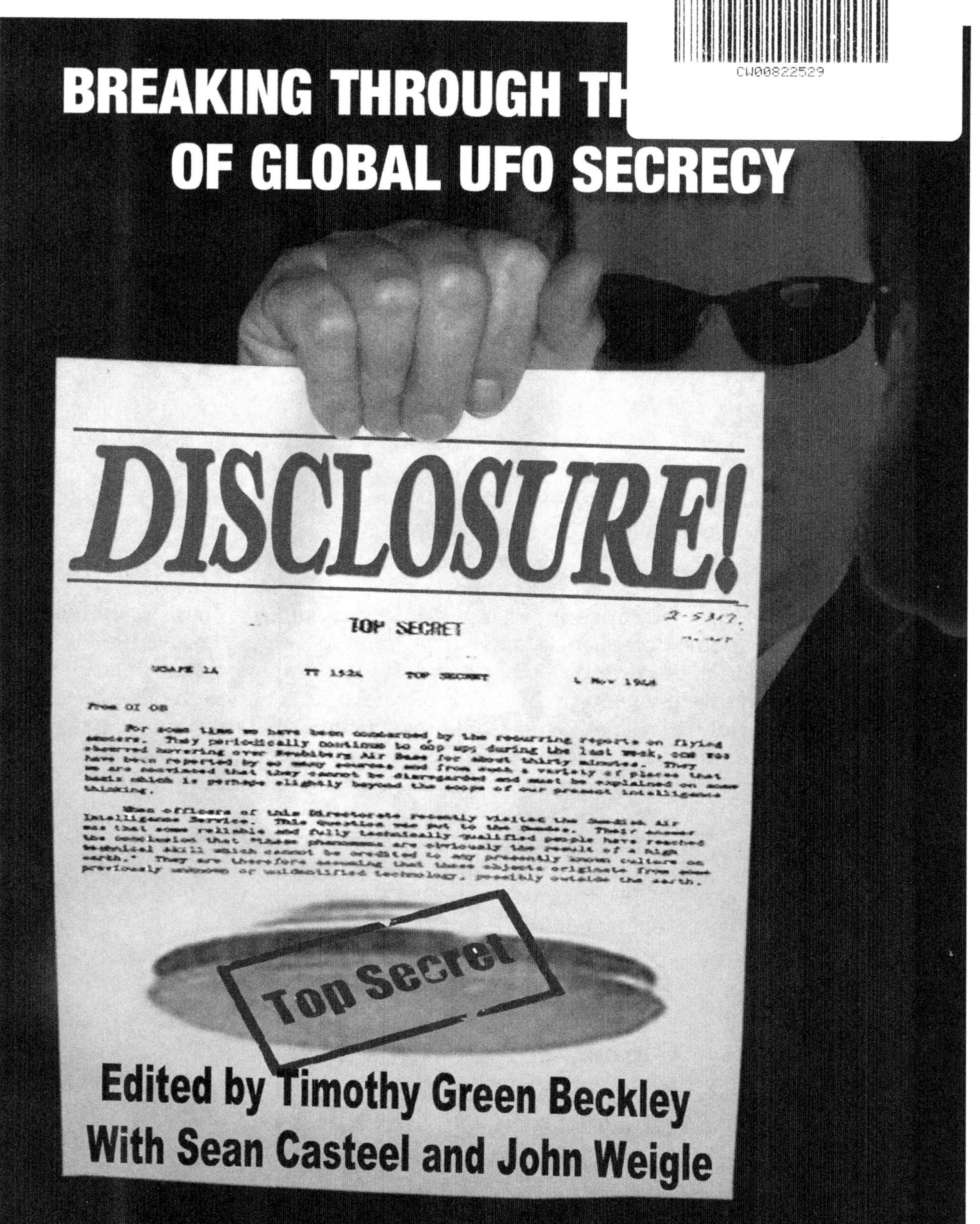

GLOBAL COMMUNICATIONS

DISCLOSURE!
Breaking Through the Barrier of Global UFO Secrecy

Compiled by Timothy Green Beckley
With Sean Casteel and John Weigle

ISBN-10: 1-60611-083-7
ISBN-13: 978-1-60611-083-6

Nonfiction

Timothy Green Beckley: Editorial Director
Carol Rodriguez: Publishers Assistant
Tim Swartz: Associate Editor
Sean Casteel: Editorial Assistant
Covert Art: Tim R. Swartz

For free catalog write:
Global Communications
P.O. Box 753
New Brunswick, NJ 08903

Contents

Authors' Bios

Sean Casteel

Sean Casteel is a freelance journalist who has written about UFOs and related phenomena for more than 20 years. He is a Contributing Editor for "UFO Magazine" and the author of several books for Global Communications. His titles include: "UFOs, Prophecy and the End of Time," "Signs and Symbols of the Second Coming" and "The Excluded Books of the Bible." Casteel has a website at www.seancasteel.com.

Photo of "Mr UFO" in Sedona by Charla Gené

Timothy Green Beckley

Tim Beckley("Mr UFO") is author of over 30 books and publisher since the mid 1960s of Inner Light Publications and Global Communications. His books include UFOs Among The Stars, MJ12 And The Riddle of Hangar 18, Our Alien Planet: This Eerie Earth, Strange Saga and Rock Raps. He has also edited over 30 newsstand publications including Front Page Disasters, Memory Lane News, UFO Review, UFO Universe, Conspiracies And Coverups. He has appeared on hundreds of radio and tv shows and is a prominent B movie host of the Mr Creepo horror series. He has spoken before the House of Lords Special UFO Group and currently hangs his internet hat at: www.ConspiracyJournal.com

John Weigle

John Weigle, who has been in the newspaper business for 46 years, has been interested in UFOs since the early 1950s. He was a member of the Aerial Phenomena Research Organization and the National Investigations Committee on Aerial Phenomena. Weigle is currently a member of the Mutual UFO Network. His email address is: jweigle@vcnet.com

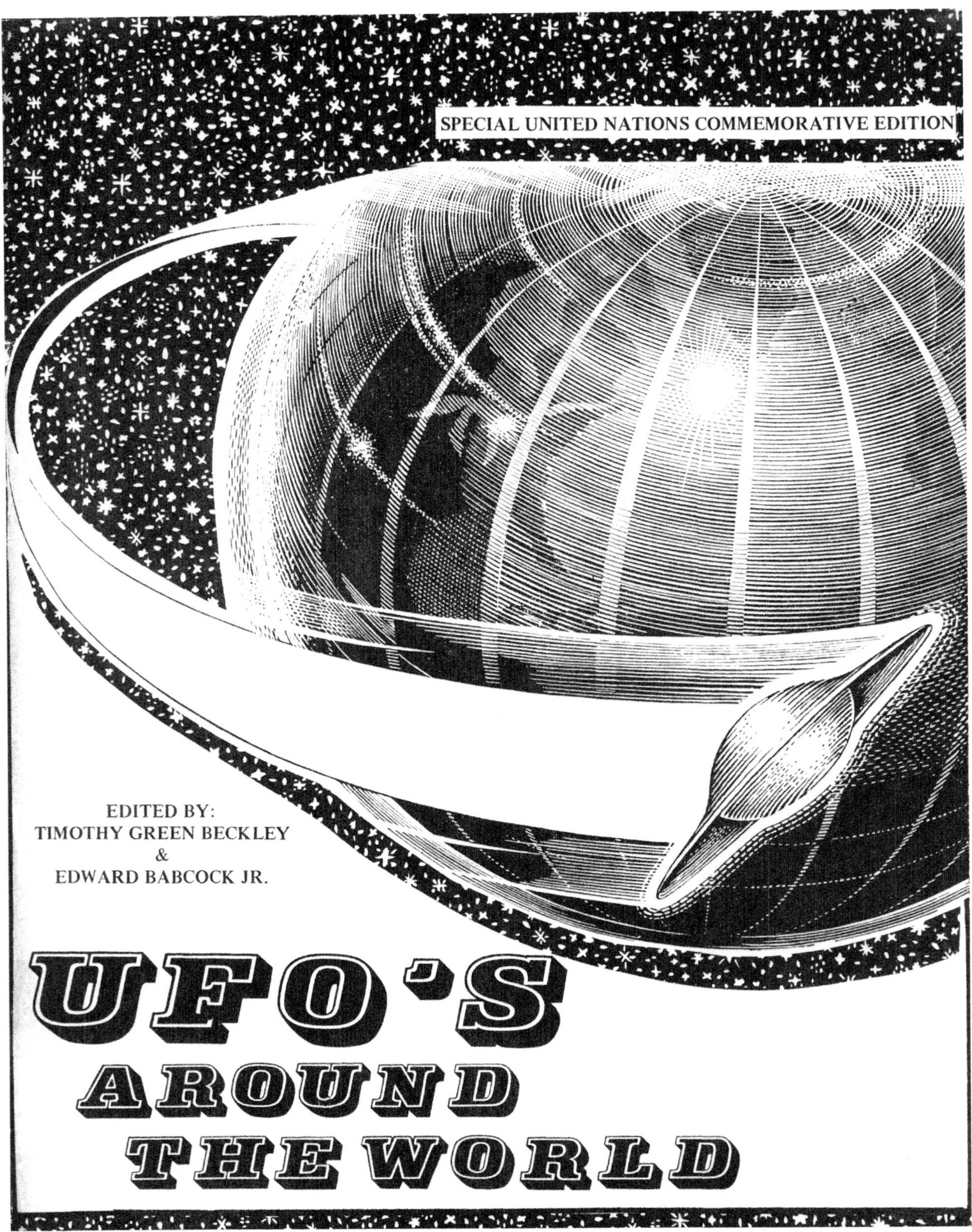

SPECIAL UNITED NATIONS COMMEMORATIVE EDITION
EDITED BY:
TIMOTHY GREEN BECKLEY
&
EDWARD BABCOCK JR.
UFO'S
AROUND
THE WORLD

This book's editor Tim Beckley acknowledged the importance of global research when he published in the mid 60's the book UFOS AROUND THE WORLD.

DISCLOSURE: WHICH EVER WAY THE WIND BLOWS

By Timothy Green Beckley

I have long been aware of the global nature of the UFO phenomenon.

Unless you are really "in tune" or on top of what's going on among the rank and file positioned on the front lines of UFOlogy, the tendency is to think of each sighting or encounter as a local anomaly with no connections to what might be happening a few miles, a half continent or a world away. If you monitor UFO activity like I have for over four decades, it will eventually occur to you that something weird is happening and not just in Denmark (though there, too, as you can see by reading the chapter on this Scandinavian nation elsewhere in the pages of this book of great cosmic illumination).

In all honesty, without tooting my horn too much, back in the 1960s I, along with fellow researcher Edward Babcock Jr., produced a book that went through several editions and was fairly well received, even if not necessarily here in the United States.

UFOS AROUND THE WORLD was crudely printed as opposed to the volume you are about to go through. But we weren't a "big press" then – not that we are in that league even now – but we were dedicated to "the cause" even if we were mere teenagers at the time. Hey, you have to get started somewhere.

The object of our primitive early effort was to offer evidence that the UFO phenomenon was international and not just localized in scope.

Thumbing through a dusty copy I just pulled down from my extensive library of esotericism, I am amazed by the table of contents and the wide spectrum of material and nations it covered in this would-be attempt for global disclosure.

Chapters with teasing titles like:

Look Out! Flying Saucers! by Edgar Simons (Belgium).

The Mysterious Chunk Of Hardware At Ottawa by the Ottawa New Sciences Club (a Canadian group affiliated with Wilbert B. Smith)

A Suggested Reason For UFO Interest by Stan Seers (Australia)

Flying Saucers In Brazilian Skies by Dr Elidio Hernandes

The Wandering Poles and Orthoteny by Hank Hinfelaar (New Zealand)

Some Tales Of "Little Green Men" by Antonio Ribera (Spain)

Mexico's Largest Flap Of All

We also delved into the UFO mystery inside the USSR, The People's Republic of

China, Cuba and the remote (then at least) nation of Ceylon. Obtaining UFO data from behind the "Iron Curtain" was a difficult task at best, in contrast to the Russia and China of today, who seem to pretty much dominate the Internet with reports on an almost daily basis, as well as providing some really fascinating photos to ponder and gawk over.

Outside of a nice note from Coral Lorenzen of APRO, in which she reflected on our attempts to ascertain the global truth about UFOs, few if any other American researchers bothered to send their congratulations. Coral wrote: "It is indeed gratifying to know that someone else realizes the importance of global sightings. We have been fighting this battle against provincial U.S. researchers for over twelve years since the weighty evidence of the 'little men' in Europe and South America made itself evident in 1954."

There were, on the other hand, positive comments from Jacques Vallee, the famed French researcher: "I am absolutely convinced of the truth of your statements concerning the need for international cooperation in the study of the UFO phenomenon. Indeed, we shall all be indebted for calling the attention of the American public not only to the excellent sightings that have been made abroad, but to the efforts that are actively exerted to conduct research on a global scale."

Even the then President (Dictator?) of the Philippines, Ferdinand E. Marcos, added his own two cents when he stated: "The possibility of our planet's receiving visitors from space is, I am certain, not remote in the face of the wonders that we, right here, have witnessed; and indeed it is a thought, an idea, that brings intense and magical excitement which I, for one, would not unduly set aside until all avenues pro and con have been examined."

Amen Brother! Regardless of your national alliance or immigration status.

SPEAKING BEFORE THE HOUSE OF LORDS

My efforts for global reorganization of a subject I hold so dear to me did not end with the publication of UFOS AROUND THE WORLD. One of my connections, beginning in the early days of my writing on the subject, was Brinsley Le Poer Trench, the 8th Earl of Clancarty. The editor of the prestigious British magazine "Flying Saucer Review," Trench had always insisted there be an international slant to the articles published under his direction.

When his brother, the previous Earl of Clancarty, passed away, the title was handed down to Trench, who stepped up from his editorial duties to become a member of the House of Lords. For several years before his own passing, Trench tried his utmost to get the British government to release its UFO files. He started an informal group that met regularly inside Parliament, inviting UFO journalists and researchers such as myself to make presentations before the House of Lords UFO Study Group. It was without a doubt a high point of my career to be greeted by Trench and about 40 members of the group who saw eye-to-eye with Trench's ideals and to be allowed to present a talk on this hallowed ground. We need to give Brinsley kudos for being far ahead of his time. His efforts were not in vain.

UFOs GO BEFORE THE UNITED NATIONS

Such international UFOlogical matters remained pretty static on the home front until a bill was placed before the General Assembly of the United Nations by the head of a small, independent, Caribbean nation. The Honorable Eric M. Gairy of Grenada proposed that a committee be formed to study and to collect verifiable UFO data from participating member nations in an attempt to correlate and provide any evidence that our planet was being visited on a regular basis by extraterrestrial nations, as he believed it had been for centuries. Sir Gairy was assisted by NBC "UFO anchorman" Lee Spiegel, who sought and received the cooperation of the likes of Dr. J. Allen Hynek, Jacques Vallee and astronaut Gordon Cooper to get the world body to yield to Gairy's request. And though they were unable to achieve even that modest goal, the handwriting was on the wall that Disclosure had to arrive eventually here on Earth in whatever form, for good or for bad (depending upon the nature and attitude of our visiting parties).

Disclosure has been no bed of roses and it does offer some particular headaches and problems we as global citizens have never had to deal with before. In this work, the culmination of many weeks of fastidious research, you will witness various attitudes and methodologies by those involved in "upping the ante" in their attempt to have their nations' leaders open those UFO vault doors and, by hook or by crook, let the chips (or angel hair) fall where it may. We don't always agree with the aforementioned methodologies of the various independent researchers interviewed and quoted in these pages...but, on the other hand, we don't manage to agree even amongst ourselves about what Disclosure means or what it might have in store for us. But as John Podesta stated while on duty for the Clinton administration, and now for Obama:

"I think it's time to open the books on questions that have remained in the dark and on the question of government investigations of UFOs. It's time to find out what the truth really is that's out there. We ought to do it because it's right, we ought to do it because the American people, quite frankly, can handle the truth and we ought to do it because it's the law."

Timothy Green Beckley, Editor In Chief

mrufo8@Hotmail.com

www.ConspiracyJournal.com

Contact us to get on our global mailing list

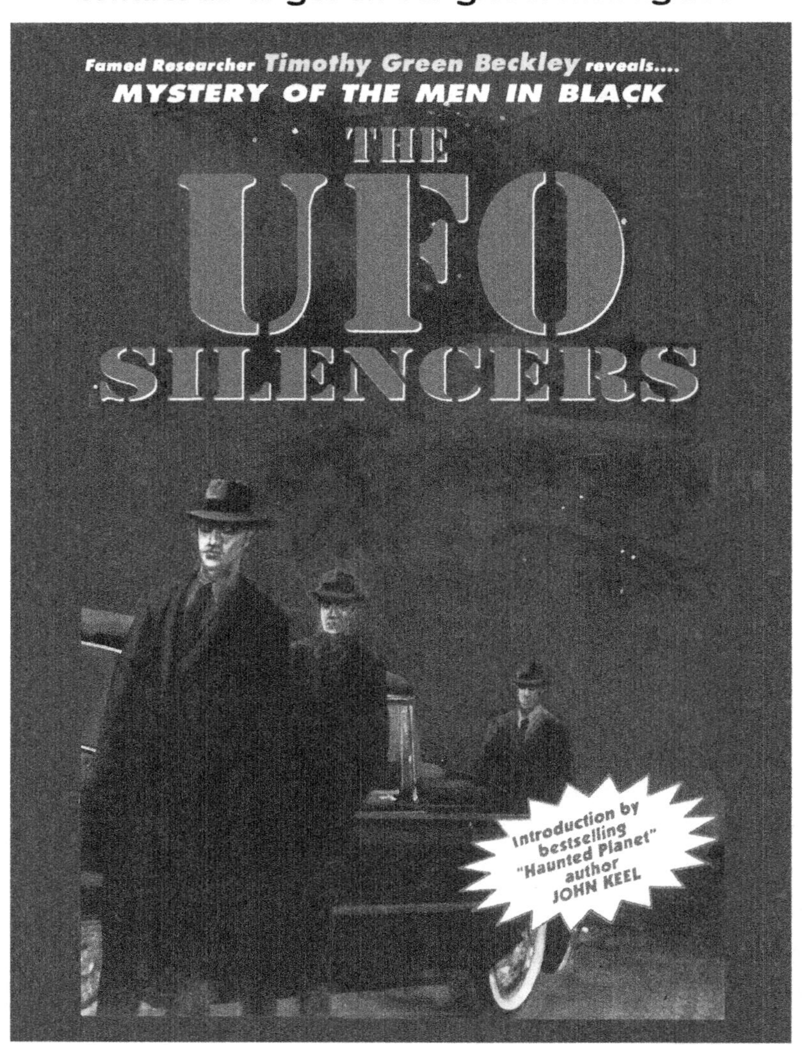

This book's editor Tim Beckley has documented the attempts at coverup of UFO information and for more than 40 years has fought for full DISCLOSURE.

Hillary Clinton

Washington / USA - The new U.S. Secretary of State Hillary Clinton has long had an interest in and been open to the UFO phenomenon. In 1995, a giant step was made to present her with the best evidence for UFOs.

A note from August 4, 1995, by President Clinton's science adviser, Dr. Jack Gibbons, confirmed that the Clintons spent their holiday near the ranch of the philanthropist Laurence Rockefeller in Teton, Wyoming. The Clintons visited Rockefeller there and also discussed UFOs: "You will probably meet Mr. Rockefeller during your vacation in Teton. He wants to talk to you about his interest in extrasensory perception, paranormal phenomena and UFOs," Gibbons wrote.

Rockefeller himself was known in his later years for his concerns about issues regarding the exploration of UFOs, declaring the information should be made available to the public. Specifically, he wanted to approach the presidential couple with his "UFO Disclosure Initiative to the Clinton White House," a request to the Clinton administration to disclose the secret UFO knowledge held by the U.S. According to the website, presidentialufo.com, Clinton tried to obtain UFO documents as part of the 1995 Injunction of the President 12958 (Executive Order 12958). EO 12958 is comparable to the recent memorandum from President Obama on "transparency and open government," in which he instructed various authorities and departments on the rules governing the release of information relating to national security.

Hillary Clinton's appearance at the Rockefeller meeting was followed by subsequent public statements on UFOs and alien life forms, saying at one point that she was obviously very concerned about the negative stereotypes of the Hollywood depictions of aliens. On January 25, 1999, she explained: "Most films about the future show aliens landing from outer space who are coming to the Earth from space to hunt. And somehow they always begin or end with Washington, DC." Later that year, on June 17, in Paris, she again commented on the reasoning behind these films: "Often, in these films, for reasons which I would like to know more about, Washington, DC, and the White House are blasted by aliens into the air." The most telling comment came during the presidential election campaign on December 17, 2007: "Do you remember that in the movie 'Independence Day,' the whole world is united against the invaders from space? Why can we not unite on behalf of our planet? That is what I want to achieve. "

Clinton's criticism of the Hollywood stereotypes of invading and conquering alien forces is for many UFO researchers, including Exo-Political expert Dr. Michael Salla (exopoliticsinstitute.org), "an allusion to their rejection of the politics of national security with regard to the UFO evidence and 'future relations' with extraterrestrial life. " From her position as Secretary of State, Hillary Clinton now offers hope for UFO researchers and interested parties that the political leaders of this planet may intend to establish a new national security policy with regard to the UFO and extraterrestrial life issue.

Hillary Clinton and Laurance Rockefeller walking at his Wyoming Ranch. Hillary is carrying a copy of Paul Davies' book "Are We Alone?"

DISCLOSURE TIMELINE

Historically:

There has not been an "official disclosure" in the United States since the 1969 demise of Project Blue Book in the wake of the Condon Committee Report, which was mostly negative in content. Some speculation has it that President Barack Obama will be the chief executive to pull the plug on the "truth embargo," but this seems unlikely in light of what we now know about his administration. The following is a Disclosure Timeline as it applies to the history of this issue in America.

1956:

The timeline of the Disclosure movement can be said to begin with Donald Keyhoe, a naval aviator and a marine who wrote numerous articles on aviation and in the 1950s became well-known as a UFO researcher. From the beginning he began to argue that the U.S. government should conduct appropriate research in UFO matters and should release all its UFO files.

He was widely regarded as the unofficial leader of the UFO movement and, in 1956, took over the helm of the National Investigations Committee on Aerial Phenomena (NICAP). He was one of several prominent professional, military or scientific figures on the board of directors, which lent the group a degree of legitimacy many of the other "flying saucer clubs" of the time sorely lacked.

Keyhoe became the director of NICAP in 1957, after the group's original director was ousted for "financial ineptitude." Under Keyhoe's leadership, NICAP pressed hard for Congressional hearings and investigation into UFOs. They attracted some attention from the mainstream media and the general public, causing their membership to swell to 15,000 by the mid-1960s, but garnered only limited interest from government officials, though for years they acted more or less as a lobbying group with headquarters in the District of Columbia. Support from some officials such as Senator Barry Goldwater did come from their hard work and tireless efforts.

NICAP joined the chorus calling for independent scientific investigation of UFOs in the wake of a widely publicized wave of UFO reports in 1966, which would eventually result in the formation of the Condon Committee and its highly suspect whitewash of UFOs, published in 1968. Keyhoe himself helped to publicize the so-called

"Trick Memo," an embarrassing memorandum written by a committee official that seemed to suggest that the Committee had had the goal of effectively debunking the UFO phenomenon well before beginning their studies. The memo was discovered by psychologist Dr. David R. Saunders, who was brought into the study thinking it would be objective and unbiased. After he made the memo known, he was fired from the Condon study group on grounds of "incompetence." Shortly thereafter, half of the remaining members resigned in protest of the obvious bias of the project.

Meanwhile, NICAP began to lose members in the late 1960s, and Keyhoe himself faced charges of incompetence and authoritarianism. He was forced to resign and by 1973 NICAP itself had closed down completely. The group eventually closed down its Capitol Hill headquarters while it still maintains a position on the internet. Keyhoe died in 1988 at the age of 91.

1960:

Gabriel Green (born 1924 in Whittier, California, died 8 September, 2001, in Yucca Valley, California) was the first – and only – UFO Presidential Candidate in 1960 and 1972. For much of his life he worked as a photographer for the Los Angeles school system. He is probably also among the least well-known of the classic 1950s contactees, individuals who claimed to have met and talked with friendly human-looking Space Brothers from other planets, and to have ridden in their spacecraft. He founded the California-based Amalgamated Flying Saucer Clubs of America, Inc. in 1957. In his 1960 run for US president, representing the Universal Flying Saucer Party, he called his political philosophy "United World Universal Economics." He also ran unsuccessfully for the U.S. Senate in 1962 in California, but accumulated over 171,000 votes. Among the highlights of his political career was a letter written by Robert Kennedy, whom he had once campaigned against for the Senate. In a letter to researcher Gray Barker, Kennedy admitted being a member of Green's UFO organization and to having a high degree of interest in the subject. A friend of the editor of this book, Gabe passed away at his home in the desert which he loved so much.

1968:

James E. McDonald, an American physicist, while best known for his research into UFOs, had an impressive background as a scientist. He was senior physicist at the Institute for Atmospheric Physics and professor in the Department of Meteorology at the University of Arizona in Tucson. McDonald campaigned vigorously in support of expanding UFO studies during the mid to late 1960s, arguing that UFOs were an intriguing, pressing and unsolved mystery that had not been adequately studied by science. He spoke to over 500 UFO witnesses, uncovered many important government UFO documents, and gave important presentations on UFO evidence. He argued that the extraterrestrial hypothesis was plausible though it remained unproven.

In 1968, McDonald spoke before the United States Congress at a UFO hearing along with Dr. J. Allen Hynek and Carl Sagan, where he offered his opinion that UFOs are real but that their true nature remained unknown because "we have laughed them out of court." He also said that he viewed the possibility that they are extraterrestrial devices and represented surveillance by an advanced technology as a very serious concern. He acknowledged he could not prove the extraterrestrial hypothesis, but that he felt the competing explanations were even less adequate.

He stated at the time that he did not accept the Condon Report since 30 percent of the cases in the document remained unexplained.

In 1970, he suffered public humiliation when he agreed to appear before a Congressional committee to provide evidence against the development of the supersonic transport (SST) plane. Like many other atmospheric physicists who testified with him, he was convinced that the plane could eventually harm the Earth's vital but fragile ozone layer. A Congressman whose district stood to gain from the development of the SST tried to discredit McDonald's testimony by bringing into the discussion the physicist's belief in "little green men." McDonald was deeply humiliated by both the Congressman's mocking attitude and by the open laughter of the other committee members. The shame of that moment, combined with marital and family issues, led to McDonald's suicide in June of 1971 at the age of 51.

1978:

Under the guidance of WNBC Radio producer Elliot Lee Speigel, a group of military, scientific and psychological experts meets with U.N. Secretary-General Kurt Waldheim to discuss their planned 1978 presentation to the U.N. Special Political Committee. Topic: the importance of establishing an international UFO study panel.

From left: astronaut Gordon Cooper, astronomer Jacques Vallee, astronomer/astrophysicist Claude Poher, astronomer J. Allen Hynek, Grenada Prime Minister Sir Eric Gairy, Waldheim, Morton Gleisner of the Special Political Committee, Elliot Lee Speigel, researcher Len Stringfield and University of Colorado psychologist David Saunders.

On December 17, 1978, the United Nations General Assembly took a vote on "Decision 33/426," inviting U.N. member states "to take appropriate steps to coordinate, on a national level, scientific research and investigation into extraterrestrial life, including unidentified flying objects, and to inform the Secretary General of the observations, research and evaluation of such activities." And while President Jimmy Carter himself had a UFO sighting in October, 1969, while he was running for Governor of Georgia, and supported the proposed U.N. study program, the resolution before the world body was almost unanimously defeated.

Despite presentations by numerous experts such as Dr. Hynek and Dr. Jacques Vallee, only the small Caribbean nation of Granada backed the resolution, which had actually originated from its nation's leader Sir Eric Gairy, later ousted in an armed revolution.

1978:

CAUS (Citizens Against UFO Secrecy) is an organization founded by lawyer Peter Gersten and a small group of anti-UFO secrecy activists which included Brad Sparks, Larry Fawcett and Larry Bryant. The main purpose of the group – which has been fairly inactive in recent years -- was to utilize the Freedom of Information Act to compel various governmental agencies to tell what they know (and when they knew it) about UFO-E.T. reality. In 1977, Gersten brought suit in a U.S. District Court against the Central Intelligence Agency. Pursuant to the FOIA lawsuit, the CIA in 1979 released over 900 pages of documents relating to the UFO phenomenon. They refused to release additional documents, claiming national security considerations.

CAUS chief honcho Peter Gersten relaxes after a hike through the beautiful mountains and creeks of Sedona where he now resides following several law suites against the CIA involving UFO Disclosure.

On June 24th, 1980 Gersten brought suit against the National Security Agency on behalf of CAUS for 135 UFO related documents. On November 18, 1980, based upon a NSA top secret affidavit, the Court dismissed the lawsuit stating that "the continued need for secrecy far outweighed the public's right to know." Based in New York at the time of the lawsuits, Gersten eventually moved to Arizona where he still maintains an esoteric web presence www.pagenews.info/, while Larry Bryant continues to serve the group's interests from his District area home office.

In the District of Columbia Larry Bryant keeps CAUS as active as can be

Bryant's most profound attempt at disclosure involved a legal action, titled "Petition for a Writ of Habeas Corpus Extraterrestrial," which sought to compel the U. S. Air Force to hand over the bodies of the alien crew allegedly retrieved from wreckage of a crash-landed "flying saucer" near Roswell, N. M., in July 1947. Bryant's blog http://ufoview.posterous.com includes a lengthy retrospective review of that seminal case within the impenetrable field of "space law."

1990:

Dr. Steven Greer, an American physician, ufologist and author, founded the Center for the Study of Extraterrestrial Intelligence, which, among other things, offered how-to training on initiating contact with extraterrestrial intelligence. Greer also teaches meditation techniques that allow for "remote viewing" and to develop cosmic consciousness. He is widely credited with coining the use of the word "Disclosure" in the context of the government's declassifying of their UFO materials and ending their cover-up. In 1993, he began an organization called The Disclosure Project, which he also uses to disseminate his belief that the government has concealed advance energy technologies obtained from the extraterrestrials.

Greer and the Disclosure Project called for Congressional hearings on all data collected on UFOs, including the information being hidden on free energy and the technology being suppressed that can produce it. He bolsters his arguments with written statements and accounts from military personnel and defense industry employees. In May of 2001, Dr. Greer presided over the Disclosure Project Press Conference, held at the National Press Club in Washington, DC. Over 20 military, government, intelligence and corporate witnesses presented compelling testimony regarding the existence of extraterrestrial life forms. The event was covered by media outlets from throughout the world.

1993:

Laurance Rockefeller comes from a family whose very name is a proverbial expression for enormous wealth. He began his public life as a venture capitalist and embraced environmental causes in the 1950s and 60s, long before they became fashionable. In his later life, he became interested in UFOs, and in 1993, along with his niece, Anne Bartley, he established the "UFO Disclosure Initiative to the Clinton White House." They asked that all the UFO information held by the government, including the CIA and the Air Force, be declassified and released to the public. Rockefeller felt the Roswell Incident should be a priority case for releasing the Top Secret files, but in 1994, the Air Force categorically denied that the event was UFO-related. However, Rockefeller was able to brief then President Clinton on the results of his UFO initiative. Clinton did indeed issue an executive order in late 1994 to declassify numerous documents in the National Archives, but this did not specify UFO-related files.

Along with helping to finance the alien abduction research of the late Harvard psychiatrist Dr. John Mack, Rockefeller also backed the Starlight Coalition, a group said to be made up of former intelligence and military men interested in UFOs. He assisted Marie Galbraith in bringing together various UFO research groups together to create a 169-page report called "Unidentified Flying Objects Briefing Document: The Best Available Evidence." The report was distributed among VIPs of the media and governments throughout the world, though Rockefeller did not personally endorse the document's conclusions, saying he was more interested in learning what the government has on file. Laurance Rockefeller died in 2004 at age 94.

1996:

Dr Steven Greer holds down the fort at the National Press Club where the first Disclosure press conference was held in 2001.

Stephen Bassett set up his advocacy organization the Paradigm Research Group in Bethesda, Maryland. The group's mission was to confront the government, by all means possible, regarding its policy of a truth embargo on the events and evidence of an extraterrestrial presence engaging the human race and the formal acknowledgement of that presence. In 1999, he worked to develop a UFO State Ballot Initiative in the 16 states that permit direct referendum. He backed Steven Greer's Disclosure Project in 2001, assisting the 2001 press conference at the National Press Club. In April of 2002, Bassett announced his candidacy for the Maryland 8th District seat in the U.S. House of Representatives.

His campaign sought to challenge voters and other candidates to engage the politics of disclosure and the facts of an extraterrestrial presence. He also proposed that the House and Senate conduct a weeklong hearing on UFOs, declaring that, "If Congress will not do its job, the people will."

Always a titan Stephen Bassett appears on CNN to get his latest Disclosure point across.

2009:

The documentary film "I Know What I Saw," by filmmaker James Fox, was aired on the History Channel. The film was primarily based on the panel that Fox and journalist Leslie Kean of the Coalition for Freedom of Information assembled at the National Press Club in November of 2007. Among the 14 speakers were two retired generals and several other military officers, a former governor, civilian pilots and government scientists from seven countries. It was called "one of the most credible UFO panels ever assembled."

Journalist Leslie Keen of the Coalition for Freedom of Information and General Letty (President of France's COMETA) stands alongside filmmaker James Fox in the streets of Paris.

"I Know What I Saw" begins with the famous Phoenix Lights of March 13, 1997. The governor of Arizona at the time, Fife Symington, was also a witness to the huge craft that crossed the skies of Phoenix that night. He reveals in the documentary why he made the decision to ridicule the event publicly, saying that he feared the incident would lead to panic and disrupt the normal conduct of state government and private business. While the film has been subjected to criticism for stopping short of frank discussions on Roswell, abductions and crop circles, Fox said his main objective with the movie had been to nail once and for all the issue of credibility regarding UFOs.

The CE-5 Initiative

Definition: CE-5 is a term describing a fifth category of close encounters with Extraterrestrial Intelligence (ETI), characterized by mutual, bilateral communication rather than unilateral contact. The CE-5 Initiative has as its central focus bilateral ETI-human communication based on mutual respect and universal principles of exchange and contact. CE types 1-4 are essentially passive, reactive and ETI initiated. A CE-5 is distinguished from these by conscious, voluntary and proactive human-initiated or cooperative contacts with ETI. Evidence exists indicating that CE-5s have successfully occurred in the past, and the inevitable maturing of the human/ETI relationship requires greater research and outreach efforts into this possibility. While ultimate control of such contact and exchange will (and probably should) remain with the technologically more advanced intelligent life forms (i.e., ETI), this does not lessen the importance of conscientious, voluntary human initiatives, contact and follow-up to conventional CE-s types 1-4.

CSETI is the only worldwide effort to concentrate on putting trained teams of investigators into the field where 1) active waves of UFO activity are occurring, or 2) in an attempt to vector UFOs into a specific area for the purposes of initiating communication. Contact protocols include the use of light, sound, and thought. Thought - specifically consciousness - is the primary mode of initiating contact.

Core Principles

There is strong evidence for the existence of ETI, civilizations and spacecraft.

ETI/ETS have been and are currently visiting the Earth.

Careful bilateral communications between ETI and humans is of continuing importance and will increase in the future.

CSETI approaches the study of ETI with cooperative, peaceful, non-harmful intentions and procedures.

The establishment of a lasting world peace is essential to the full development of the ETI-Human relationship.

Both humans and ETI, as conscious, intelligent beings, are essentially more alike than dissimilar; CSETI is dedicated to the study of both our shared and unique characteristics.

CSETI operates on the premise that ETI net motives and ultimate intentions are peaceful and non-hostile.

It appears probable that more than one extraterrestrial civilization is responsible for the ETI/ETs contact so far observed. It is likely that this represents a cooperative effort.

CSETI will attempt to cultivate bilateral ETI-human contact and relations which will serve peaceful, cooperative goals. It is NOT a goal of CSETI to acquire ET advanced technologies which may have a potential harmful or military application if disclosed prematurely.

SYMPOSIUM ON UNIDENTIFIED FLYING OBJECTS

HEARINGS BEFORE THE COMMITTEE ON SCIENCE AND ASTRONAUTICS U.S. HOUSE OF REPRESENTATIVES

Introduction by Jan L. Aldrich

On two previous occasions the Congress of the United States has conducted open hearings on the subject of Unidentified Flying Objects. On April 5, 1966 the House Armed Services Committee held public hearings, and on July 29th, 1968, the U. S. House of Representatives' Committee on Science and Astronautics convened a one-day Symposium on Unidentified Flying Objects, chaired by then-Indiana Congressman J. Edward Roush.

James E. McDonald (May 7, 1920 – June 13, 1971) was an American physicist. He is best known for his research regarding UFOs. McDonald was senior physicist at the Institute for Atmospheric Physics and professor in the Department of Meteorology, University of Arizona, Tucson. McDonald campaigned vigorously in support of expanding UFO studies during the mid and late 1960s, arguing that UFOs represented an intriguing, pressing and unsolved mystery which had not been adequately studied by science. He was one of the more prominent figures of his time who argued in favor of the extraterrestrial hypothesis as a plausible, but not completely proved, model of UFO phenomena.

However, these two occasions were not the only time that the subject was discussed by legislators. Project Blue Book documents, newspaper stories and letters in the National Investigations Committee on Aerial Phenomena (NICAP) files show that on a number of occasions UFOs had been privately discussed in executive session of various committees and subcommittees. However, the July 29, 1968 Symposium on Unidentified Flying Objects was unique in the respect that it provided Congressmen and Committee staff with the opportunity to ask questions of the participants, and the results were made accessible to the public through the government printing office.

Since the late fifties, NICAP had struggled to get Congressional attention focused on the UFO phenomenon and the official handling of UFO investigations. During this period the Project Blue Book files had only been available to a few select individuals. While the Blue Book files contained an extensive collection of UFO reports, they were hardly definitive. In fact, NICAP probably had just as many well-investigated cases in its own files. However, the denial of public access to the Project's files seemed like a cover up, and something on which to focus the request for Congressional action. NICAP developed a number of proposals they hoped Congress would help implement:

- (a) the public release of official UFO files from the USAF Project Blue Book and other agencies,
- (b) a review and reform of the USAF UFO investigation methods,
- (c) an end to the mistreatment of some UFO witnesses, who NICAP felt were unfairly categorized in press statements or ordered into keeping silent about their experiences, and
- (d) a review of possible threats to US national security, which NICAP thought were being ignored.

Congressman L. C. Wyman requested the type of hearings that NICAP proposed and entered a resolution into the House to authorize the Committee on Science and Astronautics to conduct a wide-ranging hearing, complete with witnesses and subpoena powers. Indiana Congressman J. Edward Roush, an advocate of serious attention for the UFO problem, thought the action premature, and wanted to wait until the Condon Committee, then underway at the University of Colorado, had delivered its final report. In the meantime he proposed a Symposium and became the driving force behind it.

The Symposium that resulted was not what NICAP had hoped for. Rather than examining the USAF's handling of UFO investigations, or the details of the then in-progress University of Colorado study, the discussion was confined to an exchange of views and evidence presented by the participants.

The Symposium consisted of six scientists presenting their views on UFOs to the committee:

- Dr. J. Allen Hynek, Chairman, Department of Astronomy, Northwestern University, Evanston, Illinois and at the time a scientific consultant to the USAF on UFOs for almost two decades;
- Prof. James E. McDonald, Department of Meteorology, and Senior Physicist at the Institute of Atmospheric Physics, University of Arizona, Tucson, Arizona, who had conducted a multi-year full time investigation of the UFO problem;
- Dr. Carl Sagan, Associate professor of astronomy, Center for Radiophysics and Space Research, Cornell University, Ithaca, New York;

- Dr. Robert L. Hall, Head, Department of Sociology, University of Illinois, Chicago, Illinois;
- Dr. James A. Harder, Associate professor of civil engineering, University of California; and
- Dr. Robert M. L. Baker, Jr. Senior scientist, System Sciences Corp., North Sepulveda Boulevard, El Segundo, California who had also done extensive analysis of UFO films.

These scientists also participated in discussions with the Congressmen and their staff after the initial presentations and some had written statements read into the record.

A number of other scientists who did not appear before the committee but submitted written statements were:

- Dr. Donald H. Menzel, Director of the Harvard University Observatory, author of a number of books and articles on UFOs;
- Dr. R. Leo Sprinkle, Division of Counseling and Testing, University of Wyoming;
- Dr. Garry C. Henderson, Senior Research Scientist, Space Sciences, General Dynamics;
- Stanton T. Friedman, Westinghouse Astronuclear Laboratory;
- Dr. Roger N. Shepard, Department of Psychology, Stanford University; and
- Dr. Frank B. Salisbury, Head, Plant Science Department, Utah State University, NASA consultant and author of UFO articles.

1927 - Cave Junction, Oregon, US

THE PEOPLE HAVE A RIGHT TO KNOW!

Several Countries Have Recently Put Their Best Foot Forward In The Arena Of Disclosure – But When Will Other Countries Follow Suit?

Major Players In The Global UFO Disclosure Game

- Russia: Following The Winds Of Change
- China: Enter The Dragon
- The UK Releases Its UFO Files Minus The Smoking Gun
- Canada: Fair And Balanced Reporting
- Denmark Claims It Hides No Secrets
- Disclosure Down Under; New Zealand Releases (Some) UFO Files
- Searching For UFO Disclosure In Australia
- Flying Saucers In Brazilian Skies
- Disclosure In France: Some Astonishing Revelations
- Pilot Reports Out Chilean Government: Officials Aren't Afraid To Acknowledge The Truth

1976 - Urals, Russia

Triangular UFO filmed over Moscow 2009

RUSSIA: FOLLOWING THE WINDS OF CHANGE

By Sean Casteel

Changes in the official response to UFOs are not happening only in Western countries, but also in countries not exactly known for government openness. Some disclosure advocates in the United States have even suggested that Disclosure with a big D could happen anytime in other parts of the world, which would then force the U.S. and all its many allies to follow suit, however reluctantly. Russia has always had its share of UFO "fanatics," though officially the Kremlin was – until Glasnost came about – ideologically opposed to the existence of UFOs, though it more or less tolerated independent research by its citizens as long as their study didn't have a democratic streak to it.

RUSSIAN NAVY RELEASES UFO FILES

While it is generally agreed that the worldwide release of formerly classified UFO documents represents only the tip of a very large iceberg, it is also important to note that the files that have been released are at least official government documents and not open to question in those terms. In other words, they don't represent the efforts of some hoaxer playing games on the Internet.

Just like the American media has been known to do, the Russian Press seems to make light of the hypothesis that Undersea anomalies might be for real.

A case in point is the July 2009 release of some stunning UFO documents by the Russian Navy which ended up receiving more than a small amount of media attention.

"The Russian Navy," an online posting began, "has declassified its records of encounters with unidentified objects technologically surpassing anything humanity has ever built, reports the Svobodnaya Pressa news website. The records, dating back to Soviet times, were compiled by a special navy group collecting reports of unexplained incidents delivered by submarines and military ships. The group was headed by Deputy Navy Commander Admiral Nikolay Smirnov, and the documents reveal numerous cases of possible UFO encounters, the website says."

A former navy officer and famous Russian UFO researcher named Vladimir Azhazha declared that the materials released are of great value. He also says that 50 percent of UFO encounters are connected with oceans, and another fifteen percent with lakes, so it is clear that UFOs stick close to water.

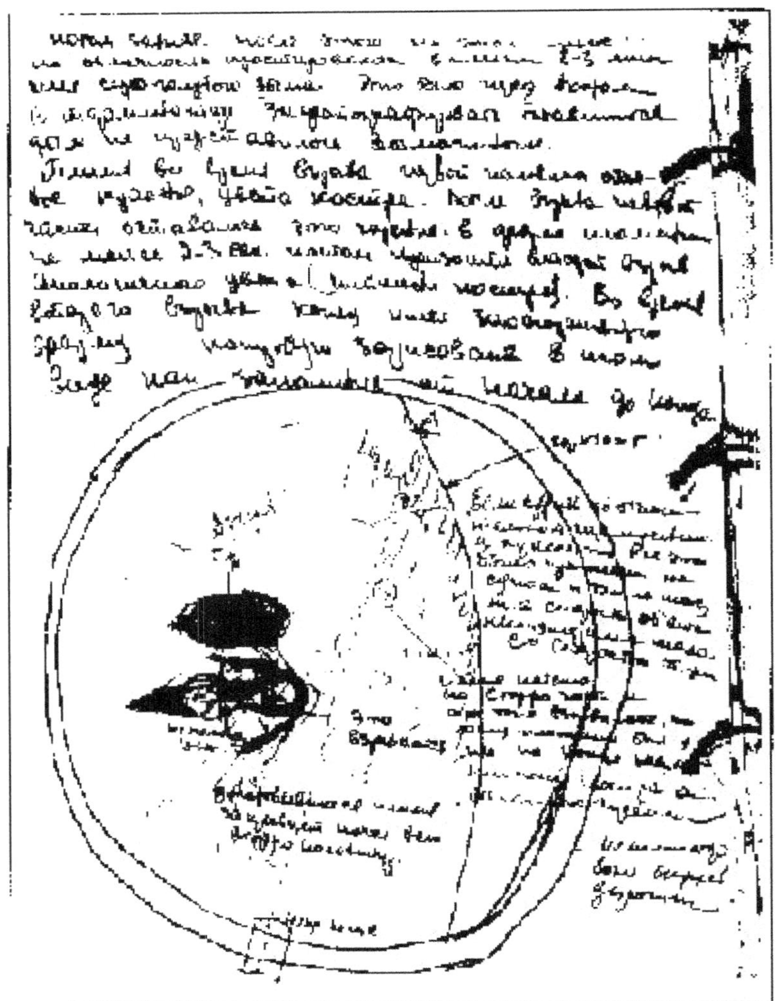

Photocopie d'une page du journal de bord.

One sketch made while in space of a UFO as seen by a Russian cosmonaut. There is no more secrecy it would seem in what former USSR residents may say - regardless if in the military or in civilian life -- than in any Western nation.

SOME BRIEF CASE HISTORIES

Among the cases released is one involving a nuclear submarine on a combat mission in the Pacific Ocean. The sub detected six unknown objects. After the crew failed to pull away from their pursuers by evasive maneuvering, the captain gave the order for the sub to surface. The objects also rose to the surface, took to the air and flew away.

A retired submarine commander, Rear Admiral Yury Beketov, claims that many mysterious events happened in the Bermuda Triangle region. He recalled that the instruments on his submarine often malfunctioned for no apparent reason or were subject to intense interference. Beketov said it could be the result of deliberate disruption by UFOs.

"On several occasions," Beketov said, "the instruments gave readings of material objects moving at incredible speed. Calculations showed speeds of about 230 knots, or 400 kilometers per hour. Speeding so fast is a challenge even on the surface. But water resistance is much higher. It was like the objects defied the laws of physics. There's only one explanation: the creatures who built them far surpass us in development."

Beketov went on to say that ocean UFOs often show up wherever Russian or NATO fleets concentrate, to include the Bahamas, Bermuda, and Puerto Rico. They are most often seen in the deepest parts of the Atlantic Ocean, in the southern part of the Bermuda Triangle, and the Caribbean Sea.

SIGHTINGS AT A LAKE IN RUSSIA

Another place where people often report UFO encounters is Russia's Lake Baikal, the deepest freshwater body in the world. Fishermen tell of powerful lights coming from the deep and objects flying up from the water.

Russia's Lake Baikal is the deepest freshwater body in the world and for decades fishermen tell of powerful lights coming from the deep and objects flying up from the water. Here is a map of the famous lake as well as a most scenic view that can only be described as breathtaking.

In one case, in 1982, a group of military divers training at Baikal spotted a group of humanoid creatures dressed in silvery suits. The encounters happened at a depth of 50 meters. The divers tried to catch the strangers, to no avail. Seven divers died during the incident, and another four were severely injured.

"I think about underwater bases and say, 'Why not?' Nothing should be discarded," Vladimir Azhazha said. "Skepticism is the easiest way. To believe nothing, to do nothing. People rarely visit great depths. So it's very important to analyze what they encounter there."

Given that the files have been released by the Russian Navy, it is only reasonable that the cases involve mainly water-related UFOs, or what are often called USOs, Unidentified Submerged Objects, a closely related phenomenon.

A RUSSIAN GOVERNOR OUTS HIMSELF

Shortly before this book was due to go to press, an astonishing story began to circulate on some hard news websites that the governor of Russia's Buddhist republic, called Kalmykia, had gone public with claims of an abduction experience.

A world class chess player and the elected governor of Russia's Buddhist republic, Kirsan Ilyumzhinov claims to have been abducted from his Moscow apartment by aliens in 1997.

The governor's name is Kirsan Ilyumzhinov, and he is also the president of the World Chess Federation. Ilyumzhinov told the host of a television talk show on Channel One Russian Television that in 1997 he had been abducted from his Moscow apartment by aliens who took him into their spaceship. He spent several hours with the ETs, according to the Moscow Times.

The details of the story go like this: Ilyumzhinov was in bed, falling asleep, and heard a voice call to him from his balcony. When he went outside, he claims he was met by humanoids dressed in yellow spacesuits, who then gave him a tour of their spaceship.

"I would probably not have believed this," he said, "if there had not been three witnesses. Those were my driver, a minister and my assistant."

He added that the alleged aliens "spoke" with him telepathically and said they had come to Earth for samples, although what kind of samples was not revealed.

Andrei Lebedev, an official with the Liberal Democratic Party, wants the Kremlin to investigate this story to determine whether or not Ilyumzhinov offered any confidential Russian information to the extraterrestrials.

The BBC reports that, in a letter to Russian president Dmitry Medvedev, Lebedev suggested that if Ilyumzhinov's story wasn't a hoax, then it must be viewed as an historic event and should have been reported to the Kremlin. Lebedev also asked if there are any government guidelines in case any officials are contacted by extraterrestrials.

With this close encounter hanging over his head, the political future of Ilyumzhinov was in doubt, to say the least, and it is not known whether Medvedev will reappoint him as Kalmykia's leader when his current term is over. According to one online report, Ilyumzhinov has long been known to have an "eccentric personality."

Dramatic sightings of UFOS have come from the vast area that used to be known as the USSR but is now divided up into many independent states. Explanations have varied from missile launches to unusual weather anomalies. Believers know better.

Crashed UFO in Russia – Soviet Soldiers Investigate

RUSSIAN COSMONAUTS AND GENERALS CONFIRM: UFOS ARE REAL

Michael Hesemann

Michael Hesemann

During his lecture at the International UFO Congress in Laughlin/NV on March 6, 2002, Michael Hesemann presented filmed interviews with four Soviet Cosmonauts and four high-ranking Soviet Generals. After he received numerous request for transcripts, here is the translation of their statements:

(Translation by Valery Uvarov, St. Petersburg)

COSMONAUT MAJOR GENERAL VLADIMIR KOVALYONOK: Saljut VI Mission 1981

Many cosmonauts have seen phenomena which are far beyond the experiences of earthmen. For ten years I never spoke on such things. The encounter you asked me about happened on May 5, 1981, at about 6 PM, during the Saljut Mission. At that time we were over the area of South Africa, moving towards the area of the Indian ocean. I just made some gymnastic exercises, when I saw in front of me, through a porthole, an object which I could not explain. It is impossible to determine distances in Space. A small object can appear large and far away and the other way around. Sometimes a cloud of dust appears like a large object. Anyway, I saw this object and then something happened I could not explain, something impossible according to the laws of Physics. The object had this shape, elliptical, and flew with us. From a frontal view it looked like it would rotate in flight direction.

It only flew straight, but then a kind of explosion happened, very beautiful to watch, of golden light. This was the first part. Then, one or two seconds later, a second explosion followed somewhere else and two spheres appeared, golden and very beautiful.

After this explosion I just saw white smoke, then a cloud-like sphere. Before we entered the darkness, we flew through the terminator, the twilight-zone between day and night. We flew eastwards, and when we entered the darkness of the Earth shadow, I could not see them any longer. The two spheres never returned.

COSMONAUT MUSA MANAROV, MIR: MIR mission 1991

It happened during a visit mission, when all our attention was focused on the slowly approaching space capsule. I was close to the great porthole, from where I could see our approaching visitors. I watched everything very carefully... When the capsule came closer, I filmed it with a professional Betacam camera. Suddenly I noted something below the spaceship, which first looked like a kind of antenna. Only when I looked closer and analyzed the situation, I realized that there was no antenna at all. But first I thought it was a part of the construction. But then this element started to move. It moved away from the ship. So I grabbed the radio and told them: "Hey, Boys, you are losing something."

Always the globe trotter UFO journalist Antonio Huneeus speaks with Russia's Dr. Vladimir Azhazha and aviation pioneer Marina Popovich about sightings made by their fellow countrymen while in space.

This, of course, alarmed them. With all my experience especially with docking maneuvers in space I can tell you that especially in this phase simply nothing can break off at all. If something would have been loose, it would have been torn off long before, during the launch, the maneuvers, the turn, all these much more energetic flight phases. Now we were just gliding slowly towards each other, without any pressure on the capsule.

But then this "something" started to remove downwards. When it flew away, it attracted all our attention. It looked like if it was rotating. It was difficult to estimate its dimensions. If it was close or far away I could not say, it was in free sight, and in space it is difficult to estimate any size and distance. I can only say for sure that it was not very close, since I set the camera for infinity. If it would have been just a screw or something close to us, it would have been out of focus. The object was quite far away. In any case at least 300 feet, since this was the distance of the space capsule, and I had the impression that it was beyond it.

It is possible that it was a kind of UFO. We can't say with any certainty what it was. It was definitely not a bigger piece of space junk, no rocket part or so, since this would have been located... the space surveillance, ours and the American, locate all bigger objects in space. They are followed, for every minute we know their position and flight direction. If such an object would have come so close to the MIR, they would have located it and informed us.

I don't think it was a piece of space junk or debris. There is a lot of that in the Earth orbit - Satellite parts, rocket parts, just everything- but our space surveillance locates them, and according to them there was nothing...

COSMONAUT GENNADIJ STREKHALOV, MIR
MIR mission 1990

On the last two flights I saw something. During the flight of 1990, I called Gennadij Manakov, our commander: "Come to the porthole". Unfortunately, but this is typical, we did not manage to put a film in the camera quickly enough to film it. We looked on Newfoundland. The atmosphere was completely clear. And suddenly a kind of sphere appeared. I want to compare it with a Christmas tree decoration, beautiful, shiny, glittering. I saw it for ten seconds. The sphere appeared in the same way as it disappeared again. What it was, what size it had, I don't know. There was nothing I could compare it with. I was like struck by lightning by this phenomenon. It was a perfect sphere, glittering like a Christmas tree decoration. I reported to the Mission Control Center, but I did not say that I have seen a UFO. I said I saw a kind of unusual phenomenon. I had to be careful with the choice of my words. I don't want someone to speculate too much or quote me wrong.

COSMONAUT GENERAL PAVEL ROMANOWICH POPOVICH
Soviet Air Force

I had only one personal encounter with something Unknown, something we could not explain. It was in 1978, when we flew from Washington to Moscow. We flew in an altitude of 30.600 feet. And suddenly, when I looked through the windshield I noticed something flying about 4500 feet above us on a parallel course - a glowing white equilateral triangle, resembling a sail. Since our speed was 600 mph, the triangle must have had a speed of at least 900 mph, since it overtook us. I called the attention of all passengers and crew-members on it. We tried to find out what it was, but all attempts to identify it as something known ultimately failed. This object looked like a UFO and it remained unidentified. It did not look like an airplane, since it was a perfect triangle. No airplane at that time had such a shape.

COL. GENERAL GENNADIJ RESHETNIKOV

Head of the General Zhukov High Command Academy of Air Defense, Tver; Former High Commander of Air Defense of the Far East

Yes, there were particularly mysterious occurrences during military practice. At times targets appeared, on which fighters in the air or radars set for anti-aircraft missiles trained themselves, but it was difficult to determine what they were exactly. There were situations when a target answered to the signal "I'm your plane" (we have such a system of inquiry.) Or the other way around, it wouldn't answer at all. It was considered incomprehensible. Moreover, I'm aware of situations when, as planes which had been sent into the air were opening their side sites, they discovered a target. But when it reached the determined distance when the automatic weapons system which dispatched missiles should have operated, suddenly the system broke down. Everything disappeared, even the target. Or maybe the plane warped through space to another position. They conducted another attack - again the same result. There were such interesting and mysterious occurrences.

Now, when I find myself in the Army Institute of Higher Learning, I know that there were attempts at similar research. There were several definite scientifically- researched studies on ufological topics. But they didn't find a wide distribution for them. Judging, in essence, by the situation of things, I mean that they couldn't find any practical applications for the incorporation of the results of the scientifically-researched developments. In this way, the problem of UFOs in the terminological sense, of how it figures into ufology, isn't followed in the affairs of the military right now. And it wasn't followed earlier. I want to emphasize, that if an unidentified target reveals itself in space, then it's displayed on our radars. Sometimes it happens that it's seen visibly. Sometimes signals are simply received from citizen eye-witnesses. Such information was also received from border posts after visual sightings, and from other sources, and we never throw it out. Verifications are absolutely conducted. But I'm not able to say that this work is taken with a scientific approach. It's conducted within the framework of the administrative attitude towards this problem. In my opinion that's how things stand in the different branches of the Armed Forces.

We try to take into account the problem of UFOs. Quite a bit of interesting material has appeared, and it's perfectly obvious it needs to be studied in earnest, and that it's necessary to address this question on a governmental level.

Right now you are more and more inclined to believe that UFOs exist. But what stands behind this? The first you think of are extraterrestrial visitors...

A bit earlier, at the end of the 1970's and the start of the 1980's, I flew to the Arctic Circle, to the place where eye-witnesses had seen some kind of cigar-shaped apparatus with portholes. This was how the press in this area was describing it. It happened in the region of Norilsk. The object was seen several times. Traces were discovered but no one conducted any kind of serious research there. When it became known to me, I flew there in a helicopter in order to examine the place, we even traveled out to the same place one more time, but we didn't succeed in noticing anything special.

Concerning the ascent of airplanes, in particular, when we were in the framework of the Soviet Union it's necessary to say, that battle duties were kept up rigidly, and we sent up planes without all kinds of restrictions. Immediately upon my order, planes went up many, many times. For example, in those situations which I just recounted during my service. Now we send up planes very deliberately on account of economic conditions. But I personally for many times have ordered aircraft to determine if something is a UFO or not - they were unidentified targets for us. Yes, there have been several cases in which they turned out to be mysterious, unknown targets on which the different detecting systems reacted, including our land-, sea- and airspace surveillance. Sometimes our weapon systems were activated because of them.

MAJOR GENERAL VASILY ALEXEYEV

Russian Air Force Space Communications Center Moscow

If we are speaking about my military capacity, it was in the 1980s when I happened to be serving not in a regular unit, but in the central staff. Work in the central staff entails close links with the units in the field and a large amount of travelling. There were many reports from unit level regarding a large number of observations of unexplained phenomena. You should bear in mind that at that time much was simply denied. The subject was to a large extent a closed one. On the ground, however, people wanted to find out what was what, to separate truth from fiction. In that period a lot of things were presented in such a way that you lost the desire to believe. Accordingly an attitude to the subject became established, where not only was there no desire to believe, it was even undesirable to believe. Nevertheless the information coming in from the bases was of interest if only because it was not merely talk and rumours; there were eye-witnesses to phenomena and that was reflected in specific documents and the reports of officials. At times this information was of such a fascinating nature that it was impossible not to believe it. Later the question no longer seemed so fantastic and began to be examined at the level not only of the Defense Ministry, but of other government departments as well. This interest specifically expressed itself in certain experts being sent to investigate, especially to those places where UFOs, let's call them that, appeared quite frequently. I know a whole number of military bases in that category. As a rule they are objects of strategic significance, rocket complexes, scientific test establishments, in other words the places where there is a high concentration of advanced science and, to some degree, danger. Because every nuclear rocket, every new Air force installation represents a breakthrough both in science and in military terms; it is first and foremost a peak, the summit of human achievement. And that is where UFOs appeared fairly often. Moreover, individual officers and commanders on the spot who knew about the phenomenon and had no official instructions on the matter, acted on their own initiative to investigate UFOs, recording data, and so on. I know that in some places they even learned to create a situation which would deliberately provoke the appearance of a UFO. A UFO would appear where there was increased military activity connected, say, with the transportation of "special" loads. It was enough artificially stimulate or schedule such a move for a UFO to appear. In other words, some kind of conditional relationship emerged. And they detected it. We're an intelligent nation, nothing escapes us. I know that at certain testing ranges - I won't name them, although it's no longer a secret - they even learnt to make contact of a kind. What did that consists of? First the UFO appeared; in most instances it was a sphere, but there were other kinds. Contact was achieved with the help of physical indications of behavior - pointing your arms in various directions, say, and the sphere became flattened in the same direction. If you raised your arms three times, the UFO flattened out in a vertical direction three times as well. In the early 1980s, on the instructions of the then Soviet leadership, experiments using technical devices (theodolites, radar stations, and others) were carried out as a result of which the unidentified objects were firmly recorded as instrumental data.

VU: Can you say on what level those researches took place? While studying the material from those observations and the contents of certain documents I formed the impression that the prime reason for circulars and orders on this matter in the armed forces was that they most likely considered UFOs a new sort of weapon belonging to some hostile country. Isn't that why orders were issued on the rigorous investigation and examination of the appearance and behavior of UFOs by all available ways and means? What was the nature of the recording, on instruments and in written documents, of the time of appearance, trajectory and other characteristics?

VA: I think that on the whole there were two reasons. First, a great deal of information of various kinds was coming in from all over. I know of a case when workers from one of the research establishments outside Moscow flew to Novosibirsk, I think it was, to investigate an air crash. When they came back they wrote a report that they had had an encounter with a UFO that accompanied their plane in the air. Being sensible people and inclined to scientific analysis, they managed to share out their roles so that during the observation some watched and dictated, others sketched, a third group kept track of time. In that way the observation acquired a certain scientific grounding. It wasn't just a sighting, but a scientific team at work, carrying out a sort of real-time experiment. Reports of UFO sightings came in regularly. And evidently somewhere nearer the core of our leadership in the sphere of the Defense Ministry, the Academy of Sciences and so on, a lot of this kind of information began to build up. And not only from ordinary laymen, but from scientists and professionals as well. Military men in general are not inclined to fantasize. They only report what they see, what actually occurs. They are people you can believe. You should not forget that the arms race was still going on at this time, a struggle for military and other priorities. New discoveries in science and technology were being made all the time. The UFOs were something new and not understood. And there really was an idea that they might be some means of gathering intelligence.

Just like the American media has been known to do, the Russian Press seems to make light of the hypothesis that Undersea anomalies might be for real.

As in other nations, UFOs have been observed over many Chinese historical and sacred sites.

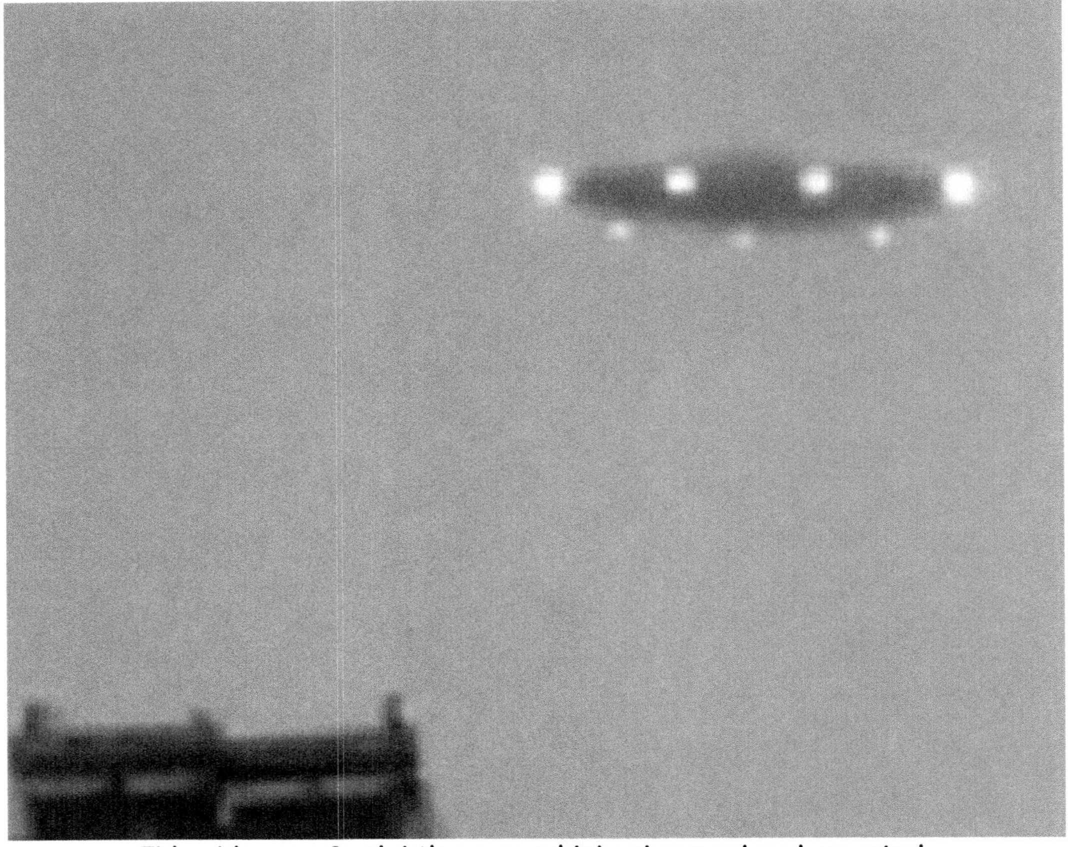

This chinese ufo sighting was widely observed and reported.

CHINA:
ENTER THE DRAGON

By Tim Beckley and Sean Casteel

The incident is referred to as **The Hopeh Incident**. It took place in Hopeh, China, and involves the alleged photograph of a UFO over that city in 1942. Masujiro Kiru had found the photograph while looking through his father's China Campaign (before World War II) photo album. His father had purchased the photograph from a Tianjin street photographer. Some sources claim that the photographer was later identified as an American serviceman on duty in that region who thought the object in question was a hat. Other skeptics identify the object as a bird. Most, however, believe the object to be truly unidentified, proving that UFOs have been with us for many decades – at least! – and definitely a global phenomenon.

What could a UFO possibly be doing over the main street of Hopeh, China in 1942?

Of course, China's history is full of stories involving flying dragons as well as all manner of unimaginable objects of a celestial nature dating back to the Shang Dinesty (2000 BC) where they have been carved into turtle shells.

For many years under Mao Tse-Tung's rule, UFOs were persona non grata. There are even rumors that those holding meetings to discuss such matters were herded up and placed in confinement because it was believed that they were traitors to the state. To some believers at the time, UFOs were considered "a symbol of freedom" and thus their experiences were not to be sanctioned by Peking. According to a report originally published in 1966, in Tim Beckley's **UFOs Around The World,** a Mr. Wu Chi-Yuan stated that someone had reported seeing "an object about the size of the moon shining behind some clouds. Our officials explained it away as a phenomenon caused by an unusual electrical discharge." At the time, Chi-Yuan says he was a member of the National Construction Troop working on maneuvers and was witness to a rather large yellow-orange colored oval-shaped disc. "We were all surprised and frightened. It came down to a very low height, like an argricultural biplane at an angle of twenty five degrees. We heard no sound and in a minute it flew upward and vanished."

Chinese folklore is ripe with stories of aerial vehicles and mysterious beings.

There are even early reports of what could be abductions.

In the "History of the Qing Dynasty" there is an incident recorded that is very similar to modern reports of an alien abduction. On July of the Third Year of Emperor Yongzheng during the Qing Dynasty, a group of villagers went into the mountains to cut bamboo in Liaojiatang of Wudu in Lingchuan. The group witnessed one villager suddenly disappear. More than 140 days later, he reappeared in his home. Fellow villagers reported that upon his return, the abducted villager was completely incoherent.

CHINESE RESEARCHER STUDIES ANCIENT CROP CIRCLES

"One of the first documented reports of crop circle formation – the unexplained geometric designs that occur in fields of wheat and corn – appeared in Stirlingshire, Scotland (UK) in 1678. But the phenomenon was largely ignored until the 1970s and 1980s when formations began to appear with increasing frequency around the globe.

"Yet is China really devoid of these unusual creations? Certainly if someone or something is trying to communicate with mankind through patterns carved into crops, China's sizable population could not be ignored.

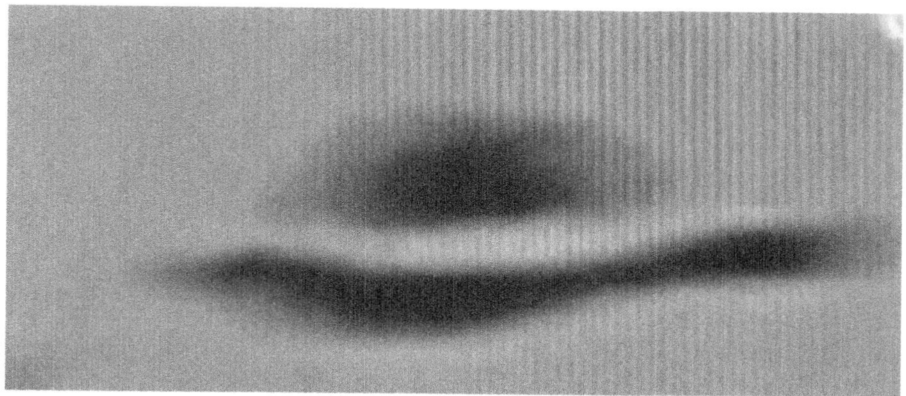

A plane load of passengers from the Peoples Republic of china observed a strange craft flying directly alongside the jet they were flying onboard.

"Western experts have obviously failed to carefully consider the data from this country (China). One has only to refer to the work of Zhang Hui, a Research Fellow at the Xinjiang Museum in Urumqui, to find evidence which suggests that China – with its long history – experienced crop circle phenomena long before any other civilization on this planet.

"Zhang claims to have discovered more than twenty stone patterns appearing to mimic crop circle formations from other countries but pre-dating them by 3,000 years."

Zhang discovered several of these stone circle patterns, which range from single circles to more elaborate shapes, in the grasslands of Qinghe beside China's border with Mongolia.

"Zhang was intrigued. He quickly headed to Beijing, China's capital, to consult Chinese translations of reference works by British crop circle experts.

"He was amazed by the similarities.

"Zhang believes the primitive people of the (Qinghe) region, after witnessing the actual formation of crop circles, concluded that the signs were a form of communication from the gods and responded in kind to the divine messages by placing rocks in the shape of the circles."

"According to Zhang, one rare eyewitness described seeing a crop circle appear in a northeastern China field in only a short time while he was in the company of Red Guards. However, the event occurred during the Cultural Revolution (1966 to 1976), when such superstition was illegal, so the account went undocumented. (See the Shanghai Star for August 2, 2002, "China says crop circles appeared there 3,000 years ago.")

(Many thanks to Chen Jilin for this newspaper article which came by way of UFO Roundup)

A SIGHTING IN CHINA WITH GOVERNMENT OFFICIALS

The Xinhua News Agency, the official government press agency of the Peoples Republic of China, reported on a UFO sighting that took place on February 24, 2009, and was seen by a number of journalists, government officials and a plane load of passengers. The event took place on a Southern Airlines flight en route to Nanjing at around 6 P.M.

Artist conception of a major UFO sighting over Beijing, China.

Nothing seems to stand in the way of these dramatic craft as they hover and than zip across the sky above mainland China.

A group of journalists were socializing during the flight when one of them noticed an unusual luminous object traveling alongside the airplane. The journalist alerted a number of security officials as well as the other journalists he was traveling with. He managed to snap a few photos before the object shot off in a northeasterly direction. The UFO had been visible for about a minute.

The witnesses were understandably stunned by what they saw and began to debate among themselves as to whether the object had been extraterrestrial. Some argued that it may have been an airplane, but when an actual plane appeared on the horizon a few minutes later, they all agreed it had little in common with the unexplainable object they had seen and concluded that they had indeed witnessed a UFO.

A noted Chinese Ufologist commented that Xinhua, the Chinese news agency, seems to be taking the UFO phenomenon rather more seriously in recent years.

"Perhaps this is the lead up to some form of disclosure by the Chinese government," he said, "who I suspect know a lot."

HALF OF THE CHINESE PEOPLE ARE BELIEVERS

According to a report issued by the Russian newspaper, Pravda, half of the entire Chinese population believes in UFOs. Hundreds of scientists and engineers conduct thorough studies of the unidentified phenomenon, giving it the kind of scientific study so lacking here in the Western world. Some Chinese ufologists claim that aliens live among us, and that the extraterrestrials are showing an increasing interest in China.

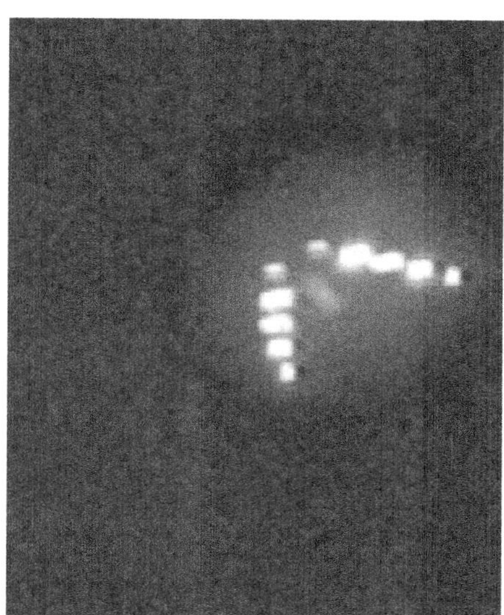

Strange objects have been photographed in broad day light as well as during the evening hours. This one from a resident's window.

One Chinese pilot reported noticing a flickering white and blue object which hovered right beside the aircraft just as he was about to land. The pilot observed that the oval-shaped object seemed to "escorting" the airplane. Then the UFO suddenly made a rapid turn and disappeared behind the clouds.

In the past few years, a considerable amount of such strange encounters with "feidi," the Chinese term for UFOs, has been reported. In one case, people saw a fluorescent orange light with an oddly-shaped object hovering above it. In another instance, people reported seeing an object no bigger than a basketball, which divided itself in half as they looked on. The two objects then started circling the area before they disappeared completely.

A Chinese newspaper ran a story saying that a hundred witnesses saw a jetfighter from the Chinese Air Force "playing cat and mouse" with a UFO not far from a military base in the town of Chinjou. A mushroom-shaped object with a rotating, brightly-lit bottom was spotted by four radar stations. While approaching the jetfighter, the object instantly moved upwards. None of the ground-based control services issued an order to open fire.

AN EXCLUSIVE CLUB OF UFOLOGISTS

China now has a record number of special clubs of UFO lovers. Many of them try to engage the extraterrestrials in a kind of conversation. Their actions are sanctioned by the National Society of Extraterrestrial Studies, which was founded in the 1980s and is financed by the government. Only professional scientists and engineers are allowed to join the society. A Ph.D. is required, and one must have published several works on UFOs. About a third of the society are also experienced members of the communist party.

A CHINESE DIPLOMAT SEES A UFO

One of China's foremost experts in Ufology, an elderly man named Sun Shili, is also a former diplomat and a translator for Mao Zedong. He informed Pravda that he had an encounter with an unidentified object in 1971, during the Cultural Revolution. Sun Shili had been undergoing physical labor at a correction facility high up in the mountains of the Tsyansi province. One day, while working in the rice fields, he spotted a strange object in the sky which he took to be a real extraterrestrial spacecraft.

As stated earlier, experts from the National Society of Extraterrestrial Studies claim that half of Chinese residents believe in such phenoemena. Sun Shili explains such interest by UFOs in China, where every fifth UFO appears, in this way: China appeals to the aliens the most because of the country's recent breakthroughs economically and culturally and its aspiration to become the world's leader. Until recently, the aliens used to focus more on the United States, he said.

Sun Shili is one among many in the National Society who believe some of the aliens live among us, having taken on human form.

THE UK RELEASES UFO FILES, MINUS THE SMOKING GUN

By Sean Casteel

In February of 2010, the United Kingdom's Ministry of Defence and the National Archives released more than 6,000 pages of material from their UFO files, covering the years 1994 to 2000. It was the fifth collection of records about UFOs to be released by the two agencies as part of a project to open the files up to a wider audience.

SOME OF THE MORE DRAMATIC CASES

One of the files included the story of a sighting by a man in Birmingham, England, who was returning from work in March of 1997 at 4 a.m. He saw a large, blue, triangle-shaped craft hovering over his back garden. The ship made no noise, but it caused the neighborhood dogs to bark, according to the report. The craft "shot off and disappeared" after about three minutes, leaving behind a "silky-white substance" on the treetops, some of which the man saved in a jar. It was not clear what happened to the jar or its contents, but to those familiar with the UFO phenomenon, it is a classic example of the "angel hair" often left behind after a sighting or landing.

Large triangle-shaped craft seen gliding silently across the British skyline have become more common that most other types of UFOs sighted in recent years

Another interesting incident revealed by the newly released files took place in January 1997. According to what had been a top secret police report, a man was driving home through south Wales one night when he saw what he called "a 'tube of light' coming down from the sky," which he at first thought was a "massive star" descending toward him. His mobile phone and car radio failed. He got out of his car and was able to walk through the light, which was very bright. He got back into his car, feeling frightened and sick. He soon developed a skin condition which he consulted a doctor about. His car was left covered in dirt and dust.

Other reports are about groups of people, including one from August 1997 in which five members of a fishing trawler in the North Sea reported seeing a round, flat, shiny object hovering in the sky. The object was visible both to the naked eye and through binoculars, with the report noting that the witnesses were "very skeptical of UFOs." They tracked the object on their radar for several seconds before it vanished.

In two towns on England's east coast, Boston (the English one) and Skegness, police caught a UFO on video at the same time that the Royal Air Force (RAF) detected an "unidentified blip" on their radar, the files show. The incident took place in October, 1996, when the officers saw "strange rotating red, blue, green and white flashing lights in the sky." A ship in The Wash, a bay near Boston, also saw the lights while simultaneously RAF air defense radars picked up the blip over Boston. Media coverage of the incident led the RAF to look into the lights, later identifying some as stars and bright planets, and attributing the radar blip to a "permanent echo" created by a nearby church spire.

In still another event catalogued in the new files, a "Toblerone-shaped" UFO was seen hovering over Annandale, Scotland, in July 1994. The Toblerone is a triangular-shaped Swiss chocolate candy bar. The files include a sketch of the object, which showed it as 35-40 feet long and about 20 feet wide. It hovered silently about 10 feet above a field with no lights and was "observed for at least 40 minutes," the report said.

Documents show that Winston Churchill was anxious to find out all he could about the mysterious objects that had plagued him even before World War 2

BRITISH INTEREST IN UFOs DOWN THROUGH THE YEARS

The British newspaper "The Daily Telegraph," in their online story about the 2010 release of the UFO files, played up the wackiness angle, headlining their report "Aliens Gave Me Weird Skin Rash." But they seemed to take more seriously a file that dated back to 1952, in which then Prime Minister Winston Churchill requested a briefing on UFOs from his secretary of state for air.

"What does all this stuff about flying saucers amount to?" Churchill asked. "What can it mean? What is the truth? Let me have a report at your convenience."

In reply, Churchill was told that alleged UFO sightings could be explained by earthly phenomena such as optical illusions, mistaken identification of planes, birds and balloons and deliberate hoaxes. In other words, the same answer the governments of the world continue to give us, a non-answer designed to pacify our supposedly childish inquiries.

Which seems as good a way as any to begin a little history lesson on British interest in UFOs. When the new files were posted online in 2010, at the UK's National Archives site, they also thoughtfully included a 14-page report by one Dr. David Clarke, a private citizen Ufologist who teaches journalism at Sheffield Hallam University in northern England. Clarke has also written a book called "The UFO Files" and was quoted in several news stories about the new files, commenting about the transition in sightings reports from disc-shaped flying saucers to higher-tech looking triangle-shaped ships that had gradually taken hold after the 1950s.

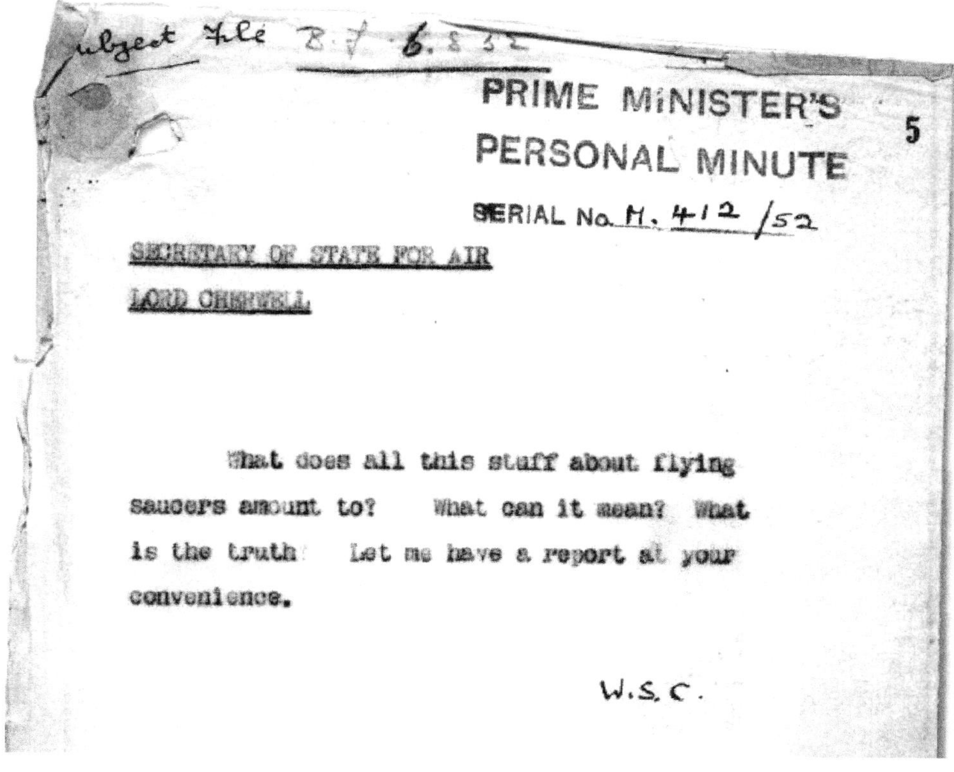

PRIME MINISTER'S PERSONAL MINUTE

5

SERIAL No. M. 412 /52

SECRETARY OF STATE FOR AIR
LORD CHERWELL

What does all this stuff about flying saucers amount to? What can it mean? What is the truth? Let me have a report at your convenience.

W.S.C.

FIG. 15 Following a 'flap' of UFO sightings over Washington DC, British Prime Minister Winston Churchill asked the Secretary of State for Air: 'What does all this stuff about flying saucers amount to?'
PREM 11/855

Clarke's briefing report gives an excellent overview of the history of UFOs, beginning with Kenneth Arnold's seminal sighting in June of 1947. Arnold, a private pilot, reported seeing nine strange objects that moved at tremendous speed across the sky like "a saucer skipping on water." His sighting triggered a wave of similar reports from North America and across the world. In July of that same year, a report was issued from the Army Air Base at Roswell, New Mexico, that a disc-shaped object had landed on a remote ranch and had been removed for examination by officers from the U.S. Eighth Army Headquarters.

"The age of the flying saucer had arrived," Clarke writes.

The term "UFO" was coined for the U.S. Air Force by Captain Edward Ruppelt of Project Blue Book, the Air Force's official "UFO Project," to replace "flying saucer." Though the term UFO, for the media and the public, came to be a synonym for "alien spaceship," to the military forces of the world it simply refers to something in the sky the observer can see but does not recognize. Some branches of the UK's Ministry of Defence (MoD) prefer the term UAP, for Unidentified Aerial Phenomena, since that term does not imply the existence of an "object" of extraterrestrial origin.

Sightings of phantom airships date back to 1909. Evidence seems to support the theory that many of these reports were due to German inovation, but there are some sightings that cannot be explained.

While much of the UK's policy was modeled after their American cousins, Clarke reports that official British interest goes back as far as the period between 1909 and 1913, when phantom airships – dark cigar-shaped flying objects carrying searchlights – were sighted at night moving over many British towns and cities. As tensions increased in the period leading up to the First World War, newspapers and some politicians accused the Germans of sending zeppelin airships to spy on dockyards and other strategic locations around the British coastline.

When sightings were made over the Royal Navy torpedo school at Sheerness, Essex, in October of 1912, the matter was discussed in the House of Commons. This led the First Lord of the Admiralty, Winston Churchill, to order an investigation. Naval intelligence failed to solve the mystery of the airships, but the Germans were widely held to be responsible. Both the War Office and the Admiralty continued to investigate sightings of unidentified aircraft and mysterious moving lights, and the aerial phenomena were further sighted over many parts of the British Isles throughout the war. In 1916, a War Office report concluded that the vast majority of reports could be explained by bright planets, searchlights and natural phenomena. The report ended by saying, "There is no evidence on which to base a suspicion that this class of enemy activity ever existed."

During the Second World War, RAF pilots, along with their American counterparts, began to see balls of fire and mysterious moving lights that seemed to pursue Allied aircraft operating over occupied Europe. The American pilots dubbed the phenomenon "foo fighters" after a comic strip whose catch phrase was "where there's foo, there's fire." Although the foo fighters did not seem to be hostile, they were still a major concern to the Air Ministry and the U.S. Army Air Force as they prepared for the invasion of France. The RAF began to collect reports on the foo fighters in 1942 and later shared their intelligence on the subject with U.S. authorities. They assumed the mysterious lights were German secret weapons, but after the war's end, no evidence of advanced aircraft or weapons that could have produced the foo fighters were found by Allied occupying forces. Ironically, it was later discovered that German pilots had observed similar unexplained phenomena and had attributed it to secret Allied technology.

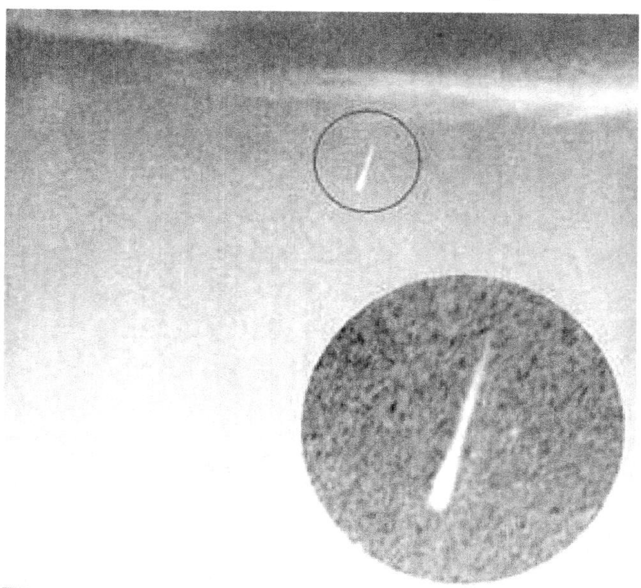

Just like the US military, the MoD in Britian was concerned about the breakout of sightings of mysterious Ghost Rockets toward the end and directly following the conclusion of WWII. Most sightings came from Scandanavia and a few were even said to have crashed into bodies of water. Over 1,000 reports have been cataloged todate by civilian researchers.

UFOs IN POSTWAR BRITAIN

When the mysterious "ghost rocket" sightings of 1946 and 1947 were underway in Scandinavia, intelligence officers of the UK's Air Ministry classified the anomalous phenomenon as modified V2 rockets captured from the Nazis and fired by the Soviets. But the British Director of Intelligence, one Dr. R.V. Jones, doubted this theory. Drawing on his wartime experiences, he believed the scare was triggered by sightings of bright meteors in countries that feared Soviet expansion. The newly released files contain reports and correspondence between the Foreign Office, the Air Ministry and the British attaché in Stockholm.

The reports of ghost rockets preceded by six months Kenneth Arnold's sighting of flying saucers over the U.S. mainland, the latter being part of what prompted the U.S. Air Force to set up a project codenamed "Sign" to investigate the growing mystery. It was around that time that U.S. Lieutenant General Nathan F. Twining made his now famous declaration that, "The phenomenon reported is something real and not imaginary or fictitious."

Following the U.S. policy, albeit a little more slowly, the British government began their own official inquiry in 1950. During the spring and summer of that year, a rash of UFO sightings were made and the media started to take an interest, which led to senior officials in the government and the scientific community to take the subject seriously for the first time. The direct result of this demand for reports of flying saucers to be studied more closely was the assembling of a small team to investigate reports under the Directorate of Scientific Intelligence / Joint Technical Intelligence Committee (DSI/JTIC).

Meanwhile, a group called the Flying Saucer Working Party was kept so secret that its existence was known to very few people. It was at this time, according to files that came to light in 1988, that Winston Churchill asked his Air Minister for the basic facts on UFOs and was given the standard debunking answers of natural phenomena, etc. Files released ten years later, in 1998, revealed how the Working Party was created in August, 1950, under the following terms of reference:

1) To review the available evidence in reports of flying saucers.
2) To examine from now on the evidence on which reports of British origin of phenomena attributed to flying saucers are based.
3) To report to the DSI/JTIC as necessary.
4) To keep in touch with American occurrences and evaluation of such.

MAKING THE DECISION TO DEBUNK

In June of 1951, after investigating some reports from the RAF Fighter Command, including a group of test pilots who had reported sightings of unknown aerial phenomena, the Working Party produced a brief final report debunking the sightings and concluding that flying saucers did not exist. The report included the statement, "We accordingly recommend very strongly that no further investigation of reported mysterious aerial phenomena be undertaken, unless and until some material evidence becomes available."

The members of the Working Party relied heavily on information from the U.S. Air Force project, now renamed "Grudge," and the CIA. It was partially under that American influence that the Working Party also chose to debunk the subject and to restrict the release of information to the public about sightings made by the armed services. The skeptical conclusions of the Working Party set the template for all future British policy on UFOs.

BUT SIGHTINGS PERSIST

However, in the summer of 1952, as Cold War tensions were increasing, a new wave of sightings took place around the world, which included the UFOs detected by radar over Washington, DC, that had prompted the U.S. Air Force to scramble jet interceptors. The scare led to headlines worldwide and was the impetus for Churchill's memo seeking an explanation from his head of Air Ministry. The Prime Minister was told that nothing had happened since the 1951 report dismissing the reality of flying saucers to make the Air Staff change their opinion, and that this was the American point of view as well.

In September of that same year, this policy was again revised after further UFO sightings took place during a major NATO exercise in Europe. The most dramatic of these was reported by a group of airmen in Shackleton who saw a circular silver object appear above an RAF airfield in North Yorkshire. One of the men said he watched as the object appeared to descend to follow a Meteor jet, rotated on its axis and then accelerated away at a speed "in excess of a shooting star."

By now the American UFO agency had changed its name to Project Blue Book, still headed by Captain Edward Ruppelt, who noted in his records that the North Yorkshire sighting had "caused the RAF to officially recognize the UFO." Soon afterwards, the Air Ministry decided to monitor UFO reports on a permanent basis.

Responsibility was delegated to a branch within the Deputy Directorate of Intelligence (DDI), and orders were issued to all RAF stations that any future UFO reports were to go directly to the DDI for further investigation. Any release of information was to be "controlled officially," and that all reports were to be classified as "Restricted." Personnel were warned not to communicate to anyone other than official persons any information about phenomena they have observed, unless officially authorized to do so. Once the Air Ministry was forced to make the decision to take UFO reports seriously, their official clampdown on the release of information followed quickly in its wake.

POLITELY UNHELPFUL

While officially the standard debunking prevailed, the Air Ministry continued to accept reports of UFOs, the reason being that "there is always a chance of observing foreign aircraft of revolutionary design." This factor remained a concern for intelligence agencies until the end of the Cold War. But the Air Ministry also added, "As for controlled manifestations from outer space, there is no tangible evidence of their existence." In 1958, a civilian wing of the Air Ministry called S6 (Air) was charged with fielding questions from the media, the public, and Members of Parliament about UFOs. The S6 desk officer decided their policy would be "politely unhelpful," the same sort of business-as-usual approach that was followed by their U.S. counterparts. While the agencies dealing with the UFO problem would shift along with changes in the structure of the British military and the occasional sightings wave would prompt Parliament to make official inquiries to no avail, the MoD chose to continue to maintain an interest in the subject so it could answer questions from MPs and where necessary assure the public that UFOs posed no threat to national defense.

The last time the government made an official public statement on its policy was in January 1979 when UFOs were the subject of a lengthy debate in the House of Lords, an event initiated by Lord Clancarty, whose given name was Brinsley le Poer Trench and who had authored several books on UFOs and related subjects. Clancarty believed that the MoD had evidence that UFOs were of extraterrestrial origin and was convinced they were hiding this truth from the public. He was able to elicit a government response to his demands in a speech delivered by Lord Strabolgi, a retired Royal Navy officer whose given name was David Kenworthy. Lord Strabolgi's closing remarks were: "As for telling the public the truth about UFOs, the truth is simple. There really are many strange phenomena in the sky, and these are invariably reported by rational people. But there is a wide range of natural explanations to account for such phenomena. There is nothing to suggest to Her Majesty's Government that such phenomena are alien spacecraft."

DOCUMENTS AVAILABLE AT THE NATIONAL ARCHIVES

The official reporting, analysis and recording of UFO sightings began in the 1950s, but there is nothing substantial there until 1962. It was standard policy until 1967 to destroy files at five year intervals because they were deemed to be of only passing interest, resulting in many records from this period being lost. Pressure from a Member of Parliament in 1970 resulted in the official review of files for eventual release to the National Archives. There exists a note attached to one file in 1988 saying that all UFO files are to be permanently preserved "in view of the public interest in this subject." The surviving records are typically made up of four categories of material:

5) UFO policy

6) Parliamentary business, including responses to Parliamentary questions and enquiries
7) Public correspondence
8) UFO sighting reports

That last category contains a mixture of letters from members of the public and reports from official sources such as the police, the Coast Guard and the Civil Aviation Authority. The most often used method of reporting a sighting was a standard questionnaire, patterned after a U.S. Air Force questionnaire.

For an extensive overview of the files available, complete with links to particularly relevant individual files, visit the National Archives website at: ufos.nationalarchives.gov.uk One can also find the complete text of Dr. David Clarke's Briefing Document, which this section of the chapter on the history of the UK's official military policy has been quite liberally making use of, at the National Archives website. To a researcher who wishes to take a "hands on" approach to studying the UK UFO files released to the public, the site is crucial to that effort.

MORE ON THE NEWLY RELEASED FILES

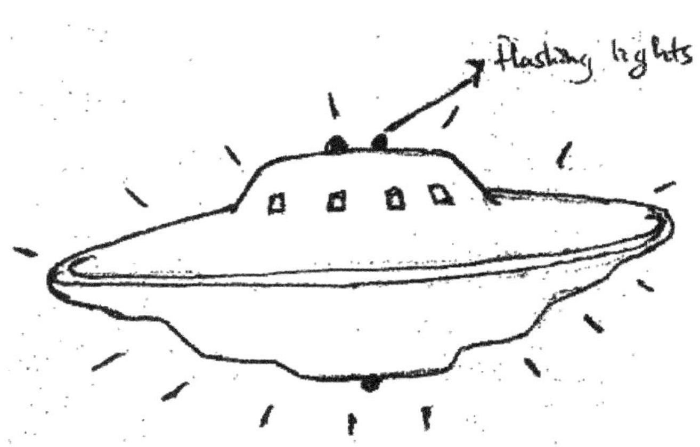

The Mod UFO files contain thousands of reports as well as some rather primitive drawings of bogies.

When the latest batch of UK UFO files was released in February of 2010, it made news around the world, and did not escape the notice of American UFO researcher Alfred Lambremont Webre, who publishes his research into disclosure on a site called the "Seattle Exopolitics Examiner.

Webre begins his reporting of the release by saying, "In a remarkable policy tour de force disclosed on February 18, 2010, a purported year of 'official extraterrestrial disclosure,' the U.K. Ministry of Defence has engaged in yet another serial data dump of multiple UFO and extraterrestrial files, without any accompanying scientific, cosmological, exopolitical narrative or framework of analysis."

Webre goes on to describe the state of mind of the MoD as "embattled," based on a MoD secret memo, dated November 11, 2009, and obtained by the aforementioned Dr. David Clarke under the UK's Freedom of Information Act, that declared that "Reported sightings received from other sources should be answered by a standard letter and should be retained for 30 days and then destroyed, largely removing any future FOI liability and negating the need to release future files post-November 30, 2009." The memo further states that "We have deliberately avoided formal approaches to other Governments on this issue. Such approaches would become public when the relevant UFO files are released, and would be viewed by 'ufologists' as evidence of international collaboration and conspiracy."

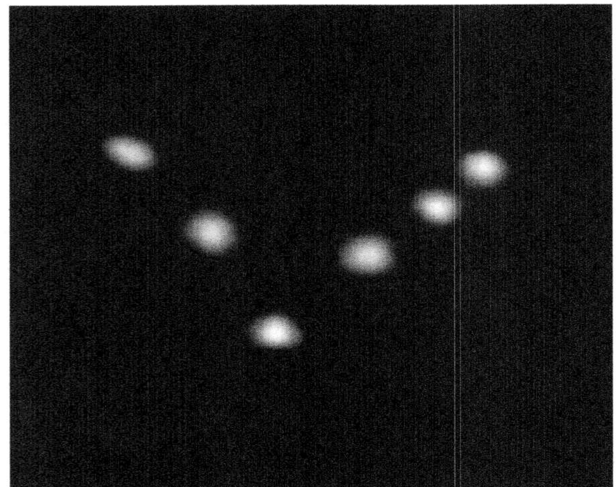

Sometimes they appear as a single object, other times they fly -- or float -- overhead in formation as these UFOs do in Cardiff.

Webre believes that the UK and its close ally the U.S. wants to concentrate on its secret compartmentalized programs with extraterrestrial civilizations while shutting down all of its mechanisms for collecting public reports of UFOs.

But publicly, of course, the reasoning is much different. A UK news report dealing with the secret memo gives the MoD's "reasons for shutting its UFO unit and ceasing to invite the public to send in details of sightings. It notes that the number of reports the department received soared last year, taking up extra resources and diverting staff from 'more valuable' defense-related activities. The MoD recorded 634 UFO sightings in 2009, the second highest annual total after 1978, when there were 750, according to UFO expert Dr. David Clarke. This compares with an average of about 150 reports a year over the past decade."

The memo also states that the UFO hotline phone and email address serve no defense purpose and merely encourage correspondence of no defense value.

"Accordingly, these facilities should be withdrawn as soon as possible."

FOLLOWING AMERICA'S LEAD

Thus it would appear that the UK's MoD is now adopting a policy similar to the 1969 cancellation of Project Blue Book by the U.S. Air Force. Dr. Clarke offers the opinion that the new UK policy is "the final rubber-stamping" of a policy whereby "they just want to totally wash their hands of the UFO business altogether. It's just been such a millstone around their necks ever since the Cold War. They have decided that whatever they do, it reflects badly on them." Clarke also said that the new policy on destroying UFO reports would make it much more difficult to uncover the truth about incidents in the future.

"It's like they're desperately trying," Clarke said, "to avoid having to answer FOI requests on this subject. Even if something quite serious happened, perhaps where there was a near-miss with an airline, the MoD will say, 'We may have had a report on it, but we've destroyed it.'"

But according to Webre, the subject nevertheless continues to have the odd whistleblower here and there who manage to keep the subject viable and relevant. For instance, British computer hacker Gary McKinnon, currently under investigation for espionage, has claimed to have found evidence of a secret U.S. antigravity space fleet which interacts with extraterrestrial civilizations.

IS THE ROYAL SOCIETY PAVING THE WAY FOR DISCLOSURE?

In January of 2010, a meeting of the UK's Royal Society dealt with the issue of extraterrestrial life. Most of the attendees at the elite gathering of mainstream scientists and scholars were largely unaware of the evidence for an existing extraterrestrial presence on Earth, but one Cambridge professor offered the opinion that "Extraterrestrials might not only resemble us, but have our foibles, such as greed, violence and a tendency to exploit others' resources. And while aliens could come in peace, they are quite as likely to be searching for somewhere to live, and to help themselves to water, minerals and fuel."

It has become rather common place it would seem for pilots to encounter unidentified foreign objects during the time they are in the air.

Lord Martin Reese, the President of the Royal Society, stated that, "They could be staring us in the face and we just don't recognize them. The problem is that we're looking for something very much like us, assuming that they at least have something like the same mathematics and technology. I suspect there could be life and intelligence out there in forms we can't conceive. Just as a chimpanzee can't understand quantum theory, it could be there are aspects of reality that are beyond the capacity of our brains."

While some argue that public conjecture on the subject by a respected academic group like the Royal Society could be a precursor, a preparation of the public for disclosure and perhaps even open contact with the extraterrestrials, to Webre it is all too obviously a campaign of obfuscation intended, like the wholesale dumping of thousands of files by the MoD, to muddy the waters surrounding the UFO phenomenon in the UK and around the world. Has true disclosure been brought closer by the 2010 release of the UK files? Or is it simply another strategic move in the ongoing war to keep the extraterrestrial presence a secret even from the people whose lives have been so obviously touched by "unidentified aerial phenomena" and their occupants?

2-5317.

TOP SECRET

USAFE 14 TT 1524 TOP SECRET 4 Nov 1948

From OI OB

For some time we have been concerned by the recurring reports on flying saucers. They periodically continue to crop up; during the last week, one was observed hovering over Neubiberg Air Base for about thirty minutes. They have been reported by so many sources and from such a variety of places that we are convinced that they cannot be disregarded and must be explained on some basis which is perhaps slightly beyond the scope of our present intelligence thinking.

When officers of this Directorate recently visited the Swedish Air Intelligence Service. This question was put to the Swedes. Their answer was that some reliable and fully technically qualified people have reached the conclusion that "these phenomena are obviously the result of a high technical skill which cannot be credited to any presently known culture on earth." They are therefore assuming that these objects originate from some previously unknown or unidentified technology, possibly outside the earth.

One of these objects was observed by a Swedish technical expert near his home on the edge of a lake. The object crashed or landed in the lake and he carefully noted its azimuth from his point of observation. Swedish intelligence was sufficiently confident in his observation that a naval salvage team was sent to the lake. Operations were underway during the visit of USAFE officers. Divers had discovered a previously uncharted crater on the floor of the lake. No further information is available, but we have been promised knowledge of the results. In their opinion, the observation was reliable, and they believe that the depression on the floor of the lake, which did not appear on current Hydrographic charts, was in fact caused by a flying saucer.

Although accepting this theory of the origin of these objects poses a whole new group of questions and puts much of our thinking in a changed light, we are inclined not to discredit entirely this somewhat spectacular theory, meantime keeping an open mind on the subject. What are your reactions?

TOP SECRET

(END OF USAFE ITEM 14)

GREAT BRITAIN: AN ORDER TO SHOOT THEM DOWN, PLUS BLUE BEAMS AND STRANGE VISITORS

by John Weigle

Great Britain, which uses the term UAP (Unidentified Aerial Phenomena), rather than UFO, has collected lots of UFO reports but seems to have had a complete lack of curiosity about any of them. Still, however, in the executive summary of a December 2000 report, "Unidentified Aerial Phenomena in the UK Air Defence Region," it drew a startling conclusion:

"That UAP exist is indisputable. Credited with the ability to hover, land, take-off, accelerate to exceptional velocities and vanish, they can reportedly alter their direction of flight suddenly and clearly can exhibit aerodynamic characteristics well beyond those of any known aircraft or missile – either manned or unmanned."

It continues, "The topic has, hitherto, defied credible description as to its actual cause. Any worthwhile study of UAP, while maintaining the study aim, has inevitably required a multidisciplinary approach and an understanding of the interaction of all the contributory factors. It is believed that the correlation of the overview of information reported over a period of about 30 years, with a more detailed examination of the last 10 years, together with the probable underlying science, may point to a reasonable justified explanation of the cause of the phenomena."

The study attempted "to determine the potential value, if any, of UAP sighting reports to Defence Intelligence. Consistent with MoD policy the available data has therefore been studied principally to ascertain where there is any evidence of a threat to the UK, and secondly, should the opportunity arise, to identify any potential military technologies of interest."

What did the report find?

"Based on all the available evidence remaining in the Department (reported over the last 30 years), the information studied, either separately or corporately contained in UAP reports, leads to the conclusion that it does not have any significant Defence Intelligence value. However, the Study has uncovered a number of technological issues that may be of potential defence interest.

"Causes of UAP Reports: In the absence of any evidence to the contrary, the key UAP findings are:

"—Mis-reporting of man-made vehicles, often observed by perfectly credible witnesses, but with unfamiliar or abnormal features, or in unusual circumstances.

"—Reports of natural but not unusual phenomena, which are genuinely misunderstood at the time by the observer.

"—The incidence of natural, but relatively rare phenomena. These may be increasing due to natural changes and possibly accelerated by man-aided factors, such as smoke and dust.

"Further:

"—No evidence exists to associate the phenomena with any particular nation.

"—No evidence exists to suggest that the phenomena seen are hostile or under any type of control, other than that of natural physical forces.

"—Evidence suggests that meteors and their well-know effects and, possibly some other less-known effects, are responsible for some UAP."

No one familiar with the subject of UFOs would dispute that most reports are exactly what the report suggests: misidentification of known objects. The question, of course, is whether the unidentified reports are simply more of the same or represent something else entirely.

U.S. readers who are familiar with the Condon report can almost predict what happened after those conclusions of the Condon report were submitted. The Ministry of Defence announced in December 2009:

"a. In more than fifty years no UFO sighting reported to the Department has indicated the existence of any military threat to the UK;

"b. There is no Defence benefit in Air Command Secretariat recording, collating, analysing or investigating UFO sightings;

"c. The level of resources devoted to this task is increasing in response to a recent upsurge in reported sightings, diverting staff from more valuable Defence-related activities;

"d. The release of existing UFO files to the National Archive is nearing completion;

"and agreed:

"e. The closure of the 'UFO Hotline' answer phone service and associated e-mail address from 30 November 2009;

"f. That reported sightings received from other sources should be answered by a standard letter and, on the advice of Corporate Memory and The National Archive, should be retained for 30 days and then destroyed, largely removing any future FOI liability and negating the need to release future files post 30 November 2009;

"g. That all UFO files dated up until 30 November 2009 should be released to the National Archive one year from the date of closure."

Here is a selection of reports from the released British files.

A pilot Says He Was Scrambled To Fire On A UFO
May 20, 1957, RAF Station Manston
Reported in July 1988

Pilot Milton Torres says he was given the order to "shoot em down" while chasing a UFO over UK in 1957.

MILTON TORRES RECEIVES SHOOT-DOWN ORDERS

One of the more dramatic documents released by the U.K. government in recent years concerns an American Air Force pilot named Milton Torres. In 1957, while Torres was based in the U.K., he was scrambled in response to an uncorrelated target being tracked on radar. He next saw the object on his own airborne radar and received an order to shoot it down. He is thought to have been flying an F-86 Saber, equipped with 24 air-to-air rockets. He came close to a position that would have put him in range to fire his rockets, but at that point the object moved away. The UFO went from a virtual hover to a speed of about Mach 10 and disappeared. At no time did Torres see the object visually; it was visible only on his radar.

Torres was ordered to tell no one what had happened, and he kept his silence until the relevant files were released to the public, at which point he was approached by both the British and American media. Torres also appeared at lobbyist Stephen Bassett's 2009 UFO conference in Washington and told his story there.

"It was a typical English night in Kent. The 406th Fighter Interceptor Wing had committed to Met sector (RAF) to have F-86D's stand alert as an operational requirement. The date was May 20, 1957, and our squadrons were considered combat qualified when they committed us to the operational requirement. My recollection seems to indicate that this function was rotated about England between the various RAF and USAF units. This particular night the 514th Fighter Interceptor had the alert duty. Two F-86D's were on 5 minute alert at the end of the runway at RAF Station Manston awaiting the signal to scramble. The hour was late as memory serves me and the weather was IFR. Looking back at the log book, a total of 30 minutes of Night Weather was logged on a 1 hour and I5 minute flight. The details such as exactly what hour the scramble occurred or what we were doing just prior to scramble totally escapes me, however, the Auxiliary Power Units (APU) were on and the power was transmitted to the aircraft. We were ready for an immediate scramble and eager for the flight time.

"I can remember the call to scramble quite clearly, however, I cannot remember specifics such as the actual vector to turn to after take off. We were airborne well within the 5 minutes allotted to us and basically scrambled to about Flight level 310. Our vector took us out over the North Sea just east of east Angtia. Normally [Redacted with handwritten note: "deleted to protect witnesses' identity"] the other member of the set of two fighters would be the lead ship. I can only suggest that I was leading due to an in place turn of some sort. I remember in quite specific terms talking as lead ship to the GCI site (who's [sic] call sign I cannot recalI). I was advised of the situation quite clearly. The initial briefing indicated that the ground was observing for a considerable time a blip that was orbiting the East Anglia area. There was very little movement and from my conversation with the GCI all the normal procedures of checking with all the controlling agencies revealed that this was an unidentified flying object with very unusual flight patterns. In the initial briefing it was suggested to us that the bogey actually was motionless for long intervals.

"The instructions came to go 'gate' to expedite the intercept. Gate was the term used to use maximum power (in the case of the F-86D that meant full afterburner) and to proceed to an Initial Point at about 32,000 feet. By this time my radar was on and I was looking prematurely for the bogey. The instructions came to report any visual observations, to which I replied 'I'm in the soup and it is impossible to see anything!' The weather was probably high alto stratus, but between being over the North Sea and in the weather, no frame of reference was available, i.e. no stars, no lights, no silhouettes, in short nothing. GCI continued the vectoring and the dialogue describing the strange antics of the UFO.

"The exact turns and maneuvers they gave me were all predicated to reach some theoretical point for a lead collision course type rocket release. I can remember reaching the level off and requesting to come out of afterburner only to be told to stay in afterburner. It wasn't very much later that I noticed my indicated mach number was about .92. This is about as fast as the F-86D could go straight and level.

"Then the order came to fire a full salvo of rockets at the UFO. I was only a Lieutenant and very much aware of the gravity of the situation. To be quite candid I almost shit my pants! At any rate I had my hands full trying to fly, search for bogeys, and now selecting a hot load on the switches. I asked for authentication of the order to fire, and I received it. This further complicated my difficulty as the matrix of letters and numbers to find the correct authentication was on a piece of printed paper about 5 by 8 inches, with the print not much bigger than normal type. It was totally black, and the lights were down for night flying. I used my flashlight, still trying to fly and watch my radar. To put it quite candidly I felt very much like a one legged man in an ass kicking contest.

"The authentication was valid, and I selected 24 rockets to salvo. I wasn't paying too much attention to [Redacted with same note: 'Deleted to protect witnesses' identity'], but I clearly remember him giving a 'Roger' to all of the transmissions. I can only suppose he was as busy as I was.

"The final turn was given, and instructions were giving (sic) to look 30 degrees to the Port for my bogey. I did not have a hard time at all. There it was exactly where I was told it would be at 30 degrees and at 15 miles. The blip was burning a hole in the radar with its incredible intensity. It was similar to a blip I had received from B-52's and seemed to be a magnet of light. These things I remember very clearly. I ran the range gate marker over the blip, and the fizzle band faded as the marker super imposed over the blip. I had a lock on that had the proportions of a flying aircraft carrier. By that I mean the return on the radar was so strong ,that it could not be overlooked by the fire control system on the F-86D. I use in comparison other fighter aircraft and airliners. The airliner is easy to get a lock on while the fighter not being a good return is very difficult and, on that type aircraft, a lock on was only possible under 10 miles. The larger the airplane the easier the lock on. This blip almost locked itself. I cannot explain to the lay person exactly what I mean, save to say that it was the best target I could ever remember locking on to. I had locked on in just a few seconds, and I locked on exactly 15 miles which was the maximum range for lock on. I called to the GCI 'Judy', which signified that I would take all further steering information from my radar computer.

"Let me explain visually what I saw on my radar screen. Once lock on is accomplished, two circles of light appear on the screen. One was a complete circle in the center of. the radar screen about an inch in diameter, the other about 3 inches in diameter with a half inch segment darkened to indicate the overtake speed. If the dark segment was at 12 o'clock it meant 0 overtake. If the segment was at 6 o'clock, then we had about 600 knots of overtake. The maximum overtake was in the 9 o'clock position. The overtake I had on this particular intercept was in the 7 or 8 o'clock position which indicate close to 800 knot overtake. I was really hauling coals. To complete the description of the radar scope there were two other significant pieces of data displayed. One is the horizontal indicator which gave a gyro stabilized reference to the horizon enabling the pilot to not have to refer to his flight instruments. The second is a steering dot, which was nothing more than computer data indicating which way the aircraft should fly to accomplish the intercept, i.e. if the dot was above the center, the stick should be pulled back to climb, if it was to the right then turn to the right to center the dot. The idea was to have the dot centered in the smaller circle.

"A normal intercept proceeds from the lock on phase with the constant maneuvering to center the dot. When the aircraft is in a position to accomplish its intercept, the dot would be centered. The outer circle will start to shrink at 20 seconds from rocket release. The circle in the center shrinks to about a quarter inch, and keeping the dot centered requires small rapid maneuvers. At about the time the outer circle reaches three quarters of an inch in diameter a small quarter inch line appears in lieu of the inner circle. This is the signal to pull the trigger for rocket release, and to make only up and down corrections as the computer calculates the point of rocket release for the azimuth. With the trigger pulled and the switches set, the rockets are released by the computer.

"Now back to the intercept of the UFO. As I said I had an overtake of 800 knots and my radar was rock stable. The dot was centered and only the slightest corrections were necessary. This was a very fast intercept and the circle started to shrink. I called '20 seconds' and the GCI indicated he was standing by. The overtake was still indicating in the 7 or 8 o'clock position. At about 10 seconds to go, I noticed that the overtake position was changing its position. It moved rapidly to the 6 o'clock then 3 o'clock then 12 o'clock and finally rested about the 11 o'clock position. This indicated a negative overtake of 200 knots (the maximum negative overtake displayed). There was no way of knowing of what the actual speed of the UFO was as he could be traveling at very high mach numbers and I would only see the 200 knot negative overtake. The circle, which was down to about an inch and a half in diameter, started to open up rapidly. Within seconds it was back to 3 inches in diameter, and the blip was visible in the blackened jizzle band moving up the scope. This meant that it was going away from me. I reported this to the GCI site and they replied by asking 'Do you have a Tally Ho?' I replied that I was still in the soup and could see nothing. By this time the UFO had broke lock and I saw him leaving my 30 mile range. Again I reported that he was gone only to be told that he was now off their scope as well.

"With the loss of the blip off their scope the mission was over. We were vectored back to home plate (Manston) and secured our switches. My last instructions were that they would contact me on the ground by land line.

"Back in the alert tent I talked to Met sector. They advised me that the blip blip had gone off the scope in two sweeps at the GCI site and that they had instructions to tell me that the mission was considered classified. They also advised me that I would be contacted by some investigator. It was the next day before anyone showed up.

"I had not the foggiest idea what had actually occurred, nor would anyone explain anything to me. In the squadron operations area, one of the sergeants came to me and brought me in to the hallway around the side of the pilots briefing room. He approached a civilian, who appeared from nowhere. The civilian looked like a well dressed IBM salesman, with a dark blue trench coat. (I can not remember his facial features, only to say he was in his 30's or early forties). He immediately jumped into asking questions about the previous day's mission. I got the impression that be operated out of the States, but I don't know for sure. After my debriefing of the events he advised me that this would be considered highly classified and that I should not discuss it with anybody not even my commander. He threatened me with national security breach if I breathed a word about it to anyone. He disappeared without so much as a goodbye and that was that, as far as I was concerned. I was significantly impressed by the action of the cloak and dagger people and I have not spoken of this to anyone until the recent years.

"My impression was that whatever the aircraft (or spacecraft) was it must have been traveling in 2 digit mach numbers to have done what I had witnessed. Perhaps the cloak of secrecy can be lifted in this day of enlightenment and all of us can have all the facts. This is my account to the best of my memory."

The text of a July 20, 1988, letter that is part of the Ministry of Defence file follows (the name of the writer and the agency he represented is blacked out):

"In the course of my investigations into the matter two suggestions have been made to me, namely:-

"A. That adverse weather conditions caused a 'bogus' blip.

"The witness concerned says the weather conditions were, apart from being cloudy, 'tranquil' and calm.

"B. An experiment in 'electronics warfare' was taking place by means of a bogus radar pulse being transmitted to create an illusion on the Pilot's radar of a solid moving target and that at the last minute before the Pilot was due to release his salvo of rockets the target was very swiftly removed off his radar screen by some technical means creating the further illusion that the target had outrun the Pilot.

"The Pilot concerned concedes that this is possible but does not think it probable for a variety of reasons which were too technical for me to comprehend fully.

"Is it possible for you to say whether, in fact, 31 years after the event, such an experiment was taking place using the Pilot as a 'guinea pig' and if it was not whether, in-deed, the technology existed in 1957 to create such radar illusions.

"The nature of my interest, and that of the Pilot, is to establish whether or not there was a genuine large Unidentified Flying Object flying at speed and performing maneuvers beyond the capability of any known Aircraft – on the other hand if the event was part of what was then part of a Top Secret Military exercise and is still To Secret perhaps you would simply say so and confirm that whatever was involved it was not an Unidentified Flying Object i.e. that you people know what it was and were in full control of the situation even though you cannot say for security reasons, be it 31 years after the event, what was going on."

More information about the case was developed by David Clarke, author of "The UFO Files: The Inside Story of Real-Life Sightings." Clarke is a regular contributor to the British magazine Fortean Times and a senior lecturer in journalism at Sheffield Hallam University. He has worked closely with the MoD to get UFO files released to the public. In his book, he identifies the pilot as Milton Torres, who was 25 at the time of the incident.

"Compounding the mystery is the almost complete lack of contemporary records relating to the incident. In the files released during 2008 the MoD admit that all Air Ministry UFO records from this period have been destroyed and there is no mention of the incident in Project Blue Book."

* * * * *

**Intense Heat, A Strange UFO, Aliens,
And A Voice In Their Head
That Said -- 'We want you ...'
May 4, 1995
Chasetown**

A report from the Staffordshire Police says that two agitated and distressed youth appeared at the police station and asked the officers to go outside and see a UFO. The officers saw "a red light visible in the far distance with white lights surrounding but these could quite easily have been a civil airline."

The report continues:

"We returned to the Police Station and both youths attempted to convey to me what had allegedly happened. They state that whilst walking up the Rugeley Road, Burntwood from the direction of the Nags Head Public House to Swan Island at approximately 2255 hours, at a point near the Fulfin School, they both experienced an intense heat. Their skin turned a glowing red. They then stated they saw a darkish silver inverted saucer shaped object in a field which was glowing red beneath (brief drawing provided at time by [redacted] Appendix A). They stated the object was about four houses high in the sky and about four foot away from them. They then, reluctantly, went on to state that a voice which came from a lemon like head (!), which appeared beneath the machine, said, 'We want you, come with us'. Both appeared upset and shocked and as it was increasingly difficult to obtain detailed information from them they were told to go home and write an account of what they thought they had experienced for our information."

The original file has been edited for clarity, and parts of the narrative still remain jumbled. The names of the two witnesses have been deleted for the sake of their privacy, but apparently the name "Mark" was not blacked out at one point, probably a clerical error made before the file was released to the public. In any case, a harrowing encounter to be sure.

Statement Made On 5/15 /1995 At 8:10 AM

Me and _____went to the grill last night and we left there about 10:30 and walked along the Rugley Road. And as we walked along, we felt this intense burst of heat which I just couldn't believe. I said, "______can you feel that?" It was so hot we stopped, turned around, and walked up again and we kept on walking. And it got hotter. Then we turned around into the field and just saw this glowing bright red object. By this time it was hard to breathe and swallow, and the sweat was just pouring off me.

We just can't believe and I still can't believe now what we actually saw. It was so hot and then we saw this disc hovering. I think it was about 40 - 80 feet away. Probably more. I mean, I just can't describe what I was feeling. My right hand was just red like it had been scalded. The color was like a kind of silver. It was about four houses high. Then _______(my friend) burst into tears.

At this time I was just looking into the sky. I wish I'd had a camera. Then

Mark (identity revealed!) said: "Look at that. Look at that." I said, "Don't f ... about! I am scared as it is." Then he stood high off in the bush and then he pointed at me and I saw this figure which was only about twenty feet away and the voice said, "Come toward me. . .I want you." Then I just said, "Run!" This time I could hardly breathe and we turned around. It just shot off in the air and the sky didn't light up. It just vanished.

Than I said to _____while we were running, "Don't say a word. I'm warning you." Because they'd think we were crazy. We got to Burnwood Island at 10:55 and we saw a bus and I said to my friend, "Stop that bus." Got the coins and it was a bus driver I knew. It was so hard because we just acted like nothing had happened. We got off at the dock and ________said, "Just forget it." Walked past into the Seven Eleven and just tried to calm down again and act as if nothing had happened.

We came out of the Seven Eleven and I was going to the phone booth to make a phone call and then I looked at ______ and the sweat was pouring (off my friend) and he was just standing still and just pointing to the sky and we saw something in the sky (again). I can't be absolutely sure that it was the same, but I just cried and said, "Let's run to the police station and tell 'em." He and I ran and the police looked as if they didn't show much interest. Probably thought we were drunk or on drugs, but when we got in the police station we gave a statement and I said, "You can test us. We haven't been on drugs and we're not drunk." We walked out of the police station and then I just had this sensation of feeling hot and this voice said, "Come here." We could see this face. It was like three stars together. We were both just [illegible] and for some reason we just started running to High Street and went into the restaurant and were just shaking and we just needed to calm down. I asked them if we could have a ____ just to calm down. But they didn't. We walked out and _____ legs gave way and I had to carry him. He was scared. We were both crying. We went to a nearby phone because we decided to call a taxi. We could hardly speak on the phone, but managed to get the dispatcher for about 12:30 and I was just thinking that what we had experienced on High Street made us shake. He caught a taxi and I just repeated not to say a word. I hardly got any sleep, but I woke up about 6:30 and I think I think I had a flashback. I saw this face in this field in front of this disc (this UFO) and it said, "Come here. I want you!"

Don't think I'm crazy. The face had all veins around the neck, and on the head it looked like it was wearing some sort of helmet. It was clear and there were holes for the eyes.

* * * * *

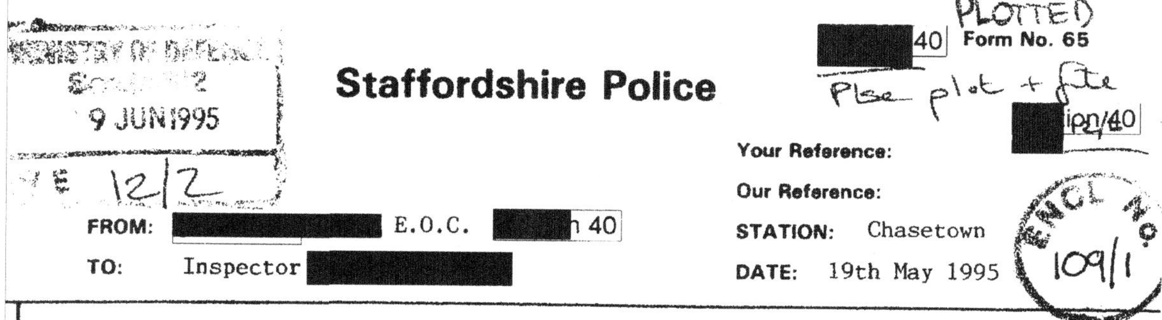

MINISTRY OF DEFENCE
9 JUN 1995
12/2

PLOTTED

40 Form No. 65

Staffordshire Police

Plse plot + file

ipn/40

Your Reference:

Our Reference:

FROM: E.O.C. h 40

STATION: Chasetown

ENCL NO. 109/1

TO: Inspector

DATE: 19th May 1995

SUBJECT: REPORT OF AN UNIDENTIFIED OBJECT

1. At 2355 hours on Thursday 4th May 1995 the following named persons visited Chasetown Police Station, both in an agitated and distressed state reporting an alleged encounter with a U.F.O.

1)

Chasetown.

2)

2. They were extremely excited and initially requested me to go outside and view a U.F.O. which was still visible. Myself and Sgt. went to the front of the station. There was a red light visible in the far distance with white lights surrounding but these could quite easily have been a civil airline.

Section 40

3. We returned to the Police Station and both youths attempted to convey to me what had allegedly happened. They stated that whilst walking up the Rugeley Road, Burntwood from the direction of the Nags Head Public House to Swan Island at approximately 2255 hours, at a point near the Fulfin School, they both experienced an intense heat. Their skin turned a glowing red. They then stated they saw a darkish silver inverted saucer shaped object in a field which was glowing red beneath, (brief drawing provided at time by h 40 Sec Appendix A). They stated the object was about four houses high in the sky and about forty foot away from them. They then, reluctantly, went on to state that a voice which came from a lemon like head(!), which appeared beneath the machine, said, "We want you, come with us". Both appeared upset and shocked and as it was increasingly difficult to obtain detailed information from them they were told to go home and write an account of what they thought they had experienced for our information.

4. On 5th May 1995 the attached written accounts of the 'encounter' were delivered to Chasetown Police Station, Appendix B from Appendix C from

5. On 6th May 1995 the two informants were taken to the area and the exact location of 'sighting' pin pointed to P.C. Enquiries locally reveal no further witnesses but a nearby resident stated a local farmer was crop spraying in a field at the material time. The farmer, has been spoken to and confirms

Cont'd Overleaf / Sheet No.

the crop sprayer being used but stated he did not see any persons in the field, speak to anyone or see anything unusual.

6. In addition to aforementioned appendices attached, please find information required in format as laid down by Force Standing Order, E.1.1. I ask that this report together with appendices be forwarded to, Department of Trade and Industry, National Air Traffic Control Services, 1, Victoria Street, London SW1H OET.

Forwarded as at 'A' above. Inspector

- 3 -

Forward to:

Ministry of Defence Secretariat (Air Staff),
2A Room
Main Building,
Whitehall,
London.
SW1A 2HB

A Tube Of Light And A Sick Driver
Jan. 27, 1997
Near Ebbw Vale

The percipient reported "a 'tube of light' coming down from the sky." The report contnues:

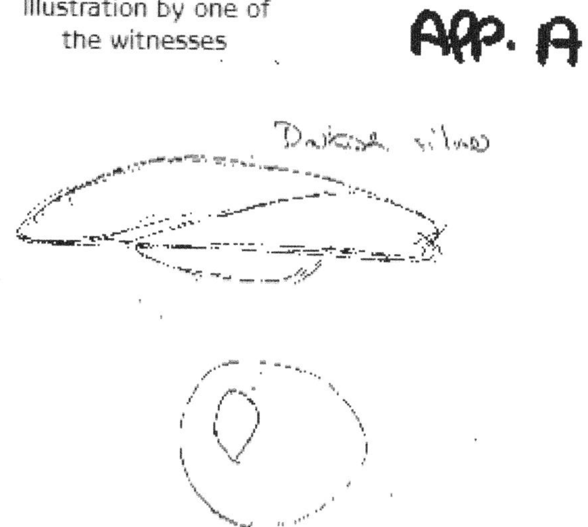

"[Redacted car radio & mobile phone failed during the incident and he felt ill & was indeed sick later on. He is still feeling ill today (28/1/97) and has developed a skin condition. Advised to see doctor ... First sighting seemed like 'massive star' moving towards car. Having stopped the car and turned the lights off, the light encircled the car, remaining for perhaps five minutes. [Redacted] was able to walk through the light which was very bright. There was no sound, no aircraft or helicopter noise. Feeling ill, he was very frightened. The car was covered in dirt & dust."

Writing in the May 2010 Fortean Times, David Clarke comments, "There is no evidence in the file to suggest the MoD followed up this startling incident or collected evidence from the scene."

* * * * *

Aer Lingus crew sighting
April 18, 1997

A hard-to-read, handwritten captain's report (see accompanying document) describes an in-flight encounter with a UFO by the crew of an Aer Lingus flight en route from Dublin to Amsterdam .

June 22, 1997, 1 a.m.

The man reporting the sighting, a former soldier, and his wife were driving from Ulverston to Silloth. "Ahead of them, at a height estimated at 1000 feet, they saw three extremely bright lights, one to the left, one to the right and one in front, forming a huge triangle. The lights were of similar brightness to a welding torch and were flickering in an irregular manner. [Redacted] described them as being identical to those he saw on a video of unexplained sightings in Scotland seen on a TV documentary on Monday or Tuesday of this week."

LOOSE MINUTE

D/Sec(AS)/64/2

14 May 97

ADGE1
DI55c

"UNIDENTIFIED" AIRCRAFT REPORT BY AER LINGUS CREW - 18 APR 97

1. As agreed in recent exchanges of correspondence concerning "UFO" policy, Sec(AS) is under remit to forward any "unidentified" aerial activity reports received by credible witnesses to you.

2. Attached please find a copy of a report (which we only received this week) of an unidentified aircraft made by the crew of an Aer Lingus flight from Dublin to Amsterdam on Friday 18 April. On the face of it this would appear to be a flight safety issue and one on which the CAA would have the lead.

3. As yet we have received no enquiries from members of the public about this matter, but should there be anything in this of particular interest to either of you then I should be grateful if you would keep Sec(AS) in the picture.

Sec(AS)2a1
MB8245

Enc.

ht Operations

Captains Special Report Form

Reference B735 | 135 | 97

For Office Use Only	Crew Details	Cat II/III Record	Regularity Report
Received ____ Urgent Y / N	Capt	S/N	Flight Date 5/7/604/5 — 18/04/97. Reg. EI-CDF
Description	F/O	S/N	Flight Number (s)
Unidentified A/C.	S/N	Airport / R/W	
	Note. Staff Numbers are not required unless a Cat II or III approach is carried out.	Practice / Actual — Successful / Unsuccessful	

From	To	Delay (Min.)	Reason for delay
CDG	DUB	–	–
DUB	AMS	+7	REMOTE STAND
AMS	DUB	+8	BAGGAGE LOADING

Special Report — Action Required — Reply Requested? (Y) N — Copy IALPA (Y) N

Assigned to: — Fax.

Airsafety ✓	Airmiss	Birdstrike	GPWS	TCAS	Incident Signal ✓

Please complete reverse of form for above, and a TCAS form for a TCAS event

ON FLIGHT , DUB – AMS cruising at FL 370 and cleared direct to GOLES POSITION when we both noticed an unusual contrail on our left hand side ~~~ – also heading in towards GOLES. We asked ATC 131.05 if this A/C was military as the trail appeared as if rolls or unusual flying was being carried out in the airway and at our level. They had no knowledge or indication of this A/C. We were in smooth conditions VMC. The wind was 310/30 [TIME 1026Z] Approaching Goles we entered and felt the wake of this trail, and then the wake paralleled our track at FL 370, heading ± 100 DEG, TRACK GOLES/BLUFA, approx 20–30 yards to our right. Further information requests from ATC about the A/C which appeared to descend/turn and accelerate away from us and on approaching the Dutch Boundary it faded into the distance. I requested if the Dutch had seen any A/C in their area which they had not. London ATC again made contact and confirm that their military had no A/C in the area and now wish to investigate the incident with this report to be sent to MILITARY SUPERVISOR, DISTRESS + DIVERSION C... RAF

Signed

Aer Lingus

In a statement reminiscent of so many other reports, this one notes that the man hesitated to make this report lest he be considered a crank, but in view of the proximity of Sellafield (approx 10 miles NW) he "decided to ring and say what he had seen in case of security implications."

The report is on the letterhead of RAF Regional Community Relations Officer (Cumbria and Tynedale).

* * * * *

A strange visitor
June 11, 1997, early evening
From a weekly activities report (preparing agency not noted):

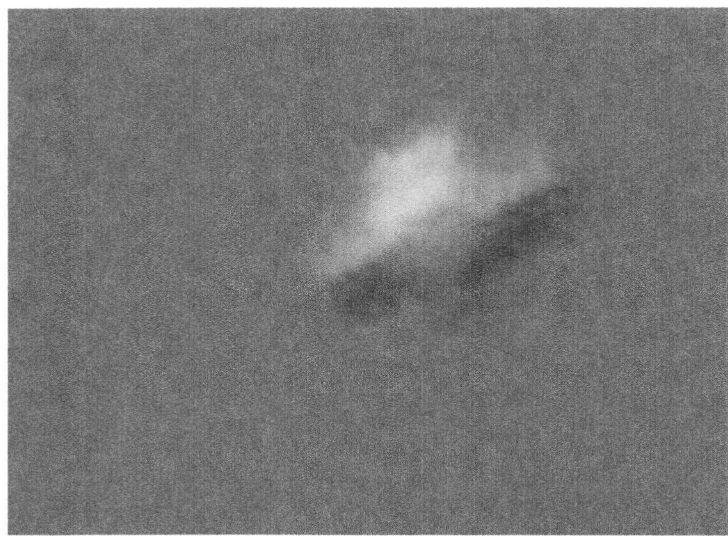

Something strange is photographed over Dorset, UK. Experts say photo has NOT been hoaxed.

"[Redacted] telephoned at 12:22. He stated that in the early evening of 11 June he was sitting in his living room when a man walked in and layed on his quilt. ([Redacted] sleeps in his living room and the bed is always made up.) The window then went all white and the man on the bed whooshed through the window. [Redacted] [Redacted] telephoned the police who wouldn't come to his house because they thought he was 'a nutter,' so he phoned Scotland Yard and the Fire Brigade. He wanted the police to see the quilt where the man had layed because the indentation showed that the person just lifted off the quilt without getting up from it in a normal way. [Redacted] stressed that he was not a crank and was not on drugs. He failed to leave an address or phone number."

* * * * *

A triangle-shaped aircraft
March 17, 1997
From a similar weekly activities report as above

"[Redacted] phoned at 10:16. She runs a UFO group in Southend, Essex and has received some information that she believes to be defence related. She stated that in the area of Machrihanish (Mull of Kintyre), the Aurora has been seen taking off, and black triangle shaped aircraft with glowing engines have been spotted which has resulted in people submitting UFO sightings reports. She also stated that stealth pilots have information projected onto the retina of their eye and can control their planes with their thoughts when wearing a special helmet. She wants the MoD to telephone her as soon as possible on [Redacted] so she knows 'which avenue to go down.'

"ACTION: [Redacted] Sec (AS)1, is aware of activity at Machrihanis and advised us to contact [Redacted] and ask her to write to Sec (AS)1 with her concerns. Sec(AS)1 will then reply to her directly."

* * * * *

A large saucer shaped object
March 1, 1997, evening
Another entry from the same activity log as above

"At 14:43 [Redacted] from the Stroud Journal newspaper telephoned. He has received reports of a large saucer shaped object with blue flashing lights around the side seen over Hampton Common on Friday evening (14/03/97)

"ACTION: Phoned [Redacted} DPO and asked him to telephone [Redacted] [Redacted] and explain MoD's role, explain that we do not provide an aerial identification service and that the MDO did not receive any other reports for 14 March."

* * * * *

Angel hair found after sighting
March 20, 1997, 4 a.m.

[Redacted] phoned at 3:16 p.m. to report a UFO. He came home from work at 4 a.m. and saw a large lit up blue triangle shaped craft over this back garden. It was silent, about 200 ft in length and was lit up at each corner. Dogs in the area were barking which he said was unusual. The object was hovering about 300-400ft in the air, then it shot off and disappeared. It left a silky white substance on the tree tops, and he has got some of this in a jar at home. The total sighting lasted for about 3 minutes. [Redacted] lives in [Redacted] Birmingham and his telephone number is [Redacted]."

The log contains no information about any attempt to examine the jar of what has become known as "angel hair" among ufologists.

* * * * *

'Circular with a bottom missing'
April 10, 1999
Near Shrewsbury

In a frustratingly brief report, a pilot reported a large object he described as "circular with a bottom missing." He reported it to the Shropshire Police and RAF Shabury (?-the writing is poor). Under the item "any background of informant that may be volunteered" is the comment "He is a pilot. Videod the object."

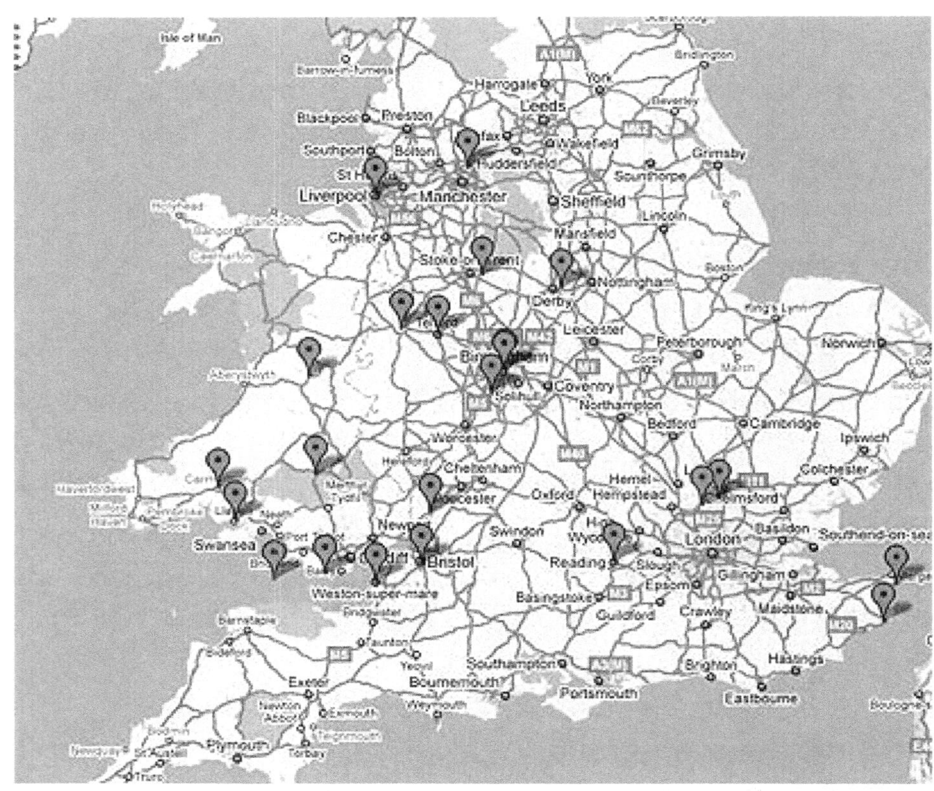

Investigators as well as tourists looking for a thrill will find a map of the best UFO sightings over UK a handy aid.

1990 - Stonehenge, England, UK

CANADA: FAIR AND BALANCED REPORTING

Compiled by John Weigle

Canada's National Archives, no doubt recognizing the worldwide interest in UFOs, prepared a website called "The Search for the Unknown," describing UFO sightings and investigations, with links to portions of the official documents they're based on. The site is at

http://www.collectionscanada.gc.ca/ufo/002029-1100-e.html.

The first item describes Canada's UFO investigations and is followed by specific UFO reports. The titles for the items have been added by the authors of this book and do not appear on the Web pages.

Information about other incidents that were filed under Communications Instructions Reporting Vital Intelligence Sightings (CIRVIS) are shown after the website reports in their original form.

Project Magnet And Other Investigations, 1952 Shirley's Bay, Ontario

In 1950, a senior radio engineer from the Department of Transport, Wilbert B. Smith, made a request to his superiors to make use of a laboratory and the department's field facilities in a study of unidentified flying objects (UFOs) and the physical principles connected to them. Smith spearheaded Project Magnet with the purpose of studying, among other occurrences, magnetic phenomena, which he believed would open up a new and useful technology.

The goals of Project Magnet were fueled by the concepts of geomagnetism, and the belief that it may be possible to use and manipulate the Earth's magnetic field as a propulsion method for vehicles. Tests conducted by Smith were reported in November 1951 and they stated that sufficient energy was abstracted from the Earth's field to operate a voltmeter at approximately 50 milliwatts. Smith believed he was on the "track of something that may prove to be the introduction to a new technology."

CANADA SEARCHES FOR THE UNKNOWN

Years of Research

1947

Canadians were still accustomed to looking towards the sky, keeping a watch for enemy aircraft. Although the war was over, people were conscious of the possibility of an attack due to the new threat of a cold war. As a result, the Royal Canadian Mounted Police (RCMP) and the Department of National Defence received reports of unidentified flying objects (UFOs). Although sightings in Canada had occurred before, it was at this time that the Department of National Defence and other government agencies began to collect information on UFOs.

1950 Project Magnet

Project Magnet began operations in 1950, with the purpose of studying, among other occurrences, magnetic phenomena. The engineer in charge of the project was senior radio engineer Wilbert Smith from the Department of Transport. The goals of Project Magnet were fuelled by the concepts of geomagnetism, and the belief that it might be possible to use and manipulate the Earth's magnetic field as a propulsion method for vehicles. Smith believed that this technology already existed in the mysterious UFOs that had been sighted so frequently in Canada. He believed that "the correlation between our basic theory and the available information on saucers checks too closely to be mere coincidence."

1952 Project Second Story

In connection with the establishment of Project Magnet by Wilbert Smith at the Department of Transport, a committee was formed by members of other government agencies that was dedicated solely to dealing with "flying saucer" reports. This committee was sponsored by the Defence Research Board and called "Project Second Story." Its main purpose was to collect, catalogue and correlate data from UFO sighting reports.

1954

The government stopped funding Project Magnet. Work continued, however, by those dedicated to the project.

1959

The RCMP was typically the front line for reports of unidentified flying objects. The records of the RCMP at Library and Archives Canada contain reports beginning in 1959. Each record contains the sighting, the location in the sky, witness statements, name and occupation of witnesses, and a credibility assessment. Some of this information is protected by the Privacy Act. A few investigations include sketches and drawings based on witness descriptions. Reports were sent to the National Research Council (NRC) for inclusion into their non-meteoric file. Researchers at NRC frequently determined that sightings were the result of natural phenomena such as fireballs, weather balloons and meteors. Other occurrences defy explanation.

1959-1960

An agreement was finalized between the United States and Canada to institute a joint reporting system of UFOs. The Cirvis/Merint reporting system was created "to extend the early warning coverage for the defence of North America . . . and to extend the reporting of vital intelligence during peacetime." Posters were created to explain that airborne and water-borne objects that appeared hostile, unidentified or that seemed to be acting suspicious, were to be reported immediately. A drawing of a saucer-like object appeared with drawings of missiles and submarines, as examples of hostile objects.

1960s

The Department of National Defence classified reports into one of two categories:

Category One: Information that would suggest the type of phenomena associated with fireballs and meteorites

Category Two: Information that does not conform to the physical patterns usually associated with fireballs or meteorite activity.

Reports in Category One were sent to the National Research Council. Reports in Category Two were kept at the Department of National Defence to be investigated.

1961

The Department of National Defence (DND) was receiving many reports of UFO sightings. As well, DND was being asked by various

Canadian individuals and organizations about its role in the investigation of UFOs. A memo dated October 18, 1961, to the office of the Deputy Minister of National Defence, outlines the typical questions asked of the department:

"Question 1: Are unsolved UFO reports in Canada kept from the Press and general public?

Answer: No. While reports are not necessarily offered to the Press in every case, they are never denied.

Question 2: Does the Defence Department share American concern that UFOs pose a possible threat?

Answer: The Canadian Government is concerned with any report which might affect national security and, undoubtedly, this would be the attitude of the United States Government also. However, to date, UFO reports which have been investigated by various departments of the Canadian Government have not revealed positive evidence of anything which might affect national welfare and which could not be attributed to possibly natural phenomena or mistaken identity.

Question 3: What is the official RCAF stand on UFOs?

Answer: The RCAF position is one of complete open-mindedness. Each reported incident is investigated to the extent that circumstances, such as the apparent reliability and competence of the observer of the incident, seem to warrant."

1966

Prime Minister Pearson said to his Cabinet that in view of the interests being shown in Parliament and the press concerning reports of unidentified flying objects, he would ask the minister or ministers responsible to provide him with reports on what had been done over recent years in connection with such reports.

1967

The Department of National Defence transferred its files to the National Research Council. It was generally believed that most of the reports did not pose a threat to national security, but that rather "a number of investigations of the reports suggest the possibility of UFOs exhibiting some unique scientific information or advanced technology which could possible contribute to scientific or technical research." ["Unidentified Flying Objects (UFOs) - Investigations", September 1967 (memo)]

Three reports were highlighted by the Department of National Defence and the files were transferred to the National Research Council as unsolved: the Falcon Lake encounter, the Duhamel crop circles and the Shag Harbour landing. The department also asked to be kept advised of matters that would threaten national security. Reports continued to be submitted to various government departments.

1968

The Department of National Defence received a letter from a German man. The man claimed to be an aeronautical engineer who in 1944, with other scientists, built a saucer-like flying vessel meant to be "Hitler's secret weapon." The Royal Canadian Air Force (RCAF) investigated and interviewed the man. Incidents such as these are examples of cases that were kept by the department for further investigation.

1970

The RCMP continued to investigate reported sightings

1978

The Department of Transport file called "Unidentified Flying Objects" contained information on UFOs sighted between 1976 and 1978. More information on the records within the Department of Transport, the Department of National Defence, the Royal Canadian Mounted Police and the National Research Council can be located in the search database.

Smith believed that there was a correlation between his studies and investigations into UFOs: "...the existence of a different technology is borne out by the investigations which are being carried on at the present time in relation to flying saucers.... I feel that the correlation between our basic theory and the available information on saucers checks too closely to be mere coincidence" (Smith, Geo-Magnetics, Department of Transport, November 21, 1950).

It was believed by both Smith and other government departments involved that there was much to learn from UFOs. Investigations into these sightings and interviews with the observers were the starting point for Project Magnet.

Researcher Wilbert Smith headed Project Magnet in the early 1950s from a small shack in Shirley Bay, Canada. He later went on to become an advocate of the "contactee" movement (see last section for his personal revelations).

In connection with the establishment of Project Magnet, members of other government agencies formed a committee solely dedicated to "flying saucer" reports. This committee was sponsored by the Defense Research Board and called "Project Second Story." Its main purpose was to collect, catalogue and correlate data from UFO sighting reports. The committee created a questionnaire and interrogator's instruction guide. The reporting method used a system intended to minimize the 'personal equation.' In other words, a weighting factor was created to measure the probability of truth in each report. Smith explained that most UFO sightings fit into two general types: "those about which we know something, and those about which we know very little."

In a summary of 1952 sighting reports, Smith noted common significant characteristics of UFOs: "They are a hundred feet or more in diameter; they can travel at speeds of several thousand miles per hour; they can reach altitudes well above those which should support conventional air craft or balloons; and ample power and force seem to be available for all required maneuvers" (Smith, Project Magnet report, 1952, p. 6).

In his closing, Smith stated, "Taking these factors into account, it is difficult to reconcile this performance with the capabilities of our technology, and unless the technology of some terrestrial nation is much more advanced than is generally known, we are forced to the conclusion that the vehicles are probably extra-terrestrial, in spite of our prejudices to the contrary." (Smith, Project Magnet report, 1952, p. 6).

Smith summed up the possibilities of studying the technology of these vehicles, and suggested that the next steps in the Project Magnet investigation should be a "substantial effort towards the acquisition of as much as possible of this technology, which would without doubt be of great value to us" (Smith, Project Magnet report, 1952).

It was with these goals in mind that Smith set up an observatory in Shirley's Bay, Ontario, 10 miles outside of Ottawa. Based on the conclusions of the 1952 sighting report, Smith thought that these vehicles would emit physical characteristics that could be measured. In October of 1952, he set up the observatory to attempt to measure magnetic or radio noise disturbances. Many more sighting reports were investigated by Project Magnet, but in 1954, the project was shut down.

Further information about Project Magnet is found in the meeting minutes of Project Second Story in the search database.

Something – A Craft Or A Meteor -- Falls Into A Lake
Clan Lake, Northwest Territories
June 22, 1960

Clan Lake, and the small community on its shoreline, is located in a remote part of the Northwest Territories, accessible only by boat or airplane. The people of the area have lived off the land -- hunting, fishing and trapping -- for generations. In 1960, when an object hit the water of Clan Lake, a month passed before the Royal Canadian Mounted Police (RCMP), located 30 miles away in Yellowknife, were called to investigate the sighting.

On June 22, 1960, an airplane dropped two campers off at Clan Lake. About 20 minutes after the plane left, the two reported hearing a loud noise similar to an airplane. As the noise grew louder, the campers looked to the sky, but saw nothing. Seconds later, however, an object fell from the sky and crashed into the water. When it hit the surface, the object began to rotate, causing a spray of water around it. There was no steam to indicate that the object was hot. According to the campers, the object was approximately 4 to 6 feet wide, with spokes coming out of it like arms. As it began to slow down, a rush of water met the campers on the shore. Finally, the object sank.

The campers rushed to the spot in the water with their canoe and saw that the reeds in the water appeared burnt, and an area approximately 20 feet by 60 feet appeared to be 'cut-up.' Poking around with their paddles, they found a channel in the bottom of the lake that corresponded with the cut path of grass. The campers, however, could not locate the object with their canoe paddles.

A statement of one camper's sighting was filed with the RCMP on July 18th, almost one month after the event. The report states that the observer was "well known in this county and is considered very reliable."

The RCMP investigated Clan Lake on July 19, 1960, through an aerial patrol. It appeared that an object did land on the east side of the lake. An area of water about 12 feet wide by 40 feet long was completely clear of reeds and grass. The water in this corridor also appeared to be deeper.

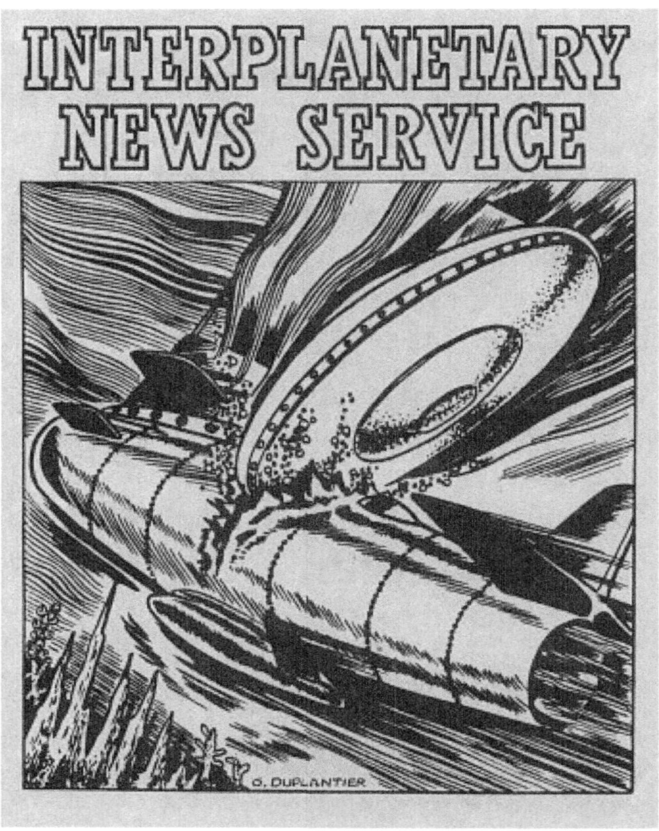

Canadian artist Gene Duplantier as far back as the mid 1960s depicted the "death" of the American submarine Thresher which may have been struck by an unknown object while patrolling the bottom of the ocean.

Another RCMP officer returned to the lake on August 15, 1960. The officer reported that the lake's water level had dropped considerably since the previous RCMP visit, with only 1 foot of water at the site in the lake where the object had supposedly landed. Officers could easily wade through the area and used metal rods to probe beneath the water's surface. A Geiger counter, used to detect the presence of radiation, returned negative results. No object was located. A local geologist volunteered to do a magnetometer check after the water froze in the fall to help locate any metal objects in the area.

It was around this time that the RCMP contacted the Royal Canadian Air Force (RCAF) for help with the investigation. As a follow-up to a phone conversation, the RCMP sent a memo to the Director of Air Intelligence of the RCAF. The memo, dated August 16, 1960, stated that the issue was likely more in keeping with the interests of the Air Force than with those of the RCMP: the "description of the object is very interesting and the whole matter seems worthy of the attention of someone such as the RCAF, who are no doubt better able to handle this matter."

The Department of National Defence responded on September 23, 1960, with a letter confirming that the object could not have been associated with space research, as no reports were made by tracking agencies within Canada or the United States. The department stated that it was inclined to believe that the object seen by the campers was a meteorite, and that the heat of the meteor when it struck the Earth would have undoubtedly caused steam and could account for the burning reeds and grass. The original observers, however, reported that they saw no steam when the object hit the water.

The department recommended that the local geologist complete the magnetometer check; he would be familiar with the reactions of the instruments, and would be able to ascertain whether fabricated metals were buried in the area. Finally, although the department doubted the object was significant as far as national security was concerned, the Department of National Defence stated that they would "be most interested in being advised of the outcome" of the investigation.

However, a document dated almost one year after the incident explains that the plan to have the local geologist complete a magnetometer check never happened. Mr. Brown, the geologist, had to be out of the area and could not complete the check. The use of the magnetometer would have been the most effective method for finding the object. The case of the flying object landing in Clan Lake was closed. No object or meteor was ever found.

Another Something Falls Into A Lake Shag Harbour, Nova Scotia October 4, 1967

On the night of October 4, 1967, officers of the Royal Canadian Mounted Police (RCMP) and six civilians witnessed an incredible, yet unexplainable, sight. Earlier in the evening, the RCMP had received many phone calls from residents reporting that an airplane had crashed into Shag Harbour. Both the RCMP and locals had rushed to the shore of the harbour, but what they encountered there was far from a conventional aircraft.

Witnesses reported seeing an object 60 feet in length moving in an easterly direction before it descended rapidly into the water, making a bright splash on impact. A single white light appeared on the surface of the water for a short period of time. The RCMP, with help from local fishermen and their boats, endeavoured to reach the object before it sank completely.

Local fishermen remember traveling through thick, glittery, yellow foam to get to where they saw the object. Bubbles from underneath the surface of the water appeared around the boats. The crews attempted to search the area for evidence of survivors, but found no one.

The Department of National Defence (DND) conducted an underwater search of the area, but failed to locate any evidence of an object.

The crashing of the unidentified flying object into Shag Harbour is still discussed today, with many articles appearing on the Internet. There is no trace of the RCMP reports of this sighting in the files. The Department of National Defence has identified this sighting as unsolved, and the only documentation that exists in the files is a DND memo.

[Note: The Shag Harbor incident is the subject of a book, "Dark Object: The World's Only Government-Documented UFO Crash" by Don Ledger, Chris Styles and Whitley Strieber. – Editor]

Prospector Sickened By landed UFO – Or Was He? Falcon Lake, Manitoba May 20, 1967

Stephen Michalak set out on a prospecting trip to Falcon Lake, Manitoba, on Friday, May 19, 1967, just as he would have for any other trip. He packed his equipment, and his wife packed him a lunch for the next day's work. He arrived in Falcon Lake at approximately 9:30 p.m. and checked into a motel. He would later report to the Royal Canadian Mounted Police (RCMP) that he went for a coffee at the motel's beverage room. On the morning of May 20th, Michalak awoke early in the morning and began prospecting in an area he later attempted to keep secret. After a morning of work in the bushes around Falcon Lake, he came across a flock of geese, a typical scene for rural Manitoba, and sat down at 11:00 a.m. to have his lunch.

It was the ruckus caused by the geese that first caught Michalak's attention. When he looked up, there were two flying saucers directly in front of him. According to his statement to the RCMP, he knelt in amazement before the two objects.

One of the objects landed about 100 feet in front of him, while the other hovered about 10 feet off of the ground. Michalak estimated the size of the hovering object to be about 30 feet in diameter.

The first object remained on the ground for 45 minutes. It made a whirling sound and gradually changed in colour from grey to silver. Then a hatch opened and the object emitted a bright violet light. Michalak claimed that he heard voices from within. He called out to the voices in English, German, Italian, Polish, Ukrainian and Russian. There was no response; instead the hatch closed quickly as if the inhabitants were spooked. Michalak reached out and touched the object as it began to revolve and take off, and he was instantly pushed back by a force of hot air. The blast burned his clothing and left marks on his chest. After he ripped off his clothing, Michalak felt ill. He began to vomit and noticed a metallic smell coming from inside his body, like the burning smell of an electric wire or an electric motor.

2 the STAR-PHOENIX Saskatoon, Tuesday, September 10, 1974

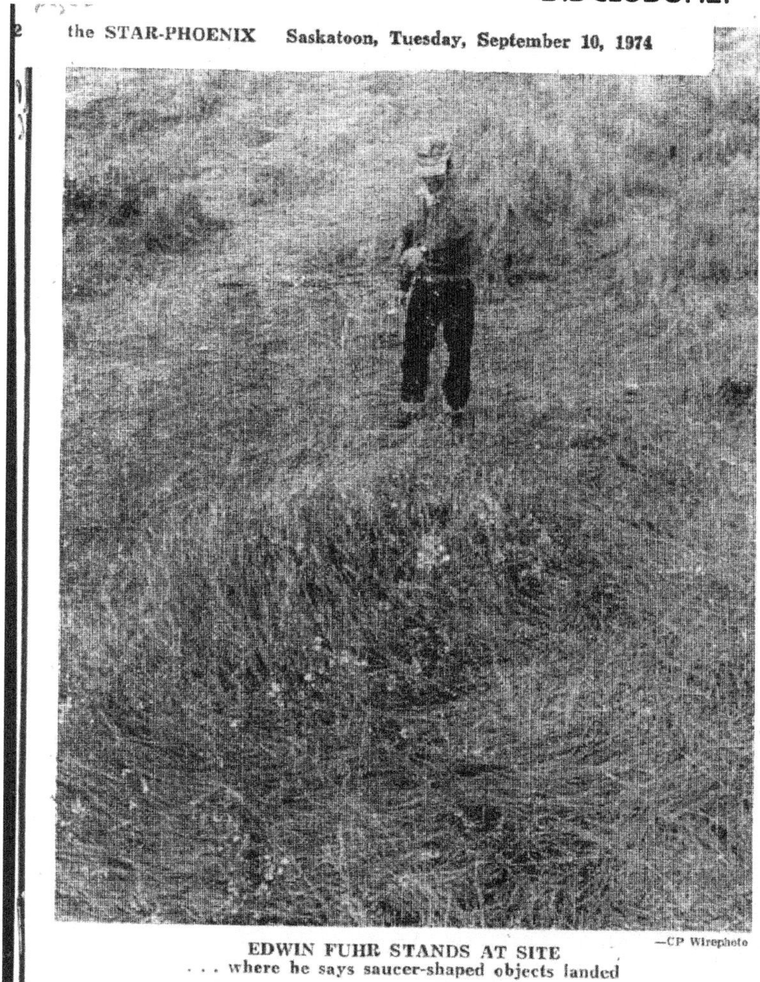

—CP Wirephoto

EDWIN FUHR STANDS AT SITE
. . . where he says saucer-shaped objects landed

'Saucers' sighted, no hoax – RCMP

LANGENBURG (CP) — RCMP Constable Ron Morier says he doesn't think a district farmer is trying to pull a hoax with his claim of seeing saucer-shaped objects hovering about a foot over a slough near his rapeseed field six miles north of here.

Edwin Fuhr, 36, claims five stainless steel objects stayed for 15 minutes before leaving. He says there were depressions in the foot-high grass about 11 feet in diameter where they had been.

Constable Morier visited the farm Monday in this community 120 miles northeast of Regina for a first-hand look.

"They took me out to where they'd seen these things in the grass. I saw the rings . . .

"Something was there and I doubt it was a hoax. There's no indication anything had been wheeled in or out and Mr. Fuhr seemed genuinely scared."

Constable Morier took photographs and measurements and sent his information to the National Research Council in Ottawa.

"Some farmers are afraid to work their fields," the constable said. "At least that's what I hear on coffee row."

Mr. Fuhr says he got down from his swather and moved to within 15 feet of the objects.

"All of a sudden I noticed the grass was moving . . . turning near this thing. I just watched it for about two minutes and then noticed that the whole thing was turning.

"I backed up slow. I wasn't going to turn my back on the thing. When I got back to the swather, I noticed there were another four to the left of me, all revolving. I just froze on the seat and didn't move.

"I was terrified. I froze. I couldn't do anything.

"Then they took off (after 15 minutes) . . . straight up. There was a grey vapor coming from underneath them and a strong wind. I had to hang on to my hat and it knocked the rape down."

It took two minutes for the objects to disappear into the clouds and another two minutes for Mr. Fuhr to come down from his swather.

"I wanted to be sure they were gone."

He then examined the circular depressions left by the objects. "I felt the grass to see if it was warm. There was nothing you could feel and there wasn't any smell."

The Royal Canadian Mounted Police took Edwin Fuhr seriously when he said he saw a saucer shaped object resting on the ground for 15 minutes, leaving a solid impression in the field.

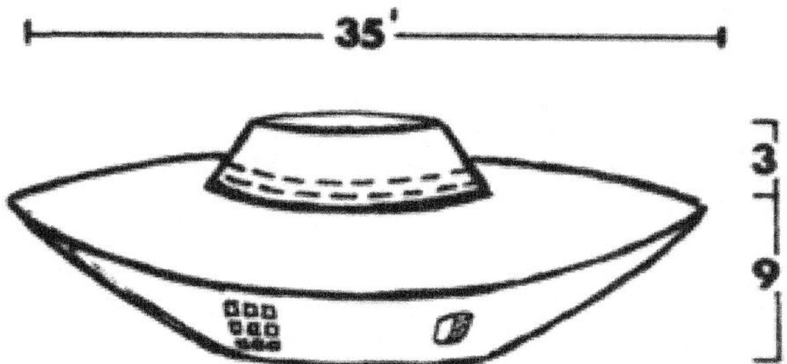

In the Northwest Territories in the small community known as Clan Lake a strange saucer-like object hovered and than hit the water frightening the people of the area who live off the land by hunting, fishing and trapping.

ROYAL CANADIAN MOUNTED POLICE - GENDARMERIE ROYALE DU CANADA

RCMP GRC 6440 | C 237 REV. 1-4-64

OTHER FILE REFERENCES / REF. AUTRES DOSSIERS	DIVISION	DATE	RCMP FILE REFERENCES / REF. DOSSIERS GRC
	"D"	18 JUNE 67	67D
	SUB-DIVISION - SOUS-DIVISION: Winnipeg		67WS-700-20
	DETACHMENT-DÉTACHEMENT: Falcon Beach Highway Patrol		67-700-2

RE. OBJET.

Stefan MICHALAK - Report of Unidentified Flying Object
Falcon Beach, Manitoba - 20 MAY 67 700-130

20 MAY 67

1. At approximately 3:00 PM, this date, I was patrolling PTH# 1, one half mile West of Falcon Beach, Manitoba, when I noticed a man walking on the South shoulder of the highway, towards Falcon Beach. He was wearing a grey cap, brown jacket with no shirt, light coloured trousers and carrying a brown briefcase.

2. This subject, upon seeing the police car, began waving his arms excitedly. I turned around on the highway and drove back to see what he wanted. He shouted to me to stay away from him. I asked him why and he replied saying that he had seen two space ships. He said I might get some sort of skin disease or radiation if I came too close. He seemed very upset. I asked for some identification and he gave me a document pertaining to prospecting, which showed his name as Stefan MICHALAK of 314 Lindsay Street, Winnipeg, Manitoba.

3. I enquired as to the circumstances surrounding his unusual experience, and Mr. MICHALAK related the following story. He apparently had been prospecting approximately one mile West and two miles North of Falcon Beach. About 12:00 Noon he sighted the two space ships. He said they were rotating at a high rate of speed and emitted a red glow. The space ships landed near him and he reportedly touched one. The exhaust or some sort of hot substances came off the space ship, burning his shirt, chest and hat. The space ships remained awhile, how long he was not certain, then flew away. He left the bush to get medical treatment.

4. MICHALAK showed me his cap, the back of which was burnt. I wanted to examine his shirt, however, he would not let me, and kept backing away every time I got close to him. As far as I was able to determine, the back of MICHALAK'S head was not burnt. It appeared to me that MICHALAK had taken a black substances, possibly wood ashes, and rubbed it on his chest. At no time during my conversations with MICHALAK would he allow me close enough to him to definitely see whether or not he was injured. I asked him why his hands were not burnt if he had touched the space ship and he would not answer me. At my request he drew a diagram of the space ship which appeared to be saucer shaped.

5. I could not smell the odour of liquor on MICHALAK. His general appearance was not dissimilar to that of a person who has over indulged. His eyes were bloodshot and when questioned in detail could or would not answer coherently. I offered to drive him to Falcon Beach and arrange for some one to treat him but he declined saying the he was alright.

6. Approximately one half hour later, he came to the Detachment Office and asked for me. He would not enter the office,

Feeling worse by the minute, Michalak headed towards the highway, where he managed to flag down an RCMP car. Michalak refused medical treatment from the officer at the time, but later went back to the RCMP detachment office and asked for a doctor. Upon learning that there were no doctors in the area, he caught a bus back to Winnipeg.

When Michalak returned home, his son took him to the hospital. He did not tell the doctor the burns were caused by an unidentified flying object (UFO), but rather by airplane exhaust. Michalak also consulted his family doctor about his loss of appetite; since the ordeal, he had experienced rapid weight loss.

On May 26, 1967, Michalak was interviewed by C.J. Davis of the RCMP. His report describes the burn marks visible on Michalak's chest: "...a large burn that covers an area approximately 1 foot in diameter. The burn was... blotchy and with unburned areas inside the burned perimeter area."By this time, the authorities had become very interested in the case. There were aspects of Michalak's story that were difficult to explain, such as the burns on his body. The RCMP wanted to find the landing site to investigate further. They first attempted to find the site on their own, on May 31st, but were unsuccessful.

On June 1, 1967, Michalak was brought to Falcon Lake to lead another search. Michalak could not find the site, causing increased speculation about the validity of his claim. The RCMP uncovered another discrepancy in his story: Michalak had reported that he went for coffee the night before the alleged sighting; however the bartender at the Falcon Lake Motel's beverage room claimed to have served Michalak bottles of beer.

The RCMP decided to close the case until Michalak could locate the landing site. On June 26th, however, the case re-opened. Michalak claimed to have found the site on his own, and recovered objects he had left there -- pieces of his burnt clothing, steel tape, and some rocks and soil samples.

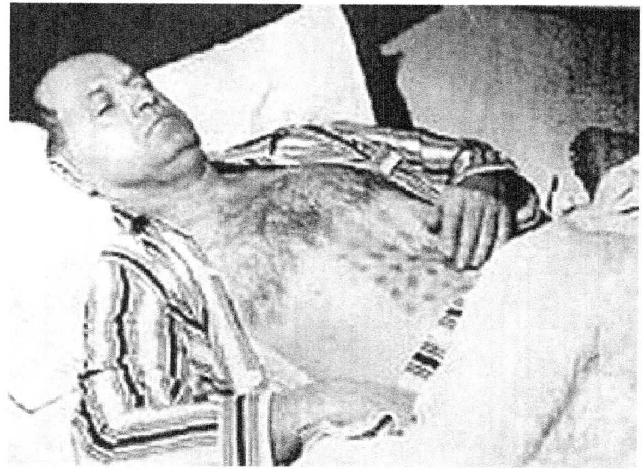

In one of the few cases of UFO injuries, Stephen Michalak ended up in the hospital with bad bums on his chest, hands and head. His gloves and hat were terribly scorched, but in a follow up document the authorities seem to show some degree of skepticism.

RCMP Squad Leader Bissky visited Michalak on the evening of June 26th and obtained samples of soil brought back from the location. The soil samples, along with samples of clothing and the steel tape, were sent to be tested for radioactive material. On July 24th, the results of these tests were sent to the RCMP along with a memo that stated, "U.F.O. reported by Stephen Michalak. Laboratory tests here indicate earth samples taken from scene highly radioactive. Radiation protection Div. of Dept. of Health and Welfare concerned that others may be exposed, if travel in area not restricted."

A second laboratory test was sent to the RCMP on July 25th. It stated that the Department of Health and Welfare would be sending a representative, Mr. Hunt, to Winnipeg to investigate.

On the evening of July 27, 1967, Michalak was visited by Hunt, Squad Leader Bissky and C.J. Davis, who explained the laboratory findings of radioactive material. Michalak agreed to take them to the landing site on the following day, July 28th. The group walked to the location in the afternoon and reported the scene to be bare of evidence except for a semi-circle on the rock face, 15 feet in diameter, where the moss had been somehow removed. Mr. Hunt found traces of radiation in a fault in the rock across the center of the landing spot. No trace of radiation was found around the outer perimeter of the circle or in the moss or grass below the raised portion of the rock. The radioactive material found in the rock fault was radium 226, an isotope in wide commercial use and also found in nuclear reactor waste. In view of the small quantity of soil contamination, Mr. Hunt determined that there was no danger to humans traveling in the area.

The Department of National Defence identifies the Falcon Lake case as unsolved. Stephen Michalak wrote a book about his experience, but claimed to never have financially benefited from his ordeal.

[The book is "My Encounter with the UFO." published in 1967. – Editor]

Crop Circle Investigation Duhamel, Alberta August 1967

Today, crop circles are part of the popular imagination. But back in 1967, when crop circles appeared in a farmer's field in Duhamel, Alberta, the Department of National Defence conducted an investigation to determine who or what was responsible.

Duhamel is a small hamlet near Camrose, Alberta. For several weeks before the crop circles appeared, Duhamel had been plagued with strange occurrences. Reports of unidentified flying objects (UFOs) had made it into the local papers weeks before the crop circles were discovered.

The crop circles were discovered by accident. A local farmer, Mr. Schielke, went out to his fields to collect his cows. The cows normally came back from the pasture on their own, but on Saturday, August 5, 1967, after a night of heavy rains, the animals didn't come home. Bringing home the cows was something Mr. Schielke rarely had to do, so this was the first time he had been to his fields in weeks. It was therefore the first time he noticed the bizarre imprints on his land -- four circular marks approximately 30 feet in diameter. Mr. Schielke made it very clear to the investigator that the marks on the field could not have been made by his equipment, nor did he believe in UFOs.

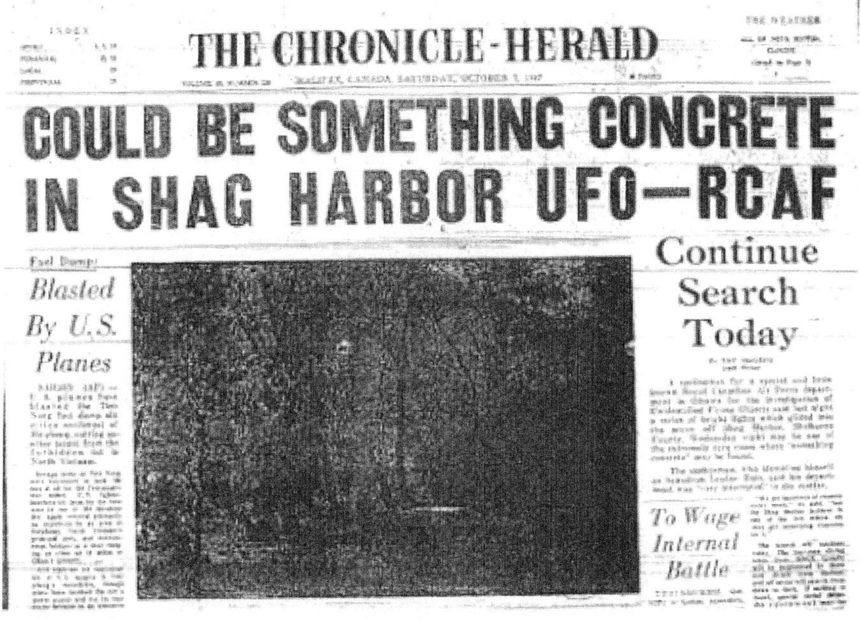

THE CHRONICLE-HERALD

COULD BE SOMETHING CONCRETE IN SHAG HARBOR UFO—RCAF

Fuel Dump Blasted By U.S. Planes

Continue Search Today

To Wage Internal Battle

Canada seems to have an affinity with USOs - objects seen emerging or shooting into the sky from a body of water. The most famous being the incident at Shagg Harbour witnessed by sane and sober observers as it slowly sank to the bottom of the harbor as this front page story describes.

The investigator sent to the site admitted that the marks left him perplexed. He described the four marks: "The mark varies from five to seven inches wide, and the smallest circular mark is 31 ft., 9 in. in diameter. Three of the rings are essentially circular, with the largest mark being slightly elliptical, varying from 34 ft., 5 in. to 36 ft., 3 in."

According to the investigator, there was no evidence outside of the circular marks. There were no exhaust blasts, scorch marks or disturbances of the loose surface material. Within the circles, there was evidence that thumbnail-sized pieces of vegetation had been removed by the object that made the marks.

Although the investigator talked about the possibility of the marks being left by a wheel, it is clear in the report that the marks were more likely left by a 135-ton aircraft or spacecraft.

The crop circles in Duhamel, Alberta, are considered unsolved by the Department of National Defence.

The curious and serious UFO researchers as well stop by the Shagg Harbour Museum while in town.

Crop Circles started showing up fairly early on being associated with UFO appearances. One of the first such cases was in Duhamel, Alberta in August, 1967 (see map inset). Today, the Canadian Crop Circle Research Network keeps taps of the situation as with the case of one such formation that appeared near the edge of a major roadway.

Prince George, British Columbia January 1, 1969

Though there have been thousands of reports involving sightings of lights in the sky, Canada has its landing cases as well. This photo has been authenticated by Naval scientist Dr. Bruce Maccabee.

Just as the sun was about to set on the first day of the New Year in 1969, the residents of Prince George, British Columbia looked to the sky and saw something they could not explain. Many were prompted to call the Royal Canadian Mounted Police (RCMP). Three unrelated witnesses reported a strange, round object in the late afternoon sky. The sphere radiated a yellow-orange light and appeared to ascend from 2,000 to 10,000 feet. Further reports by other residents were made to the RCMP on January 3, 4 and 5.

Mrs. William Dow may not have been aware of these reports when she called the RCMP to investigate an object that landed in her back yard on January 9, 1969.

An official RCMP investigation report made on January 30, 1969, includes a photograph to explain the object that was recovered.

THE CIRVIS REPORTS

Many UFO researchers have long been convinced that JANAP 146 directives were used to cover up reports by military and civilian pilots. Under JANAP 146 pilots were required to submit reports of CIRVIS reports of UFOs (CIRVIS stands for Canadian-United States Communications Instructions for Reporting Vital Intelligence Sightings). The security provision read, "All persons aware of the contents or existence of a MERINT Report are governed by the Communications Act of 1934 and amendments Thereto, and Espionage Laws. MERINT reports contain information affecting the National Defense of the United States within the meaning of the Espionage Laws, 18 U.S. Code, 793 and 794. The unauthorized transmission or revelation of the contents of MERINT reports in any manner is prohibited." (See instructions poster on next page.)

FOR EARLY WARNING IN DEFENCE OF THE NORTH AMERICAN CONTINENT

CIRVIS-MERINT REPORTING PROCEDURE

1. MESSAGE IDENTIFICATION

(a) Reports made from airborne and land-based sources will be identified by **CIRVIS** (pronounced SUR-VEES) as the first word of the text.

(b) Reports made by waterborne sources will be identified by **MERINT** (pronounced MUR-ENT) as the first word of the text.

2. WHAT TO REPORT

Report immediately all airborne and waterborne objects which appear to be **HOSTILE**, are **UNIDENTIFIED** or are acting suspiciously.

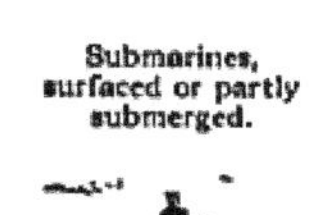

Submarines, surfaced or partly submerged.

Surface warships positively identified as not Canadian or U.S. Other ships or boats acting suspiciously.

Aircraft or vapour trails which appear to be directed against Canada, the United States, their territories or possessions.

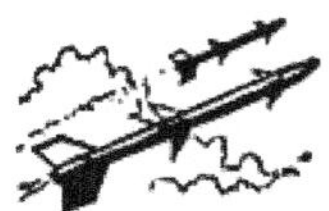

Guided Missiles

Unidentified Flying Objects or unidentified objects in the water.

3. SEND TO ANY

Canadian Military Establishment,
RCMP Post,
Department of Transport or Fisheries Representative,
Hudson's Bay Company Northern Radio-Equipped Store, or
The nearest open Canadian Telegraph Office. (By telephone if necessary.)

Use the quickest possible means to make your report.

4. SEND THIS KIND OF MESSAGE

(a) Begin your message with the word "CIRVIS" or "MERINT" as applicable.
(b) Give the identification of the observer, aircraft or vessel making the report.
(c) Describe briefly the objects sighted.
(d) Indicate where and when the objects were sighted.
(e) If objects are airborne, estimate altitude as "low", "medium", "high".
(f) Give direction of travel of sighted objects.
(g) Estimate and give speed of sighted objects.
(h) Give other significant information.

5. SEND IMMEDIATELY

DO NOT DELAY YOUR REPORT DUE TO INCOMPLETE INFORMATION.

NOTE

There are no charges to the originator in the handling of CIRVIS or MERINT messages.

Authorized by Department of National Defence
Authorized for display in Post Offices by the Postmaster General

SHIRLEY BAY LOOKOUT STATION OUTSIDE OTTAWA, ONTARIO, CANADA
Detecting UFOs in the 1950s

The original SETI program (Search for Extra-Terrestrial Intelligence) was set-up by Canadian Department of Communications engineer and scientist Wilbert Brockhouse Smith in 1953. The main difference? Smith was not looking at distant stars, he was looking a lot closer to home - like the skies over Ottawa, Ontario, Canada.

The Canadian government was quite concerned about flying saucer UFOs over Canadian skies at the time, so Wilbert Smith designed instruments that would detect when a UFO flew over. He set up a UFO detection station at Shirley Bay ten miles outside Ottawa, Ontario.

Based on the idea that the UFOs operate by manipulating gravity, Smith's equipment was set-up to detect and record changes in the gravity field. The device was also connected to an alarm should some exotic technology manage to change the gravity field over Shirley Bay.

On Sunday, August 8, 1954 the station detected something in the skies. Wilbert ran outside, but the sky was overcast, so he could not see what sort of aerial phenomena or UFO had altered the gravity in the area.

Immediately after Smith announced the detection to the press, he was heavily reprimanded. Within days he reversed himself in the press and said no UFO was detected. By the end of the month the government told the press that it had not only shut-down the detection station, but all UFO research including Project Magnet.

It's interesting to read between the lines of the press release of August 10, 1954 that states, while the government is officially out of the UFO business, they still want people to forward their UFO information to Wilbert on an "unofficial" basis. They even go to the point of including his mailing address in the press release. So while they wanted the press off their backs regarding the UFO issue, it's obvious they were still interested in studying UFOs.

Machine 'Records Saucer'

OTTAWA — (CP) — Is Canada the first country in the world to record a flying saucer with instruments?

That question is being debated here today after the transport department's flying saucer sighting station reported that it had detected an unexplained object in the atmosphere over Ottawa Sunday.

Wilbert B. Smith, engineer in charge of the broadcast and measurement section of the transport department, said the saucer station's gravimeter was tripped at 3:01 p.m.

The gravimeter is designed to detect and record gamma rays, magnetic fluctuations, radio noises and gravity and mass changes in the atmosphere.

Based on the intense government interest in solving the UFO problem at the time, it's most likely that UFO projects went top-secret from this point on. Some of it may have been taken out of the hands of Smith, who had the problematic tendency of sharing his UFO findings with the press, who would then descend on his superiors.

CONTENTS OF DOSSIER:

1. [ELECTRONIC OBSERVATORY] *Globe and Mail* Nov. 12, 1953
2. [OTTAWA OBSERVATORY] *Winnipeg Free Press* Nov. 12, 1953
3. [THE DAY] *Wilbert Smith* Aug. 8, 1954
4. [CANADIAN FIRST] *Globe & Mail* Aug. 10, 1954
5. [SHUTDOWN] *Press Release* Aug. 10, 1954

ELECTRONIC OBSERVATORY TO WATCH FOR FLYING SAUCERS

Toronto Globe and Mail
Thursday, November 12, 1953

OTTAWA Nov. 11 (Staff) -- an engineer engaged in a scientific hunt for flying saucers says there is a 90 per cent change the numerous saucer sightings are justified by physical somethings and better than a 50-50 chance that the somethings are alien vehicles.

He is Wilbert B. Smith, engineer in charge of the Department of Transport's broadcast and measurement section of the Telecommunications Division, which, at Shirley Bay. 10 miles west of Ottawa, had the worlds first flying saucer sighting station

The scientific watch for saucers began five years ago as a hobby among some of the telecommunications people engaged in ionospheric studies. It since has been given official recognition and there is a small appropriation for it within the Department of Transport.

The departmental directive on the subject says the station is to see what it can prove of disprove the existence of flying saucers.

The Defence Research Board, which has been gathering flying saucer data for some time, is co-operating in the project. Among those associated with it are Dr. James Wait, the board's physicist, and John H. Thompson, technical information expert of the telecommunications division.

Professor J. T. Wilson, the University of Toronto, and Dr. G.D. Garland, specialist in gravitational studies at the Dominion Observatory assisted with some of the equipment for the station.

"From our point of view," says Mr. Smith, "this is nothing more than part of our routine work. At Shirley Bay we have an ionosphere observatory in connection with our radio wave studies."

Specifically, for the flying saucer work there is additional electronic equipment, some of it unique.

The purpose of the setup according to Mr. Smith, is to gather measurements, information as to the type of propulsion used, and other data, if a saucer should be sighted and if it should prove to be an alien vehicle.

Those associated with the project do not subscribe to the view that the saucer sightings can be explained as optical illusions. Engineer Smith states that he has not yet found one reported sighting which wholly could be put down to illusion.

Statistically it has been worked out, on the basis of past sightings, that the object, phenomenon, or whatever, may be expected to be seen within a year or so. The people at Shirley Bay are confident that maintaining an around the clock watch, the [group] should see something in a year.

Although it did not produce the results expected, an experiment tried here some time ago proved one thing. Not many people are sky-watchers. A weather balloon, 10 feet in diameter, lighted from the underside so a to have a saucer-like appearance from the ground, was released over Ottawa. It was estimated that a minimum of 5,000 people were in a position to see it.

The saucer scientists waited for the reports to come in. For one thing, they wanted to see what sort of descriptions were given. They didn't hear a word.

In a negative way, the test seemed to support the existence of saucers if a 10-foot lighted balloon could pass unnoticed, or cause no comment, among 5,000 people, at least some of those who reported seeing flying saucers must have seen something.

OTTAWA OBSERVATORY TO SIGHT FLYING SAUCERS

The Winnipeg Free Press
Thursday, November 12, 1953

OTTAWA (NYHT) -- The Canadian government is building an observatory near Ottawa to watch the skies for flying saucers.

The observatory, first of its kind in the world, will be manned by government scientists headed by Wilbert B. Smith, an engineer of the Canadian department of transport.

"There's a very high degree of probability that flying saucers are real objects." Mr. Smith said Wednesday night, "and a 60 per cent probability that they're alien vehicles."

He discounted the optical illusion explanation of the phenomenon. He said that in every one of many reports of flying saucers seen in Canadian skies, there is some factor precluding writing it off as an optical illusion. The sighting station will use specially built electronic devices to track saucers.

Co-sponsor of the observatory, with the transport department, is the Defence Research Board of Canada. Dr. O. M. Solandt, chairman of DRB, and Dr. C. J. Mackenzie, former president of the national research council, have consistently refused to ridicule flying saucer reports.

The Day Magnet Detected a Flying Saucer

Wilbert B. Smith

August 8, 1954 started out as a rather typical day at Project Magnet. Since the project had started it was hoped that the instruments on hand would sooner or later pick up an unidentified flying object and track and analyze its movements.

For months I and my tiny group of likeminded associates had watched the sensitive gravimeter in vain. On occasions when large commercial airlines would pass over, our hearts would skip a beat, as the instruments would register aerial activities.

But on August 8 at 3:01 P.M. the gravimeter began acting strangely. First it waved, drawing a thin dark line on the graph paper being used to measure the movements of the instruments. Without further warning the gravimeter went wild. All evidence indicated that a real unidentified flying object had flown within feet of the station.

Alarm systems connected to the instrument panel began to ring, alerting us to the UFO. After watching the instruments a few seconds, we ran outside to see what was causing the odd reaction.

Unfortunately our area was completely fogged in, and whatever was up there could not be seen visually.

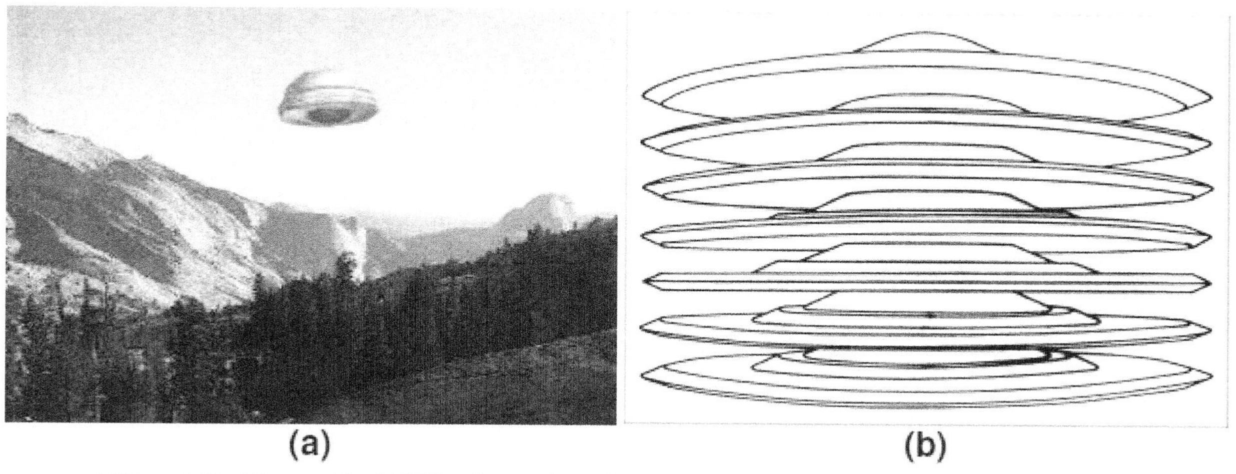

Wilbert Smith studied UFOs from the view point of magnetic propulsion as well as certain magnetic grids that he believed circled the earth, especially strong around the area of the Bermuda Triangle. Though not identical Prof. Dr Eng. Jan Pajak of Poland believes that UFOs have a certain magnetic property that makes them appear differently under various sets of circumstances.

CANADIAN SCIENTISTS FIRST!

DID WE TRIP A FLYING SAUCER?

The Globe and Mail
August 10, 1954

OTTAWA, Aug 9 (CP) -- Is Canada the first country in the world to record a flying saucer with instruments?

That question is being debated today after the Transport Department's flying saucer sighting station reported that it had detected an unexplainable object in the atmosphere over Ottawa Sunday.

Wilbert B. Smith, engineer in charge of the broadcast and measurement section of the Transport Department, said the saucer station's gravimeter was tripped at 3:01 p.m.

Mr. Smith said he is convinced that the deflection on the gravimeter was not caused by an aircraft. It was either something scientists did not know about or an instrument failure.

"We now are attempting to find out if there was a failure somewhere in the instrument." he said.

If it turns out that there was no failure then I don't know what it was that passed overhead."

Mr. Smith said it is not possible for anyone to state that the gravimeter recorded the presence of a flying saucer.

However, he added "it also is not possible to say it wasn't a flying saucer."

Mr. Smith, who built and operated the sighting station, said the deflection on the gravimeter was the first that could not be explained since the instrument was installed last October.

The gravimeter is designed to detect and record gamma rays, magnetic fluctuations, radio noises and gravity and mass changes in the atmosphere.

Mr. Smith was on duty at the station when a set of alarm bells tripped by the deflection of the gravimeter -- rang.

"I dashed over to look at the instrument," he said. "The deflection in the line (drawn by an electronically operated pen) was greater and more pronounced than we have seen seven when a large aircraft has passed overhead.

"I ran outside to see what might be in the sky. The overcast was down to 1,000 feet, so whatever was up there, whatever it was that generated the sharp variation, was concealed behind clouds.

We must now ask ourselves what it could have been."

PRESS RELEASE

Controller of Telecommunications
Ottawa, Ontario, August 10, 1954
Dear Sirs:

1. For the past three and a half years the Department of Transport has carried on an investigation of Unidentified Flying Objects. Considerable data was collected and analysed and many attempts were made to fit these data into some sort of pattern. However, it has not been possible to reach any definite conclusion, and since new data appear to be similar to data already studied, there seems to be little point in carrying the investigation say further on an official level.

2. It has therefore been decided that the Department of Transport will discontinue any further study of Unidentified Flying Objects and Project Magnet, which was set up for this purpose, will be dropped. However, Mr. W.B. Smith, P.O. Box 51, City View, Ontario will continue to receive and catalogue any future data on a purely unofficial basis.

Your very truly,

Controller of Telecommunications

1937 - Vancouver, BC, Canada

October 8, 1981, Kelsey Bay, Vancouver Island,Canada

DENMARK CLAIMS IT HIDES NO SECRETS

By Sean Casteel

In January of 2009, the Denmark Air Force, following the example of the U.S. and U.K., declassified and released its secret archive on UFO sightings.

"At just 329 pages," a publication called the Copenhagen Post Online writes, "the newly released 'X-Files,' detailing previously secret unexplained UFO sightings in Denmark, might not at first glance seem to offer much in the way of sustenance for the legions of hopeful stargazers out there. But detailed within the slender volume are over 200 unsolved UFO sightings which provide plenty of food for thought for the old question: are we alone?"

The Copenhagen Post quotes a captain in the Danish Air Force, one Thomas Pederson, as saying, "We decided to publish the archives because frankly there is nothing really secret in them."

As in many other countries discussed in this book, the Danish Air Force has simply become tired of journalists requesting a look at the UFO files.

"The Air Force has no interest," Pederson continued, "in keeping unusual sightings a secret. Our job is to maintain national security, not investigate UFOs."

The archives cover unexplained events occurring between 1978 and 2002. The files reveal that most cases have never been solved, but also that many are precise and detailed enough to be explained by other phenomena. Military aircraft, weather balloons, bright planets and, in particular, Chinese lanterns, all of which can explain away the bulk of reports by worried observers.

After 2002, the job of chronicling UFO sightings was taken over by a group called Scandinavian UFO Information (SUFOI).

A KID ON HIS BICYCLE

One of the unsolved cases concerns an incident that happened on Funen in 1982. A 15-year-old boy was cycling through the countryside early in the morning one summer's day when he noticed something unusual in a field. Dismounting his bike, he walked towards what appeared to be a large, brightly-lit object that resembled two discs placed on top of one another. Intrigued, the boy walked closer and was amazed to see five humanoid figures next to the object.

The files state that the figures were about 60 centimeters tall and had large heads and chests compared to their puny legs.

"Whether the boy was making it up or not," the article continues, "we can't be sure, but his story is one of the more detailed examples contained in the dossier."

ANOTHER UNEXPLAINED DANISH SIGHTING

The online report goes to relate another unexplained sighting in the Danish Air Force files.

In August 1991, two police officers on a night patrol in the northern Copenhagen suburb of Ordrup had an unusual experience. Sitting in their patrol car at 2:30 A.M. they suddenly saw a strange object hovering about 75 to 150 meters in the air above the car. The officers thought it looked like the underside of an airplane, and then they noticed that their communications systems had ceased to function. Now thoroughly fascinated, the officers followed it as it moved slowly away, eventually disappearing behind some tall trees a few minutes later.

Less than 24 hours after the policemen had filed their report of the incident, a report came in from southern Funen of a silently moving UFO with bright lights that the observer was able to keep in sight for five minutes.

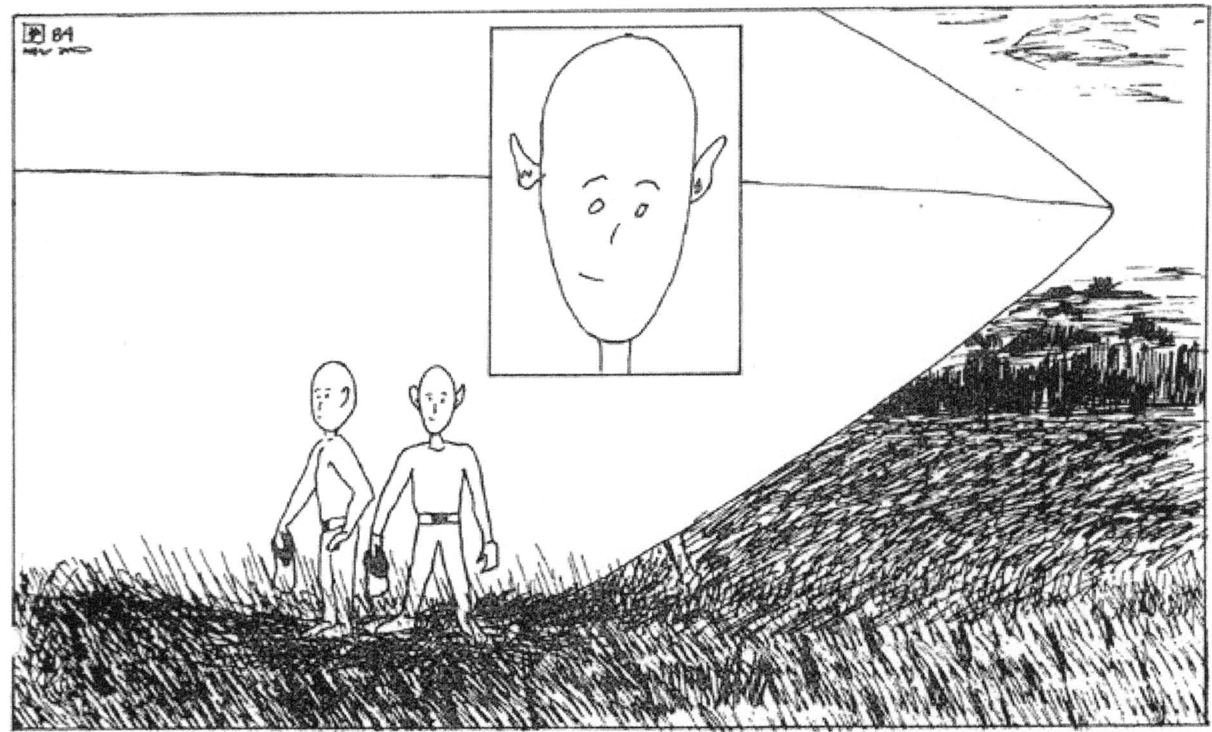

The Danish archives contains the remarkable tale told by a 15 year old boy of almost riding his bicycle into a UFO complete with two alien beings standing nearby.

NO SHOOT DOWN ORDERS IN DENMARK

Unlike the British Royal Air Force, which it was recently revealed has a penchant for attacking UFOs on sight [see the Stephen Bassett and Nick Pope interviews in this book], the Danes are more cautious. Captain Thomas Pederson denies the Danish Air Force has ever fired on a UFO.

"Personally, I think it would be a stupid thing to do," he said. "With their superior technology, our attacks would be like a mere catapult to them and we would surely be defeated. Haven't you seen 'Independence Day'?"

Pederson's statements about the UFOs having superior technology seems to contradict his earlier statement that the Danish Air Force harbors no secrets about the subject. Is it an inadvertent admission of some kind? Or just a setup to another "Independence Day" joke?

SUFOI - The most recognized UFO organisation in the world

The headlines could give the impression that we have bugged down by the summer heat and have started fantasising. It is, however, not totally fiction!

SUFOI has carried out a survey of the Danish population with regard to their knowledge of SUFOI and what our activities are (and a whole lot of other questions). It turns out that about every **third Dane** knows of SUFOI, which absolutely was more than anticipated by SUFOI.

In the survey we interviewed a high number of randomly selected Danes about their knowledge about UFOs, known sky phenomena etc. Some of the results were highly disappointing, such as people's knowledge about ordinary sky phenomena. Other results were more positive. In particular we are satisfied with the fact that many people – **31%** to be exact – know about our organisation.

At the same time it came evident, that most people know reasonably well the type of activities that SUFOI have. According to the Danish average person, SUFOI first of all is doing field investigations and is publishing a magazine. After this followed meetings for members, research and conferences. This view of SUFOI is actually very precise relative to our actual activities.

This position is, of course, not something out of the blue (so to speak!). First of all SUFOI has had permanent contact to the Danish press over many years – as mentioned elsewhere we in 1997 could celebrate our 40 years anniversary. Secondly, there has been a lot of focus on SUFOI through the many different media that exist in Denmark.

SUFOI's strong mindshare in the media was very well illustrated recently at the public event in Vanløse on May 27 where people were invited to listen to different presentations. This event lead to a new media record for SUFOI as it was mentioned the same evening on the prime time new of each of the two major national channels (DR1 and TV2). Between them the two appearances had more than 1 million viewers (compared to an adult population of about 3.5 million)!

To this we can add an appearance on national radio the same morning and major features in both Politiken and Berlingske Tidende – the two major newspapers in Denmark. Within the same week SUFOI appeared in no less than 4 television broadcasts, 2 radio broadcasts and numerous articles in the press!

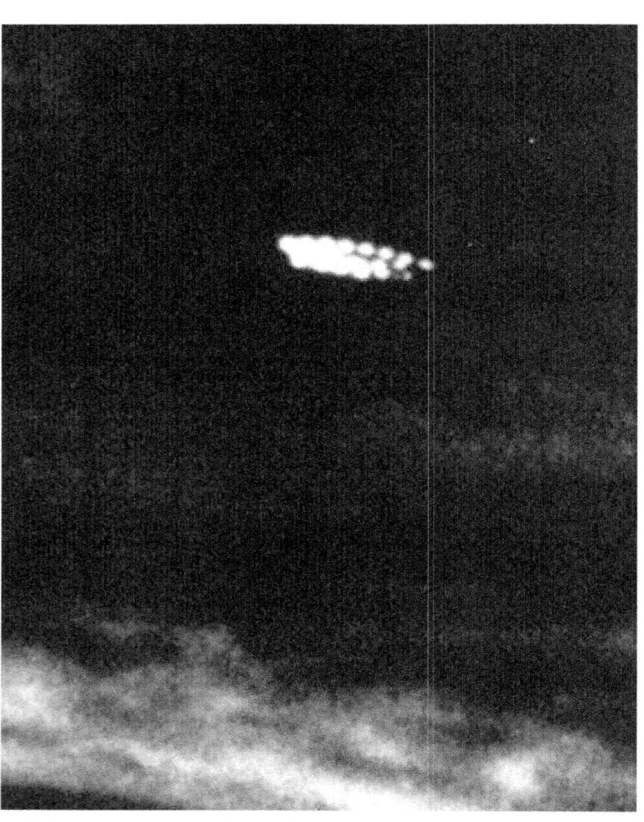

This photograph taken on Oct 27 1979 in Montonau is said to be among the most authentic ever taken in NZ.

In order words it is through active work with the press that SUFOI is getting close to one important objective: to become widely recognised as a serious UFO organisation in Denmark. Being recognised by 31% of the population is not bad and probably more than most other UFO organisations in the world. I will dare to claim that no other UFO organisation is known by more than 31% of the population in the home countries.

There are no reasons, however, to become complacent. We also want to create awareness among the remaining 69% of the Danish population!

DISCLOSURE DOWN UNDER: NEW ZEALAND RELEASES (SOME) UFO FILES

By Sean Casteel

The intent to release formerly classified UFO documents in New Zealand happened largely because of the efforts of Suzanne Hansen, the Director of a civilian UFO group called UFOCUS NZ. In her campaign to make the files public, Hansen negotiated for over a year with the Chief of Defence Force NZ, Lt. General Jerry Mataparae.

Chief of Defence Force, Lt. General Jerry Mataparae assisted in the UFO Disclosure movement in NZ.

Mataparae was initially unwilling to cooperate. He told Ms. Hansen, "It would require a substantial amount of collation, research and consultation to identify whether any of that information could be released." The Lt. General further stated that he was not in a position to deploy staff to undertake that task given their other work priorities.

However, the Chief of Defence also acknowledged his own feelings on the subject, saying, "In the longer term, recognizing the ongoing public interest in this topic, I would like to see a summary of information held about UFO sightings produced, in much the same way as that which was produced by the United Kingdom Ministry of Defence. Given the existing constraints, however, I cannot predict when that objective could be achieved."

Which sounds like Lt. General Mataparae was sympathetic to the cause of Disclosure and even a little apologetic about having to withhold the files from UFOCUS NZ.

Then, in December of 2009, after many months of ongoing communications, the Chief of Defence sent another letter to the New Zealand UFO group.

"I am pleased to be able to inform you," Mataparae wrote, "that two New Zealand Defence Force officers have begun the task of assessing classified files held in relation to this topic with a view to declassification. I would expect that files which are transferred to Archives New Zealand would be subject to extensive embargo periods in terms of access by the general public."

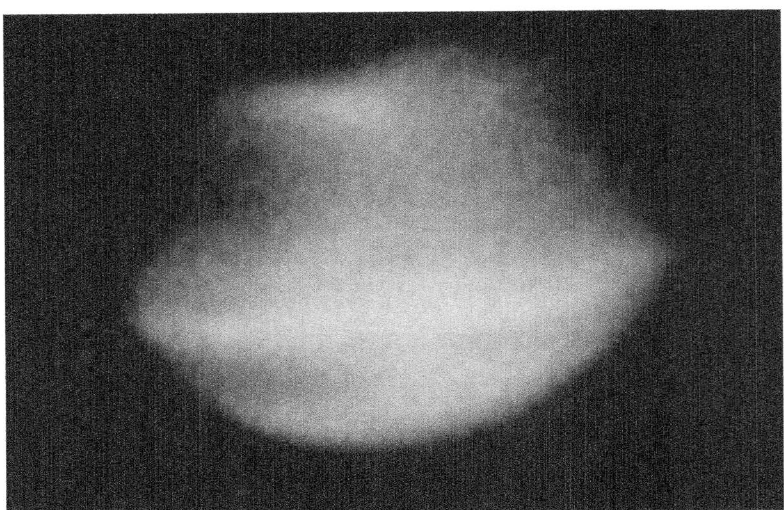

In this frame of the Christchurch footage the UFO looks like a typical "flying saucer."

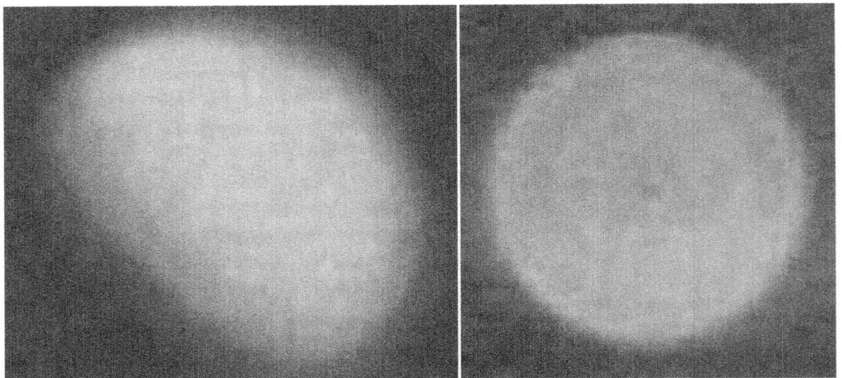

Close up of what appears to be a spinning disc photographed over Christchurch circa Dec. 1978.

THE MORELAND SIGHTING

(This account of the Moreland sighting written by F & P Dickeson, diagrams by Mr. B. Dickeson, is posted on UFOCUS NZ with the kind permission of Mrs. P. Dickeson and Mr. B. Dickeson. It appeared in the NZSSR group newsletter in 1959, and also in Xenolog 100, Sept-Oct 1975.)

Blenheim, New Zealand.

Date : Monday 13 July 1959
Time : Between 0530 - 0545 hrs.
Duration : 2-3 mins.
Witness : Mrs. Eileen Moreland
Weather conditions : Dark morning, cold and still, with thick cloud layer at approx. 2,000 ft. (Estimated)

On 13 July 1959 at 5.30 am Mrs. Eileen Moreland was walking across a flat paddock to bring in the small herd of cows for milking. The paddock where the cows were, was surrounded by trees After turning on the milking shed light, Mrs. Moreland set off across the paddock, torch in hand, to collect the cows. She was well-clad as the morning was cold and there was a thick layer of cloud over the district at an estimated height of 2,000 feet. Half-way across the paddock, some 50 yards from the shed, she noticed an unusual green glow, emanating from the cloud above and bathing the area in a ghastly light. She stopped and looked directly upwards, thinking that it could not be the moon, as it was in the wrong place. Then suddenly, two green lights, "like eyes", appeared through the clouds, circled by a band of orange lights. All about her the ground was illuminated by the sickly-green light, and, looking at herself and her hands, she saw that she too was bathed in this green glow.

Feeling that she did not want to stay put, she bolted for the pinus radiata trees bordering the paddock. The cows could be seen plainly in the light and she ran among them and stood against the trunk of one of the pine trees. Turning around from the shelter of the trees, she saw a flatish, saucer-shaped object slowly descending from about 50 feet above the ground. It stopped it's smooth descent some 30 feet above the ground and hovered about 15 feet above a group of peach trees (10-15 feet high.)The ratio of height to width of the object was about 1:3 - it was between 7 ½ - 8 ft high and some 20 - 25 feet across. There were two circumferential rows of orange-green 'jets' set into bands at the top and bottom of the main body of the object. The jets were brilliant orange in colour, with greenish centers, and faded to the outside, through orange to yellow. They made a faint hissing noise and were located on metallic bands about 1 ½ feet in towards the center from the upper and lower edges of the object. (If the bands had been 2 ft wide, say, there would have been about 1 ½ ft between the two - the total depth of this arrangement being about 4 ½, possibly 5 ft.)

The motionless object hovered some 30 feet above the ground, about 40 yards out in the center of the paddock, and was perfectly visible. On stopping, the jets immediately shut off and reappeared, at a slight angle. Each band of jets then began to counter-rotate at high speed, the top band from right to left and the bottom from left to right. The speed became so great that the bands of light became continuous, "like halos". There was none of the 'revving-up' noise associated with a car or plane engine, but a loud humming could be heard, and the noise of the 'jets' hissing. Mrs. Moreland became apprehensive when she noticed that the object was occupied. There was a clear, glassy dome-like structure on top, filled with a pure white light, the source of which was not visible itself, but seemed to arise from the center of the object. She could see two figures seated, one behind the other and facing the same way, a little over an arm's length apart. The two figures were dressed in almost skin-tight metallic-looking suits that crinkled and creased with each movement, and reflected the light. The 'man' at the rear suddenly stood up and leaned forward on his hands, and appeared to be observing something between himself and the figure in front - possibly the brightly flickering light source. Mrs. Moreland thought that he must be a little over 5 feet in height, but she could not make out any facial characteristics as he was not facing in her direction, and the large silvered helmet covered from shoulder to shoulder. The rear figure then sank back to his former position - the front figure remained motionless throughout the period of observation.

The object then tilted slightly, the bands of jets stopped whirling and went out, then back on again without rotation. There was a loud 'whoosh' of air and the object rose vertically (the body still at a slight angle) and vanished into the cloud at tremendous speed. This movement was accompanied by a high-pitched whine - "The screech was almost unbearable", the movement "unbelievably fast". A moment or two later a wave of warm air reached Mrs. Moreland, and there was a strange hot pepper smell of ozone.

After several more moments, Mrs. Moreland "pulled herself together", and collected the cows, which had been little affected by the episode (one or two did get up), and drove them to the yard. At this point she heard the town clock striking a quarter to six, "so the visit could not have lasted longer than two or three minutes, though it seemed ages."

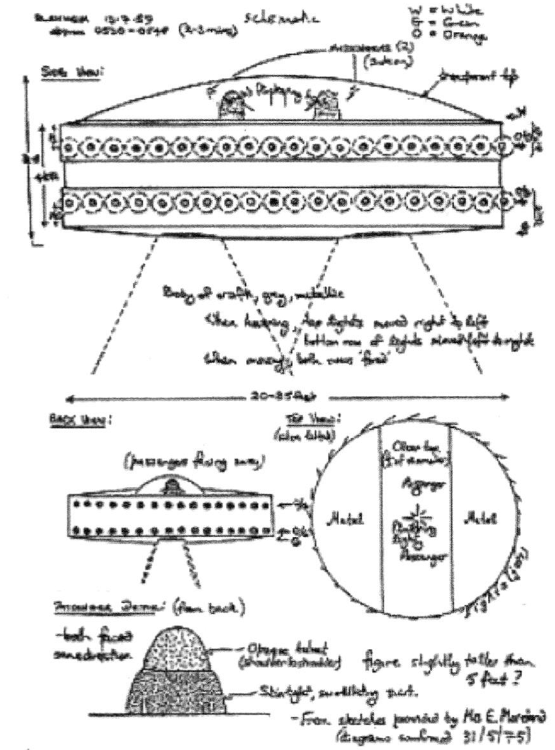

'Sketches provided courtesy of Bryan Dickeson and Mrs. Phyllis Dickeson, redrawn by Bryan from sketches provided by Mrs. Moreland, and confirmed by her on 31/5/1975.'

The milking was completed as usual, and the milk left at the gate, before Mrs. Moreland flew inside with her account. Her family was soon awake, and her husband, a member of the Royal New Zealand Air Force based at Woodbourne nearby, told her she should ring the police. Although a little reluctant to do this at first, (she thought no-one would believe her), she did telephone and said that they seemed to be interested. Her husband notified the Woodbourne authorities, who took the story seriously.

Mrs. Moreland was questioned by Air Force personnel who visited the area. Furthermore, they indicated that residual radiation had been detected where the object was seen. Brown pigmented areas developed on her face, and she referred these conditions to her doctor. The brown patches on her face persisted - the last blotch, over her right eyebrow, washed off some six years afterwards. An account of Mrs. Moreland's experiences made its way into the papers and created such interest that their farm was plagued by hordes of inquisitive sightseers. People wandered all over the property, uninvited, leaving gates open, upsetting the cows and generally creating such a nuisance that, should either of the Morelands see another object, they would prefer to just 'shut up' about it. Later on, it was noticed that the row of fruit trees beneath the position where the UFO had hovered, died and had to be pulled out. However, grass in the vicinity grew at a much faster rate, was several times taller and much greener than grass elsewhere.

Mrs. Moreland underwent a series of audiotone readings in Wellington, supervised by Air Force personnel, to determine the noise levels of the object. These placed hovering noise at 15,000 cycles, and climbing noise (a high-pitched scream) at 150,000 cycles. The 'Moreland UFO' remains a classic case in UFO lore. Enquiries still come in about it from all over the world. Mrs. Moreland spoke to Professors McDonald and Hynek during their respective visits to this country - both were very impressed by her account of the incident.

Locally, the Moreland UFO raised questions against the Adamski approach to UFOs (still the most fashionable influence to ufologists in NZ during 1959), which were not readily answerable.

("The Moreland material is particularly important and interesting. The case directly contributed to the collapse of the Adamski groups throughout New Zealand because what Mrs. Moreland saw was nothing like the Venusian or Saturnian spacecraft promoted by Adamski. The case was widely re-reported in overseas UFO newsletters." - B. Dickeson, 2006.)

www.ufocusnz.org.nz

There was also this from a spokesperson for the Lt. General's office: "The declassification of the UFO files is now a 'work in progress' in conjunction with Archives New Zealand. The files must be amended to meet new requirements of the Privacy Act."

Meaning it will be necessary to edit the files so that no personal information on the private citizens who made the sightings reports to begin with, for example, is made open to the public. Many people, given the stigma often attached to the subject, may not appreciate having the fact that they once reported a UFO announced to the world.

The process of removing personal information from the files was to take several months with the expected release date sometime in 2010. The Defence force agreed to notify UFOCUS NZ when the process was complete and to give them the opportunity to actually access the files as soon as they became available.

UFOCUS director Susanne Hansen deserves credit for having pushed the NZ government to release its UFO files.

Meanwhile, Hansen states on the group's website that the archives of UFOFOCUS NZ already contain "credible and detailed UFO sightings reports from New Zealand pilots, air traffic controllers and military personnel. In addition, the research network holds sightings reports from members of the public who experienced significant UFO sightings dating as far back as 1908. Some of these prominent cases were investigated by NZ Air Force personnel."

A particularly important case that happened in New Zealand is called "The Kaikoura Lights," which made headlines throughout the world in 1978/79. John Cody, currently a member of the NZ UFO group, is a former Chief Air Traffic Controller of Wellington International Airport. Cordy was a witness to the Kaikoura Lights and saw the event transpire on radar there at the control center.

"I hope the files will validate the reality of the sightings," Cody said, "and vindicate key witnesses who observed them and faced 'trial by media.'"

UFO sightings are on the increase in New Zealand, with patterns and characteristics that parallel reported sightings and flaps occurring worldwide, according to Hansen. The increase in sightings reported to UFOFOCUS NZ is a direct result of heightened public awareness and growing interest in the subject in New Zealand.

The mainstream non-UFO press in New Zealand also made note of the fact that the military there would be releasing UFO files. An online newspaper called "The Press" based in New Zealand said the release would include hundreds of pages on sightings from 1979 to 1984, and will include files on the aforementioned Kaikoura Lights.

In that incident, lights were seen in the sky over Kaikoura in December 1978 and were filmed by an Australian news crew. Aircraft tracked the lights, which were also seen on radar. A man who was working at Christchurch International airport at the time said he also saw United States Air Force planes with unusual call signs touring the area and believes the full story about the lights has not been disclosed.

"For the U.S. Air Force to come all that way," said the man, who prefers to remain anonymous, "and spend three days here, there must have been something going on."

In any case, the New Zealand Defence Force seems willing to cooperate.

"At the moment, we are working on making copies of these files, minus the personal information," a Defence Force spokeswoman said. "Once this work is completed, we are hoping to be able to release a copy of all the UFO files, including some ahead of their release time, within the year."

The publication "The Press" also made its own request to the Defence Force for access to the UFO files under the Official Information Act and was given the same answer as UFOCUS NZ, that the public files were available from Archives New Zealand. When "The Press" requested access at the Archives, they were told they were currently unavailable because they had been borrowed by the Defence Force. The article also stated that Suzanne Hansen of UFOCUS NZ was frustrated by the delays but understood the privacy reasons.

"We have been in discussion with the New Zealand Defence Force for many years," Hansen said. "It is frustrating from a research perspective because we would like to collate these sightings with international research."

Some sightings could have been of alien technology, she said.

"There are cases that are certainly not our technology. It has been scientifically proven that this is entirely possible."

If you're interested in visiting the Archives New Zealand, the website address is www.archives.govt.nz. For more information on current and historical activity on NZ activity we highly recommend: www.ufocusnz.org.nz

Members of the film crew who took motion picture footage over Christchurch are from left to right: Quentin Fogarty, David Crockett and Ngaire Crockett.

MORE ON THE KAIKOURA CASE

An Internet survey of New Zealand UFO cases quickly leads to the conclusion that the Kaikoura incident of 1978 is the most controversial in the region to date. Entries on the case abound and there is much interest and anticipation as to what the eventual release of files to the Archives New Zealand will have in the way of comment on the event.

UFO Casebook webmaster Billy Booth provides a capsule history of what happened:

"An extremely rare case of a plane flight for the express purpose of filming a UFO occurred on December 30, 1978, in New Zealand," Booth writes. "For some time, there had been a spate of UFO sightings in the area, and an investigation was called for."

With an Australian television film crew onboard, the plane soared over the Pacific Ocean, northeast of South Island, and a UFO was sighted. One of the television crew members stated that he saw "a row of five bright lights, which were pulsating and grew from the size of a pinpoint to that of a large balloon." The whole sequence was then repeated and the lights then appeared over the town of Kaikoura, between the aircraft and the ground.

Air traffic control at Wellington radioed the pilot that they had a return for an unknown object following the plane. The pilot made a 360 degree turn in an attempt to confront the UFO, which could still not be seen by crew members aboard the plane. Air traffic control again confirmed a target near the plane, which they said had now increased in size. The flight crew then made visual contact with the UFO, but the plane's navigational lights made it impossible to film the object. After the pilot turned the lights off, the crew members could see a large, bright light. The television crew managed to film the object for 30 seconds with a handheld camera.

The pilot turned the plane around and the UFO was no longer visible, although the airport was still seeing the radar target there. Finally, the plane landed at Christchurch with the UFO still visible on radar.

The same plane was sent aloft the very next night, and this time two UFOs were sighted. One of the news crew observed one of the objects through his camera, describing it as a spinning sphere with lateral lines around it. Near the end of the flight, two lights could be seen, and as the plane landed the airport ground control still had both objects on radar.

The film taken by the Australian news crew would be seen around the world, with the BBC even making it their lead story on an evening news show. Although the film was quickly debunked by skeptics, the Royal New Zealand Air Force had planes on full alert to confront the UFOs if it became necessary.

A U.K. newspaper called The Daily Telegraph, noted for businesslike and scientific observations, remarked, "The scientist who suggested that all on the aircraft were seeing Venus on a particularly bright night can be safely consigned to Bedlam (an insane asylum)."

Subsequently, the Royal New Zealand Air Force, the police and the Centre Observatory in Wellington conducted a joint investigation into the sightings. The results were stamped "Top Secret" and archived in the Wellington National Archives. The sightings have never been adequately explained.

* * * * *

Interestingly enough, when the story first broke the initial media coverage in the U.S. came about partly due to the efforts of the editor of this book. Tim Beckley working in association with the late publicist Harold Salkin informed the American Press of the matter by organizing a press conference in Manhattan where Naval optical data expert Dr Bruce Maccabee put forward a strong case that the object phographed was not part of a fishing fleet or any other optical illusion. Mcaccabee has had a long time interest in UFOs dating back to the days of Nicae and is highly educated in his profession having received a B.S. in physics at Worcester Polytechnic Institute in Worcester, Mass., and then at American University, Washington, DC, (M.S. and Ph. D. in physics). In 1972 he began his long career at what is now the Naval Surface Warfare Center Dahlgren Division, in Dahlgren, Virginia, finally retiring from government service in 2008. He has worked on optical data processing, generation of underwater sound with lasers and various aspects of the Strategic Defense Initiative (SDI) and Ballistic Missile Defense (BMD) using high power lasers.

ATMOSPHERE OR UFO?

by Dr Bruce Maccabee

NOTE: This is a greatly abridged version of a paper that was written as a response to the 1997 Review Panel of the Society for Scientific Exploration (sometimes called the "Sturrock Panel" after Dr. Peter Sturrock who convened the panel with support from other SSE members and Laurence Rockefeller.) It was published in the Journal of Scientific Exploration,Vol. 13, pg. 421 (1999) The complete text can be found on Dr. Maccabee's Research Web Site http://brumac.8k.com/index.html

HISTORY OF THE SIGHTINGS

In order to fully understand the significance of the radar event (#16 below) to be discussed it is necessary know the events leading up to that event. A history of the various sighting events represented by the numbers in Figure 4 will now be given. At point (1) the aircraft passed over Wellington at about midnight. It reached a non-geographical reporting point just east of Cape Campbell at about 10 minutes past midnight (point 2 on the event map) where the plane made a left turn to avoid any possible turbulence from wind blowing over the mountains of the South Island.

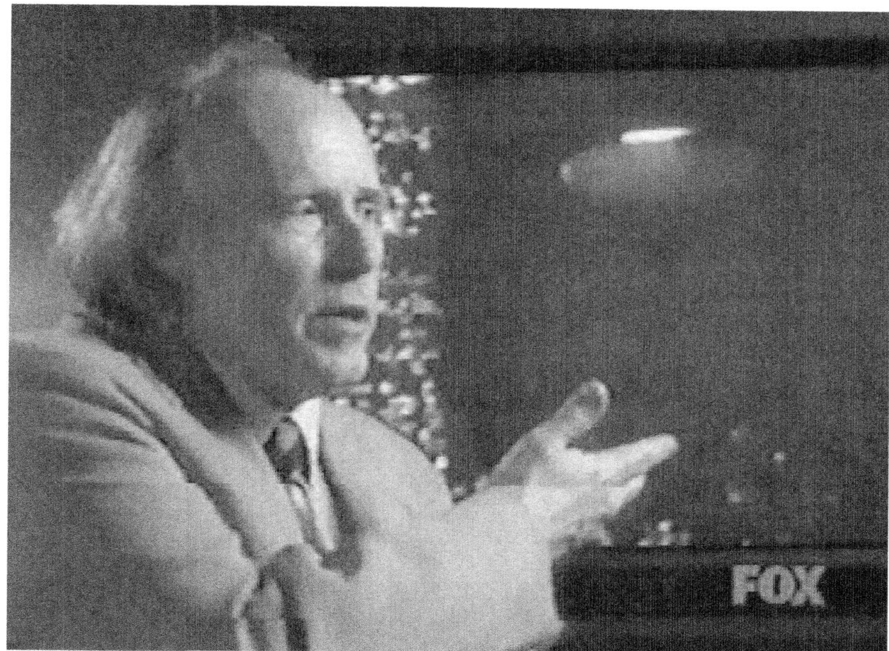

Optical expert Bruce Maccabee is frequently interviewed by the media. He proclaimed the Christchurch footage to be authentic.

This turbulence had been predicted by the flight weather service, but was not detected at all during the trip. The captain reported that the flying weather was excellent and he was able to use the automatic height lock, which would have automatically disengaged had there been turbulence that would change the altitude of the aircraft. The sky condition was "CAVU" (clear and visibility unlimited) with visibility estimated at over 30 miles. (Note: the definition of visibility is based on contrast reduction between a distant dark object and a light sky. Thus a black object could barely be seen against a bright sky at 30 miles. However, a light could be seen in the night sky for a hundred miles or more, depending upon its intrinsic intensity.) The air crew could see the lights along the coast of the South Island, extending southward to Christchurch about 150 miles away.

At about 0005 (12:05 A.M., local time), the captain and copilot first noticed oddly behaving lights ahead of them near the Kaikoura Coast. They had flown this route many times before and were thoroughly familiar with the lights along the coast so they quickly realized that these were not ordinary coastal lights. These lights would appear, project a beam downward toward the sea, and then disappear, only to reappear at some other location. Sometimes there was only one, sometimes none and sometimes several. After several minutes of watching and failing to identify the lights the pilot and copilot began to discuss what they were seeing. They were puzzled over their inability to identify these unusual lights and their odd pattern of activity, which made the captain think of a search operation. (Similar activity of unidentified lights nearer to Cape Campbell had been seen by ground witnesses during a series of UFO events that had occurred about ten days earlier. See Startup and Illingworth, 1980)

At about 0012 they decided to contact Wellington Air traffic Control Center radar to find out if there were any aircraft near Kaikoura. At this time, point (3) on the map, the plane was traveling at 215 nm/hr indicated air speed and had reached its 14,000 ft cruising altitude. There was a light wind from the west.

The average ground speed was about 180 nm/hr or about 3 nm/minute. Since the copilot was in control of the aircraft on this particular journey, the captain did the communicating with WATCC. "Do you have any targets showing on the Kaikoura Peninsula range?" he asked. The controller at WATCC had been busy with another aircraft landing, but had noticed targets appearing and disappearing in that direction for half an hour or more. He knew it was not uncommon to find spurious radar targets near the coast of the South Island. These would be ground clutter effects of mild atmospheric refraction so he had paid little attention to them. About 20 seconds after the plane called he responded, "There are targets in your one o'clock position at, uh, 13 miles, appearing and disappearing.

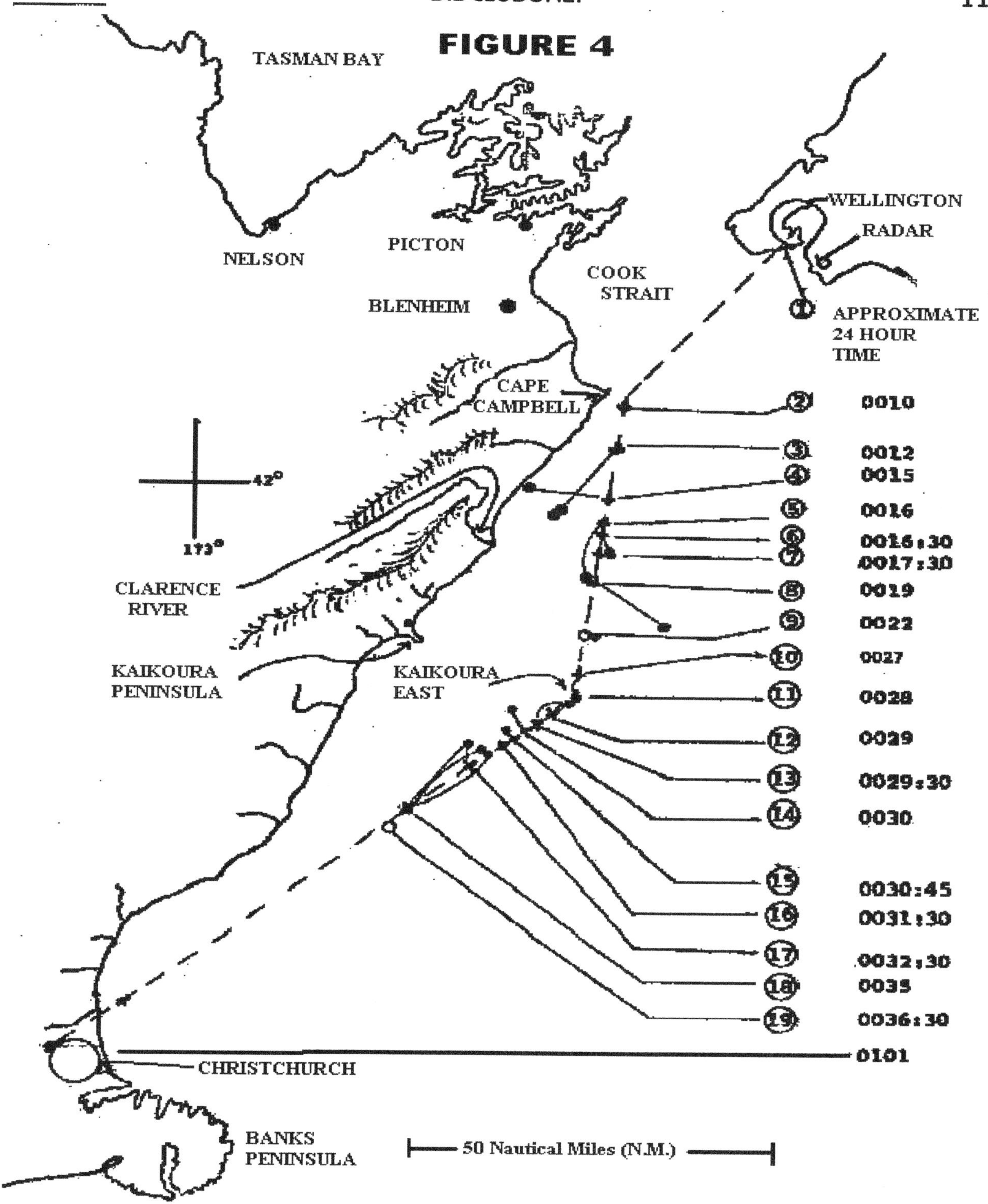

At the present moment they're not showing but were about 1 minute ago." (Note: directions with respect to the airplane are given as "clock time" with 12:00 - twelve o'clock - being directly ahead of the aircraft, 6:00 being directly behind, 9:00 to the left and 3:00 to the right. The "1:00 position" is 30(+/-)15 degrees to the right.) The pilot responded, "If you've got a chance would you keep an eye on them?" "Certainly," was the reply. Shortly after that the other aircraft landed and from then on the Argosy was the only airplane in the sky south of Wellington.

At about 0015 (point 4) WATCC reported a target at the 3:00 position on the coastline. According to captain (7), at about that time the TV crew, which had been below deck in the cargo hold of the aircraft filming a short discussion of the previous sightings, was coming up onto the flight deck. The air crew pointed out to the TV crew the unusual lights and the ordinary lights visible through the windshield. The crew did not see the target at 3:00.

The TV crew had to adapt to the difficult conditions of working on the cramped and very noisy flight deck. The cameraman had to hold his large Bolex 16 mm electric movie camera with its 100 mm zoom lens and large film magazine on his shoulder while he sat in a small chair between the pilot (captain) on his left and copilot on his right. From this position he could easily film ahead of the aircraft but it was difficult for him to film far to the right or left and, of course, he could not film anything behind the aircraft. He was given earphones so he could hear the communications between the air crew and WATCC. Occasionally he would yell over the noise of the airplane to the reporter, who was standing just behind the copilot, to tell the reporter what the air crew was hearing from the WATCC. The sound recordist was crouched behind the cameraman with her tape recorder on the floor and her earphones. She was not able to see anything. She could, of course, hear the reporter as he recorded his impressions of what he saw through the right side window or through the front windows of the flight deck. She heard some things that were more than just a bit frightening.

At approximately 0016, the first radar-visual sighting occurred. WATCC reported "Target briefly appeared 12:00 to you at 10 miles," to which the captain responded, "Thank you." (The previous target at 3:00 had disappeared.) According to the captain (7), he looked ahead of the Argosy and saw a light where there should have been none (they were looking generally toward open ocean; Antarctica, the closest land in the sighting direction, was about 1,000 miles away; there were no other aircraft in the area). He described it as follows: "It was white and not very brilliant and it did not change color or flicker. To me it looked like the taillight of an aircraft. I'm not sure how long we saw this for. Probably not very long. I did not get a chance to judge its height relative to the aircraft." This target was not detected during the next sweep of the scope. (Note: each sweep required 12 seconds corresponding to 5 revolutions per minute.)

About 20 seconds later, at about 0016:30, WATCC reported a "...strong target showing at 11:00 at 3 miles." The captain responded "Thank you, no contact yet." Four radar rotations (48 seconds) later (at point 7) WATCC reported a target "just left of 9:00 at 2 miles." The captain looked out his left window but saw nothing in that direction except stars. Eighty-five seconds later, at about 0019, WATCC reported at target at 10:00 at 12 miles. Again there was no visual sighting. The captain has written (7) that he got the impression from this series of targets that some object that was initially ahead of his plane had traveled past the left side. He decided to make an orbit (360 degree turn) to find out if they could see anything at their left side or behind.

At about 0020:30 the captain asked for permission to make a left hand orbit. WATCC responded that it was OK to do that and reported "there is another target that just appeared on your left side about 1 mile....briefly and then disappearing again." Another single sweep target. The captain responded, "We haven't got him in sight as yet, but we do pick up the lights around Kaikoura." In other words, the air crew was still seeing anomalous lights near the coast.

At this time the plane was about 66 miles from the radar station. At this distance the 2.1 degree horizontal beamwidth (at half intensity points) would have been about 2 miles wide (at the half power points on the radiation pattern). The radar screen displays a short arc when receiving reflected radiation from an object, such as an airplane, that is much, much smaller than the distance to the object (a "point" target). The length of the arc corresponds roughly to the angular beamwidth. Hence in this case the lengths of the arcs made by the aircraft and the unknown were each equivalent to about 2 miles. If the controller could actually see a 1 mile spacing between the arcs, then the centers of the arcs, representing the positions of the actual targets (plane and unknown) were about 2 + 1 = 3 miles apart.

As the plane turned left to go around in a circle, which would take about 2 minutes to complete (point 9), WATCC reported "The target I mentioned a moment ago is still just about 5:00 to you, stationary."

During the turn the air crew and passengers could, of course, see the lights of Wellington and the lights all the way along the coast from the vicinity of Kaikoura to Christhurch and they could see the anomalous lights near Kaikoura, but they saw nothing that seemed to be associated with the radar targets that were near the aircraft.

During this period of time the WATCC controller noticed targets continuing to appear, remain for one or two sweeps of the radar, and then disappear close to the Kaikoura Coast. However, he did not report these to the airplane. He reported only the targets which were appearing near the airplane, now about 25 miles off the coast. The TV reporter, who was able to watch the skies continually, has stated (8) that he continually saw anomalous lights "over Kaikoura," that is, they appeared to be higher than the lights along the coastline at the town of Kaikoura.

By 0027 (point 10) the plane was headed back southward along its original track. WATCC reported "Target is at 12:00 at 3 miles." The captain responded immediately, "Thank you. We pick it up. It's got a flashing light." The captain reported seeing "a couple of very bright blue-white lights, flashing regularly at a rapid rate. They looked like the strobe lights of a Boeing 737..."(Startup and Illingworth, 1980)). At this time he was again looking toward the open ocean.

From the time he got seated on the flight deck the cameraman was having difficulty filming. The lights of interest were mostly to the right of the aircraft and, because of the size of his camera, he was not able to film them without sticking his camera lens in front of the copilot who was in command of the aircraft. When a light would appear near Kaikoura he would turn the camera toward it and try to see it through his big lens. Generally by the time he had the camera pointed in the correct direction the light would go out. He was also reluctant to film because the lights were all so dim he could hardly see them through the lens and he didn't believe that he would get any images. Of course, he was not accustomed to filming under these difficult conditions.

Nevertheless, the cameraman did get some film images unidentified lights. He also filmed known lights. He filmed the takeoff from Wellington, thereby providing reference footage. The next image on the film, taken at an unrecorded time after the takeoff from Wellington, is the image of a blue-white light against a black background. In order to document the fact that he was seated in the aircraft at the time of this filming he turned the camera quickly to the left and filmed some of the dim red lights of the meters on the instrument panel. Unfortunately the cameraman did not recall, during the interview many weeks later, exactly when that blue-white light was filmed, nor did he recall exactly where the camera was pointed at the time, although it was clearly somewhat to the right of straight ahead. The initial image of the light is followed by two others but there are no reference points for these lights. They could have been to the right or straight ahead or to the left. The durations of the three appearances of a blue-white light are 5, 1.3 and 1.9 seconds, which could be interpreted as slow pulsing on and off. After this last blue-white image the film shows about 5 seconds of very dim images that seem to be distant shoreline of Kaikoura with some brighter lights above the shoreline.

Unfortunately these images are so dim as to make analysis almost impossible.

Although it is impossible to prove, it may be that the cameraman filmed the flashing light at 0027. Unfortunately the camera was not synchronized with either the WATCC tape recorder or the tape recorder on the plane so the times of the film images must be inferred by matching the verbal descriptions with the film images. The cameraman did not get film of the steady light that appeared ahead of the aircraft at 0016.

Regardless of whether these blue-white images were made by the flashing light at 0027 or by some other appearance of a blue-white light, the fact is, considering where the plane was at the time, that this film was "impossible" to obtain from the conventional science point of view because there was nothing near the airplane that could have produced these bright pulses of light. The only lights on the flight deck at this time were dim red meter lights because the captain had turned off all the lights except those that were absolutely necessary for monitoring the performance of the aircraft. There were no internal blue-white lights to be reflected from the windshield glass, nor were there any blue-white lights on the exterior of the aircraft. The only other possible light sources, stars, planets and coastal lights were too dim and too far away to have made images as bright as these three flashes on the film. These images remain unexplained.

There is a similar problem with determining exactly when the reporter's audio tape statements were made since his recorder was not synchronized with the WATCC tape. Therefore the timing of the reporter's statements must be inferred from the sequence of statements on the tape and from the content. Recorded statements to this point mentioned lights seen in the direction of the Kaikoura Coast, as well as, of course, the normal lights along the coast. But then the reporter recorded the following statement: "Now we have a couple right in front of us, very, very bright. That was more of an orange-reddy light. It flashed on and then off again...... We have a firm convert here at the moment." Apparently he underwent a "battlefield conversion" from being a UFO skeptic to believer.

The probability is high, although one cannot absolutely certain, that the air crew, the reporter and cameraman all saw and recorded on tape and film the appearance of the light at 3 miles in front of the aircraft. If true, then this might have been a radar/visual/photographic sighting. (A radar/visual/photographic sighting did occur about an hour later as the airplane flew northward from Christchurch.)

As impressive as this event was, the radar/visual event of most interest here was still to come. At about 0028 (point 11) the Argosy aircraft made a 30 degree right turn to head directly into Christchurch. WATCC reported that all the radar targets were now 12 to 15 miles behind them.

Then at about 0029 (point 12 on the map) WATCC reported a target 1 mile behind the plane. About 50 seconds later (after 4 sweeps of the radar beam) he reported a target about 4 miles behind the airplane. Then that target disappeared and about 30 seconds later he reported a target at 3:00 at 4 miles. Two sweeps of the radar beam later he saw something really surprising. He reported, "There's a strong target right in formation with you. Could be right or left. Your target has doubled in size."

The extraordinary condition of a "double size target" (DST) persisted for at least 36 seconds. This duration is inferred from the time duration between the controller's statement to the airplane, made only seconds after he first saw the DST, and his statement that the airplane target had reduced to normal size. This time duration was about 51 seconds (four radar detections over a period 36 seconds followed by a fifth revolution with no detection plus 3 seconds) according to the WATCC tape recording of the events. The radar aspects of this DST event will be discussed more fully below.

The pilot and copilot and the cameraman were able to hear the communications from the WATCC. The reporter and sound recordist could not hear the WATCC communications, but the cameraman would occasionally yell (loudly because of the extreme engine noise) to the reporter what he heard from WATCC. The cameraman told the reporter about the target flying in formation and the reporter started looking through the right side window for the target. The copilot was also looking and after some seconds he spotted a light which he described as follows: "It was like the fixed navigation lights on a small airplane when one passes you at night. It was much smaller than the really big ones we had seen over Kaikoura. At irregular intervals it appeared to flash, but it didn't flash on and off; it brightened or perhaps twinkled around the edges. When it did this I could see color, a slight tinge of green or perhaps red. It's very difficult describing a small light you see at night."

The captain had been looking throughout his field of view directly ahead, to the left, upward and downward to see if there could be any source of light near the aircraft. He saw nothing except normal coastal lights and, far off on the horizon to the left (east), lights from the Japanese squid fishing fleet which uses extremely bright lights to lure squid to the surface to be netted. Neither the captain nor copilot saw any running lights on ships near them or near the coast of the South Island, which implies that there were no ships on the ocean in their vicinity.

When the copilot reported seeing a light at the right the captain turned off the navigation lights, one of which is a steady green light on the right wing, so that the reporter wouldn't confuse that with any other light. There were lights along the coast but the city lights of Kaikoura were no longer visible, hidden behind mountains that run along the Kaikoura Peninsula. Ireland (1979) suggested that the witnesses saw a beacon at the eastern end of the Kaikoura Peninsula. This beacon is visible to ships at a range of 14 miles from the coast. It flashes white twice every 15 seconds (on for 2 seconds, off for 1 second, on for 2 seconds off for 10 seconds). The plane was about 20 miles from the beacon and at an elevation angle of about 7 degrees, which placed it above the axis of the main radiation lobe from the beacon. The combination of the distance and off-axis angle means that it would have been barely visible, if at all. Moreover, the light seen by the copilot and others appeared to be at about "level" with the location of the navigation light at the end of the wing which, in turn was about level with the cockpit, or perhaps a bit above since the plane was carrying a heavy load. Hence the light was at an elevation comparable to that of the aircraft and certainly above ground level. Many months later, at my request, the air crew attempted to see the Kaikoura beacon while flying along the same standard flight path from Kaikoura East into Christchurch. Knowing where to look for the beacon they stared intently. They reported seeing only couple of flashes during the several trips they made past the lighthouse. The copilot has stated very explicitly that the unusual light he saw was not the lighthouse.

During this time the reporter also saw the light and recorded his impression: "I'm looking over towards the right of the aircraft and we have an object confirmed by Wellington radar. It's been following us for quite a while. It's about 4 miles away and it looks like a very faint star, but then it emits a bright white and green light." Unfortunately the light was too far to the right for the cameraman to be able to film it (he would have had to sit in the copilot's seat to do that). The captain was able to briefly see this light which the copilot had spotted. This event was a radar-visual sighting with several witnesses to the light.

About 82 seconds after Wellington reported that the DST had reduced to normal size, when the plane was approximately at point 17, the captain told WATCC, "Got a target at 3:00 just behind us," to which WATCC responded immediately, "Roger, and going around to 4:00 at 4 miles." This would appear to be a radar confirmation of the light that the crew saw at the right side.

Fifty seconds after reporting the target that was "going around to 4:00 at 4 miles" the WATCC operator was in communication with the Christchurch Air Traffic Control Center. He told the air traffic controller that there was a target at 5:00 at about 10 miles. He said that the target was going off and on but "...not moving, not too much speed..." and then seconds later, "It is moving in an easterly direction now." The Christchurch radar did not show a target at that location. This could have been because the Christchurch radar was not as sensitive as the Wellington radar, because the radar cross-section (reflectivity) in the direction of Christchurch was low (cross-section can change radically with orientation of an object) or because the target may have been below the Christchurch radar beam, which has a lower angular elevation limit of about 4 degrees.

At about 0035, when the plane was about at point 18, WATCC contacted the plane and asked, "The target you mentioned, the last one we mentioned, make it 5:00 at 4 miles previously, did you see anything?" The captain responded, "We saw that one. It came up at 4:00, I think, around 4 miles away, " to which WATCC responded, "Roger, that target is still stationary. It's now 6:00 to you at about 15 miles and it's been joined by two other targets." The reporter heard this information from the cameraman and recorded the following message: "That other target that has been following us has been joined by two other targets so at this stage we have three unidentified flying objects just off our right wing and one of them has been following us now for probably about 10 minutes." Unfortunately, as already mentioned, the reporter could not hear the communications with WATCC so he did not always get the correct information. These targets were behind the plane and one of them had been "following" the plane for 7 - 8 minutes.

Then the WATCC reported that the three targets had been replaced by a single target. The captain, wondering about all this activity at his rear, requested a second two minute orbit. This was carried out at about 0036:30 (point 19). Nothing was seen and the single target disappeared. From then on the plane went straight into Christchurch. The Christchurch controller did report to the aircraft that his radar showed a target over land, west of the aircraft, that seemed to pace the aircraft but turned westward and traveled inland as the aircraft landed. The copilot looked to the right and saw a small light moving rapidly along with the aircraft. However, copilot duties during the landing itself prevented him from watching it continually and he lost sight of it just before the aircraft landed.

* * * * *

LARGE ORANGE BALLS OVER TAUPO

A website called UFOINFO provides a wealth of UFO reports from New Zealand. The organization provides a sightings report form for witnesses to fill out, with the reports then helpfully posted on the Internet.

One report, dated April 24, 2010, comes from Taupo, Waikato.
Time: 10:30 P.M.
Number of witnesses: 3
Number of objects: 5

Shape of objects: Large orange ball leading light with dark saucer-shape attached behind, and large orange ball with dimly lit elliptical shape above.

Weather Conditions: High clouds, moonlit balmy night. Sightings were below the clouds and flying cross-wind.

Description: First appeared as large orange light attached to large saucer-shaped body, followed within a minute by two more similar balls. Two minutes or so later two more followed with the last looking a little more like a dimly-lit hot air balloon above a bright orange light-ball, but flying cross-wind to the north, northeast. The wind was blowing from the west at six mph. There was no sound except for neighborhood dogs howling. We thought we were getting a good film clip, but the camera (or operator) malfunctioned.

Additional information: I realize I can't explain my sighting very clearly, but I feel I must add that the body of the first craft was frighteningly large, and all the sightings I would estimate to be within 2000 feet above us.

A NEW YEAR'S VISITATION

Another New Zealand case happened on January 2, 2009 in McLaren Falls, Bay of Plenty, Tauranga.

Time: 2:23 A.M.
Number of witnesses: 4
Number of objects: 7
Shape of objects: Yellow balls

Description: Hi. My name is Doug. While celebrating the New Year at McLaren Falls Campground on the 2nd of January, 2009, at 2:23 A.M., four of our group were just gazing at the stars, looking toward 70 degrees east in line with the Milky Way, six yellow balls arose from the horizon in formation. They darted towards the north, then forming in a diamond gem-type shape then descended down in the horizon. They only traveled in a northeasterly direction. After they descended, another yellow ball arose same as the first and with the same motions as the first. It began to descend, only it started to flash. So we, being cheeky, flashed our torches back. It seemed to stop in midair for a while and then carry on its way. I have some videos taken on my cell and a photo which is attached. Would love to get some info back.

A BEWILDERED SKEPTIC

On January 23, 2009, in Ongley Park, Palmerston North, a skeptic had a bewildering UFO experience.

Time: 5 A.M.
Number of witnesses: 2
Number of objects: 2
Shape of objects: Rectangle
Weather Conditions: Clear, first quarter moon.

Description: First, I would like everyone to know I am not claiming to have seen aliens, merely exactly what UFO stands for, objects I cannot identify. It was a hot night, a friend and I decided to go for a walk as we couldn't sleep. As we walked across Ongley Park, looking into the sky, we both noticed a rectangle shape much larger than any star in the sky, with the source of white light being on the two longer sides, sitting stationary in the sky. After about 30 seconds, it started to move away, darting side to side to the east and getting further away very fast, considering the distance required to travel to have that affect on the eye. After approximately one minute the object faded out of eyesight in the east of the sky. To the best of my knowledge, it was too high and sporadic for a plane, too fast and again sporadic for a satellite and heading away from the earth, so clearly not a typical meteor. We caught the second object in the later phases of exactly what I just described from the northwest to disappear in the north. I am by no reach of the imagination a conspiracy theorist. In fact, I'm rather the opposite, but I cannot explain this. If someone can, please do so, as I have looked at every site I can about balloons, satellites and the International Space Station.

A REAL MYSTERY

On September 26, 2009, in Timaru, South Canterbury, the following event occurred.

Time: 8:15 P.M.
Number of witnesses: 2
Number of objects: About 10 visible
Shape of objects: Bright orange, glowing like a star.

Description: About 10 bright orange glowing objects like a star shape were moving in the night sky. Three or four across the top and four or five fanning out below on both sides. Two then veered off to the left. This was witnesses by two people for about five minutes, then the objects disappeared into the cloud. We looked many times over the next hour but didn't see them again. What did we see? A real mystery. I rang the Timaru police to report what we'd witnessed.

PULSATING SHAPE-SHIFTERS

Location: Mairangi Bay, Auckland, New Zealand.
Date: February 3, 2006
Time: 8:30 A.M. to 8:55 A.M.
Approach Direction: North, heading east.
Departure Direction: Disappeared straight upwards.
Witness Direction: Northeast.

Description: At 8:30 this A.M., my mother was hanging out the washing when she called me outside to look at some objects in the sky. At first, I suggested that they were a cluster of weather balloons and counted ten altogether. As we continued to watch, some of them started to change colors from the original shining bright silver to reddish orange to luminous violet-blue. They started to make formations. Almost pulsating and changing shapes from round to oval, and some moved into clusters. The clouds were wispy and the objects were moving in the same northerly direction as the clouds but slightly faster. Then they changed direction and moved slowly east and stopped directly above our house. Some of them formed the Southern Cross constellation and the pointers turned red.

I phoned the Auckland Observatory and asked if anyone could see them from that location in Royal Oak. Unfortunately, they could not see them. Eventually, after 25 minutes, they disappeared directly upwards. Perfectly round and silver in colour again.

Color/Shape: Changing shape from round to oval and back to round again. Sometimes pulsating and making formations. Colour shining silver initially then a couple went to red-orange and violet-blue. Then back to silver again.

Height and speed: Difficult to assess.

TV/Radio/Press: I phoned the Observatory while watching them at about 8:40 A.M. Then I phoned TVNZ at approximately 1:45 P.M. and spoke to the newsroom to see if there had been any other reported sightings. None had been reported, and unfortunately we did not have any footage as proof.

Thirty years ago today, strange lights were filmed in the night skies over the Kaikoura coast. Theories ranged from squid boat lights to sightings of Mercury and Venus. Former television producer Leonard Lee recalls his involvement in the Kaikoura UFO mystery.

The lights were captured on film.

On the morning of December 31, 1978, I received an early-morning call from Neil Miller my chief-of-staff in the newsroom at Channel 0 (now Channel Ten) in Melbourne.

He was babbling, telling me one of our reporters and a freelance film crew had filmed UFOs from a freight plane in the skies over Kaikoura the previous night.

My friend - and fellow Kiwi - Quentin Fogarty was the reporter. I had sent him to recap another apparent encounter by two pilots 10 days earlier.

The objects were also seen by the two pilots, Bill Startup and Bob Guard, Quentin's cameraman, David Crocket, and his wife, Ngaire, the sound recordist.

They were also confirmed on ground radar in Wellington and Christchurch, and further confirmed by the plane's radar.

We also had 16mm film footage of the lights. As news of the sightings spread through the media, Quentin was holed up in a Christchurch motel with his family, and I knew we had to get him back to Melbourne with the footage as quickly as possible.

I was nervous the film might be confiscated before we could get our hands on it.

It was New Year's Eve and almost all the airline seats had been sold out.

Luckily, I managed to get him a first-class ticket on an Air New Zealand flight into Melbourne that night.

I was very nervous by then, concerned the film might be blank or unusable.

Later, I stood with Quentin in a darkened editing room as the film editor began spooling the footage through his machine.

And there they were: lights dancing and changing shape, lots of them - unidentified flying lights.

None of us slept that night as we worked into New Year's Day trying to pull together for international release a news story we knew nothing about.

Unlike other news stories we had absolutely no reference points for this, most of us having previously believed that UFO sightings were akin to spotting hobgoblins down the back of the garden.

Telephone calls were coming from all over the world.

The BBC asked us to feed them the story, and at one point I spoke with Walter Cronkite from the American CBS News, which was prepared to pay US$5000 for the film.

It was after the screening of a 30-minute documentary on the sightings that the sceptics - numerous scientists among them - started screaming at us from around the globe.

We had, they said, filmed Venus, Mars, Jupiter, squid boat lights, mating mutton birds, everything in fact except UFOs, whatever they were.

The media also seemed to turn on us and began slyly insinuating we had somehow hoaxed the whole thing.

It was then I decided the footage needed to be examined scientifically, so a judgment could be made as to what the objects were - or weren't.

I travelled to the United States where I gave the film to Bruce Maccabee, an optical physicist who specialised in laser technology for the US Navy.

I also persuaded Channel 0 to spend some of the proceeds of the story on flying Dr Maccabee to New Zealand to interview witnesses, check radar equipment and review other material concerning the sightings.

He also came to Melbourne to interview Quentin.

Dr Maccabee returned to the US, releasing his preliminary findings a couple of months later.

He disputed all the various theories put up by the so-called experts, although he later wryly agreed the lights could have come from squid boats, but only if they were "flying squid boats".

He believed the lights were generated by an unknown source, and as such fulfilled the UFO criteria: "unidentifiable, flying solid objects".

Dr Maccabee's interim findings notwithstanding, the "Kaikoura UFO" story has never been fully told.

Further scientific research on the sightings was shut down in April 1979.

For 30 years now the Kaikoura story has lain mainly dormant, only resurrected now and then in segments of sensationalised documentaries produced to cater for the so-called UFO crazies.

I still hold ambitions that one day the complete story will be told.

This was reinforced during a visit to Renwick last week, where producer Paul Davidson has the decommissioned old Argosy Safe Air freighter - the Merchant Enterprise - on show on his front lawn next to the main highway to Nelson.

I spent a lot of time looking out at that old, historic aircraft, reliving the extraordinary events of December 30, 1979.

During my time there I had the pleasure of meeting Captain Bill Startup for the first time and reading his book The Kaikoura UFOs.

It wasn't until I read his book that I realised how courageous the witnesses had been on that night. Not only did they fly south from Wellington to Christchurch, they then flew back through the UFOs to Blenheim.

I would have jumped off in Christchurch and bloody stayed there.

For 30 years I have lived almost every day with this story. The trouble is that no story can ever match.

NZherald.co.nz

* * * * *

This has been but a brief, partial sampling of UFO reports from New Zealand in recent years. As Suzanne Hansen of UFOCUS NZ stated earlier in this chapter, sightings are increasing there as awareness of the phenomenon grows.

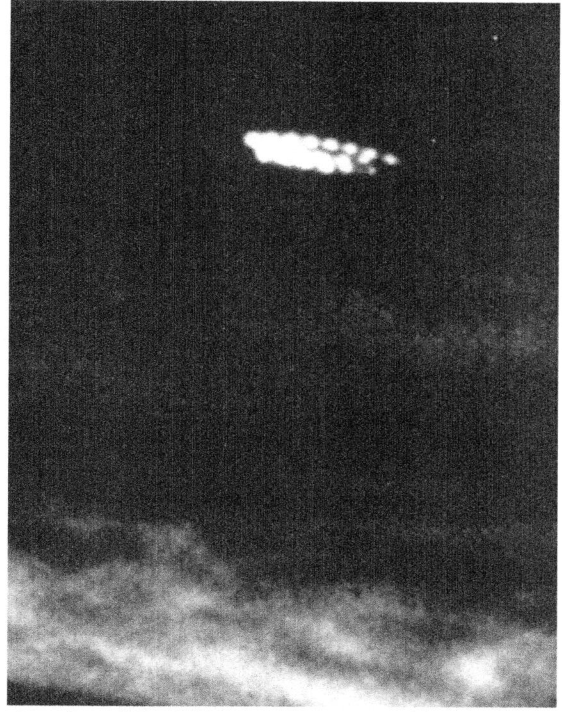

October 27, 1979 - Motonau, New Zealand

March 28, 1992 - Brunchillii, Australia

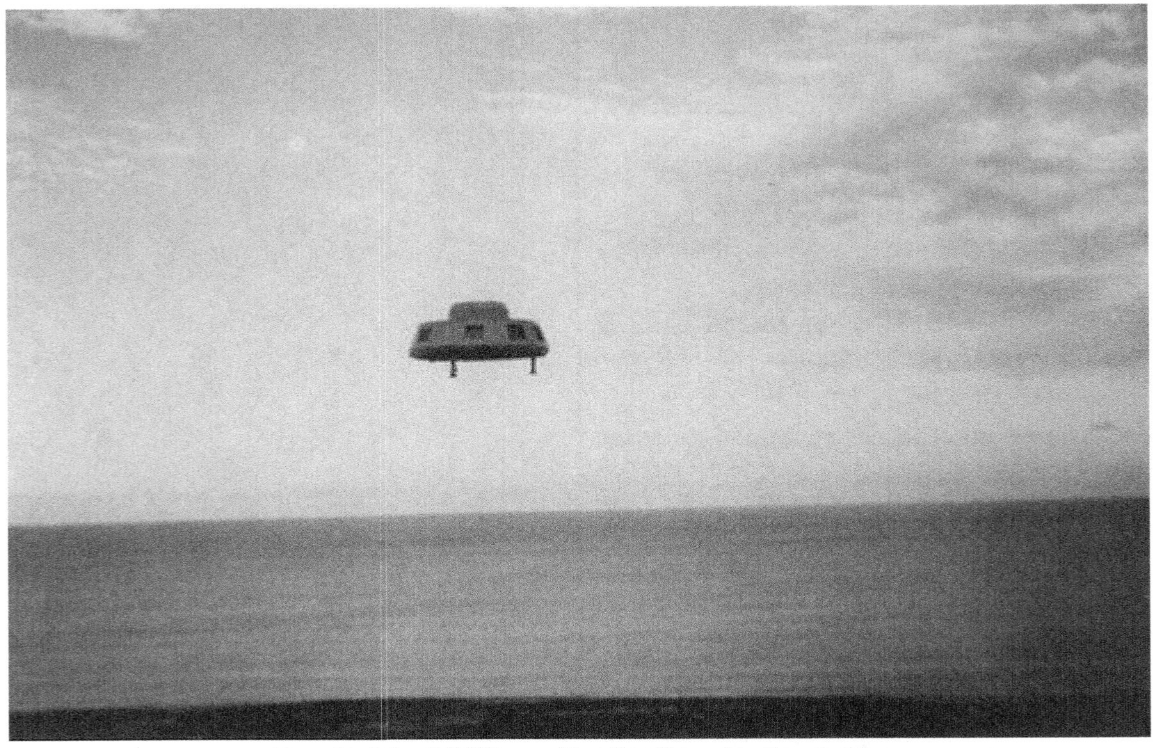

March 10, 1993 - Maslin Beach, Australia

SEARCHING FOR UFO DISCLOSURE IN AUSTRALIA

Without a doubt, Australia has a rich history of UFO sightings, landings and even abductions. And starting back in the early 1950s they have had a legacy of organizations devoted to the study of the phenomenon. There have been pilot reports, sightings by the police, and all sorts of credible citizens have seen these mysterious craft as well. So what is the obstruction – why can't these organizations break through the code of silence? It's not that they aren't trying.

A civilian disclosure advocacy group in Australia called The Disclosure Australia Project, between June 2003 and November 2006, searched for, located and examined Australian government files relating to the UFO phenomenon.

According to an online posting by the group, the search was as thorough as possible but "there is no doubt it is incomplete.

"To begin with," the report continues, "the electronic Record Search system of the National Archives of Australia (NAA) indexes only about 10 percent of their collection. Secondly, the search was undertaken using both the Archives Act and the Freedom of Information Act, where the expense of the latter precluded broad spectrum requests such as 'for all material held on UFOs.' In addition, unlike the detailed and indexed UFO fact sheet available for the U.K. Government Archives, which guides researchers through file numbers, searching the NAA's Record Search is a very hit and miss affair. Quite often, a slight adjustment of words or even letters would reveal yet other files."

Among the many frustrations the Disclosure Australia Project endured was confusion over what words to search for. Were they to restrict their search to just UFOs? Searches for the term UFOs then led to other keyword searches for terms like "flying saucers" or "unusual aerial sightings." There was also confusion as to which laws applied at a given time, the Archives Act or the Freedom of Information Act. In addition, if one of the files the group requested was shown as "not yet examined," it meant that the file had to go from the archives back to whatever authority originated the file in order to be cleared and released. Getting such a clearance could take up to a year.

"Despite the issues related above," the group's posting says, "the staff of the NAA could not have been more helpful in their efforts to assist us. Thanks must also go to the Royal Australian Air Force's FOI staff for their professional approach to what, to them, must have seemed a trivial topic of inquiry. In the end, it is believed that a representative collection of files has been uncovered which allows researchers to gain some insight into how the Australian government viewed the UFO phenomenon."

Without a doubt one of the strangest UFOs ever photographed over Australia this picture shows an unknown object along the coastline. The photo was taken within an hour of a young pilot's disappearance.

The Project has found records of 146 files which are, or were, in whole or part, about UFOs or UFO organizations. The files originated with various departments, including the former Department of Civil Aviation and the current Department of Transport and Regional Services, as well as the Australian Security Intelligence Organization. Of course, the Australian Department of Defence, and the Army, Navy and Air Force also keep files on UFOs, some of which were found by the Project's search efforts.

After examining over 10,000 documents, the questions that still arise for the Project involve such issues as, "What did these government departments do with the material they gathered, and why? Did any government agency conduct scientific research into the subject? Were there any interesting unknowns to be found in government files?"

It appears that the government of Australia is playing the familiar sort of "cat and mouse" game with its inquiring citizens and is a long way from the openness on the UFO mystery that the Disclosure Australia Project is so earnestly seeking. But perhaps continued diligence in searching the archives there will produce the kind of surprising "unknowns" that keep everybody in the game to begin with.

INSIDE THE AUSTRALIAN TERRITORY OF PAUPUA NEW GUINEA -- THE BEST CLOSE ENCOUNTER CASE OF ALL TIME

According to renowned UFO investigator, Dr. J. Allen Hynek, one of the most well-documented "close encounters of the third kind" occurred in the Anglican mission village at Boianai, Papua, New Guinea, which was, at the time of the incident, still a territory of Australia. The Australian Anglican Church was very involved in missionary work, and ardent in sending its heralds to the island nation.

One of these was the Father William Booth Gill. Gill was highly thought of by his co-hearts, and all those who knew him. As far as the occurrence of extraordinary events was concerned, Gill was skeptical, to say the least, especially being a devoted Church worker.

The first hint of the events to come, began on April 5, 1959, when Gill saw a light on the uninhabited Mount Pudi. This light, Gill stated, moved faster than anything he had ever seen.

A month or so later, his assistant, Stephen Moi, saw an "inverted saucer-shaped object" in the sky above the mission. Gill dismissed these sightings as some sort of electrical or atmospheric phenomena.

Little did he know, that these events, whatever they were, had drawn their attention to the sky above them, and soon William Gill would have one of the most celebrated UFO sightings to ever be documented, which was validated by a whole group of additional witnesses.

This extraordinary event would take place at 6:45 P.M., June 26, 1959. Father Gill saw what he described as a bright white light to the Northwest. Word of the sight spread quickly, and within a few moments, Gill was joined by no less than thirty-eight additional witnesses, including Steven Moi, Ananias Rarata, and Mrs Nessle Moi. According to sworn statements, these thirty-plus individuals watched a four-legged, disc-shaped object approximately the size of 5 full moons lined up end to end. This unbelievable craft was hovering over the mission!

To their utter surprise, they saw four human-like figures that seemed to be performing a kind of task. Now and then one of the figures would disappear, only to reappear in a moment or two.

A blue light would shine up from the craft at what seemed to be regular intervals. The witness watched the craft and its activities for a full forty-five minutes, until the shining ship rose into the sky, and disappeared at 7:30 P.M. Glued to the sky, the witnesses would see several smaller objects appear at 8:30, and twenty minutes later, the first craft reappeared. This phenomenal occurrence would last an incredible four hours, until cloud cover obscured the view at 10:50. Father Gill prepared a full written report of this event, and 25 other observers signed the document.

This first sighting, a once in a lifetime occurrence, would incredibly be followed by another sighting the very next night. At 6:00 P.M., the larger object appeared again, with its occupants. It was shadowed by two of the smaller objects.

In William Gill's own words: "On the large one, two of the figures seemed to be doing something near the center of the deck. They were occasionally bending over and raising their arms as though adjusting or "setting up" something. One figure seemed to be standing, looking down at us."

(In a moment of anticipation, Gill raised his arms and waved to the figure.)

"To our surprise the figure did the same. Ananias waved both arms over his head; then the two outside figures did the same. Ananias and myself began waving our arms, and all four seemed to wave back. There seemed no doubt that our movements were answered..."

Gill and Ananias continued to occasionally wave, and their waves were returned. Another witness, Eric Kodawara, waved a torch, and there were acknowledgments from the craft. Gill went inside to eat, but when he came back, the craft was still there, only farther away (smaller).

After a Church service, at 7:45, Gill again came outside to look for the craft, but clouds had appeared, and there was no sight of the object. The very next evening, the shining craft would make one more appearance.

Gill counted eight of them at 6:45. At 11:20, Gill heard a loud bang on the roof of the mission. Going outside to see what had happened, he spied four UFOs in a circle around the building. These four craft were extremely high in the sky. The roof was checked for damage the next morning, but none was found.

The aftermath of the event would bring unsubstantiated explanations. The noted UFO debunker Dr. Donald H. Menzel offered his explanation thus: He claims that Father Gill, who suffered from myopia (nearsightedness), had "probably" not been wearing his corrective lenses, and misidentified the planet Venus, which was prevalent in the evening skies during this period. This was NOT true; Gill WAS wearing his glasses, and in either event, what about the other witnesses to the event.

Menzel also asserted that the Papuans were ignorant, native people who worshiped Gill, and believed anything he told them. This was a surefire way to debunk the 30+ witnesses.

As to the Venus connection, Gill knew where Venus was during this sighting, and had even pointed it out separately to the unknown craft. Gill would be criticized for "leaving such an extraordinary sight" to go eat dinner, but his response is that he did not think of the craft as extraterrestrial at the time. He believed that it was an American or Australian craft, and that if it did land, that ordinary human beings would emerge.

Gill was scheduled to return to Australia soon, and it afforded an excellent opportunity to get his documentation of the case to the appropriate authorities.

All investigators found Gill to be an intelligent, impressive individual. One of the most respected civilian groups, the Victorian Flying Saucer Research Society stated:

"Gill's reports constitute the most remarkable testimony of intensive UFO activity ever reported to civilian investigators. They were unique because for the first time, credible witnesses had reported the presence of humanoid beings associated with UFOs

The Papua, New Guinea Sightings (2)

The sighting at Papua brought about an unlikely allegiance among UFO research groups in Australia. The groups distributed copies of Reverend Gill's report to all of the members of the House of Representatives of Australia's Federal Parliament. An accompanying letter urged the leaders of government to request the Minister for Air to issue an opinion on the subject, not being satisfied with their initial, negative reaction. This letter did exact a reply.

On November 24, 1959, E.D. Cash, who was a Liberal member of Parliament, asked the Minister for Air, F.M. Osborne, if they had even investigated the sightings at Papua. Osborne's response was that they were still waiting for more evidence before making an "official" report. In his own words; "Most sightings of UFOs are explained and only a very small percentage-something like 3 per cent-of reported sightings of flying objects cannot be explained."

The response of the Australian Minister for Air was to be taken lightly, considering the fact that they had not even interviewed Gill, until the Minister of Defense requested an investigation into the matter. The RAAF finally interviewed Gill in December 1959, some six months after the sightings. Gill related that the interview consisted of two officers who talked about stars and planets, and then left. He heard no more from the two. The RAAF finally released an opinion on the case... and a negative one at that. Squadron leader, F.A. Lang stated:

"Although the Reverend Gill could be regarded as a reliable observer, it is felt that the June/July incidents could have been nothing more than natural phenomena coloured by past events and subconscious influences of UFO enthusiasts.

During the period of the report the weather was cloudy and unsettled with light thunder storm.

Although it is not possible to draw firm conclusions, an analysis of rough bearings and angles above the horizon does suggest that at least some of the lights observed were the planets Jupiter, Saturn and Mars."

Since the unusual events of 1959, there have been many "explanations" of the event, all by individuals who had not witnessed the event. Most of these are, as you would expect, panaceas for the general reports of sightings. Among these are hoax, planets, stars, astronomical misidentification, Gill's myopia, etc. None of these really address the event as it happened. Dr. J. Allen Hynek investigated the sighting at great length, and gave his usual well thought out conclusions.

His "Center For UFO Studies" research included well-respected Allen Hendry, who was, at the time, the Center's top investigator. Their conclusions were as follows:

"Though the smaller UFOs seen by Gill

could be attributable to bright stars and planets, the primary object COULD NOT. "its size and absence of movement over three hours ruled out an astronomical explanation.

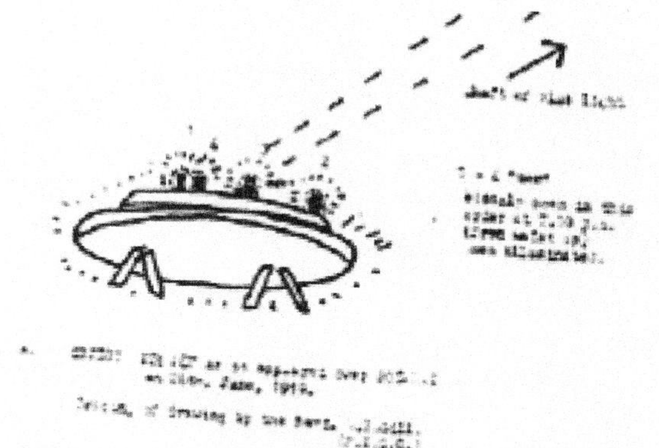

Drawing made by Father Gill of the humanoid beings on top of the craft who were said to have waved at the witnesses. „

The inclusion of the Boianai case in the well-known Australian book of fiction, Randolph Stow's 1979, "Visitants," would become a double-edged sword. Although it brought the details of the case to a larger audience, its inclusion in pure fiction lessened the appeal of the events as being REAL. Stow was a cadet patrol-officer in Papua, New Guinea, and an assistant to the Government Anthropologist. His novel begins with this sentence, "On 26 June 1959, at Boianai in Papua, visitants appeared to the Reverend William Booth Gill, himself a visitant of thirteen years standing, and to thirty-seven witnesses of another colour."

The events of New Papua in 1959, at first glance, seem to be too unbelievable to be true. It is just too good of a sighting, compared to hazy photographs, reports of abductions by unreliable witnesses, and the designation of any undefined light in the sky as a "flying saucer." To be respectable, open-minded individuals, we must NOT compare one report to another. Each case must be viewed on its own merits. Many of the so-called explanations are by those who never interviewed Reverend Gill, never visited the site, and never read Gill's actual reports, but relied on third party explanations to draw their own conclusions.

Dr. Hynek and his staff members actually interviewed Gill, they visited the site, they searched weather reports, and they stood in the same spot that Gill stood. They interviewed other witnesses of the events. They followed up initial inquiries with subsequent visits, and interviews, allowing the passage of time to shed its light on the witnesses, and what they had seen. Fourteen years after the fantastic events at Papua, Dr. Hynek revisited Papua New Guinea, Australia, and re-interviewed six of the initial witnesses.

They all supported William Gill's initial reports, and still believe what they saw to be a REAL craft of unknown origin. The Papua, New Guinea sighting is one of the best documented cases of an unidentified craft of unknown origin in UFO annals.

Compiled by B.J. Booth

www.UFOCASEBOOK.COM

* * * * *

SPECULATIVE HISTORY OF UFOS IN AUSTRALIA

Courtesy Australian UFO Connection

It may surprise some to know that Australia has had a long and exciting history with UFOs, or as they are known as in Australia, Unusual Aerial Sightings (UAS). Officially it is our esteemed RAAF who are responsible for investigating these delicate matters but departments like the Australian Security and Intelligence Organisation (ASIO), and the Directorate of Scientific and Technical Intelligence (DSTI), also actively monitor the situation. In 1968 an ASIO scientist even made an official proposal for a special team to be commissioned to investigate UFO incidents around Australia. There does not seem to be any record of a response so one can only wonder whether or not the 'rapid intervention team' was ever formed.

Positively one UFO that should be given a speeding ticket for it erratic movements over highway.

The DSTI, which is a branch of Australia's Joint Intelligence Organisation, rely on the Directorate of Air Force Intelligence (DAFI) to make initial investigations which they follow up if necessary. Thus DAFI would hold the majority of UFO files. The RAAF also make their UFO investigations in conjunction with DAFI (Directorate of Air Force Intelligence). Nearly all RAAF files are held at the Department of Defence Russel Offices in Canberra. The RAAF have three categories of UFO files;

1. Unidentified Flying Objects - Reports of Sightings.
2. UFO - Enquires from members of the public / Organisations.
3. Investigation of Flying Saucers - Policy.

It has been reported that the RAAF keeps it's most highly classified reports and an extensive collection of UFO video films at East Sale, Victoria. But some UFO files are not held with the others. This list includes all incidents prior to

1955, which may have been officially destroyed, as well as several famous incidents in 1973/74, during a documented UFO 'flap' period in Australia. Also missing are government files relating to the North West Cape UFO sighting, wherein a full nuclear alert was issued at the base. Full nuclear alerts are about as serious as they come! On 25 October 1973, two US Navy personnel saw a UFO hovering near the US Naval Communication Station there. It was a large , black UFO sighted around 8km out to sea. One of the witnesses, a Lieutenant Commander, said; "After about 20 to 25 seconds the craft accelerated at unbelievable speed and disappeared to the north."

A UFO also hovered over the former British nuclear test site at Maralinga, South Australia, for fifteen minutes after several nuclear tests in September and October of 1957. The corporal at the base who made the report said the craft was a silver-blue metallic saucer, with portholes around it and was only 150 feet away at one stage. The UFO was also witnessed by several other military officers and a private air traffic control officer. The corporal had this to say; "I swear to you as a practicing Christian this was no dream, no illusion, no fairy story - but a solid craft of metallic construction."

UFO / UAS records submitted through the Department of Aviation by non-military air traffic are held at the Bureau of Air Safety Investigation, in Melbourne. Australia also has it's own SETI (Search for Extra-Terrestrial Intelligence) operation which is based at the Faculty of Informatics, Science and Technology, at the Campbelltown campus of the University of Western Sydney Macarthur. The centre's current SETI project is called Southern SERENDIP, and they use CSIRO's 64-metre radio telescope at Parkes, NSW. Southern SERENDIP was first connected to the Parkes Radio Telescope on 20 March, 1998 with the ability to scan eight million channels per second. This has now been upgraded to scans of 58 million channels per 1.7 seconds. Obviously the centre handles huge amounts of data and millions of slight radio signals so the equipment only registers radio signals in outer space that are at least twelve times the average of the closest 8,000 or so other signals.

Whatever all these government departments are interested in, one thing is for certain, they do not wish to share their findings with us, the public. In 1952, officers of the Department of Civil Aviation sought to establish a special bureau to collect and collate the facts on UFOs. The Government Cabinet directly issued instructions that the subject was a Security Service matter.

CONFIDENTIAL

2A

COPY

M.518.1

24th July, 1960

UNIDENTIFIED LIGHT - WEWAK AREA.

The Range Commander,
Maralinga.

At Wewak, the site of the Vixen "A" tests, approximately 15 miles from Maralinga Village, are a number of static balloons used in instrumentation. At 7.15 p.m. on 15th July, 1960, a telephone report was received from Constable Hubert Dave SCARBOROUGH, who is stationed on the site, that a balloon had burnt in the air. The Balloon Officer made an inspection and found that all balloons were intact.

2. The Constable was questioned and said that he was sitting in his caravan at approximately 7.5 p.m. when his attention was drawn to a light, of approximately the power of bright moonlight, playing on the ground. He left the caravan and saw what he described as a white light travelling from East to West. As it appeared to come nearer, or grow larger, it turned to a red colour. Because of its position and height he thought, at first, that it was a balloon afire and reported it as such. Owing to lack of knowledge as to distance away it was found difficult to estimate the size of the light. The only fact contributed that could assist was that the light appeared to occupy 1½ to two degrees of the horizon. The Constable thought that the light burned for thirty seconds.

3. Constable Richard Henry MAXWELL who was outside the caravan at Roadside, thirteen miles from the Village, saw a light out of the corner of his eye at about 7 p.m. He thought that the light appeared to come from the direction of Wewak a distance of 2½ miles. As far as he knows the light did not play on the ground in his immediate vicinity. The light had made so little impression on his mind that he failed to mention it to his companion when he returned to the caravan and recalled it only when he received a telephone call from the Constable at Wewak inquiring if the light had been witnessed at Roadside.

4. The light was observed from the Village at about the same time by the following personnel -

2/345 Capt. Keith Angus ROSS, Catering Officer.

Trevor James HOSKINS, Technical Assistant, Health Physics Group,

Russell McFarlane KINGSLEY, Fitter, Department of Mines, and

Ian Kenneth HASKARD, Supervising Technician, P.M.G's Department.

All gave, more or less, the same description. They saw a light over the R.E.M.E. Workshop Building in the Village and coming from the general direction of Wewak. There was some disagreement as to the duration of the light; this varied between two and fifteen seconds. The discrepancy could be explained by some people seeing the light some seconds after it had first appeared. The person who saw it for fifteen seconds was able to reconstruct his movements at the particular time and it is thought that his estimate is reasonable. While an agreement could not be reached as to the exact time all agree that it was some time after 7 p.m.

5. Inquiries, with negative result, were made of Woomera in case a firing had taken place and was witnessed in this area. The same source was used to contact a survey party from Exoil Pty. Ltd. who were camped in the vicinity of Emu in an effort to discover if they had witnessed any phenomenon such as a meteor. The result was negative.

/6. A

CONFIDENTIAL

CONFIDENTIAL

-2-

6. A suggestion that the light could have been produced by a photo-flash from a high-flying aircraft was discounted. No aircraft was heard at the time and, in any case, no known photo-flash has a duration of anything like fifteen seconds.

7. Scientific personnel who would have the "know-how" were questioned in case the light was the result of a practical joke. Assurances were given that no member of the Scientific parties were responsible.

8. One practical suggestion was made by a Scientific Officer that the light could have been caused by "St. Elmo's fire". The Balloon Officer said that, although the balloons are "earthed" sometimes static electricity does build-up sufficiently to electrify the anchor vehicle. Three balloons are in line with the position where the light was observed from Wewak and approximately half a mile distant from the caravan. At such a distance it is understood that 1½ degrees of the horizon could be calculated to approximately 40 feet. Opportunity was taken during a visit to Adelaide to attempt some research into static electricity at the Adelaide Public Library. No reference book produced gave much useful information. The following description of "St. Elmo's fire" was extracted from an encyclopaedia -

> "...the glow accompanying the brush-like discharges of atmospheric electricity which usually appears as a tip of light on the extremity of pointed objects such as church towers or the masts of ships during stormy weather. It is commonly accompanied by a crackling or fizzing noise."

9. Mr. Oliver Harry Turner, Health Physics Officer, who possesses an inquiring mind, made an independent investigation and extensive calculations. He is of the opinion that the light was not the result of a natural phenomenon but caused by an unidentified flying object; either a cone from a satellite or a "flying saucer."

10. It is felt that all avenues of inquiry at Maralinga have now been covered and that it is not possible to positively identify the source of the light. It is felt, however, that the light was the result of either a meteor or static electricity.

11. Submitted.

SGD. J.J.A. [illegible]

Security Officer, Maralinga

CONFIDENTIAL

Though most of Australia's UFO archives are still not available, one from 1960 tells of unidentified lights that baffled authorities.

All the Security Service spokesman said was that the Government were currently involved in some matters that required the aid of scientists from the Commonwealth Scientific and Industrial Research Organization (CSIRO). In 1963, Senator J. L. Cavanagh asked for the Federal Government's dossier on UFOs to be made public. His request was refused by the Minister for Air at the time.

But there were many other influential people who believed that there was a cover-up in operation. Dr. Harry Messel, Professor of Physics at Sydney University, made the following report in 1965; "The facts about saucers were long tracked down and results have long been known in top secret defence circles of more countries than one." Also, in September 1952, the Civilian Saucer Investigation published an article about alien artifacts. In the article the editor, J. Sullivan, referred to a top-level meeting between western scientists and the 'gray' aliens that took place in the "Australian bush". But the current Government UFO Policy documents are simply not available for public access. Our worried governments throughout the twentieth century never saw fit to enlighten us with a confirmation of the existence of extra terrestrial life though one is not really necessary nowadays is it? We all know that they exist, aliens from other worlds and galaxies ARE here, today, now! They come and go as they please. They are hovering out in space asking themselves the same question our governments are (maybe), and that is, are the people of Earth ready for the big news, are we ready for the Intergalactic Age? Would the timid-minded slip into insanity? Would there be a revolution? Would we go to work on Monday? The problem is this; were we to enter the cosmic arena we would most certainly be a 'third-world' player. We would have nothing to offer unless perhaps our very moist planet, or maybe our artists and musicians? I wonder did some famous rock-stars really die early or were they in actual fact 'taken'? Of course we are joking but see the many theories in Who Are These Aliens Anyway to really get you wondering.

In Australia our government has deemed that only 3-4% of sightings could be possibly associated with possible aliens from other worlds. Even so, at the rate of well over a hundred UFO related cases per year, that still adds up to at least three or four real alien crafts per year dropping in. Yet nobody seems to be panicking! Satellites in orbit are commonly mistaken for UFOs all over the world so get to know what one looks like, there are plenty to see. That way you will know if it is a UFO that you are seeing, even if the authorities disagree (and they will!).

One place in Australia that has seen its fair share of UFO activity is Bass Strait. First the SS Amelia J. and then a search aircraft disappeared here in 1920, at the same time that strange lights were reported in the skies above. There were many unexplained reports of unidentifiable aircraft here especially during the early to mid 1900s. It is interesting to note that during World War 2, a total of seventeen aircraft vanished without a trace over Bass Strait yet there was never any enemy fighting anywhere close to the area.

There are also many incidents concerning WWII pilots who reported UFOs pacing them, even showing off with incredible maneuvers, before zooming off out of sight at speeds up to five times faster than that of our fighter planes capabilities at the time...

In 1944, a Beaufort bomber flying over Bass Strait was joined by a UFO that flew alongside, some 150 feet away, for 18 minutes before quickly leaving. It was described by the pilot as a dark object with a flickering light/flame coming from the rear. The most famous and dramatic disappearing act though was performed by Frederick Valentich in his Cessna 182, the Delta Sierra Juliet, in 1978. Valentich, a civilian pilot, had flown the 69 minute journey from Moorabbin, Victoria, to King Island, Bass Strait, many times. Please see the official transcript between him and the Melbourne Flight Service Unit as he flew then disappeared off the radar over Bass Strait. He reported being tailed by a strange craft before his transmission was abruptly cut off.

There have also been several famous sightings by commercial pilots from private airlines. On a flight from Brisbane to New Guinea in 1965, a UFO paced the Ansett-ANA DC-6b aircraft for approximately fifteen minutes. It was seen by the pilots and crew and was described as oblate in shape with exhaust gases. Some of the flight crew actually hurt themselves in the cockpit as they panicked on seeing the flying object. The pilots took photos of the object which were immediately confiscated, even the camera, on returning to Australia. As per normal officials denied anything unusual had occurred though the pilot Captain John Barker had this to say; "I had always scoffed at these reports, but I saw it. We all saw it. It was under intelligent control, and it was certainly no known aircraft."

In 1968 during a flight between Perth and Adelaide the pilots witnessed a formation of UFOs including a main ship which split into two and connected with the other ships in the formation before joining back together. Check the details but their eight-seat Piper Navago lost communication to ground control which was restored after the UFOs had departed. In their statements the pilots ruled out explanation by balloons or tricks of light; "We conclude that the UFOs were in fact aircraft with the solidity of aircraft, except perhaps for the fact of the ability of the larger UFO to split and change shape slightly." There were many more famous sightings so please see Our Sightings Database for a catalogue of 100 Australian UFO sightings over the last century, and our recent (1990s) sightings pages.

Australia has a rich history of UFO pop culture. Photos of strange twirling and whirling objects are often printed on the front pages of the dailies. (Credit: UFO Casebook)

During all these sightings our governments were not idly standing by. They have had their fair share of UFO cover-up accusations, perhaps not to the extent of our American counterparts, but almost certainly always warranted. One organisation that springs to mind is the Defence Science and Technology Organisation (DSTO), which is part of Australia's Department of Defence and operates the primary defence research facility in Australia. The organisation's main role is to give professional advice to Australian Defence Forces on science and technology that is best suited to Australia's defence needs. The DSTO has a staff level of 2600, and an annual non-classified operating budget of around $235 million. The organisation has two major laboratories headquartered in Melbourne and in Salisbury, South Australia. DSTO also has outposted staff in various parts of Australia, and representatives in London, Washington and Bankok. They have had much success and have contributed greatly to our defence and tracking capabilities. But they have also discreetly contributed to the US Star Wars Program and receive additional funding from the Australian Government for their involvement. Government supporters include Robert Ray and Ian McLachlan, and Gareth Evans actively supported Canberra's participation in US missile defence programs during his term as Foreign Minister. In fact the former Labor Government was one of the most active foreign supporters of the US program. The Star Wars, or Strategic Defence Initiative (SDI), was meant to produce a system of lasers in space that would destroy missiles before they reached America. However, $40 billion later they still have not achieved such a system. In 1995 DSTO invited the US to test anti-missile equipment at South Australia's Woomera rocket range and another test is scheduled soon.

There have also been allegations that DSTO is directly involved in the UFO situation. There was a report by a mechanic who had worked at the facility on a number of craft with unfamiliar mechanical systems. Most were strangely-shaped and one was round. He was verbally told that some of these were UFOs and that alien bodies had been recovered from them. This same officer then informed him that there were several different species of alien, but two of them were externally like human beings though with different internal structures.

AUSTRALIAN FLYING SAUCER MAGAZINE

Facts Stranger Than Science Fiction

EDITORIAL

MT. PALOMAR INVESTIGATING SATELLITES, TOO

Publications have come and gone in Australia that have been devoted to the subject. Flying Saucer Magazine came out decades ago and vanished, while the publication UFOLOGIST is still a very active publication - perhaps one of the most popular in the world.

Another story, by a well known journalist involves a television camera crew which was allowed into the Edinburgh branch of DSTO to make part of a corporate video for the RAAF, and they entered an off-limits building by mistake. They saw a saucer-shaped aircraft, and were about to examine it when military personnel noticed them and ushered them away, insisting that they not disclose what they had seen. There is another matter which concerns a document describing an Australian TOP SECRET operation called Project Apotheosis, regarding the transport of aliens from DSTOs' Salisbury facility to an unknown destination. Perhaps these aliens are the same ones that were aboard a saucer that crashed near Eyre Highway, Western Australia in December, 1977? The two witnesses saw two aliens, one dead and one badly injured. They were immediately arrested by a military team that arrived soon after.

Another notable Australian UFO related mystery is the purpose of the SIGNIT Satellite gathering station at Pine Gap, near Alice Springs. Our government insists it is simply a 'defence space research facility' but much evidence points to this station being much more than that. Pine Gap is one of the largest ground satellite stations in the world with massive capabilities and is operated by, and under the jurisdiction of the US. The site is essentially US soil. There is a drill-hole 8000m deep that contains a massive antenna capable of sending electronic charges outward into the ocean to recharge submarines. The station receives data from many geostationary SIGNIT satellites but in particular a group of satellites controlled by the CIA. Since 1969 there have been twice weekly flights to the US to deliver the thousands of reels of SIGNIT satellite data gathered at Pine Gap. It has been said that the Australian Government does not know exactly what goes on at Pine Gap, or chooses to ignore the extremely illegal intelligence gathering that takes place here.

1954 - Australia

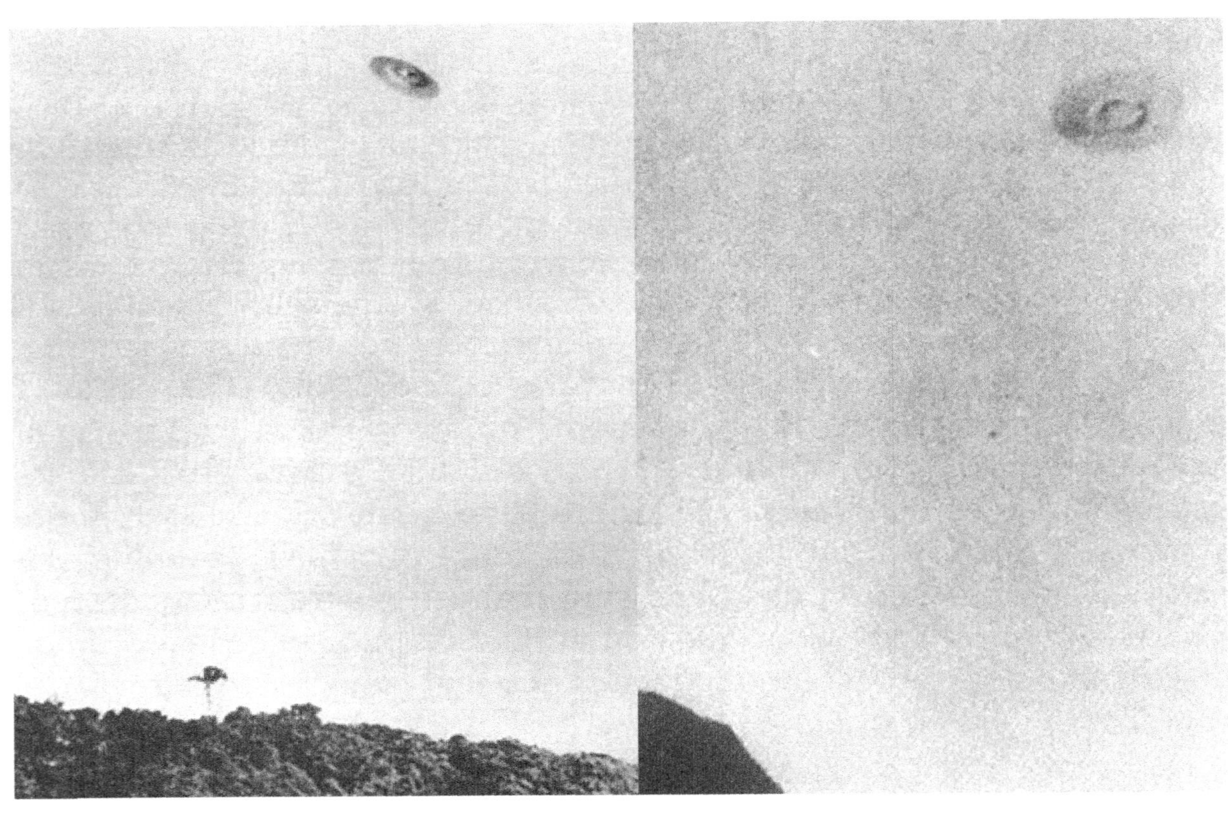

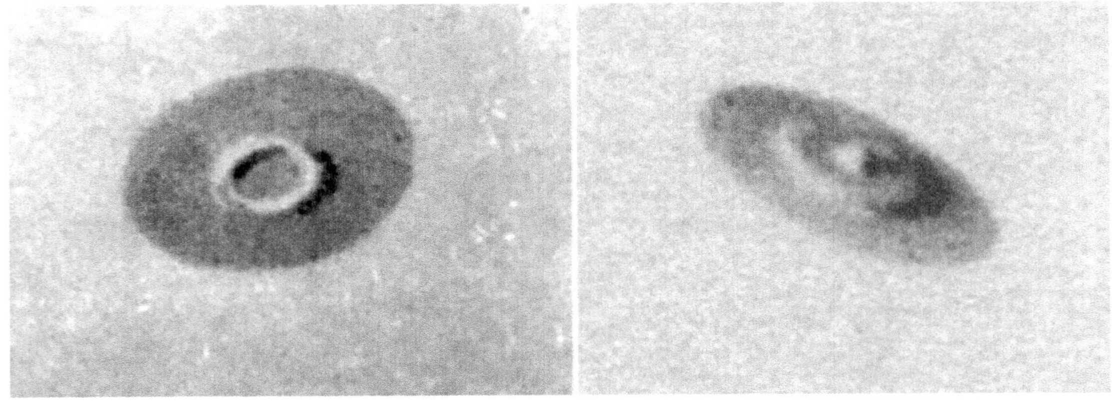

May 7, 1952 - Barra da Tijuca, Brazil

FLYING SAUCERS IN BRAZILIAN SKIES

By Timothy Green Beckley

For decades, I have been collecting and studying what I consider to be probably some of the most exciting reports of UFO encounters and sightings ever made – and the majority have come my way from the land of beautiful waterfalls and tropical jungles.

Already back in the mid 1960s I had been in touch with several highly professional UFO researchers from Brazil who were publishing their reports widely, and even translating them into English to share with the rest of the world. Brazilian UFOlogists were among the first to realize the relevance of UFOs as a global phenomenon. It was with this in mind that I was corresponding with the likes of Dr. Walter Buhler of the Brazilian UFOlogy group SBEDV who filled me in quite regularly on what seemed to be a rash of encounters with humanoids. I utilized quite a bit of this material in various articles for UFO Report, Ray Palmer's Flying Saucers Magazine and my own little publications. There were one-eyed giants, dumpy little men who could roll better than they could walk, and a few congenial human looking entities who could have passed for soap opera stars instead of extraterrestrials. But it was all part of the UFOlogical soap opera in Brazil and American researchers would just have to put up with the many oddball differences they were likely to encounter along the Amazon or in the urban areas of the country.

Dr. Elidio Hernandes, Director Circulo da Amizade Sideral Curitiba, agreed that, "Flying saucer activity in Brazil has included a large percentage of landing and contact reports. These reports for the most part have been written up in the press," he acknowledged, "but because of censorship and other factors, for the most part, have not reached America."

According to Dr Hernandes, sightings of humanoids went back as far as the summer of 1947, which would have been the same timeframe where UFO activity had started in the States with the Maury Island incident , Kenneth Arnold's sighting over Mount Rainier and of course the crash of something outside of Roswell.

Dr Hernandes shared with us this early episode in which a Mr. Jose C. Higgins appears to have had his life altered forever due to the circumstances of his encounter.

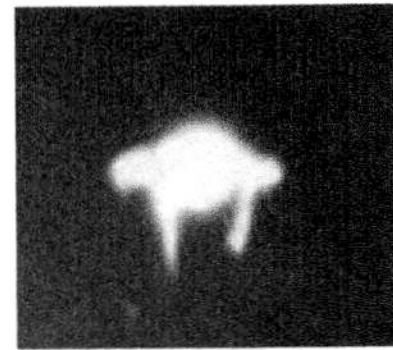

A dozen witnesses saw this strange object low in the sky over Rio De Janeiro on Oct 1, 1971.

"On July 23, I was near the small village of Goio-Bang, northwest of Pitanga and southwest of Campo Mourao, all in the stata of Parana. I was doing some topographic work, when I heard a deep hissing sound which made my hair rise on my head. A strange object of circular shape and looking like a medicine capsule was coming down from the sky. My men, all simple country people, ran far away at the sight of the strange object. I still do not know why I decided to stay and see what was to happen. The object circled the clearing and landed softly about 50 meters from where I was. It was an amazing thing. It was about 30 meters in diameter and it had a border of some 1.5 meters and was approximately 5 meters high. It had pipes crossing it in several directions, from six of which came the hissing sound, but no smoke whatsoever. The part that touched the ground had bent leg-like supports, which bent even more when the ship landed. It seemed to be made of a white-gray metal which was not silver. While taking an overall look at it, I noticed a wall on which there was a window made of glass or something like glass. Then I saw two people look at me with curiosity. They were very strange looking.

"After a while one of them turned to the inside of the ship and appeared to be talking to someone. Presently, I heard a noise and a door opened from under the border. Three people came out. They were dressed in a kind of transparent overalls which wrapped around them completely, including their heads, and which were inflated like an automobile pneumatic. At the back they carried a kind of metallic sack which appeared to be part of their outfit. Through the transparent overalls I could see perfectly well that they were wearing undershirts, trunks and sandals made not of cloth material but of something that looked like aluminum paper. I also noticed that their strange appearance was due mainly to their round eyes with no eyebrows and long eyelashes and because they were almost completely bald-headed. They had no beard and their hands were big and rounded and their legs were longer than the proportions we know."

After this initial period of awkward curiosity wore off they began to converse in an unknown tongue. "They spoke," says Higgins, in a language that sounded very nice and pleasant. In spite of their great size they moved with great swiftness and formed a triangle around me. The one holding a tube-like metal piece motioned at me to get into the ship. I approached the door and all I could see inside was a small den in which appeared another door and the end of a pipe that came from inside. I also noticed several rounded planks on the base and border.

"I started to talk, asking them where they were taking me, using a lot of mimics. They understood me and the one who seemed to be the leader drew a circle on the ground showing the sun in space surrounded by seven other circles. He pointed to the seventh circle and then to the ship and repeated this several times. I was dumb-founded. Leave the earth alive? No, that was not for me! I thought over the situation for a while. I could not fight them and that was obvious. They were much stronger and there were a lot of them. Then I had an idea. I noticed that they avoided the sunlight. I went over to the shade and took my wallet from my pocket showing them my wife's photograph and explaining through mimics that I would like to fetch her. They did not stop me. I left and giving thanks to God went into the bushes from where I watched them. They played like children, jumping around and flinging stones of great size from long distances. After half an hour more or less, having looked around the neighborhood carefully, they went inside the ship which took off with the same peculiar noise and headed north until it disappeared into the clouds. . ."

A disc on its side flaunting observers over Parana, Brazil, Dec. 14, 1954.

One hardly knows how to take this episode, though there was no reason to suspect that the witness was telling a tall tale as he would have nothing to base it on at this point as certainly there was no foreknowledge of such beings or even such a ship existing anywhere in his known world.

Over the ensuing decades there have been so many sightings by reliable witnesses in Brazil and entire books have been written on the subject, most in Portuguese, but a handful in English. The best known is by ace reporter Bob Pratt, called UFO DANGER ZONE, which provides some pretty explosive evidence that the nation of Brazil has been a focal point for what many have seen as an "interplanetary invasion" of some sort, with some witnesses even being burned and possibly mutilated by all manner of flying oddities, a great many of which defy explanation.

There have been USO – unidentified submerged objects – chases by pilots, radar reports and a nice collection of UFO photos, some of which have appeared on the front page of the country's most popular dailies. Later on in this edition, we will interview Brazil's foremost UFOlogist at length. But as part of the world sweeping Disclosure program we wish to first off publish a most important interview with Brazil's former minister of Aeronautics, Brigadier Socrates da Costa Monteiro.

Unidentified cigar glides silently above San Paplo.

BRAZIL'S FORMER MINISTER OF AERONAUTS PROCLAIMS. . . UFO TECHNOLOGY IS FAR AHEAD OF OURS

"Over decades the military have been reporting UFO activity within the Brazilian territory. However, due to the lack of a reasonable explanation, these reports are left aside awaiting for the time when their nature and the identity of their crew can be understood", says former Brazilian minister of Aeronautics, Brigadier Socrates da Costa Monteiro to the Brazilian UFO Magazine.

Exclusive interview given to A. J. Gevaerd, editor of Brazil's UFO Magazine (www.ufo.com.br)

Introduction:

The latest military to join the UFO disclosure enthusiasm in Brazil states that the country's ufologists are on the right path by searching for the official acknowledgement of UFO existence and their activities in Brazilian skies. Furthermore, Lieutenant Brigadier Socrates da Costa Monteiro admits his wish to know our visitors' technology by saying: *"If, at my term as the Minister of Aeronautics, I were asked to disclose our secret files, I'd have that done".* Such stance only adds to the list of officials who no longer agree with the secrecy involving the alien presence on Earth.

From 1990 to 1992, during the Collor administration, Monteiro served as a minister. He also occupied different high positions in the Brazilian armed forces. Even after years of retirement from the Brazilian Air Force (FAB), he maintains his links with acting officials in numerous ranks in the military. As a commander of the Brasilia-based I Centro Integrado de Defesa Aérea e Controle de Tráfego Aéreo (Cindacta I) our interviewee was in charge of the recording of UFO information for the whole country, especially for the Central and South-Eastern parts of Brazil. Monteiro reveals that UFO sightings and radar detections were already common much before he took office. He further says that all cases were thoroughly registered by the Aeronautics and some were even investigated.

Having served as a pilot for the Brazilian Postal Service and a commander of important divisions such as the VII Comando Aéreo Regional (Comar VII), Monteiro keeps a vivid memory of his times in the military and talks for the first time about his interest in Ufology. He further explains how the country dealt with the issue during his times as an officer on duty. Just like any other minister before him, Monteiro also had access to serious information on the presence of other cosmic species in his country. In this interview, he even shares some of those cases with the readers. Despite his more than 5,000 hours flying several types of aircraft, his experiences were never onboard, but on the ground with his wife, in Rio de Janeiro.

Brigadier Monteiro was also a commander at the Sao Paulo-based IV Comando Aério Regional (Comar 4), a body in control of South-Eastern air space in Brazil. Therefore, he was in charge of the area affected by the so-called Brazilian Official UFO Night, on 19 May 1986. This incident is one of the pillars to our campaign *UFOs: Liberdade de Informação Já.* As well known, in that occasion Brazilian states of Rio de Janeiro, Sao Paulo, and Goias were swarmed by some 20 luminous flying circles with estimated 100 meter in diameter each. Those lights were chased by Brazilian F5E and Mirage jets which took off from Santa Cruz (RJ) and Anapolis (GO) airfields. *"I was reported that those objects reached 4.000 km/h, but such speed is too high for our radars and cause them to loose accuracy"*, he states.

In this exclusive interview to Revista UFO Monteiro reveals a striking occurrence within Cindacta facilities at the city of Gama (DF) when he realized the crew of that object were in possession of highly advanced technology. Even without authorization and not knowing how to act, his men at the base decided to open fire against an intruder. By knowing of the incident, the brigadier ordered for an immediate cease-fire, *"They have a much more advanced technology. We don't know how they would react to our actions"*. Throughout the interview, Monteiro referred to our visitors as a more advanced species, but that didn't seem to be a comfortable assertion from him. At the beginning of the talk, he called the phenomenon as "magnetic abnormalities", *"since we lack a more appropriate term"*. As the interview went on, the brigadier felt more comfortable and, laughing of his previous interpretation, acknowledged he was always aware of the extraterrestrial nature of the UFOs.

As a friend of other military involved with UFO incidents, such as former Embraer's chairman Ozires Silva and former minister of Aeronautics Octavio Moreira Lima, Monteiro confesses his immense curiosity about flying saucers. *"I wish I could enter that 'thing' at once and see how it is"*. He is also said to have made controversial comments on the Brazilian Official UFO Night, an occurrence now brought to light with the disclosure of important official documents by Brazilian government *[See UFO 160]*. The Brigadier is quoted as having stated that, *"the Aeronautics have been recording these events for so many years"* and that UFOs *"went from 250 to 1.500 km/h in less then a second"*. Monteiro may also have admitted that, *"FAB recorded the whole incident in magnetic tapes"*. All these facts are now further elaborated by him.

The interviewee is open to the idea of other forms of intelligent lives, but is also cautious when talking about that. After much insistence from his interviewers, Monteiro admits that not only him, but also other high ranking officers, are quite aware that we are being visited by more advanced cosmic species. *"We know that they do not represent any threat. I am convinced that their approach is aimed to know us"*. Such words become even more meaningful when uttered by the man responsible for the implementation of the Amazon Surveillance System (SIVAM) and the privatization of Embraer.

This remarkable interview published by Revista UFO shows readers that Lieutenant-Brigadier Socrates da Costa Monteiro is another important figure in the Brazilian military to acknowledge the seriousness of ufologists' mission in researching alien activity on Earth. He also expresses his support to the campaign *UFOs: Liberdade de Informação Já*, an initiative conducted by the *Brazilian Committee of Ufologists (CBU)*. Following colleagues who previously spoke through this magazine, Monteiro states that official institutions should support ufologists in their task to determine the nature of the UFO phenomenon.

Brigadier, I should start by thanking you for being so kind in receiving us.My first question is: Have you ever experienced any ufological event, be it in your military career, as a minister, or in your private life?

Well, it depends on what you call a "ufological event". But I can say I've seen things that caught my attention. Even my wife was present at one of those occasions. It occurred at that night in which many objects were seen flying over Rio de Janeiro, Sao Paulo, and Sao Jose dos Campos *[The Brazilian Official UFO Night]*. She was watching the Copacabana beach from the balcony of our flat in Rio and spotted a bizarre light in the sky. She was surprised, looked to me and said: *"It's a flying saucer"*. When I saw the scene, especially my wife's reaction, I joked: *"I don't know what that is, but if you tell someone I'll punish you. You didn't see anything, you don't know anything. If you don't keep quiet, you'll get into trouble. I won't say anything either"*. Then I took my powerful Navy binoculars to better see that light.

What did you think that was? As an Air Force expert you must have rejected any known explanation...

Actually, I can't say what that was. Ozires Silva had a similar experience that same night. You know his story, right?He was travelling from Brasilia to Sao Jose dos Campos and saw an unidentified light following his aircraft, an Embraer's Xingu. Ozires was interviewed by a TV channel the next day and declared, *"That's true. The light stood beside me following me for a long time changing from one side of the aircraft to another"*. When I heard that I told him: *"Now you're in trouble. You won't be able to hide it from anyone anymore"*. He only laughed. Ozires was a colleague of mine at the military school and is a very close friend. When my wife heard his account, she said to him, *"That's it, Ozires. Socrates and I saw that too"*. In another interview he even mentioned that experience I had with my wife. In the end, the case became well known. However, it would be difficult for me to give a personal account on the issue, since I have never seen anything really clear or something I could affirm was not of human nature. There was never anything I could address by saying: *"You are not a human being. You are an extraterrestrial"*. Therefore, I've never seen anything like that, but I've seen things in the sky which I call "electronic anomalies".

And what would be "electronic anomalies," Brigadier?

Those should be phenomena seen in the sky for which we do not have a reasonable explanation. Let me explain it better, when I was a commander to the Centro Integrado de Defesa Aérea e Controle de Tráfego Aéreo (Cindacta), in Brasilia, there were many cases. As you know, Cindacta has a very sophisticated operational system. At the time of its implementation Latin America had only two similar ones – one was in Mexico City subway, the other one was in Sao Paulo subway. Cindacta used to integrate all of Brazilian territory in real time by means of a powerful computer system. We recorded everything spotted by our radars and all was kept for 30 days. After that we used to clear the tapes in order to reuse it for new recordings. Sometimes we had signals on the screen, objects that stopped and moved. We didn't know what they were. So we only took notes of all that and, by lacking a better definition, we only called those artifacts as "electronic anomalies" *[At that time the term "hotel traffic" was not in use]*. We did so because they were electronic signals which we didn't know how to interpret.

Monteiro describes de UFO scenario in the Amazon, where He helped to implement a special air traffic ontrol system

Besides this phenomenon, have you ever received any reports from locals about UFO sightings?

Yes, yes. Sometimes people came to me telling of things they had seen, both military and civilians. One case was special, since it seriously involved our facilities. Cindacta had radar and telecommunication facilities based in Gama, a Brasilia neighbor city. The commander in that base was Captain Joao Bernardo Vieira. I had just taken office at Cindacta's command two months before. So, one night around 22h00, Vieira called me to report that radars in Gama had been spotting strange objects. *"Commander, it's full of flying saucers around here"*, he said. Then I told him: *"Don't be a fool, man. What's really going on there?"* He insisted: *"I'm no fool, they are really here, commander. They are throwing stones at us"*. Vieira even said some soldiers had shot at the object so I ordered them to stop immediately. *"Don't shoot anything. Get your people inside the barracks, I don't want anyone close to that thing"*. The objects had glowing lights that changed in color and moved slowly around them.

This is impressive, but how could the aircraft throw stones at the soldiers? Do you have any explanation for that?

That I don't know, I only heard Vieira reporting: *"They are throwing stones at us"*. I think that a propulsion object may have raised stones from the ground then soldiers around it might have thought they were being assaulted. Or it may be that pilots in that "thing" propelled a strong blast in order to raise stones and scare the soldiers in order to prevent them from a stronger response. They have a much more advanced technology and we don't know how they would react to our response. Vieira told me around 25 soldiers were present, so I ordered them to get inside the base and receive a piece of paper in order to describe exactly what they had seen. *"They are forbidden from talking to one another and you take measures to enforce that"*, I told him. I wanted the soldiers to make their description of the events and Vieira to bring me their papers at Cindacta at 08h00 the next day. That's what he did.

Did the shots hit the flying saucers?

No.

What was the outcome of your investigation? Was it possible to determine what object was that over Cindacta radars in Gama?

Well, our soldiers are very primitive. As you know, soldiers are not very educated persons and have difficulties in precisely describing what they see. But it was possible to tell from their descriptions and drawings that they had witnessed something weird. It was something with changing colors that approached them very closely. One of them asked permission to open fire and that's how the shooting began. All told the same story and I wrote that all down in a report which I sent to the Aeronautics Armed Forces (EMAER). I never expressed my opinion or made any guesses. The envelope I sent to EMAER contained all information I had and it was kept somewhere.

What does Captain Vieira says about it?

I lost contact with him. But recently, in a medical appointment I met a familiar face who asked me if I still remembered. Before I could answer, the person smiled and said, *"I am Vieira, Captain from Cindacta in Gama"*. Of course I remembered, although many people had served under my command.*"Vieira of the flying saucer?"*, I said. *"That's me"*, he replied. The funny thing is that it happened this week, only a few days before this interview. That was such a coincidence because I haven't seen him for the last 20 years or so. I even told him about our interview and asked if he would also talk and he agreed, *"Tell them to call me" [His interview will be done in a few weeks]*.

Do you have any other case to tell?

Yes. There is another story from a doctor in Sao Paulo. I had to undergo a medical procedure called cinecoronoriography which is basically the ingestion of contrasts in order to visualize whether arteries are open or blocked. I didn't want to do that in Rio, so I went to Sao Paulo to be examined at Hospital Sirio Libanes whose directors I know. I had helped them with problems regarding the clearance of equipment withheld by Infraero. They imported machines for medical examination, but didn't have the money to collect them at the customs. So we entered an agreement: I would authorize the clearance provided that they offer free treatment to a number of poor people. And so we did. They performed well their part in the deal.

Then how about the story you have to tell us?

The day following my exams many doctors came to my room to thank me for that agreement and so we talked. When most of them had left, one stood in the room and started a chat about UFOs. I don't remember his name, but he was very straight to the point, *"Brigadier, can I ask you a question?"* I said yes and he went on to say, *"Do you believe in UFOs?"* I was surprised and said, *"Ah, doctor, that's a very common question. I don't know whether they exist or not, people believe what they want to believe"* .So he told me he was from a countryside town in the state of Sao Paulo and had witnessed something there by 02h00 from the balcony of his hotel room, *"It was a huge thing simply descending at the city's square"*. I asked what huge thing was that and he replied straight away, *"It was a flying saucer!"* Then he looked for my advice on what to do and asked if he could tell his story. I told him yes, he could do as he pleased, but I didn't want to make any comments. He described the object and said to be close to it, no more than 30 meters away. I was impressed by his assertiveness and his will to state that what he saw was a flying saucer. I have never met him again and do not even know if he is still at the Hospital.

Have you heard of any cases regarding UFOs escorting airplanes?

Yes, sometimes Cindacta radars spot strange things. For example, pilots flying Brasilia-Sao Paulo route used to report sightings of lights following their aircraft. We used to make them the usual questions such as the duration of the event, the altitude of the objects, things like that. Our questions over the radio aimed to get more details on what they were claiming to have seen. Then we reported everything back to the Aeronautics without expressing an opinion, which was the recommended procedure.

The procedure of reporting to EMAER was an established guideline or was it done at your own will?

Well, actually we did like that because we didn't know what else to do. And we didn't express any opinion because we also didn't know what to say. If I told them I'd seen a flying saucer, they *[EMBAER officers]* would ask me to describe it and I couldn't describe anything, since they were all dots on the radar screen. So I only used to say, *"Look, there's a light here spotted by the radar. I'll call it an 'electronic anomaly'"*. That was always the name I used to give to those phenomena, as I didn't have a better definition to give.

Are there any cases involving pilots and UFOs that you could tell us?

Some colleagues had told me about lights which changed colors and followed their aircraft.The lights seemed to come and go suddenly and at incredible speed. I heard many of these stories and researched about some as I'm a curious person. For example, I learned from the USAF's Blue Book project that many pilots were followed by anomalies. Some of them even lost their lives, such as the case with Thomas Mantell, in January 1948. He disappeared after intercepting an undetected UFO. His aircraft was found in wrecks a few kilometers beyond the point in which he lost radar contact. Some people don't believe it, some others do. Some people believe these are merely meteorological phenomena. As for myself, I believe that anything is possible.

Brigadier, as you know, the Brazilian Committee of Ufologists(CBU) launched a campaign five years ago aiming to have an official disclosure of government archives. The campaign *UFOs: Liberdade de Informação* has already achieved good results. On 20 May 2005, we were even invited by the Air Force commander, Luiz Carlos da Silva Bueno, to go to Brasilia and visit Cindacta and Comdabra facilities.

Yes, I know. You were received by Brigadier Atheneu Azambuja and were allowed to see some documents in a room.

Yes, but the authorization was only to see those documents. We were not allowed to copy any of them. That is why the campaign still goes on. After a successful beginning we want to move further. In 2008, the government finally started to release some files. Those were classified documents and we would like to show them to you.

I am aware that some papers are being disclosed.

Right, and among them there are files concerning Operação Prato, an operation carried out in the Amazon, in 1977, under Colonel Uyrange Hollanda. At the time he was a Captain, then was promoted to the rank of Colonel. Among the documents, there are some from the defunct National Information Service (SNI), which we did not even know about.

As I can see, you've probably had access to documents from EMAER, who starts to disclose their archives. As a Cindacta commander, I sent alone 25 UFO sighting statements which must remain there till this day.

Were you ever aware of the involvement of the SNI in cases such as Operação Prato or any other UFO sightings in Brazil?

No. I knew only about EMAER.

How about Operação Prato? What do you know about it?

Not much. I only know it occurred in the Amazon, in 1977, and was under Brigadier Protasio *[Lopes de Oliveira]*. As you know, I was a commander to the VII Comando Aéreo Regional (COMAR VII), in Manaus, and that all happened at the I Comando Aéreo Regional (COMAR I), which is in Belem.

Exactly. Operação Prato was prepared at COMAR I and carried out at the island of Colares, 80km from Belem. Documents disclosed show routes, formats, and sizes of UFOs.

All these *[pointing to papers shown to him]* are official government documents? Did you have access to all that?

Yes, we did. These are copies from the originals and tell of all that happened at that time. Similarly interesting are the documents recently declassified which account for the occurrence of 19 May 1986, which had Ozires Silva as a main figure involved, the so-called Official UFO Nights in Brazil.

That's interesting. I can see here among the documents regarding that night there's an incident report signed by Brigadier Jose Pessoa Cavalcanti de Albuquerque.

Yes. In that report he describes how the objects zigzagged, stopped, reached incredible speed, and so on. It also states that the objects both chased and were chased by Brazilian jets*[See UFO 160]*.

I see. Decisions at the time were made by the Comando de Defesa Aérea (CODA), a body responsible for the monitoring of any non-identified objects which could pose a threat to the country. CODA was the body in charge of the taking-off of Mirages and F-5Es and the interception of intruders. There (CODA) is where the search for anything unusual starts.

Now we know that thanks to this document disclosed by the government. However, there are still some topics missing in order to illustrate that night. For example, you were the commander of the IV Comando Aéreo Regional (COMAR IV), in Sao Paulo, which was the body directly in charge of the occurrence. Did you follow the development of the incident?

No, I did not. That was the same night my wife witnessed those objects in Rio and I was with her when Mirages and F-5Es were launched against the objects in Rio and Sao Paulo. At the same time, Ozires Silva was on his way from Brasilia to Sao Jose dos Campos and witnessed the phenomenon.

As the commander of COMAR IV didn't you follow on the facts? There were statements published at the occasion which were quoted as being yours. You were quoted as saying that those facts were long being

reported and that FAB was aware of that. That was all published. What do you have to say about that?

Yes, now I remember. What I'm saying is that I didn't have the opportunity to witness the event in real time. I only knew that radars had spotted unusual objects or, again, "electronic anomalies". We put that all down in reports that were sent to EMAER, which was the appropriate reporting mechanism.

Did you get any answers from EMAER about that case or any other event reported to them? Also, did you receive any instructions as to how to behave in those circumstances?

No, but I know how they dealt with it. When there was nothing to say or no plausible explanation to give, the reports were sent to the archives awaiting for the day when a possible explanation could arise.

Do you know if at any given time the government, EMAER or even CODA had established a committee in order to address these cases?

When I was a minister of Aeronautics and received that kind of reports, I just did as usual: sent them to the appropriate files containing all of those similar cases. That was a single folder so that we do not loose the origin of the reports. All was kept there. When we lacked an explanation, we simply waited for it to come up one day. I used to give orders for a research, but it was not an investigation or an inquiry. It was just an informal check-up.

Those check-ups were routine or were applied in only special cases?

It happened only in a few cases, when we consider it worth to investigate. When the description of the event was a credible one, I tried to search for more concrete data.

How were those check-ups conducted?

I used to send someone to talk with locals from the place where the event occurred. We talked to people who might be linked to what was reported. We also inspected the area followed by the witness, because such cases normally happened in the rural area or small cities, not in large urban centers. At least this is what we normally got. If I'm not mistaken, it has been happening in Brazil since the 1950s, when officers from Gravataí Air Base, state of Rio Grande do Sul, saw strange objects in the sky at broad day light. I believe that was in 1954.

The former minister describes sightings of UFO in several areas of Brazil

Were you already in the military at that time? What was your rank?

Yes, I was a Lieutenant at the Air Force. The event was registered in Gravatai and caused great commotion, since high-ranking officials like Brigadier Jose Hernani were involved.

Brigadier, I'd like to resume the Brazilian Official UFO Night when jets were sent to intercept the objects. In that occasion you've said that FAB had been recording such cases for years. You also said that the artefacts went from 250 to 1500 km/h in less than a second, which is confirmed by the documents recently disclosed by the government. What else can you say about it?

My technicians mentioned 4000 km/h, but that speed is too much for our radars. It makes them loose accuracy. Therefore, we can not really state that they flew at that speed (4000 km/h). However, they disappeared from radar screens so quickly that Cindacta's system registered a not much reliable velocity assessment. We could not precisely assert 4000 km/h technically speaking. What was certain is that the objects were at more or less 800 km/h, then suddenly sped up so quickly that they disappear from radar screens. Our technicians said that happened at 4000 km/h, but I do not endorse this assumption.

When radars showed that the objects disappeared in that fashion, did you still think of "electronic anomalies" as an explanation?

Well, I still called it "electronic anomalies", because I didn't have any other name to give to it*[laughing about his own definition]*.

But what do you think those objects were? What is your opinion?

I don't think anything and do not have a personal say on that.

Have you ever considered those might be ships from another planet crewed by a superior intelligence?

I'd like to think like that. I'd like to be able to say I believe it, that I'm sure, but I'm kind of skeptic about things I can not prove. However, if you ask me if I think that is all fabrication, I'd say no. I don't think this is the case. But the point is I can not say what those things are.

I would insist in asking you: What do you think they are?

I think it's very hard to say that nothing can exist beyond our knowledge or beyond our world. That would be false. I wish I could say "they" are there, but I still had no opportunity for a close look. I have no concrete data to give to you regarding those objects. Believe me, I wish I could join you in order to research this "thing", but I'm in no conditions for that.

As you said before, FAB had been recording UFO sightings. Can you tell of any case which had this same proportions?

Yes, I consider the Gravatai case as a significant occurrence.

Besides Gravatai incident and the Brazilian Official UFO Night, do you remember any other case in which jets were sent to intercept UFOs?

No, there were none that I remember. Besides, we had the habit of not commenting on things we could not prove. So we avoided talks on those cases because we lacked concrete data in order to identify the nature of those objects. There was also the issue of meteorological phenomena to be taken into consideration. Some balloons might reach incredible altitudes.

You're right, but Cindacta radars and experienced jet pilots wouldn't take one thing for another...

Sure, but every aspect must be considered. There is a meteorological phenomenon called St. Elmo's fire, for example, which is a strong bluish light that can stood still or move. This one is often seen in cemeteries due to the decomposition of organic matter. The gas resulting from it generates a bluish light when in contact with the air. This is what we call St. Elmo's fire.

There were many reports from pilots seeing the St. Elmo's fire. However, what they usually describe are more likely to be associated with ufological occurrences. The *foo-fighters* at the II World War are an example.

All pilots have already seen the St. Elmo's fire in the sky. I have seen it many times. It might even enter the aircraft and cross through it. I've seen it very often over the Amazon when flying a C-47 or a DC-3 for the Brazilian postal service. I have more than 2000 hours of flight in that region and witnessed many electrical storms, which may generate strange phenomena. There is a number of atmospheric effects to be considered – the electric fire or the St. Elmo's fire is only one of those. The light rests at the tip of the helix, then jumps from one side to another before going away. We got even afraid of being burned. That happens to me several times. This is why pilots always think, *"It's the St. Elmo's fire again, get ready"* when there's a light in the sky. However, not everything can be explained like that, since the St. Elmo's fire is just a small luminous ball inside the cockpit. There are much larger lights. Anyway, any commercial pilot flying over 10.000 meters have experienced that.

There is another statement allegedly yours regarding the Brazilian Official UFO night. It says that FAB had recorded the event in video. Is it true?

No. Actually the whole event was registered in magnetic tapes, not in video. Radars have the ability to record everything they detect. Then we keep these recordings for 30 days, as I said before. After that we clear the magnetic tapes not to let them pile up.

Even recordings of an event which triggered an interception operation in 19 May 1986 were deleted?

When there's something like that we normally wait a little more before deleting the recordings. Maybe 2 or 3 months. After that, recordings are deleted for the reasons I've already mentioned. But Cindacta has recorded things like that many times. Not once or twice, but many times. We always prepared reports and sent them without any comments, since we didn't know what or how to explain.

Regarding this event or any other, have you ever been pressured by foreign governments to share information?

No. During my time as a minister that never happened, or it happened without my knowledge.

Brigadier Jose Carlos Pereira *[See UFO 141 and 142]* (EMAER) has already recorded hundreds of ufological sightings since the 1950s. Do you confirm that?

Well, Pereira was a chief of EMAER. Therefore, these materials were in his desk for him to access anytime he wanted.

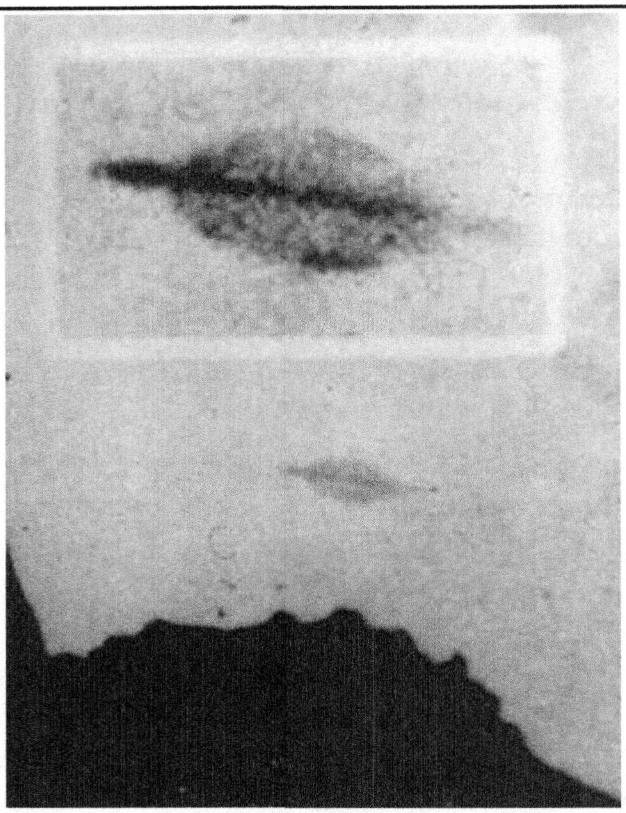

The 1958 Trindade Island Brazil "saturn"-shaped UFO was photographed while being seen by more qualified observers than any other 1950s sighting.

When ufologists can't find strings, shadows or signs that a UFO photo is faked, they question the credibility of the photographer and witnesses. Trained observers -including pilots, ship captains etc- are generally considered good witnesses. It is the corroborating testimony of the crew members on the deck of the Brazilian Navy ship "Almirante Saldanha" that makes the Trindade, Brazil UFO photos so interesting.

As part of its contribution to the 1957-58 International Geophysical Year, the Brazilian

In recent interviews he states that "*it's time to end UFO secrecy*", and "*secret files on UFOs should be disclosed*". He firmly supports our campaign *UFOs: Liberdade de Informação Já*. What do you think about these statements?

Navy set up a weather station on the small rocky island of Trindade, in the south Atlantic Ocean. Observers began spotting unusual aerial activity visually and on radar. At noon on 16-Jan-1958, the UFO shown here appeared for a few seconds within view of the ship's company. The incident was not isolated, but at least five other sightings had occurred in the island or near the water during the end of 1957 and in January 1958.

The crew onboard saw a bright grey object approach the island, fly behind a mountain peak and then do a acute-angle turn around and head back the way it came, disappearing at high speed over the horizon. Among those present was civilian photographer Almiro Barauna, who snapped a series of 6 photos, of which 4 showed the UFO. After the ship returned to port, the photos, which had been developed on board in a makeshift darkroom, were turned over to the Brazilian Navy Ministry. Analysts determined the photos to be authentic and concluded they showed a diskoid object moving at 900-1000Km/hr.

According to Capt. Viegas, the object was like a flattened sphere encircled at the equator by a large ring or platform. In Barauna's words, "...it made no noise, although with the shouting of the people on the deck and the noise of the sea, I cannot be certain. It had a metallic look, of an ash color, and has like a condensation of a green vapor around the perimeter, particularly in the advancing edge. Its motion was undulating, like the flight of a bat." The photos were later released to the Press by the President of Brazil, Mr Juscelino Kubitschek.

I think there are two possible interpretations. First, we need to disclose the files in order to clarify what the phenomenon is. Second, this is necessary in order to avoid people saying we are hiding the truth. I can anticipate people saying, *"the government hides mysterious phenomena from its people"*. This is not true. So files must be opened at once in order to avoid this idea. We can not remain in an uncomfortable position regarding this issue.

Brigadier Pereira says exactly the same. He even says that people do not fear what is transparent, they fear what is opaque instead. He further says that the documents can not affect national security, do not pose a threat to the population and do not harm the privacy of people involved. Files must be disclosed. Do you agree with that?

No doubt about that. Actually, I didn't open (the files) before, as a minister, because I was never asked to do so. If I were ever asked, I'd have them opened.

Would you do so even though they contain serious incidents such as the Official Night, in which FAB jets were sent to intercept objects of unknown nature?

Yes, even those cases must be disclosed. Note that jets were launched but could not even approach the objects. We are talking about UFOs *[not mentioning "electronic anomalies" anymore]*, and our aircraft could not even get close to them.

Do you think such impossibility to intercept the objects was due to their alleged superior technology?

Yes, *[that's why]* we could not even get close to those things which reach thousands of kilometers per hour in less than a second. Ozires Silva saw that, my wife did, and so did I. As I described before, there was a bright light standing still in the sky. I was watching and waiting for it to turn left or right, but it didn't. My conclusion was that it was flying directly towards me, although it seemed to be not moving.

What did you think that time?

I'm realistic about these matters. All I wanted was to enter that "thing" and see how that works. This idea had already gone through my mind long before.

What do you mean? When did that happen?

In 1950, when I was still a cadet. I was flying a training session over Barra da Tijuca and saw something similar to a balloon, as I can describe it. My trainer saw that as well and agreed that that could be a balloon, but the object suddenly disappeared. Not long after that, the magazine *O Cruzeiro* published a report entitled *Disco Voador na Barra da Tijuca (Flying Saucer over Barra da Tijuca)*. If you check the magazine archives, you'll get to the description of what was seen that day. I think that was the same object I saw during my training along with other colleagues. *O Cruzeiro* even mentioned that a group of aircraft flying that zone might have spotted the object. They were talking about us.

Indeed, a passage in Fernando Cleto Nunes Pereira's book *A Bíblia e os Discos Voadores* (*The Bible and the UFOs*) *[Editora Ediouro, 1986]*, says that a cadet from Campo dos Afonsos would have seen the UFO pictured by magazine *O Cruzeiro*.

It might be me or any other cadet. I saw that "thing" at Barra da Tijuca, which could be a balloon. That happened at the same time and same place in which the UFO was photographed. To my understanding, that was a balloon. However, when *O Cruzeiro* hit the stands the next Sunday, the report defined that as a flying saucer. I didn't see anything that seemed like a saucer, but only a balloon, as I can describe it. *[When inquired about it, the interviewee revealed he was never aware of the controversy surrounding Ed Keffel's pictures of an alleged UFO. Ed Keffel was a reporter for* O Cruzeiro *and worked in partnership with Joao Martins. Those pictures are considered to be a hoax by most of the Brazilian ufology community].*

Was the object just hanging still in the air? Didn't it move to any direction?

When you are flying, it's difficult to observe the movement of other things in the sky. It's hard to tell if that moved or not.

Brigadier, you already know that our main wish today is having government acknowledgement of UFOs existence as well as the disclosure of official archives. Brazilian ufologists also want to establish a research committee to work in cooperation with Air Force officials, be them retired or not. We wish to conduct joint operations for case analysis aiming both military and civil data files. Can we count on your support for that?

Of course you can. Sure. As for the Aeronautics as an institution I think that, if you're able or lucky to reach most concrete data, they will use you in order to find explanations or collect more information.

How do you suggest we could approach the Aeronautics with such a proposal for a joint work?

It maybe by finding out more new facts.

We have hundreds of facts. What we need now is an institutional and bureaucratic breakthrough so that our idea is officially made into effect.

How did you get access to all these information you've just brought to show me?

We made formal requests to the Aeronautics and many other bodies as part of procedures put in place after the *Carta de Brasilia* and, later on, by the *Dossiê UFO Brasil [See UFO 155 and 158]*. Most of materials were released by the Centro de Documentação e Histórico da Aeronáutica (Cendoc).

If that was the case, I believe you should follow on the same path. The body you said to have released most of materials is, in fact, the most accessible one to that kind of proposal. I'll see what I can get to you in that sense.

We thank you very much for that. Regarding the time you served in Manaus as a commander to the VII Comando Aéreo Regional (COMAR VII), was there any UFO sighting you could tell us about?

No. Despite the intense air traffic in that area, I didn't get any information of that kind. Roraima's Boa Vista airport used to be the most requested one in Brazil that time due to mining activities in the region. There were more than 200 daily flights, normally monometers. There was a huge exploration of cassiterite at that time.

Such an aircraft traffic demands extreme caution on the part of controllers, isn't it?

Yes. That's the reason why after two months in office as a minister I took the president to the region and proposed him the implementation of a surveillance system in order to keep track of anything that happens in the Amazon. This is what we know today as Sistema de Vigilância da Amazônia (SIVAM). It was prepared by the Armed Forces in order to monitor the air space in all of that area. The initiative has its civil part, which is denominated Sistema de Proteção da Amazônia (SIPAM). The president accepted the suggestion and the system was put in place years later.

When SIVAM started operations you were not at the Ministry anymore, correct? Despite that fact, didn't you know of any occurrence in the Amazon, either through civil or military pilots?

No, nothing. That time there was nothing in the Amazon, only rains.

Regarding the Official Night, there is another question. Some sectors in the press attempted to discredit the importance of the case, while others argued that the Air Force would never launch 7 jet fighters to intercept something of little importance. In fact, an operation like that would be too expensive.

Of course they wouldn't. However, this kind of interception operation is short. There's no interception lasting 2 or 3 hours. It normally takes no more than 30 or 40 minutes. The aircraft goes, checks, identifies the target or not, then returns to the base. But you're right, the costs are really high.

So you mean the Aeronautics would never deploy jets if the case was not very serious?

They would not, but let me tell you a story. During the conflict in Malvinas islands, in 1982, I was a commander at Cindacta when we spotted an aircraft entering Brazilian air space from the North, through Belem region. We knew that was a Russian Ilyushin flying from Havana to Buenos Aires whose route crossed Brazilian air space. We didn't know the pilot, but we knew the Cuban ambassador to Argentina was onboard carrying US$ 200,000 – and that I don't know what for. The aircraft entered Brazilian skies without contacting controllers in Brasilia. The Military Operations Center immediately launched two Mirage against the intruder. It was a Thursday, a day before Good Friday, with a heavy storm falling over Brasilia. The air strip was dark, we had lost the lights. So we put lamps on in order to make the taking-off possible. The Mirage would take off at 22h00 in order to intercept the Cuban aircraft. They ordered the intruder to come back and land in Brasilia, but their pilots pretended not to listen. Then the Mirages turned on their lights behind the Cuban aircraft and its pilots understood they had no other choice. So they returned and landed in Brasilia. What I want to say is that our system for interception really works!*[emphatic]* However, if the HIlyushin had not landed in Brasília, we wouldn't know what to do, because none of our authorities would have the courage to authorize an attack against the intruder. Now it's a different situation because we have a legislation regulating the possibility of putting an intruder down.

On 19 May 1986, Brazilian jets could not force the UFOs to land. The recently disclosed report tells how every jet was launched, what they saw, and how they unsuccessfully tried to approach the objects. There were times when they turned from hunter to prey. One of the UFOs reached 180 km in a matter of seconds going Atlantic Ocean inwards at Sao Paulo coast, then turned back to chase Brazilian jets.

That's true. What we see is that one can not approach these objects. During this specific incident, pilots tried many times, but UFOs simply sped up and left them behind.

Impressive. And all was recorded by ground and cockpit radars. The UFOs were being observed both by the pilots and Ozires Silva.

Those were "visual electronic anomalies" *[laughing each time more when quoting the term].*

Have you had the chance to talk to those pilots or other military involved, such as the commander of Comando de Defesa Aérea (CODA), Major Ney Cerqueira, now a retired Colonel? Or have you talked to the then minister of Aeronautics, Brigadier Octavio Moreira Lima?

No. I didn't talk to them because I had no intentions of carrying out a profound investigation on that. I knew it would lead us nowhere.

How did you know it would lead you nowhere?

Because it was always like this, at least here in Brazil.

But researching takes us somewhere, at least.

Yes. One day we're going to get there.

Sources say that 21 round-shaped objects, 100m in diameter each, were involved. Such a massive manifestation of UFOs wouldn't be a threat to national security, to civil air traffic, especially at the time of the occurrence?

No, we knew there wasn't any threat. We were convinced that their intention was to know better.

To know what or who? Us?

Yes, to know us.

So it means you admit "they" exist and are intelligent beings trying to know us.

Well, they were electronic anomalies *[laughing even more]...*

At a time when even the government discloses information it's becoming more and more difficult to deny it, isn't it?

My friends, I can assure you one thing: if I had any concrete evidence about the reality of UFOs, I would pass it on to you immediately. Unfortunately I don't have any, but I do know a lot of credible people who experienced the phenomenon and I can give you their names. For example, Jose Aluizio Borges, a general manager to Banco Real. He was at his farm near Campo Grande (MS) and saw a flying saucer. *"It was a huge light that crossed in front of us in the middle of the night"*, he told me *[that witness was not found to give his interview]*.

So your friend was impressed just like you when you saw that light together with your wife?

Yes. Humans are naturally inclined to look for the unknown. Brazilians have such inheritance from the Portuguese people. Some 300 years ago, someone called Bartolomeu Gusmao did something incredible. He made a small balloon go up inside the Portuguese royal palace, so that he could prove his point that flying was possible. Before that, when he was only describing what he would do, everybody laughed. Then, when people saw the balloon going up, they started to clap. Gusmao then asked the king's permission to develop that means of transport. After him, how many people got inspired to conduct similar experiments? Would you believe that someone thought about that means of transport 300 years ago?

You have mentioned the event within Cindacta facilities in Gama. Do you know of any other case in which UFOs were shot at by the military? Do you know of any jet fighters having targeted objects in the air?

I don't know any case of that. Actually, at the time we followed the doctrine of non-aggression.

That doctrine was enforced by whom?

By no one. That was just a logical conclusion, once we knew that an artefact capable of such flying maneuvers could never be hit. It would be even crazy on our part to attempt anything against it. We knew that and no one would be fool enough to try an attack. That "thing" could simply pulverize us with a beam of light. However, we were never prevented from trying to approach the ships in order to see them closely. Actually, all the military were dying to see a UFO at close range.

Was that a formal doctrine within your regulations?

No, it was rather informal. It was a natural behaviour for pilots and commanders. One would ask, *"Hey, would you shoot that?"* and the other would reply, *"Of course not. I'm not stupid"*. In fact, as we didn't believe one could get even close to those objects, we never had a procedure to be adopted in these cases.

Brigadier Jose Carlos Pereira confirms that on the Official Night Mirages and F-5Es were carrying missiles. Didn't they have the intention to fire?

No. They had missiles because that was a mission for interception when all aircraft take off carrying weapons. That was just in case, because if force is needed we must be ready whether to defend or to attack.

Wasn't there any fear on the part of the military that the jets could be viewed as a threat by the UFOs?

Yes, I feared that. I wanted we to check, but not to get much closer *[The interviewee falls into contradiction, since we previously stated he couldn't have followed the Official Night because he was in Rio]*. Also, how could they know we carried weapons?

Maybe they have technology enough to detect it.

Yes, it can be. Technology is an interesting point. We know that our limit is the speed of light, for now. However, we shall cross that frontier one day. Only then maybe we can understand what is happening today.

Brigadier, what do you say about all the huge amount of documents still held at official archives? What should be done about that?

What should be done is what is being done, that is, the disclosure triggered by ufologists. The government should call for intelligent people who are interested in the subject and put those materials in their hands – or at least facilitate their access to those files.

Do you support our campaign *UFOs: Liberdade de Informação Já* which calls for the government to open those files?

You can be sure about that! Files must be opened and you should go on with your campaign towards the government in order to make that happen *[emphatic]*. Then you come to tell me what you've got besides what you already have now.

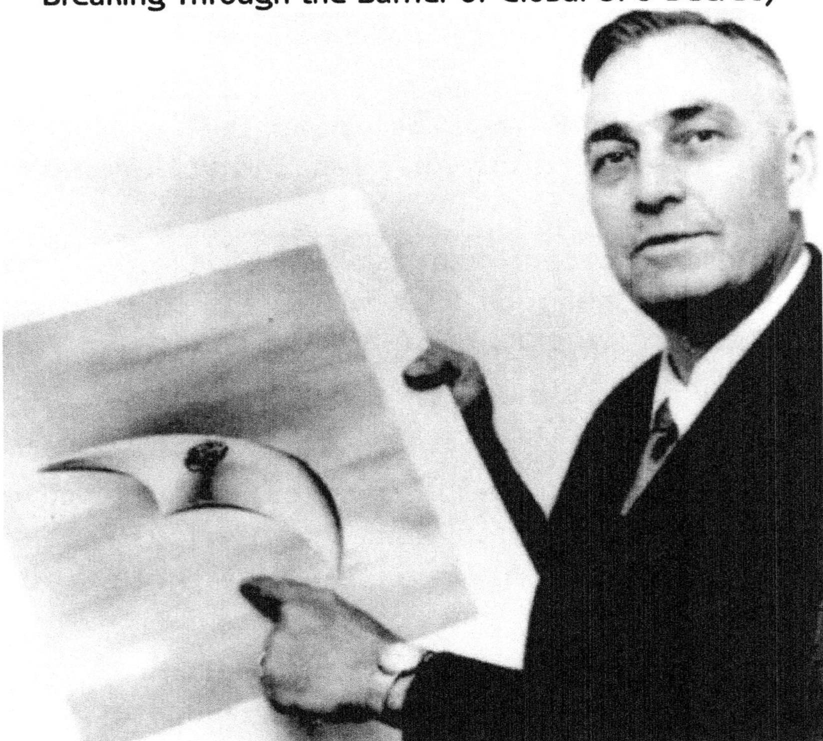

Crescent-shaped UFO, one of objects pilot Kenneth Arnold said he saw on June 24, 1947

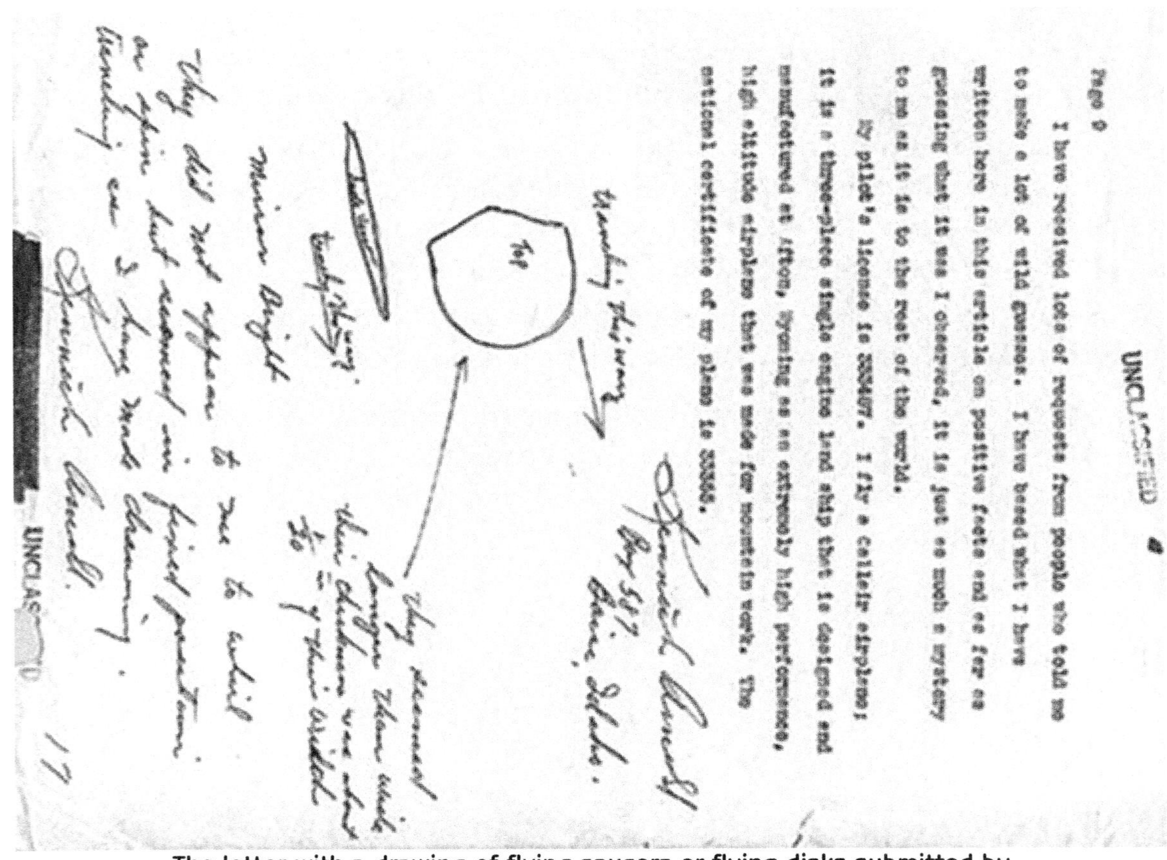

UNCLASSIFIED

Page 9

I have received lots of requests from people who told me to make a lot of wild guesses. I have based what I have written here in this article on positive facts and as far as guessing what it was I observed, it is just as much a mystery to me as it is to the rest of the world.

My pilot's license is 333487. I fly a Callair airplane; it is a three-place single engine land ship that is designed and manufactured at Afton, Wyoming as an extremely high performance, high altitude airplane that was made for mountain work. The national certificate of my plane is 33355.

Kenneth Arnold
Box 587
Boise, Idaho.

traveling this way

Top

they seemed longer than wide their thickness was about 1/20 of their width

traveling this way

Mirror Bright

They did not appear to me to whirl or spin but seemed in fixed position traveling as I have made drawing.

Kenneth Arnold.

17

UNCLASSIFIED

The letter with a drawing of flying saucers or flying disks submitted by pilot Kenneth Arnold to Army Air Force intelligence on July 12, 1947

DISCLOSURE IN FRANCE: SOME ASTONISHING REVELATIONS

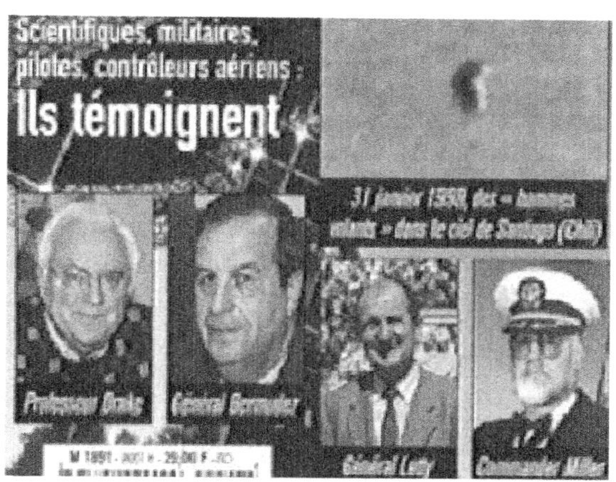

Many French admirals and generals are among those who take Disclosure seriously.

The French have a history of UFOs. The average citizen doesn't mock the subject. Going back to the early and mid-1950s aliens of one type or another – usually small, but tough as nails, humanoids – were landing and fighting the French as if it were the end of the Great War. A lot of these dramatic incidents made it into the press and the subject was more or less taken seriously from the get go. Landing pads were found in the soil out in the countryside and mushrooms and other vegetation was growing to exceptional size after being zapped by the extraterrestrials, or however we wish to define the place of their origin. The French have always had their UFO experts – for example Jacques Vallee – and numerous authors whose sensationalistic words no doubt kept many a French reader up late at night. So when the French government decided in March of 2007 to release some of its classified UFO files, your typical Parisian might not have been overly impressed, but the rather effete Washington Post did take notice.

Under intelligent control, a UFO lifts off in Beamunder.

"On an August day," an article in the paper begins, "two children tending a herd of cows outside a village in central France reported seeing 'four small black beings' fly from the ground and slip headfirst into a sphere that shot skyward in a flash of light and left behind a trail of sulfuric odors.

"It was made in the 1680s in France and the design on one side certainly looks like it could be a flying saucer in the clouds over the countryside," said Kenneth E. Bressett of Colorado Springs, Colorado, a former President of the 32,000-member American Numismatic Association and owner of the curious coin.

"The alleged extraterrestrial sighting, described by the French government as 'one of the most astonishing observed in France,' is among 1,600 UFO case files spanning the last half century that the country's space agency opened to the public for the first time Thursday [March 22, 2007]."

In what the venerable American newspaper called "an unprecedented move," the voluntary decision to release the files in France made available more than 100,000 pages of witness testimony, photographs, film footage and audiotapes from its secret UFO archives.

Most Western countries, the article said, the U.S. included, consider such records classified matters of national security.

UFOs STILL AN OPEN QUESTION

Within three hours of posting the first cases, the French space agency's web server crashed, overwhelmed by the flood of viewers seeking a first glimpse of the official government evidence on a subject long a target of both fascination and ridicule. The material dates back as far as 1954 and is being posted to enhance scientific research into what the French government calls "unexplained aerospace phenomena."

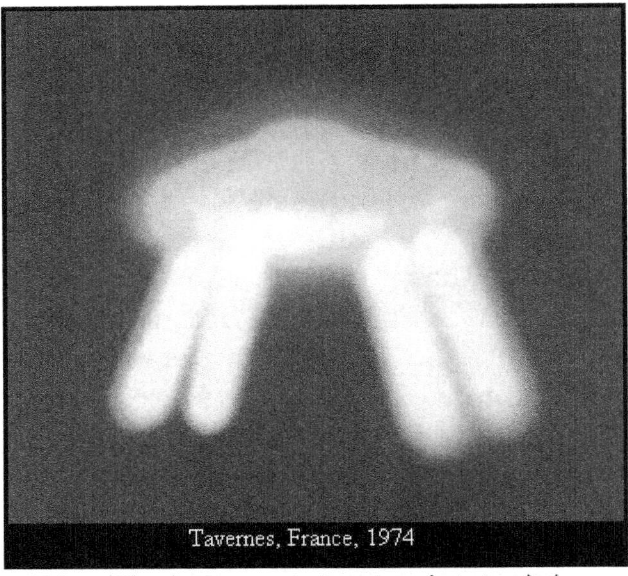

Tavernes, France, 1974

UFO emitting beams seems to get ready to touch down.

"The data we are releasing," said Jacques Patenet, who heads the Group for the Study and Information on Unidentified Aerospace Phenomena, "doesn't demonstrate the presence of extraterrestrial beings. But it doesn't demonstrate the impossibility of such a presence either. The question remains open."

Patenet also said that a few dozen cases among the 1,600 to be opened to the public "are very intriguing and can be called UFOs."

Most of the cases in the files were determined to be caused by atmospheric anomalies or the mistaken perception of such things as airplane lights or simply hoaxes. One file case described how investigators proved that a man was lying about being abducted by aliens when blood tests failed to prove he had recently experienced the weightlessness of space travel.

A STRUGGLE WITH HELMETED HUMANOIDS

The publication Nord Éclair, September 16, 1954, announced the encounter of Marius Dewilde. On the night of September 10, 1954, Dewilde was at home in Quarouble, Nord, France. His house was built near some train tracks. At 22:30, his dog started to bark desperately. Dewilde went outside with a flashlight and the dog itself. He walked towards the tracks, where he saw an object some 6 or 7 meters away from him. Behind him, he could hear some steps. When he pointed the flashlight, Dewilde saw two small humanoid figures who were as short as children. When the light was pointed to their heads, it was reflected as if they were wearing a mirror helmet or some kind of shiny material.

Suddenly, a light beam shot off the object he saw on the tracks and left him totally paralyzed. He slowly looked back and saw a door opening in the object behind him. The beings boarded the object and it took off towards the sky, changing its colors as it flew.

When he recovered his ability to move, he attempted to tell his wife and then his neighbor what he had just seen, but neither of them had seen nor heard anything. He then tried the local police, who sent some police officers to his home. Dewilde could not approach the point where everything happened because it made him feel sick, giving the officers a certainty that his story was not a hoax. Also, objects which are energized by batteries, like Dewilde's flashlight and telephone, stopped working. Before sunrise, investigators were already thoroughly covering the scene of the strange event.

AFTERMATH

The Evening Star, October 19, 1954, reported the encounter of Marius Dewilde and the other minor incidents that happened on the following days.When people were investigating the location of the object's appearance, an approaching train produced a very loud noise when passing by, making it stop. A six meter depression was found on the exact point where the object had landed, and was immediately said to be the cause of the noise.

During daylight, more details were discovered: the small rocks placed under the train tracks were all carbonized on the depression. The pieces of wood between the steel lines also featured some symmetric marks.

The incident was made famous by the local magazine RADAR.

More small incidents were added to this main happening: Dewilde suffered from respiratory problems, his dog died three days after the encounter, three cows died on farms nearby (and their autopsies revealed that their blood had been totally and unexplainably removed). Also, several local people claimed sights of objects and creatures similar to the ones witnessed by Dewilde.

FRENCH CHILDREN ARE VISITED

Here comes the fleet? Well at least two UFOs recorded over Chantureine, France in 1973.

"In one of the cases investigators consider most credible," the article continues, "a 13-year-old boy and his 9-year-old sister were watching over their family's cows near the village of Cussac on August 29, 1967, when the boy spotted 'four small black beings' about 47 inches tall, according to documents released Thursday. Thinking they were other youngsters, he shouted to his sister, 'Oh, there are black children!'

"But as they watched, the four beings became agitated and rose into the air, entering the top of what appeared to be a round spaceship, about 15 feet in diameter, which hovered over the field. Just as the sphere rose up, one of the passengers emerged from the top, returned to the ground to grab something, then flew back to the sphere. The sphere rose silently in a spiral pattern, then 'became increasingly brilliant' before disappearing with a loud whistling sound. It left a 'strong sulfur odor after departure,' the report said."

RADAR

VALENCIENNES

RECONSTITUE LA FANTASMAGORIQUE APPARITION "MARTIENNE" QUI SIDÉRA Marius DEWILDE

A French tabloid illustrates the encounter adding to the sensationalism of the event.

The children raced home in tears and their father called the local police, who duly noted the sulfur smell and the dried grass left behind when the sphere took off. Investigators said they were impressed at how consistent the stories told by the children and other witnesses were under further questioning. The investigators concluded that, "No rational explanation has been given to date of this exceptional meeting."

AIR FRANCE SIGHTING

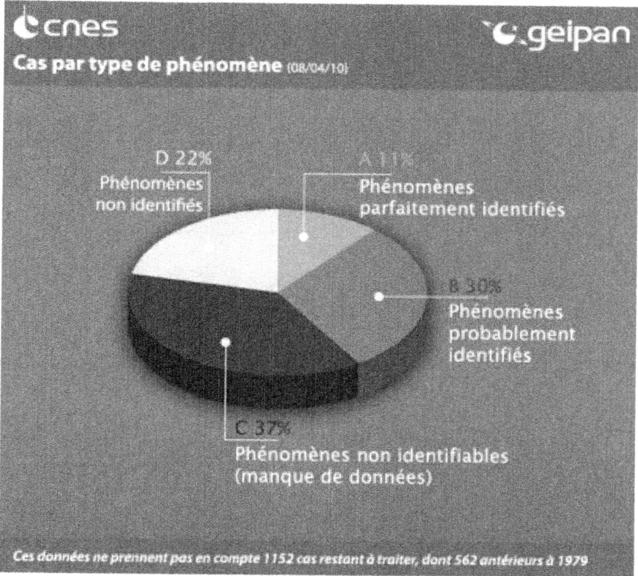

France's official UAP group openly admits that a sizeable percentage of unknowns they have cataloged.

One of the most detailed inquiries involved the report of an Air France crew flying near Paris on January 28, 1994.

"Three crew members spotted a large, reddish-brown disk 'whose form is constantly changing and which seems very big in size.' As the passenger plane crossed its trajectory, the object 'disappeared on the spot.' Radar signatures confirmed an object of the same size and location described by the crew and led investigators to conclude that 'the phenomenon is not explained to date and leaves the door open to all the assumptions.'"

MORE COMMENTS FROM PATENET

Patenet, the lead investigator for the French space agency's team, said he and his colleagues receive about 100 new cases every year, of which only 10 percent lead to further investigations.

"In 99 percent of the cases," he said, "the witnesses are perfectly sincere. They saw something. Most of the time, what they saw is a perfectly natural phenomenon that has been perceived in an erroneous way."

Jacques Patenet heads the Group for the Study and Information on Unidentified Aerospace Phenomena.

Patenet said he has never seen a UFO, though he believes it is unlikely that we are alone in the universe.

"But the probability of various civilizations coming across each other is also very slim," he said.

To read some of the French files in English, go to http://geipan-english.blogspot.com.

SOUCOUPE VOLANTE?

Rien n'est invraisemblable dans les déclarations du garde-barrière de Quarouble

...ET LA POLICE DE L'AIR A PRIS AU SÉRIEUX TOUTE CETTE AFFAIRE

De notre envoyé spécial
MICHEL DUFOREST

POUR la première fois depuis l'apparition de mystérieux engins baptisés « soucoupes volantes », on a pu relever, à Quarouble, près de Valenciennes, des traces laissées par l'un de ces appareils. Six griffes, disposées en demi-cercle sur des traverses d'une ligne de chemin de fer peu fréquentée, semblent prouver qu'en cet endroit un contact ou un frottement s'est produit entre le bois et une matière plus dure.

C'est tout ce que l'on peut affirmer pour le moment. Mais les services de police de l'armée de l'Air qui ont photographié chacune des empreintes et prélevé quelques-uns des cailloux épars sur le ballast ont peut-être déjà tiré d'autres conclusions qu'ils garderont jalousement à l'abri du secret militaire.

Car si le public demeure sceptique vis-à-vis de tout ce qui se rapporte aux « Soucoupes volantes », il n'en va pas de même de la police de l'Air dont une des sections est spécialement chargée des enquêtes les concernant. Jusqu'alors, aucun fait matériel n'était venu corroborer les dires des témoins et c'est pourquoi les marques faites à Quarouble permettront peut-être de lever un coin du voile.

MARIUS NE GALEGE PAS TOUJOURS

Sans doute, l'histoire commence bien pour les incrédules puisqu'elle est racontée par... Marius Dewilde. Mais l'éclat de rire qui accueille ce prénom cesse lorsque l'on entame le récit.

Pour obtenir plus de garanties, ce n'est pas à M. Dewilde que j'ai demandé de raconter les faits dont il fut témoin le vendredi 10 septembre. Car depuis ce jour, il a pu être influencé par les questions des enquêteurs et des dizaines de journalistes qui ont défilé chez lui. Les interrogatoires qu'il a subis pour vérifier s'il ne mentait pas ou s'il n'était pas victime d'une hallucination, ont pu travailler son imagination, et, involontairement, il serait susceptible aujourd'hui, d'ajouter des détails au récit primitif. Ce phénomène normal chez l'homme le plus équilibré s'expliquerait d'autant plus facilement que depuis bientôt une semaine, M. Dewilde lit dans une « presse à sensations » des histoires qui n'ont absolum nt plus rien de ressemblant avec ses propos.

La suite en dernière page

« La soucoupe était posée en travers de la voie, spécifia M. DEWILDE. Sur ces traverses de bois, vous pouvez voir les traces laissées par les béquilles de l'engin. La police de l'air a relevé des traces en même temps que des cailloux et pierres qui se trouvaient sous l'appareil, aux fins d'examens ».

Witness stands on the stop where the struggle with strange beings took place.

PILOT REPORTS OUT CHILEAN GOVERNMENT: OFFICIALS AREN'T AFRAID TO ACKNOWLEDGE THE TRUTH!

The time to start Disclosure in Chile seemed to be mounting for over a decade. And finally on April 2, 1997 the South American country found it exceedingly hard to tell their citizens that UFOs couldn't possibly exist. For it had been just a month earlier that a legitimate UFO wave seem to have hit the country and its territories. Luis Sanchez, Chilean Director of Skywatch International said this was the first time such an organization had attached its name to a confirmed UFO observation statement. La Direccion General de Aeronautic Civil wrote that they publicly recognized that Chile was experiencing UFO sightings and that the phenomenon was real, not a natural, conventional phenomenon such as meteoritic or climatic.

Huge mothership passes over Santiago, Chile in recent UFO wave.

The event that started this official recognition was a very seriously documented observation by the staff of an air traffic control tower at the Chacalluta International Airport in Arica, the northernmost city in Chile. On Monday, 31st March, 1997, at 12:55am, three UFOs were visually seen by the staff from the control tower and recorded on radar. They were tracked at speeds up to 8,000 mph according to the eyewitnesses, over the Pacific Ocean, near Morro de Arica. They remained there for two hours. At about 3.00am, the objects "flew away at very high speed," heading for the Andes.

The Airport's director, Julio Schettner stated that the UFOs hovered "at an altitude between 3,000 and 4,500 meters and emitted blue, red, green and yellow lights which made them clearly visible to the naked eye. In our tower, it was not possible to track them on radar, so we contacted the radar control rooms in (Arequipa) Peru and Santiago (de Chile). None of them had flights registering in Arica at that moment."

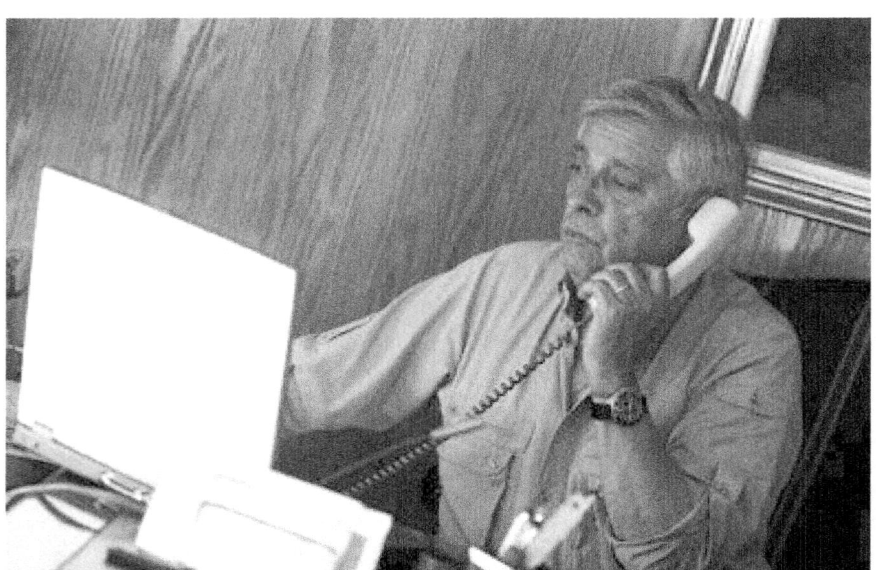
Retired General Vega was one of the first officials to endorse Disclosure in Chile.

Schettner said that he had been doubtful about the existence of UFOs, but not anymore," adding that they left Arica "at an astonishing speed."

On Wednesday 2nd April 1997, the Direccion General de Aeronautica Civil (DGAC), Chile's civilian aeronautical ministry, announced that the three UFOs in Arica had been confirmed on radar, DGAC radar and Fuerzas Aereas de Chile (FACh) Air Force radar tracked the Arica UFOs "travelling at speeds of up to 12,800 kilometres (8,000 miles) per hour."

In the capital, Santiago de Chile, a DGAC spokesman said, "Chile is experiencing OVNIs" (Spanish acronym for UFO).

Apparently, Chile has had a very high number of documented reports from pilots --- private, commercial and military. John Wigle managed to translate these high altitude encounters, and no doubt there are others still to be published in English.

1. Place: Chacalluta Airport, Arica
Date: 19 May 1972
Time: 01:30 UTC
No. Of Witnesses: Aircrew
Type of A/C: B-727
Duration: Unknown
Radar Detection: No

Description: Lan 90 close to the airport informed that over the city, approximately 4000 ft, observes to amber light with medium size making revolutions. The pilot describes that the speed and type of revolutions resemble a medium size helix plane. Near the city the object could not be observed anymore because the Lan 90 passed below a stratus-cumulus cloud formation, in north position of the city.

2. Place: Chacalluta Airport, Arica
Date: 16 September 1972
Time: 02:30 UTC
No. Of Witnesses: Aircrew
Type of A/C: Curtiss 46
Duration: Unknown
Radar Detection: No

Description: LASA registration CLA was flying in approximation at South reports a luminous orange object above the city, approximately at 2,000 ft.

3. Place: Cerro Moreno Airport, Antofogasta
Date: 02 February 1979
Time: 03:08 UTC
No. Of Witnesses: Aircrew
Type of A/C: Unknown
Duration: Unknown
Radar Detection: No

Description: Army aircraft who had taken off with flight plan IFR to Iquique, called traffic control at 80 level. The crew reported a strange object at left side position, at the same level. The object had an orange color and an inverted "V" shape. The object moved South at high speed. A fishery aircraft in lateral flying at Coloso observed the object at North position in approximation, confirming the report of Army aircraft. The crew commented that the object has a great dimension. The object disappears to the South at great speed.

4. Place: Cerro Moreno Airport, Antofogasta
Date: 26 February 1979
Time: 07:36 UTC
No. Of Witnesses: Aircrew and ATC's
Type of A/C: Cessna 310
Duration: Unknown
Radar Detection: No

Description: Airship registration CFM, in fishing prospecting to the South of the field, reports an object of yellow color at great speed moving from South to North, then hovering to the West of the airport. It disappears toward the East diminishing in size. Phenomenon was witnessed by the personnel of shift of the ACC and TWR. The airport was covered with 8/8 Sc to 235 measured meters.

5. Place: Chacalluta Airport, Arica **Date: 09 June 1983**
Time: 23:55 UTC **No. Of Witnesses: Aircrew and ATC**
Type of A/C: Cessna 337 **Duration: 45 minutes**
Radar Detection: No **EM: Possible EMI – communication interference**

Description: Shift ATC observes a ray of light coming from the West that points toward the airport. The brightness is produced by an object in cone form, of big dimensions, suspended on the sea that carried out horizontal quick movements among the radial 240 and 270 of the VOR of Arica. Airship of fishing prospecting, flying to 20 NM to the West of Corazones observes the same phenomenon. It describes it as a luminous circle that later transforms into a cone of white color. It is not detected by the radar of the airplane. In a moment the airship suffers interferences of the communications among the fishing schooners and with the control tower. In an instant the phenomenon is observed by the personal ATC of the Iquique airport, 104 miles to the South. The object remains stationary and then at great speed moves toward the South. The airplane recovers the communications.

6. Place: La Florida Airport, La Serena **Date: 30 August1 1983**
Time: 23:57 UTC **No. Of Witnesses: Aircrew**
Type of A/C: Cessna 337 **Duration: Unknown**
Radar Detection: No **EM: Possible EMI – communication interference**

Description: Airship registration CGF in works of fishing prospecting in the sector West of the radio station Tongoy gives notice of having a non-identified object visible flying in a Northerly direction. It describes it like a nebula in an egg shape with a brilliant disk in center. The phenomenon is observed jointly with pilots of other fishing airship registration CEA and captains of fishing craft in the area. The object moved to great height, it varied its direction heading for the city of Vallenar. It moved toward the NW and then got lost toward the North. Pilot of the CGF informed that when the object approached the radio station Tongoy with direction 020° position that the airplane flew over, lost contact with all the fishing ships, with the control tower and with the other airship, in HF and VHF. As the object went away contact was slowly recovered.

7 . Place: Terminal Area of Santiago **Date: 17 August 1985**
Time: 19:00 UTC **No. Of Witnesses: Aircrew and people in the city**
Type of A/C: Cessna 172, B-727 and DC-10 **Duration: More than 4 hours**
Radar Detection: Yes

Description: Airship CC LHL (Cessna 172) with flight plan Limache --Tobalaba reports having seen an object (globe type in shape) visible, seemingly metallic and very luminous. Same observation is reported by the Ladeco 061 (B-727) at level 370 who indicates that the object, very brilliant, is higher. The radar shows a blank unidentified target at 20 NM to the West of the radio station El Tabón. One hour later the object appears again on the radar to 38 NM at East position of Umkal. The personnel of Mendoza's airport (Argentina) communicates to Santiago's ACC (Chile) that they are seeing the object. The phenomenon is observed by hundreds of people and is filmed by a television channel. The flight 423 of Canadian Pacific (DC-10), with flight plan Ezeiza-Santiago, on position Umkal, informs that ten minutes before it detected with the onboard radar, at 39,000 ft., an object 92 miles to the South of the position and seemingly with its own light. The object stayed for more than four hours in the space of Santiago's TMA, the biggest static time, although it also displayed very slow displacement toward the West. Although the gross sign of the primary radar was intermittent, it was possible to calculate its speed at 33 knots.

8. Place: El Tepual Airport, Puerto Montt **Date: 01 June 1988**
Time: 00:10 UTC **No. Of Witnesses: Aircrew and ATC's**
Type of A/C: : B-737 **Duration: 10 to 15 minutes**
Radar Detection: No

Description: Flight Lan 045 next to begin descent for an approach. IFR reports having traffic to the front with an opposed direction that forces him to make an abrupt turn to avoid an imminent collision. Minutes before the object was seen by the personnel ATC of the airport, stationary and some 10 miles to the North of the threshold 17, then moving at great speed toward the North, in contrary direction to flight 045. The phenomenon was described for the controllers as being an object that exhibited several white lights in the upper part and four purple and green lights in the lower parts; the base seemed to be flat and of an approximate diameter of 60 meters. The white lights were steady and the lower lights flashed strongly. The aircrew observed a great white light that changed colors to purple and green.

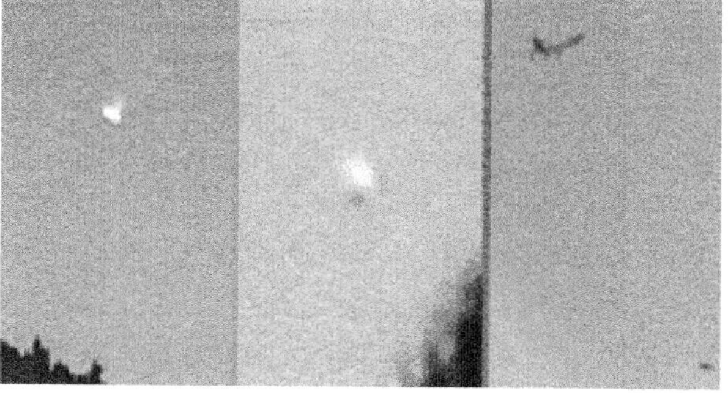

Unidentified security guard took this photo circa 2010 by the shoreline.

* * * * *

Chile is no stranger to aerial anomalies . . . hundreds of documented reports have become the norm as witnesses from all walks of life add to the weight of the testimony for truth in disclosure. Scott Corrales editorial director of Inexplicata-The Journal of Hispanic Ufology has a team of Spanish speaking correspondence worldwide who send him a constant flow of material for release over the internet at inexplicata.blogspot.com/

Among the aerial abnormalities Corrales has been collecting data on as of late is the increase in UFO sightings since the advent of the recent earthquakes in the nation. These are two such reports he translated and filed.

Chile: Sixteen UFO Cases Reported on Earthquake Night

By Natalia Heusser

Source: www.publimetro.cl/nota/noticias/van-16-casos-de-avistamientos-ovni-solo-en-la-noche-del-terremoto/xIQjcs!mayYEkZFm7I3A
Date: 03.18.10

The earthquake was followed by a boom in UFO sightings, but sixteen cases occurred on the night of the tragedy alone (some of them accompanied by significant visual material) which have been subjected to study by UFO researchers.

Researcher Rodrigo Fuenzalida told Publimetro that the highest concentrations of reports appear to be Las Condes, Peñalolén, Providencia and Colina. "We have eyewitness testimony from a couple that refused to sleep in their apartment on the night of the earthquake, choosing instead to spend the early morning hours in the street. They were able to see an object that looked much like the moon, but immediately realized that the moon was on the other side. This event may have been seen by residents of other communes," said Fuenzalida.

Another major sighting took place on Isla Robinson Crusoe, part of the Juan Fernandez Archipelago, where people witnessed an object emerging from the sea shortly before the earthquake.

Regarding the case involving a humanoid -- reported by passengers on a bus in Iquique -- Fuenzalida notes that while startling, he is aware of other similar cases, but people "do not dare report them, fearing that they will not be believed.

"I've heard of the manifestations of these "luminous men", said the ufologist. "We are in an ideal period for sightings. I would ask everyone to be alert, but be mindful to avoid confusion, or a state of hysteria."

A followup interview with a respected Chilean researcher bought the subject more into light. . .

Given the important UFO and high-strangeness events taking place in Chile, we contacted researcher Rodrigo Fuenzalida of AION to get a sense of the magnitude of the situation. Chile has an extended history of UFO sightings and was considered – for decades – one of the most reliable sources of reports involving ground traces and non-humans presences. Mr. Fuenzalida took time from his busy schedule to answer a few questions posed by INEXPLICATA.

Hi, Rodrigo. What's going on in Iquique?

The fact is that all of the symptoms of a UFO Wave are emerging in Iquique. Since the month of December [2009] we have been getting UFO reports – some of them very well documented, with photographs and even videos taken in broad daylight. In the months that have elapsed since, the amassed information has been more consistent, especially because a considerable number of cases have not been made known to the press, thus eliminating any "contamination" of the communications regarding sightings.

Do you think the current wave is in any way related with the earthquake?

The earthquake occurred over 1600 kilometers away from Tarapacá, although UFO reports have emerged from areas affected by the quake, and there's even material collected by various sources, such as the CNN video on a fallen building in the city of Concepción. However, sightings were frequent in the city of Iquique. We know that an earthquake is coming to northern Chile, but we don't know when. It's a challenge to see the measure in which seismic activity could be related to UFO manifestations.

Is the wave currently experienced in Tarapacá greater than others in the past?

Yes, indeed. I believe it's the most widely documented wave in the region. Several of these reports have included records, multiple witnesses, manifestations occurring at different times of day, and sometimes low-flying objects. We've received reports from truck drivers in the Atacama Desert who have been a short distance away from these UFOs. We also have coastal reports involving objects being seen over the sea. With such a track record, it's possible to consider this as the most important UFO wave in northern Chile in recorded history.

What's your take on worldwide movements that seek the "disclosure" of UFO information?

I think these movements serve the purpose of institutional legitimating of the UFO phenomenon, confirming the widely known secret that several of our world's governments have expressed concern over the subject of UFOs. Probably as a subject tied to defense, aimed at sensing the degree to which these reports involved secret prototypes belonging to some world power or another. I think they should contribute toward the challenge we face at the moment: trying to ascertain what in fact are UFOs. In order to achieve this, efforts must be focused on bolder scientific research projects regarding the subject.

Any thoughts you'd like to share with your readers in the U.S.A.?

We are highly alert to what's going on in Chile, and we are also monitoring the phenomenon's behavior all over the planet in order to observe patterns of behavior. The Internet has become a major tool in obtaining information on UFO activity all over the world. We ask that ufologists give our hypotheses an adequate review and break with the dogmas that are often created around the subject, and which are not based upon reliable information. We invite our friends to visit us at www.aion.cl

UFO Photographed Over Chilean Desert by Bus Passengers in Chile

DISCLOSURE PATTERNS, PROFILES AND PERSONALITIES

- Lobbyist Stephen Bassett: Seeking A Political Solution
- Grant Cameron And The UFO Legacy Of The Presidents
- A. J. Gevaerd: Making A Big Dent In The Wall Of Silence
- Antonio Huneeus: Meeting A General And Working With A Giant
- Nick Pope: The Quiet Brit And The Perfect Storm
- John Greenwald: NORAD And UFOs

91-F01-1030
JANAP 146(E)
32 pgs.

CANADIAN - UNITED STATES COMMUNICATIONS INSTRUCTIONS FOR REPORTING VITAL INTELLIGENCE SIGHTINGS

(CIRVIS/MERINT)
JANAP 146(E)

THIS PUBLICATION CONTAINS US MILITARY INFORMATION AND RELEASE TO OTHER THAN US MILITARY AGENCIES WILL BE ON A NEED-TO-KNOW BASIS.

THE JOINT CHIEFS OF STAFF
WASHINGTON, D.C., 20301

MARCH 1966

FOR OFFICIAL USE ONLY
UNCLASSIFIED

I

#392

CHANGE NO. 2
(REVERSE BLANK)

LOBBYIST STEPHEN BASSETT: SEEKING A POLITICAL SOLUTION

By Sean Casteel

He's positively the head honcho of the Disclosure movement. When I interviewed Stephen Bassett, I came away impressed with both his determination to wrest the truth of the UFO phenomenon out of the hands of the secret keepers in Washington and his seemingly indomitable belief that he can succeed where so many information seekers have previously failed. His indefatigable efforts in that regard may one day lead to the Disclosure with a big "D" that he feels is so inevitable and so right for this country and the world at large. While he readily acknowledges that America is still a force for great good in the world, Bassett also feels that ending what he calls the government's "Truth Embargo" on UFOs is a necessary component of the process of restoring our trust in our leaders.

*****

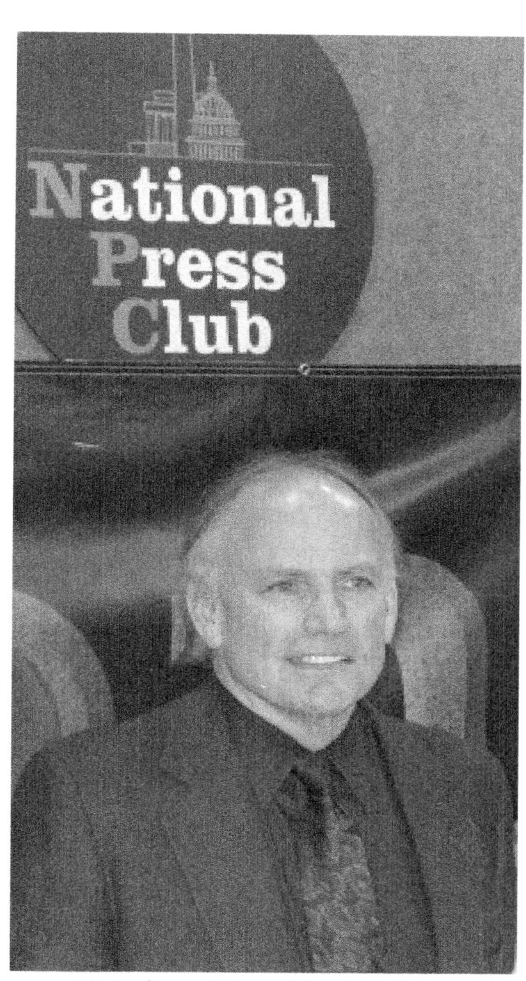

Stephen Bassett at the National Press Club

Q. Can we start with some biographical background? When and why did you become interested in UFOs? Have you personally had a sighting experience?

Bassett: Not such an easy question to answer. I was aware of the subject my whole life, but I did nothing about it. I was pretty convinced, just on what I'd been able to read from articles and various things that turned up, that the ET hypothesis was the only thing that made sense. I was probably in that position by the time I was 22. But I didn't do anything about this. I studied science and physics and stuff and I was going to go off and possibly work with NASA, but that didn't work out. So essentially, when I made the decision back in 1995 that I really wanted to get into something that for me was meaningful and had some interesting possibilities, this issue came to mind. I started doing some research and I read [the late Dr. John] Mack's book "Abduction," which had an enormous influence on me. The fact that a Pulitzer Prize-winning Harvard psychiatrist was engaging this issue in a formal way was a very big deal. So I did some other research, and the upshot was that I could sense very strongly that the issue was getting ready to pop, that something was going to give on this.

It was obviously incredibly significant, and the potential implications were profound. So I made the decision that this is what I wanted to do. I was able to persuade John Mack's organization in Cambridge, Massachusetts, the Program for Extraordinary Experience Research (PEER), to let me come out and work with them on a volunteer basis, which I did, for about four months. That was my entrance into the field, so it was kind of a very high-end and very energizing initial engagement to start getting involved. But it wasn't a fit for me. It really wasn't where I needed to be, and I understood that after a while. Then I moved down to Washington and started up the Paradigm Research Group. So that's how I got involved. It was kind of an intellectual process. I've never had a UFO sighting of any consequence. I have not had any kind of contact, or for that matter, any paranormal experience whatsoever. I'm afraid I've had a rather boring life in that regard.

Though I'm surrounded by people, as it happens, who, well, their lives are not boring. They're picking up stuff from all over the place and having all kinds of experiences and encounters. But not myself. I'm kind of meat and potatoes.

Q. What led to your work in the Disclosure movement? Why did the politics of Disclosure attract you so much?

Bassett: Well, I was in Cambridge, and this was kind of a research setting, somewhat academic, a lot of academic people on the board. That wasn't my mindset and I knew I really had to leave. I couldn't stay. It's funny, but it just sort of came to me. I was in the office there one day, this was I think in late May of 1996, and it just came to me, what I could do, what my niche would be in this. It was because I had lived off and on in Washington for many years. I've lived all over, but I've been in Washington, and I had family that had been based just outside of Washington since the 1930s. I knew that I could go back and have a place to live and a place to work out of and that what I would do is really try to engage this issue from a political perspective and try to get it resolved politically. And that's just what I did. I went down to Bethesda, I moved in with a family member, set up the Paradigm Research Group and registered as a lobbyist. I knew that it was going to be the first lobbying registration of its kind ever and I knew that would attract attention, that the political press would immediately find out about that. It would generate some media discussion, thus giving me a door into this and some exposure. That's exactly what happened. From that point forward, it was increasingly clear with each passing month or so that this was in fact what I wanted to do, that this was the way to go about this.

Getting a point across at the National Press Club.

By the time I'd been up in Cambridge for a while, I had developed a pretty strong sense that the scientific approach to the issue, which had come to be called "Ufology" by the citizen-scientists who were slaving away trying to understand this, trying to prove it per se, in spite of the government's policy that there was nothing to prove, had gone as far as it could go. It simply wasn't going to finish the job – it couldn't, because this was not an even playing field. This was a rigged game based upon a formal government policy. So it was going to take a political solution, and no amount of field work, and no amount of logging in sightings or anything else was going to get that done. It was going to take politics. So that's why I realized that's what I wanted to do. I felt even then, but even stronger now, that the only way to resolve this is through political policy change.

Q. Do you hold any degrees?

Bassett: I have a degree in physics from Eckert College. I had a couple of years at Georgia Tech, but I finished up at Eckert College. It was called Fordham Presbyterian back then. That degree is in 1970 and at that school in St. Petersburg, Florida. A bachelor's in physics.

Q. I've talked to other researchers in the field of disclosure, but none of them seem to take your activist approach to the subject. Please discuss some of your activism through the PRG. Just tell us some of your stories of approaching members of Congress and the straight media. Do you encounter a lot of ridicule and hostility in your work?

Bassett: Not really. You said you talked to a number of researchers. Do you mean ufologists or researchers in the political stuff?

Q. I meant more the political stuff. I've talked to John Greenewald and Grant Cameron. We're going to be talking to A.J. Gevaerd.

Million Fax on Washington
Phase - II
White House in Transition
The First 100 Days - January 20, 2009 - April 30, 2009

Bassett was behind the Million Fax Disclosure effort.

Bassett: Okay. Well, John is an activist of sorts, but now he's really involved in media, he's involved in production work. And Grant is a researcher who doesn't want to be an activist, which is appropriate. He's trying to maintain an objective position. Though occasionally he says something that I consider of an activist nature. That's what they do, and I think it's understandable that they can't match doing what I do. An activist, an advocate, is not neutral. There is a goal; there is a purpose to what you're doing. And you're driven by strong views about the way things are. This is the nature of activism. It's nice if you're right and, generally, if you're right, there's the chance that it will produce perhaps good results. But sometimes activists are completely wrong, and what they're pursuing is actually not going to be helpful at all. But that's it. Have you picked well and do you know what you're doing? So the advocacy work has developed somewhat of a rift or a fault line between the ufologists, those who pursue the science, that come under that nomenclature and often refer to themselves as that, and the activists. There is definitely a separation there. The ufologists, particularly the ones who are committed to the science of it and trying to understand it that way, are very concerned that the political advocacy is going to damage their work or lower the probability of making a breakthrough. It will be counterproductive. In other words, they think it should be pursued along the lines that they have pursued it. And a lot of these guys, these activists, are new in town, they're new guys on the block, and they don't go back that many years. So there is some concern there. I understand it and I don't think it's going to go away.

The Paradigm Research Group was created with one purpose only, and that was to end the Truth Embargo by helping to bring about the Disclosure Event. That is the simplest way to say that. The Truth Embargo is a formal policy of the government to contain this issue, deliberately, by whatever means possible, sometimes not legally. That policy was formulated between 1947 and 1952, and then in 1953 I think it was hardened, and it's still in place. It's been 62 years since Roswell. And it involves all manner of things. Misinformation, disinformation, undermining research, harassing people, putting out false reports, straight, flat denial, lies when appropriate, you name it. Whatever it took, including using their assets, like "The National Enquirer," which was actually a product of the CIA as well as "The Weekly World News," to plant stories and all that kind of stuff. And just contain the issue, ghettoize the issue, as I like to say, so it couldn't go anywhere. That it wouldn't be able to get money or a proper media response or the schools would have nothing to do with it. Thus it would not get to the point where it could force a government policy change. That was the Truth Embargo. Ending it is the goal of the political activism of the disclosure process. Disclosure, with a capital D, is the goal. It's the formal acknowledgement of the ET presence by the world governments. It's not the release of information. That's small d disclosure. It's not witnesses coming forward. That's small d disclosure. It is the formal acknowledgement. When President Obama, when President Sarkozy, when Gordon Brown, when Putin, when the Chinese premier, when they tell their people that the ET presence is real, that is Disclosure. Everything that PRG does is aimed at that one fundamental goal, to get that done. Now whether it's registering as a lobbyist, whether it's talking to people on the Hill, whether it's lobbying the political media, whether it's launching the X Conference, the Exo-Politics World Network, the United States Network, running for Congress as an Independent candidate, all of that. The speaking engagements, the tens of thousands of press releases, all of that is designed to end this Truth Embargo.

As far as talking to people on the Hill, I talked to some people on the Hill in the early days and it was pretty clear that the Congress was virtually a block of cement. It sort of congealed into an impenetrable mass and it couldn't get anything done. This I sensed early on in 1996, 1997. And that was during the Clinton administration, when supposedly things were a little better. Nothing that's happened since has changed my mind. Congress is almost impossible to deal with and it's fundamentally dysfunctional. Which is why its approval rating as of two weeks ago was 16 percent, two percent off the all time low of 14 percent. A 16 percent approval rating for an institution is phenomenal. I mean, mass murderers – Ted Bundy had a better approval rating. If they couldn't do anything about regular, mainstream issues, then they certainly weren't going to do anything about this issue.

So I shifted my focus to the media because it was clear that in the modern era the process of anything happening is really a joint process going on between the government and the political media. If you've got an issue and you want it to go somewhere, then you get it to the media. The media starts dealing with it. They start writing it up. They start talking it up and they put it in play. Then you can step forward and move on it. If the media doesn't get onboard your train, you're not going anywhere. So the political media are like a second Congress, and it's a lot easier to lobby them frankly than it is to lobby the Congress. So I really started focusing on the political media in Washington, just pumping information to them for years, trying to get somebody to move. It wasn't easy but it was more promising. The media's job is to cover the news, to get information out, so what you're giving them is exactly what they want: major news stories. They can choose to cover it or not cover it. Congress is a whole different ballgame. They're supposed to make laws, but of course really their whole job is to stay in office. So getting information is not primary to them at all. Telling the truth is not primary to them at all. The journalists, under the journalistic oath, are supposed to be objective and tell the truth. That's not the case with Congress. Lying is an institutional tool there. So again I felt that the political media was the most promising route and I put a lot of emphasis there.

Q. Your website says that secrecy is a hostile act. Is the government's keeping the UFO secret really an act of hostility?

Bassett: It's a contentious maneuver. We see that in our lives all the time. We understand that. Withholding information that somebody needs, or could use, withholding information that could benefit others, withholding information that protects your own actions, culpabilities and everything else – these are contentious acts. And in the prosecution of the Cold War, as we saw the emergence of the vast intelligence structures, they became the new tools of war. Since we couldn't use nuclear weapons, we spied on each other. We spied on each other to death. Fortunately, it's a good thing we did because by spying on each other we sort of knew what each other was doing so nobody got overly paranoid and launched 30 or 40 nuclear missiles.

But fundamentally, the whole act of spying and secrecy became important tools of war. So secrecy is generally hostile. We know that it can serve National Security and it's used to serve National Security, and one can sort of justify it, right? But let's make a point. When the government classifies a bomber program, no one is supposed to know about it, not even a fine, upstanding American citizen. If you find out about that and start telling people, they'll prosecute you for treason. And that's hostile. Then of course the reason they're keeping it a secret is because they have an enemy that they want to use that bomber against and so they don't want them to know about it. So hostility is everywhere in the secrecy world one way or another.

If the U.S. doesn't disclose, and another nation does instead -- China particularly would be annoying – and ends this Truth Embargo outside the U.S., and the U.S. has to be sort of shamed into following suit – meaning, "We were going to lie to you for another 25 years but oh, my God, Communist China just told you the truth so I guess we'll have to come forward." I don't know where trust levels will go frankly. It may drop to five percent and you may want to be living in another country because when it gets down to those levels this is not a place you want to be.

Q. There has recently been a great deal of formerly classified UFO reports released in the UK and Brazil. Are those newly released files of interest to you and the PRG?

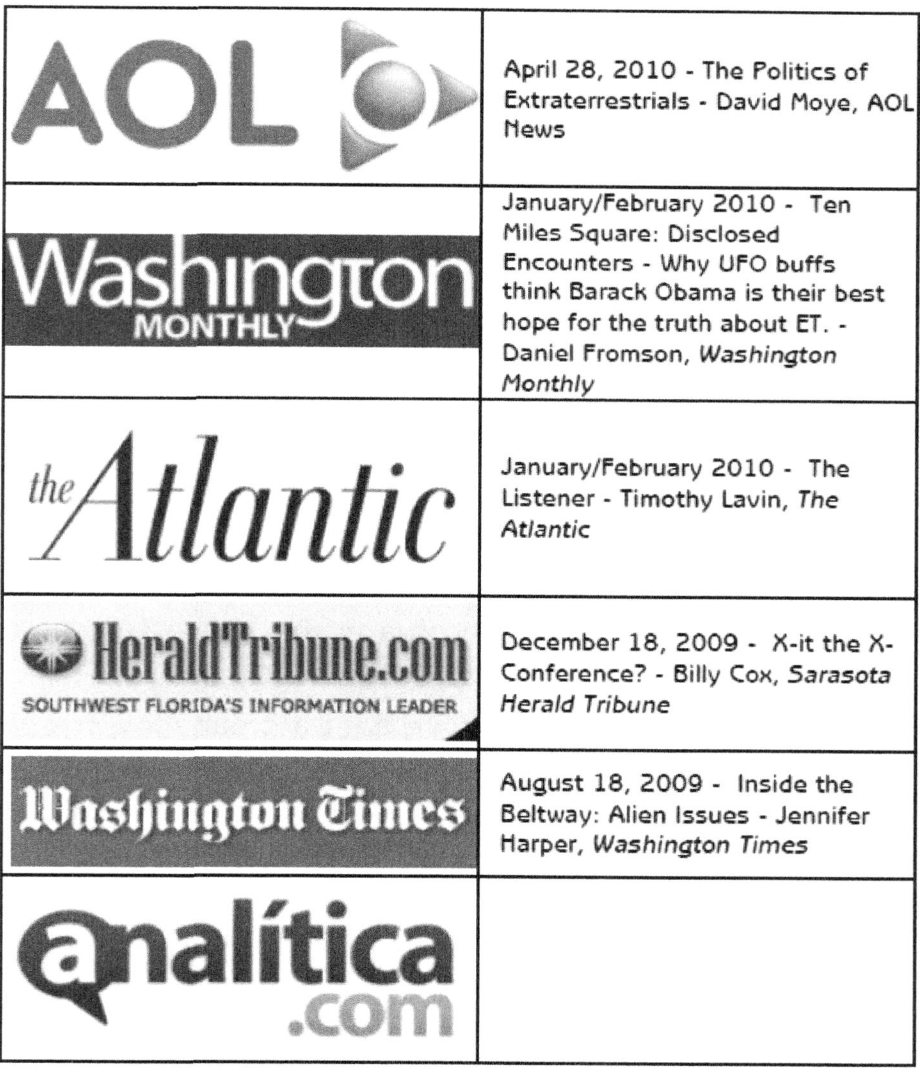

AOL	April 28, 2010 - The Politics of Extraterrestrials - David Moye, AOL News
Washington Monthly	January/February 2010 - Ten Miles Square: Disclosed Encounters - Why UFO buffs think Barack Obama is their best hope for the truth about ET. - Daniel Fromson, *Washington Monthly*
the Atlantic	January/February 2010 - The Listener - Timothy Lavin, *The Atlantic*
HeraldTribune.com SOUTHWEST FLORIDA'S INFORMATION LEADER	December 18, 2009 - X-it the X-Conference? - Billy Cox, *Sarasota Herald Tribune*
Washington Times	August 18, 2009 - Inside the Beltway: Alien Issues - Jennifer Harper, *Washington Times*
analítica.com	

Just some of the media that has paid attention to Stephen Bassett and his attempts at Disclosure.

Bassett: Well, yeah. But it's not just the UK and Brazil. Since 2000, a number of nations have started breaking ranks with the U.S.-led Truth Embargo. Which is to say, while they're not prepared to unilaterally break it themselves, they're indicating that they're quite fed up with it and it's time to end it. And this, for me, begins with the COMETA report issued in late 1999 by the French non-governmental organization called COMETA. They issued a report that basically said that the ET explanation was the only one that made sense and talked about why the U.S. has had to maintain secrecy on the issue. It was not a formal government agency or entity. started releasing files, and then Sweden, Denmark, Uruguay, recently New Zealand – it's up to about 11 countries.

Most of these files are not particularly profound, though they do kind of show the scope of the reports, which we knew. There were many and it's only a fraction of the reports that have been made and certainly only a fraction of the number of sightings and events that have taken place. But there were some good gems. There were some very interesting things in some of these files. More importantly, in most cases, they are on the Internet and are being downloaded all over the world. Millions of file downloads are taking place into computers all over the world, thus spreading the core sightings evidence worldwide.

But that's not really what's going on. What's going on is that these countries are doing two things. One, they're sending a message to the U.S. that the Truth Embargo needs to end. And while they have deferred to the U.S. as the leader of this embargo, and sort of agreed long ago that the U.S. would be the one to end it, they're losing patience. And secondly, they're positioning themselves on the right side of the issue. They're releasing their files, they're putting them out to the public. So when Disclosure takes place, the public will go, well, great, you've been trying to advance this issue. You've brought the files out. The U.S. of course has not released anything because its embargo is its policy. So the pressure is growing. There will be more countries. New Zealand was the last one, I think it was about a month ago. But there'll be more. You can count on it. And so the question is, what's the U.S. going to do?

Now in many different ways, we have sent a clear message to President Obama. If he does not disclose, very soon, then this embargo is going to be his, and his name is going to be written all over it, just like the previous 11 presidents that have dealt with it. And he's going to have to answer for that and of course it's going to destroy his open, transparent government concept. Just put the lie to it. But more importantly, if he does not disclose, there's a second thing that could happen. Another nation is going to disclose. That's going to be a major blow to American prestige and it's not going to make life any easier for his administration. And there's a third possibility. Something is going to break. A significant figure, a former secretary of defense, someone who just can't be ignored, is going to come forward and flat out say in front of some cameras, "Look, this is real and I know it." And it's going to launch a media storm. Or some of the work that I'm doing, in the Fax on Washington, is going to trigger some reporters among the White House press corps. They're going to bite into this and they're not going to let go. It's going to break out and it's going to trigger a media storm. What's going to happen is that the U.S. government is going to be driven to Disclosure. You're going to have hoards of press chasing Barack Obama down Pennsylvania Avenue with their pads waving in the air and their cameras clicking away. Or they'll be chasing Secretary of State Hillary Clinton up, you know, 15th Street. Or Bob Gates over at the Department of Defense. Or Leon Panetta. They're going to be running around town, chasing them down, trying to get them to answer questions about this because the media storm will have begun. The U.S. government is literally going to be hounded into the Disclosure Act by the media, and it's going to look goddamn stupid.

Q. This phrase occurred to me when I was writing up questions for all of this. The idea of "Disclosure With Honor." They used to say "Peace With Honor" about Vietnam. How about "Disclosure With Honor," where they're able to disclose the reality of UFOs without some sort of apocalyptic event forcing their hand.

Bassett: Thank you, Sean. I intend to steal that. The best stuff is always stolen.

Q. You're welcome to it.

Bassett: But you're absolutely right, "Disclosure With Honor." I'll use it. In fact I'll use it in a press release that I intend to put out very soon. It's a good phrase, and that is what we're talking about. It was our decision to embargo this. We got our allies in line. So we do have to answer for this embargo and how it was conducted. I think they have the answers. I think they'll be able to, quote, "defend their position."

Q. My editor and I were wondering, don't you think that, outside of Brazil, that the majority of the material that has been released so far is basically worthless from an academic and scientific viewpoint?

Bassett: Well, first of all, there is no academic viewpoint. The entire university and college system in America and pretty much all of Europe went along with the Truth Embargo, hook, line and sinker. How many courses are taught on this subject matter in American colleges and universities? You can count them on one hand with fingers left over. They're really limited. They're not part of a degree program. One professor was able to get one in and they've allowed it. Now that's 5,000 colleges and universities, filled with, over the last 60 years, millions of professors. The issue was all around them and they have not taught it at all. Period. That's the greatest academic and intellectual failure in all of human history. So, that's one point.

Secondly, the government releases the files that it wants to release. No one should be naïve enough to think that because France or the UK or Brazil or Denmark or Norway or Uruguay are releasing files, that that's all they have. That's ridiculous, right? Nevertheless, these are the basic filing reports. They come from sightings that have occurred over many years and most of them are of no particular note. You see a light in the sky. It could very well be a UFO. So what? You see another one. So what? So, yeah, the vast majority are not particularly significant, but there are embedded in there some reports that refer to things we do know about that are very interesting. A simple example was the Milton Torres case that was released in one of the UK batches, confirming that in 1957 he was ordered by the British government, while he was serving as a U.S. Air Force pilot there, to go out over the Channel and track a bogie. At some point they asked him to shoot it down. He was upset about that because the thing was the size of an aircraft carrier on his radar. Finally, the thing made some pretty radical maneuvers and took off at high speed. Not bad for a flying aircraft carrier. He was ordered by the intelligence people the very next day to keep his mouth shut and talk to nobody the rest of his life. And that's exactly what he did. He never said anything to anybody until that report was released. Then he was approached by the British papers and the U.S. papers and he was actually at my conference on April 20, 2009, calling for President Obama to end the Truth Embargo.

If someone were to take the time to review all of the files that were being released, what they would see from the collective is simply a fundamental confirmation of the research that has been done since 1947, that the extraterrestrial presence is a lock-solid, one hundred percent fact. It's just as much a fact as it is that the earth goes around the sun. It's not up for debate. If you want to debate, you can debate until hell freezes over. You can debate that the earth is flat if you want to, or that gravity doesn't exist. I don't care. It's a waste of my time and I'm not going to indulge in it. It's been proven many times over. What those files, of course, contain is not all that we know. There is a great deal of information that's been accumulated that's not necessarily in those files. What those files are doing is just confirming that this nonexistent issue has been a significant subject of collection and that there is plenty of material there that certainly reinforces what we already know to some degree or another.

Or to put it another way, if one took the time to review the entire tens of thousands of documents, they would clearly find some extremely interesting material. All of that is in the context of all the research results and the witness testimony that's been brought forward. You put it all together and you've got a massive amount of evidence. So some debunker can grab a few files that have been released by, say, Brazil and say, "Well, there's really not much here. Therefore, why are we talking about UFOs?" Well, that's debunkers. And debunkers are of no use to anybody. They have added nothing to this and they've accomplished nothing, except to make fools of themselves and obstruct the proper engagement of the most profound issue in human history. They all should be ashamed of themselves and I'm sure history will treat them appropriately.

Q. We also wanted to ask about your Million Fax Program. What was that all about?

Bassett: Well, it was another of PRG's advocacy projects and initiatives. It's a serious one. Essentially, as we approached the 2008 election – I knew this was a watershed election and I knew that Disclosure was getting pretty close. So I wanted to initiate a project that might possibly help to close the deal. This was cooked up in late 2007. The game plan was, one, to try to grow the Exo-Politics World Network, to try to get that going and up and just spread the Exo-Political approach and build up the movement worldwide to make it more international. We had some success there. And the other plan was to do everything we could during what we knew was going to be one of the longest presidential campaigns in history, to try to get the UFO issue attached to the campaigns, to the actual election process. And we did. We connected up some candidates to the issue, we got news coverage. I was on FOX, that kind of stuff.

So we were able to do that, but that was all preliminary. The game plan was simple. I did a huge amount of media in October announcing that we would start the Million Fax on Washington the day after the election. And the day after the election, the site went up and from that website, faxonwashington.org we were directing people to send letters, faxes and emails – we couldn't send faxes because there was no fax number – to the Transition Headquarters. We also got them active in the change.gov website, which was the transition website, which actually was very interesting. They were doing lots of things to engage people and get their views about things, so we infused the UFO issue quite a bit into that website's activities. But most importantly we rained letters and emails onto the Transition Headquarters. That was Phase One, and that went on through 77 days, until the inauguration. After the inauguration, on January 21, the target changed. We had the same information up on the website, the same talking points, the same points to raise, but the correspondence was then directed at the White House. Faxes, letters, emails. And that went on until we entered Phase Three.

At the April 20 press conference, after the X Conference in 2009, former astronaut Edgar Mitchell called for the Obama administration to end the Truth Embargo, and Major Torres called for it, and I of course called for it. That was one of those opportunities where you could reach out to the government because it was live-streamed by CNN, so I said to the administration, "You need to disclose." And I gave them the reasons I just gave you. If you don't, another nation is going to do it. And if you don't do it pretty soon, it's going to be your Truth Embargo and your hope in your transparent government initiative is going to turn to ash. And if you don't do it by the end of May, we're going to turn up the heat.

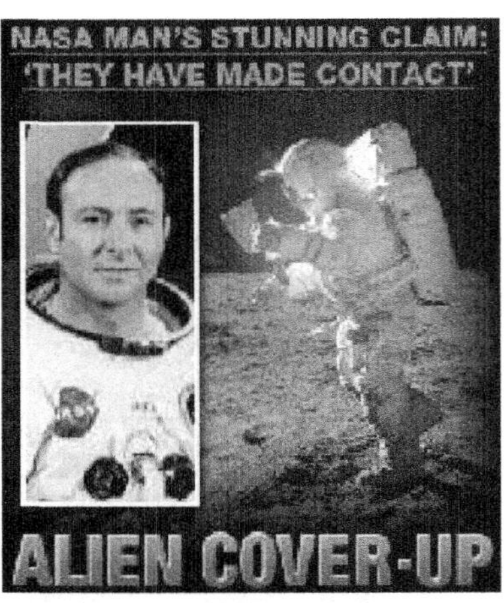

Astronaut Edgar Mitchell has been among those with credentials who have lectured at the annual X Conference organized by Stephen Bassett

And that's what we did. When Disclosure hadn't taken place by May 31st, we went to Phase Three of the Fax On Washington, and what's been going on since then, it's been a while now, is that we changed the talking points. The emphasis of the website, faxonwashington.org, was shifted from the president to the White House press corps. What you find up there are talking points regarding legitimate political questions that could be asked of the administration. All those questions that are listed right there are backed up by documents and photographs and everything else. Any reporter could figure that out in five minutes. So we've been telling everybody, okay, now we're going to send, as long as it takes, letters, faxes and emails to the White House press corps care of the White House Correspondents Association demanding that they step up and do their job and start asking these very tough but provable questions and demand answers instead of hiding and cowering, like, "Oh, I'm so sorry I mentioned UFOs. I'm so sorry."

Clinton aid (now on Obama's team) John Podesta says with no apologies that the public deserves to know the truth about UFOs.

There are several hundred people covering the White House. There's also a political corps covering the Secretary of State as well as the Department of Defense and Panetta at the CIA. And we're just going to keep pounding them until we get a couple of them to break ranks. We only need two or three. If two or three reporters have finally had enough, based on just the talking points we have at the site, and start asking those questions, there are no satisfactory answers that the administration can give. If that happens, if two or three of these reporters break ranks, when the answers come back, the rest of the reporters are going to just suddenly snap their heads up and go, "Hello? What was that?" And we could literally trigger a media storm. Also, we're still doing a lot to continue to connect Hillary Clinton, John Richardson, Leon Panetta, and John Podesta to this issue. The stuff is all over the net. You can find open letters to Hillary, open letters to Obama. You can find barackobamaufo.com or hillaryclintonufo.com

It's all over the net. Just Google Hillary Clinton UFO or Google John Podesta UFO. Now, admittedly, the press hasn't seized on it. But they will. This is why it's the final phase. This was the message I was trying to send. We're going to pound this until we trigger the media. And they will chase you down Pennsylvania Avenue with their cameras clicking and their pads in the air. And they will not stop until they run you to ground. Because we have seen, just in the last 20 years, what a media frenzy looks like, what an eating frenzy on the part of the media looks like. And once it starts, nothing stops it. Phase Three of the faxonwashington.org will continue unabated until Disclosure takes place, whether it be by Obama or another nation. But we're not going to let up, and they have to understand that the press is not going to remain silent forever. They're not going to sit down on this forever. There are too many Pulitzer Prizes to be had. It's the biggest news story of all time. So unless they've got every single investigative reporter in this country in their back pockets, on the CIA payroll, I'm sorry. They're going to finally turn on them and they're going to come after them and it's going to be pretty astounding. So they need to come forward with "Disclosure With Honor."

Q. There are some who think that there is a group of insiders who want the truth to come out.

Bassett: That is a consensus. They don't send us emails. There are no newsletters. But the sense we get from some of the witness testimony, and just an overall perception, is that within the management groups that run this, deep down in the Secret Empire, you don't know who they are, you don't know where they meet, you don't know what kind of lunch they have catered in, but they're the ones who are running this show. There may be some civilian contractor types from some of those defense contractors on some of those committees, whatever, but this idea that the corporations now run Disclosure is nonsense. It's run by the military intelligence communities, because their job is National Security, and this is a big National Security issue to them. We believe the consensus is that they would like to Disclose, they want to get this out of the way, they want to get it done. But it's not that easy, and there are logistical issues, there are concerns about the president.

The president in power on the day of Disclosure is a non-trivial matter for them. And one of the reasons that we did not pull off Disclosure, in the 18 years since the Cold War, in my opinion, and this is not easy to support, is that, one, Bill Clinton was not acceptable to them. They did not want this event taking place on his watch. And neither was George W. Bush. They were extremely concerned about him, on many levels, and the idea of him being the Disclosure president was not attractive. And believe me, considerable effort was made to unseat Bush after his first term and unseat Clinton after his first term. But they won second terms. So that to me is one of the principle reasons why we've gone through those 16 years without disclosure. But one of the reasons that we launched the faxonwashinton.org is that we figured out pretty early on that the three likely candidates that could win that election, McCain, Clinton or Obama, unlike Bill Clinton and George W. Bush, were acceptable to the military intelligence complex. Which meant that, whoever won, that would at least not be a barrier and so we would be closer to Disclosure.

So we're keeping the pressure on. We're not going to let up. We're not going anywhere. We're just going to literally pound them until they yield, hopefully in a professional and practicable way. But the idea that they're going to keep this Truth Embargo going much longer is ludicrous.

Q. There are some who have been critical of your work because you seem to accept everyone at their word, even those who make claims with very little to substantiate them. How do you answer that kind of criticism?

Bassett: Well, first of all, what does it mean, "accept people at their word?" They have to come up with very specific things. For most people, what they're really saying is, "You don't publicly condemn this person. You don't publicly excommunicate that person. You don't ostracize this person." Right? So therefore, you "accept" everything that they say. That's ridiculous. There are a lot of people out there writing a huge amount of material and engaging this issue and it's going to grow, no question. There are a lot of ufologists out there that have theories about ETs. Some think they come from another dimension. They come from the future. They come from the past. They come from the Inner Earth, whatever. There are a whole lot of people doing a whole lot of things, and my attitude is this: You do your thing. If I feel the work has relevance and value to the advocacy process, I draw on it. Whether I believe it or don't believe it is not particularly that important. In most of the cases, you can't prove one way or the other. If some researcher comes and says, "Look, based upon my understanding, these ETs must come from the future." What am I going to say? You're nuts? They don't? How do I prove they don't come from the future? Or anything else that goes on? This is now an extremely complex arena involving a lot of people, and we're at the point where the prudent thing to do is to look at each individual's work and decide what merit it has, and either draw on it or don't draw on it. If you think a person is off in leftfield, then basically you're not going to be working with that. You're not going to be using it. Another way to state this is, whatever problems anybody has with somebody's theories, works or writings, take it up with them. If someone has a problem with what I am saying, what I am writing, my positions, my statements, my interviews, then definitely take it up with me. But I am not going to be put in the position where I have to somehow judge, condemn, or provide running reviews about, quote, "my views of the validity of everyone else's work." It simply doesn't work that way. Now in the mainstream academic world, which of course as I've told you has failed this issue spectacularly, there are these structured review and peer review processes that exist. You have committees at schools and universities that look over people's work and you have peer review magazines. This does create a way to sort of build perhaps a more orderly structured body of information.

But in case anybody hasn't noticed, we don't have any universities, we don't have money for peer review journals, or what we have is modest. We have no funding, no philanthropy, we have no government support. We've had to do this out of our back pockets and most of us are broke. We don't have those structured peer reviews, so we have to be a little more, essentially, on our own. And a little more tolerant, right? Because there's another problem. Everyone in this field is operating in a ghettoized, polluted arena, meaning the information has been corrupted by their own government – direct government intervention to subvert the truth. If the government did this in real science, or major science, it would cause a major scandal. Can you imagine the government going in and sabotaging people's experiments in the genome project or undermining studies at the NIH in order to get a government result? Just screw up the research or make the researcher look like a fool? If they were doing that, it would be a massive scandal. Heads would roll and people would go to jail. Well, in this field, the government has had carte blanche to disrupt, misinform, disinform, undermine, ridicule, and isolate the efforts to try to get to the bottom of this, from the beginning.

Q. Is there anything you wish to add? Some question I haven't asked or some kind of final comment you'd care to make?

Bassett: We're going to try to reach larger and larger audiences. It is now possible to do that. The bandwidth is there. The ability for this issue to spread worldwide grows and grows. More countries coming onboard, more Exo-Politics World Network countries coming onboard. The U.S. is increasingly isolated, and increasingly looking awkward. It's got to do something. It is still a strong force for good in the world when it sticks to its values. A lot of people look to it for leadership. There are significant competing segments of the geopolitical world out there with different agendas. If we don't address this issue and get it right, it's going to have global impact. Not just on us, but to a lot of other people. And it's not going to be good.

So, on that basis alone, this issue must be resolved. It is a political issue. It will be resolved politically. We're not going to stop until we get it, and we will get it. Some people have been predicting Disclosure and the day it will happen and all that stuff, I don't do that and never have, but this is the best way to think of it: Disclosure is inevitable and soon. And the question that remains for us is: will it be soon enough?

White House Briefed on UFOs

Sarah McClendon,

White House Correspondent, McClendon News Service, March 30, 1998

Summary: (This article is written by Sarah McClendon, the nation's longest-serving White House Correspondent, who passed away on 9 January 2003.) Unidentified Flying Objects, a term given for many years to unexplained sightings of craft in the skies over every state in the Union, are actual visitors from other worlds, believe a community of scientists and technicians employed by government.

Washington, D.C. -- Unidentified Flying Objects, a term given for many years to unexplained sightings of craft in the skies over every state in the Union, are actual visitors from other worlds, believe a community of scientists and technicians employed by government.

The real danger to the U. S. and perhaps this whole planet is the government has placed such a heavy blanket of secrecy upon this issue. So much secrecy, those in government who have knowledge showing UFOs are identifiable feel the subject cannot be discussed by those in the know without serious repercussions. Others are afraid their friends and co-workers will think they are crazy if they even so much as insinuate that UFOs are identifiable as manned craft from outside the earth. This particularly applies to newspaper editors and publishers, reporters and analysts. Thus the U. S. is denying itself the chance to learn more about UFOs or to encourage research despite the fact the U.S. stands to gain form such discussions.

Not publicized but true is that the Clinton administration, soon after coming to office, had many briefings on the subject. Laurence Rockefeller provided the information for the President and Mrs. Clinton. Others provided documents and verbal briefings to presidential advisors Jack Gibbons (science), Bruce Lindsay (personal), Anthony Lake (national security) and Vice President Albert Gore. About the same time a three hour briefing was given by Dr. Steven Greer to the sitting Director of the CIA, Admiral Woolsey.

Subsequently, Clinton instructed Webster Hubbell, when naming him to the position of Associate Attorney General at the Justice Department, that he wanted him to investigate and report back to him on two things, circumstances surrounding the death of President John F. Kennedy, and the existence of UFOs. Hubbell, despite his position and the presidential imprimatur, was boxed in at Justice Department and never was able to find out. All of this was disclosed in Hubbell's memoir Friends in High Places.

Now the lid on UFOs is gradually coming off. There is a national drive underway to get one million signatures on a petition calling for an open Congressional hearing for government employee witnesses. Dr. Steven Greer, Director of the Center for the Study of Extraterrestrial Intelligence (CSETI), devotes most of his time seeking disclosure of government evidence proving the existence of craft manned by non-humans. Another who feels that positive proof exists within government, is Lt. Col. Philip J. Corso (retired), who reveals in a recent book, The Day After Roswell, that he was in charge of the Roswell files during his tenure as head of the Army's Foreign Technology Division. He states unequivocally that these files confirm the crash which occurred at Roswell, New Mexico was an alien space craft. This completely refutes the Air Force denials and subsequent explanations. Corso says that the crashed vehicle was studied and proved to be manufactured of materials unknown as to source and usage in this country. In time, he says, this and other UFOs provided technologies which were "worked into the commercial world via front companies." Incidentally he vouches for the fact that this has proven to be a valuable contribution to U.S. aircraft design and other commercial products.

After the Roswell incident, the Air Force replied to reporters' inquiries that this was all part of research using weather balloons and other equipment. Corso and hundreds of others who work or have worked in secret defense and scientific agencies, are willing to swear under oath that alien craft are repeatedly penetrating our airspace.

Whenever the military agencies are asked to look into this matter further, the answer is always the same - "We do not investigate UFOs."

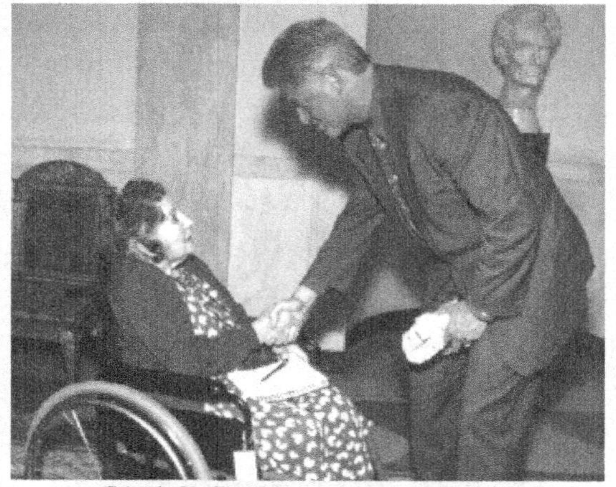

Sarah McClendon being greeted by President Bill Clinton (Official White House Photo)

GRANT CAMERON AND THE UFO LEGACY OF THE PRESIDENTS

By Sean Casteel

Canadian Grant Cameron has made a career out of seeking the publicly available truth of the presidents of the United States and their official UFO policy. The string of former American presidents runs its twisted way back to Franklin Delano Roosevelt, and it seems that each of them in turn had to struggle with the notion of what to say publicly and what to enshroud in the dark secrecy still at play today.

The UFO phenomenon found Grant Cameron and not the other way around, as is so often the case. His personal relationship with the subject began with a sightings flap in May of 1975, when he was a university student in Winnipeg, Manitoba, Canada. The wave of UFO appearances was written up in the local newspaper, and Cameron and some fellow students were eager for some excitement.

Grant Cameron

"We used to drive around the city," Cameron recalled. "We didn't have much to do. There were quite a few stories about what was going on. This was occurring about 35 miles southwest of the city, toward the American border. I kept on pressing my friends, 'Well, let's go and see what everybody's looking at.' I really didn't have any interest in UFOs or anything like that. We went out and drove around for an hour and we didn't see anything."

At the end of that first hour of seeking the unknown, something flew right in front of the school chums' car. For Cameron, it was indisputably real.

"I've always told people," he explained, "that there's believing, there's disbelieving, and then there's knowing. I knew what I saw and it wasn't anything from this Earth or anything I'd ever seen. My father's a pilot, my son's a pilot. I live on the Winnipeg flight path into the international airport here. I've seen a lot of planes, I've seen a lot of stuff, but I've never seen anything that even came close to what this thing looked like. So I was hooked from the word go."

After that watershed event with his friends, Cameron immediately began to do further research and wrote a manuscript that was later rejected by a publisher, leaving him depressed about the whole UFO business.

"I decided at that point," he said, "that sightings were kind of a waste of time. I mean, they were nice things to tell people and people liked to listen to them, but they never really changed anybody's mind."

Cameron moved on in his search for the truth, turning his attention to finding out what the Canadian government knew about the subject. That led to the his pursuit of the presidents of the United States, in what Cameron called going from one level to the next trying to figure out who was behind it all.

"It was basically to answer the question of what I had seen," he said. "I thought it was a fascinating thing and I figured that somebody must have the answer to what's going on here. I thought it would be very simple, and never in my wildest dreams did I ever believe that 35 years later I would know no more than I knew the first time I saw it. In terms of what's actually concrete evidence, in terms of what's provable, we are no further ahead then we were 35 years ago."

WHAT DID FDR KNOW?

There is mainly only conjecture, according to Cameron, about exactly what the presidents knew and when they knew it. We began with Franklin Delano Roosevelt, who is the first on the list of presidents that Cameron has done extensive research into.

UFOs themselves seem to be lobbying for Disclose as they pass over the District of Columbia during the summer wave of 1952.

"I think he knew more than the presidents of today," Cameron said. "He and Truman and Eisenhower – the story in the UFO community has always been that these guys had control of the situation. Then it was sort of moved out of the White House and transferred to private contractors and black budget organizations and international cabals, who made the decisions on this thing."

But before that transfer of responsibility, Roosevelt was forced to confront what has come to be thought of as the legendary "air raid" on Los Angeles in 1942. The L.A. event happened shortly after the start of the Second World War, when residents were very jittery about a possible Japanese attack by air or submarine. It has often been argued that what really happened in the

Southern California skies was a massive over-flight of flying saucers. Roosevelt was directly involved in the situation.

"There was documentation in his archive," Cameron said, "that shows a brief correspondence going back and forth between him and General Marshall. So he would have been much more involved. Whereas, in the Big Government that we have today, the president would not see it unless it really got out of hand. Very little is really brought to the desk of the president. That's just my opinion. There are so many issues and so many things going on that only a small percentage of one percent of anything actually reaches the president. It's stuff they need a decision on. Most of the information is dealt with at very low levels of government."

But Roosevelt, like Truman, who governed in a different age, would most likely have had more direct knowledge. Meanwhile, Cameron had an interesting story to tell about some relations of the longest serving Secretary of State under Roosevelt, Cordell Hull.

Cameron got the story from two Ohio women, now in their eighties. Their father, who was Hull's cousin, claimed that Hull took him to a room below the Senate building, a sub-basement, and showed him three alien bodies in glass jars and a crumpled up, disc-type, very light metal contraption.

"One of the women knows for sure that it was 1948 when she was told the story," Cameron recounted. "Her father was a minister. She had her young children out in the yard and her father came up and said, 'Well, now that the new generation is here, you should probably know something that happened to me.' And he told her the story about being shown these beings while in Washington, being taken by his cousin Cordell Hull to this room where he was shown these bodies."

The woman's older sister later confirmed the story, saying she was told the same thing by her father independently and at a different time. This adds to Cameron's belief that the earlier presidents like Roosevelt were more in the UFO loop than the ones who came later.

KEEPING BILL CLINTON IN THE DARK

On the other hand, former president Bill Clinton was apparently considered to have no "Need To Know." Cameron referred to a You Tube video that was recovered in Hong Kong after a lengthy search.

"Bill Clinton talks about the fact," Cameron said, "that he tried to go after the Roswell secret and to sort of quote him, he said, 'Well, I'm probably not the first president they've kept in the dark, or that bureaucrats have tried to wait out. I did try to find out even though I'm embarrassed to tell you.' He did try to find out about Roswell but was unable to get anything.

"There's a story," Cameron went on, "which I've never been able to document, where somebody actually yelled at him as he was coming out of a building and said, 'Mr. President, when are you going to tell us about Roswell?' And Clinton yelled back, 'When they tell me!' That's sort of the impression you get numerous times from Bill Clinton. I think that if you got him into a room and did an interview, he would actually be very open about the fact that he's fascinated with the subject, the fact that he's read a lot of the literature and tried to get the material and was basically cut out of the loop."

Another Clinton story comes to Cameron by way of fellow disclosure researcher Steven Greer, who had a lot of contact with the Clinton people. Greer claims that the president was afraid he'd end up like John F. Kennedy, and reiterated the fact that Clinton had been stymied in his efforts to find the truth. Greer asked R. James Woolsey, the CIA head under Clinton, why there was no UFO disclosure. To which Woolsey replied, "How can we disclose what we don't control?"

Cameron believes it all relates to the closing of Project Blue Book in 1969, after which the presidents were given to know less and less.

"They didn't need the sightings or the documentation anymore, and it was at that point that Nixon handed over the whole thing to the military/industrial complex and UFOs went into the dark. Probably since 1969 the government has basically been out of the situation. It's not a government problem anymore. There may be people in the government who know something about it, but it's my impression now that it's run by international groups that have more to do with business than to do with the government."

GIVE 'EM HELL HARRY

For Harry S Truman, there was no choice but to act.

"He had to deal with it," Cameron said. "He had the situation where he had to do something. Like all presidents, there is a structure, there is a protocol to take, and he would have gone through the National Security Council, the National Security Agency. And he would have followed the protocol to set up a group. The idea of him using the people named in the MJ-12 document – whether the document is legitimate or whether it's the right people – that concept is the way they would have done it, because it was done that way with everything else.

"You've got to remember," Cameron continued, "that Truman was the president right after World War II and the Americans were very successful in that war in developing technology by using committees, by using secrecy. The atomic bomb, radar, all this sort of thing was developed by these groups where everything was held very tightly. So this is the way they would have handled UFOs. You have scientists and military people operating to come to a conclusion or to try to develop something and solve a problem. It had worked during World War II, so it made perfect sense that that's the way it would have been done with Truman."

One should also recall that the over-flights of UFOs over Washington in the summer of 1952 took place on Truman's watch.

"We know for a fact that he knew a lot about it," Cameron said. "No doubt Truman knew a lot about Roswell and no doubt that he definitely knew about the '52 over-flights."

The 1952 flap led to the American government's policy of shutting down discussions and conjecture about UFOs in the media. The UFO phenomenon was said to be jamming intelligence channels and otherwise interfering with the smooth running of the government. A lid of some kind was needed immediately.

"That was basically what really got the cover-up going," Cameron theorized. "It's fine for UFOs to be flying around in Washington State or California, but once they're flying over the White House, then you have a situation where it's sort of like they're attacking the federal government."

The director of Project Blue Book at the time of the crisis was Air Force Captain Edward Ruppelt, who stated that he was on the phone with his superior, a General Landry, the Air Aid to Truman, and that Truman himself was listening on another line. Landry had phoned Ruppelt to get an assessment of the situation and to see what Ruppelt's investigation had turned up.

"We know, from a number of indirect sources," Cameron said, "that Truman was very upset about this whole thing and that they considered the over-flights to be very, very important. Something had to be done, and that's when the real cover-up started."

EISENHOWER'S EERIE WARNING

"Eisenhower's significance," Cameron said, "was his knowledge of the military, his knowledge of secrecy. He was a person very much into secrecy, very much into doing things by protocol, and had the connections inside the military in order to do the kind of things he needed to do. There are various stories about him actually having contact with aliens at Edwards Air Force Base, so he was a president who some say was the last president to have control over the situation.

"Of course in his last speech," Cameron went on, "he talked about 'Beware the military/industrial complex,' which has always been repeated numerous times in ufology. He was sort of losing control and the military and the military/industrial complex were taking control of the government. That may be the situation that exists today, that the black budget or the military is out of control and it's very hard to get that control back. Twelve percent of the people today are employed by the military or the military/industrial complex contractors. It's pretty hard to cut that part of the economy out. It's sort of a world unto themselves."

EISENHOWER'S ALIEN ENCOUNTER – A STORY LONG TOLD

The base was closed for three days and no one was allowed to enter or leave during that time. The historical event had been planned in advance. Details of a treaty had been agreed upon. Eisenhower arranged to be in Palm Springs on vacation. On the appointed day the President was spirited to the base. The excuse was given to the press that he was visiting a dentist. Witnesses to the event have stated that three UFOs flew over the base and then landed..

President Eisenhower met with the aliens on February 20, 1954, and a formal treaty between the alien nation and the United States of America was signed. We then received our first alien ambassador from outer space. Four others present at the meeting were Franklin Allen of the HEARST NEWSPAPERS, Edwin Nourse of BROOKINGS INSTITUTE, Gerald Light of METAPHYSICAL RESEARCH fame, and CATHOLIC BISHOP MacIntyre of Los Angeles. Their reaction was judged as a microcosm of what the public reaction might be. Based on this reaction, it was decided that the public could not be told. Later studies confirmed the decision as sound.

An emotionally revealing letter written by Gerald Light spells out in chilling detail: 'My dear friends: I have just returned from Muroc. The report is true -- devastatingly true! I made the journey in company with Franklin Allen of the Hearst papers and Edwin Nourse of Brookings Institute (Truman's erstwhile financial advisor) and Bishop MacIntyre of L.A. (confidential names for the present, please). When we were allowed to enter the restricted section (after about six hours in which we were checked on every possible item, event, incident and aspect of our personal and public lives), I HAD THE DISTINCT FEELING THAT THE WORLD HAD COME TO AN END WITH FANTASTIC REALISM. FOR I HAVE NEVER SEEN SO MANY HUMAN BEINGS IN A STATE OF COMPLETE COLLAPSE AND CONFUSION, AS THEY REALIZED THAT THEIR OWN WORLD HAD INDEED ENDED WITH SUCH FINALITY AS TO BEGGAR DESCRIPTION. THE REALITY OF 'OTHER-PLANE' AEROFORMS IS NOW AND FOREVER REMOVED FROM THE REALMS OF SPECULATION AND MADE A RATHER PAINFUL PART OF THE CONSCIOUSNESS OF EVERY RESPONSIBLE SCIENTIFIC AND POLITICAL GROUP. During my two days' visit I saw five separate and distinct types of aircraft being studied and handled by our Air Force officials -- with the assistance and permission of the Etherians!

I have no words to express my reactions. It has finally happened. It is now a matter of history. President Eisenhower, as you may already know, was spirited over to Muroc one night during his visit to Palm Springs recently. And it is my conviction that he will ignore the terrific conflict between the various 'authorities' and go directly to the people via radio and television -- if the impasse continues much longer. FROM WHAT I COULD GATHER, AN OFFICIAL STATEMENT TO THE COUNTRY IS BEING PREPARED FOR DELIVERY ABOUT THE MIDDLE OF MAY.

This incident has been discredited over the years though now researcher Art Campbell has added a degree of legitimacy to this supposed meeting with the former President.

KENNEDY AS A DEMOCRATIC WEAKLING

"I see Kennedy as a very weak president," Cameron opined, "because of the fact that he was a Democrat. The belief inside the UFO community has always been that the Democrats are not friends of the military. They're not friends of the military/industrial complex. They're more into, like Obama, Health Care and education, that sort of thing. Therefore, Democrats are told very little. Jimmy Carter complained greatly that he wasn't told anything. Bill

Clinton complained that he wasn't told anything, so Kennedy would have been in the same sort of boat."

Kennedy would have had two problems, according to Cameron. Since he could not be viewed as a military "hawk," he likely would not have been trusted by the people who controlled the UFO secret and therefore would not have been told very much. Secondly, since Kennedy did not finish his first term in office, he simply would not have had time to learn who actually held the secret and how to get to it.

"There were stories told about Bill Clinton trying to get to the secret," Cameron said, "that he would call in these admirals and say, 'I want to know what you know about UFOs,' and the admiral would just sort of look at him like, 'Are you crazy? I don't know anything.' And that's the thing, you've got to figure out who knows the secret."

Cameron said there is an audio recording on Kennedy's presidential website where the space race against the Russians to get to the moon is cast not as a scientific challenge for its own sake but rather a struggle simply to beat the U.S.S.R. to the moon. Obama similarly has no interest in furthering our achievements in space, which again is a reflection of a more socially focused political agenda. Meanwhile, Kennedy's knowledge or lack of knowledge regarding UFOs had nothing to do with his assassination.

"A lot of it has to do with the conspiratorial thing," Cameron explained, "where everything gets lumped together, and Kennedy is seen as being assassinated for his UFO beliefs. But I think it has much more to do with other issues, the Bay of Pigs, that sort of thing. He had lots of enemies all over the place. My personal opinion is that I don't think UFOs had anything to do with it and I don't think he really knew much of what was going on."

LBJ AND THE KECKSBURG CRASH

Something crashed in the woods outside Kecksburg, Pennsylvania, in December of 1965. It is claimed that a military group descended on the crash site immediately and drove away with a large acorn-shaped object on the back of a flatbed truck. Cameron says that the Blue Book files of the time recount several phone calls going back and forth trying to track what was happening.

Calls were also placed from Lyndon Johnson's presidential bunker, a shelter where the president is taken in the event of a nuclear attack. Cameron said he made his usual search of the presidential files to see where the president was at the time of the UFO crash. According to the records he found, Johnson was at his ranch recovering from gall bladder surgery.

"Very mysteriously," Cameron said, "the morning after the Kecksburg crash, the entire Joint Chiefs of Staff landed at his place in Texas and there were meetings. The meetings were described in the presidential daily diary as meetings on the Vietnam war. It was very strange."

The head of NASA and the Secretary of Defense also joined the group.

"So all of the key people were at the Johnson ranch, and it did give some indication that the right people were in the right place and that Johnson may have been tracking what was going on at Kecksburg. Johnson did claim, whether it was women or secrets – he claimed he had more women than any other president and more secrets than any other president. And he was the type of guy that if he did have a lot of secret knowledge, he was able to keep it to himself."

TRICKY DICK SHOWS OFF

Cameron said that in the case of Richard Nixon, rumors and stories abounded. For example, Cameron spoke to a woman in Florida who claimed to have had a house in Key Biscayne just down the road from Nixon's vacation retreat. (The Key Biscayne residence was called the "Southern White House" at the time.) The woman said she conversed with Nixon numerous times as he stood on his porch.

"They had discussions, though not detailed discussions, about the fact that he was very interested in outer space and UFOs," Cameron said.

Another Nixon anecdote came to Cameron by way of Larry Warren, a former serviceman who was one of the primary witnesses to the Bentwaters incident in England in 1980, and involved the comedian Jackie Gleason. As the story goes, as told by Jackie Gleason's second wife, Beverly McKittrick, Gleason had come home very late one evening to his Florida residence and he looked like something "wrong" had happened.

"He told his wife that Nixon had come in a private car, had picked him up, and taken him to an Air Force base in Florida and had actually shown him the bodies," Cameron related. "So we asked her, do you really believe that could actually happen? She said, 'Well, maybe he was out with another woman or whatever, but he was really shaken up by this whole story.'"

People often argue that Nixon could never have been separated from his Secret Service bodyguards, but Cameron says he has documented at least one occasion when Nixon actually did evade his security people.

Larry Warren, after the publication of his book "Left At East Gate," about his UFO experiences in England, was contacted by Gleason himself when they were both residing in New York. Warren shot pool and had some drinks at Gleason's home, and Gleason told him the same story of having been shown the dead alien bodies by Nixon.

GERALD FORD SOUNDS THE ALARM

Gerald Ford is famous for his demand that Congress hold hearings on the UFO problem after a frightening UFO flap had occurred in Ford's home state of Michigan in 1966, when Ford was still a member of the House of Representatives. When the then chief government investigator into UFOs, astronomer Dr. J. Allen Hynek, ludicrously declared that the sightings were caused by "swamp gas," a lot of people had suddenly had enough of the government's stonewalling.

But the Congressional hearings convened to study the subject never went anywhere. After listening to the testimony of a few believers, the UFO secret went back under wraps.

"The key thing is," Cameron said, "that once Ford became president, like all the rest of them, he suddenly shut up and didn't say anything. It sort of died away."

Ford did write a letter to UFO researcher George Filer, whose Internet news service is called Filer's Files, in which Ford said that he had asked questions about UFOs as a congressman, vice president and president and had not been able to get anything.

Meanwhile, a contact whose name Cameron prefers to keep secret told him a different story. The contact claimed to have had a conversation with Ford.

"Ford confirmed to him that he has been briefed on UFOs," Cameron said, "and that he was shown the Holloman Air Force Base film, a fifteen minute film where the aliens land, they come out of the craft, they're met by high-ranking Holloman Air Force Base officials, they walk down the tarmac, etc. So Ford confirmed that he had seen the film, and he confirmed that he had been briefed on UFOs even though his letter to Filer said he never could get anything."

The contact declined to say on what date the briefing had occurred because that would make it possible to know who was in the room and to make specific FOIA requests based on that knowledge.

"So although Ford claimed he didn't know anything," Cameron said, "there are inside stories from people, people that I believe, who indicate that Ford knew what was going on. And for whatever reason, he shut up. I think that's basically what a president is all about. The president doesn't release the UFO secret; the president doesn't release any secrets. The president keeps his mouth shut. That's what the game is all about. Jimmy Carter said he was going to release it and he didn't release it. Barack Obama said it was going to be an open administration and he was going to release all the secrets. He released no secrets.

"When you're briefed," Cameron continued, "you're brought into a room, you're given a paper to sign, you sign off that this is Top Secret, it's National Security information, and you keep your mouth shut. You're suddenly brought into the thing and nobody talks. None of the presidents talk. So whether they know or they don't know, part of the game is that they're not going to tell stories about the presidents before them or what happened or how many people they assassinated. It's all secret, UFOs and everything else."

CARTER RETREATS TO SKEPTICISM

Jimmy Carter is well known for having filed a UFO sighting report in the days before he became Governor of Georgia. He promised during his presidential campaign that he would release all the government files on the subject, a promise on which he later reneged. But Carter was allegedly still willing to tell the truth to actress and New Age activist Shirley McClain.

"Shirley McClain, who is a pretty reliable source as far as I'm concerned, stated that she was told by Jimmy Carter, 'Yes, it's true. Why should we be the only people in the universe?' And that he wouldn't and couldn't tell the people."

McClain made the claims about Carter on the Larry King Show in 1995, which Cameron was able to track down a copy of. But according to fellow actor Nicolas Cage, McClain had told Cage that Carter had actually seen the bodies. McClain denies she ever told that story to Cage and will confirm only that Carter did believe in life elsewhere.

In the years since his 1976 disclosure campaign promise, Carter has shifted, publicly at least, to a much more skeptical position.

"Jimmy Carter is telling a completely different story now," Cameron said. "He's basically playing the skeptic. He's saying, 'I don't believe it. Yes, I had a sighting but it didn't mean anything.' But he's sort of in a box. He has to keep the thing going. He's sworn to secrecy, and you can't break a secrecy oath. I think that's what it comes down to."

KEEPING REAGAN QUIET

"Ronald Reagan was fascinated with the subject," Cameron said. "He was fascinated with astrology; he was fascinated with all sorts of very esoteric things. Reagan was interested and he talked at great length about how he wanted to get rid of nuclear weapons and he talked about how the world must unite if faced with an alien threat."

One story that Cameron has gleaned in his research is about Reagan's National Security Advisor, General Colin Powell. Powell told presidential biographer Lou Cannon that part of Powell's job was to stop Reagan from talking about aliens.

"Reagan was talking about them in cabinet meetings all the time," Cameron said, "and that was part of Powell's job, to stop him from doing this."

In 1987, Reagan made the famous address to the United Nations that has come to be called "The Little Green Man Speech." Reagan not only prophesied that the world must unite against a future alien threat, he also asked casually, "And is not an alien presence already among us?"

When Cameron visited Reagan's presidential library he accidentally stumbled across material that indicated that Reagan's references to creatures from another planet had initially been removed from the speech.

"They pulled it from the speech," Cameron said, "and Reagan writes to the speechwriter and says, 'Oh, by the way, I'd like my little fantasy of how the world will unite put back in the speech.' So they put it back in the speech and he does it a number of times, which is something people don't realize. He did it on at least five occasions. One was at a school in Maryland, where Reagan did the same sort of thing."

Reagan had a photographic memory, according to Cameron, so he spoke of the extraterrestrials in nearly the exact same words on those five occasions. The references are deleted from the speeches on file in the presidential library, which meant they were most likely "adlibbed" at the end of the speech.

The former Russian president Mikhail Gorbachev was also given the alien pitch by Reagan. Gorbachev said in an interview that he met with Reagan in a small cabin where the Gipper talked about the alien invasion. Gorbachev told Reagan that he agreed with the basic premise but that Reagan's concerns were a little premature.

"Gorbachev was basically agreeing with the fact that aliens were here," Cameron said, "but he really didn't think the threat was as serious as Reagan thought it was.

"So it's an interesting scenario of a guy who just kept putting it out there and putting it out there. It was sort of a utopian thing where I think he was using it to play off of nuclear weapons, saying that we shouldn't be fighting between ourselves. That we're one people, and if someday we were invaded, then we would all suddenly be one united world. Reagan had this utopian idea of how things should be."

GEORGE BUSH WEIGHS IN ON THE UFO SECRET

The first George Bush is often labeled the president who likely knew it all. When Jimmy Carter won the 1976 election, Bush, as the then Director of the CIA, was charged with the task of briefing Carter during the transition period from the Ford administration on various intelligence matters.

"I guess Carter asked for the UFO files," Cameron said, "and Bush said, 'No, I can't give them to you. You don't have the need to know. Even being president is not sufficient need to know. If you want to know about the UFO stuff, you have to contact the House Committee on Science and Technology and get it through there.'"

The story came to Cameron through Danny Sheehan, who was a Harvard-educated Civil Rights attorney based in Washington. Sheehan claimed to have heard it from Marcia Smith, who worked for the Congressional Research Office and had produced reports for Carter on UFOs and extraterrestrial intelligence.

"So that was another story that indicated that Bush Senior had the knowledge," Cameron said.

In his time as president, the elder Bush met with Mikhail Gorbachev. One of the subjects they discussed was the recent failure of a Russian satellite called Phobos Two, which had made the journey to Mars and was sending back photos and information. The satellite had picked up a huge elliptical object in its sites and then immediately went blank and essentially disappeared.

"A Russian cosmonaut, who went public with this, stated that Gorbachev and Bush had discussed this in Malta. It was one of the conversations they had, as to what had happened to the Phobos Two satellite. So from time to time, things have come up that indicate that international leaders do discuss this kind of thing."

Bush is always considered a major player because of his intelligence background, and is a trusted insider with the Skull and Bones credentials in his favor. According to Cameron, if one were to name a present day list of members of the latest incarnation of MJ-12, Bush would definitely be on that list of people with a controlling interest in the UFO game.

CLINTON'S MASSIVE FILES

This chapter has already dealt with Clinton's admission that he sought the UFO secret but was denied access to the hidden truth despite his continued efforts as president. But surprisingly, Cameron was able to find thousands of pages on the subject in Clinton's presidential library and got some good responses to his FOIA requests.

"I have about a hundred FOIA requests," Cameron said. "I have the one file that hasn't been released yet which is 2,500 pages of UFO material. I got a thousand pages from the Clinton administration when he was still in office."

Those numbers are significant because of the paucity of material generally available at presidential libraries. Cameron's visits to the Eisenhower and Truman libraries, which contain upwards of 60 or 70 million pages, yielded only an average of 10 UFO-related documents.

"I thought this was very strange," Cameron said. "This is the most important subject in the world, a president is the most powerful guy in the world, and it doesn't make any sense that the most powerful guy in the world doesn't deal with the most important subject. Why are there no documents in the presidential libraries? That includes the Reagan Library. Ford has quite a bit but it's mostly from his Congressional days when he was making a big thing about UFOs. Even in Carter's, there's very little there. Nothing official.

"And so the importance with Clinton is, if you get a thousand pages, this is more than all the other presidential libraries combined. There's all sorts of material there, like Area 51, files on that. There's a lot of material at the Clinton Library. I think I've got 29,000 pages under review based on all my FOIA requests. And the key to that is, because I got a thousand pages in 2000, from Clinton, through the Office of Science and Technology Policy, where they were keeping all this material, I know who was involved. We know all the people in the Clinton administration who were involved in this, and so what we do now is file for all their papers. It mushrooms. So Clinton really did try to get it and came up against a brick wall."

Hillary Clinton is also known to have a background in UFOs, probably more than any previous American politician, according to Cameron.

"She's very much into esoteric stuff," Cameron said. "but you'd never get to talk to her about it because it's absolutely the end of your career as a politician to start taking about that. And Dennis Kucinich is a prime example. His presidential bid was over the minute he was faced with a UFO question in a national debate. So the Clintons are very interested, have been very much involved, all their people were involved. Bill Clinton has openly stated that he tried to find out about the alien at Area 51. The rumored story was that there was an alien underground there and he says quite openly, it's on videotape, that he tried to get that answer as to whether there was an alien at Area 51, but nothing really came of it.

"I doubt the documents are going to show him getting anywhere with it, but that's the Clinton story. It's by far the longest story on my website. It's 60 or 70 pages, and I have a lot more material that's never been put up there."

BUSH AND CHENEY AND UFOs

The junior Bush was confronted about UFOs on a couple of occasions, and in both instances referred the question to Dick Cheney. Cheney had been the Chief of Staff for Gerald Ford, Secretary of Defense under the first George Bush, and was then the junior Bush's Vice President.

"Cheney has always been the guy," Cameron said. "He's almost like George Bush Senior or Henry Kissinger; he's one of the guys who we think really knows what's going on."

Cameron was able to question Cheney himself once during Cheney's appearance on a Washington call-in radio show.

"I asked him, 'Mr. Cheney, in all your jobs in government, have you ever been briefed on the subject of UFOs? And if so, when was it and what were you told?' The idea of that question was: I don't care if you've seen one and I really don't care what you think about them. What I want to know is, did someone walk into your office and brief you? Did an official who knows what's going on read you the briefing of what, to their best knowledge, U.S. intelligence is on the subject?"

Cheney replied by saying that if he had been briefed on the subject, it would probably be classified and he therefore wouldn't be talking about it.

"Which just floored me," Cameron said, "because he basically said, yes, this is for real. He didn't laugh it off and he didn't walk away. Then the host went after him after what he said and asked, 'Well, Mr. Vice President, have you had any meetings on UFOs since you've gotten to the White House?' By then, Cheney had caught his footing and he said, 'No, I've had no UFO meetings since I got to the White House.' Which of course is probably true. This was April, just a couple of months after they'd got in.

"But Cheney is the guy who knows. Bush did make some jokes about it. He was in Roswell at one point and he made a joke about a UFO. He would have some general knowledge, but I don't think he really has any interest in it, which is the same as the general populace and a lot of politicians."

BARACK OBAMA SIDESTEPS THE ISSUE

After Stephen Bassett's 2007 UFO conference in Washington, Barack Obama's campaign manager was asked about ending the UFO Truth Embargo. The answer came back, "We're more interested in ending the embargo of information on the war in Iraq."

"That's how he handled it," Cameron said. "Later, Obama was confronted by a Chicago reporter. It's on You Tube. A Chicago reporter asked, 'Mr. Obama, if you get into the White House and you find out that aliens are for real, will you release it?' And Obama uses the same old technique that all politicians use: they make a joke out of it, to walk around it. He said, 'It depends on what they're like. Whether they're Democrats or Republicans.' That's how he answered the question.

"Obama, as I stated long before he got elected, is simply not interested in this. It's not his thing. He's the type of guy who in the late 1960s would have said it's a total waste of money putting a man on the moon when there are poor people on Earth. He's going to shut down a vast majority of NASA. He's not interested in outer space, as many times as he's claimed he is. He's interested in earthly problems, which is fine. Poor people, health care, education, all these kinds of typical Democratic issues. He's a good politician, and that's what people have to realize. People think that somebody comes along, that they're the Messiah and that they're going to give you all the things you're wishing for. They are politicians. They're there to get elected.

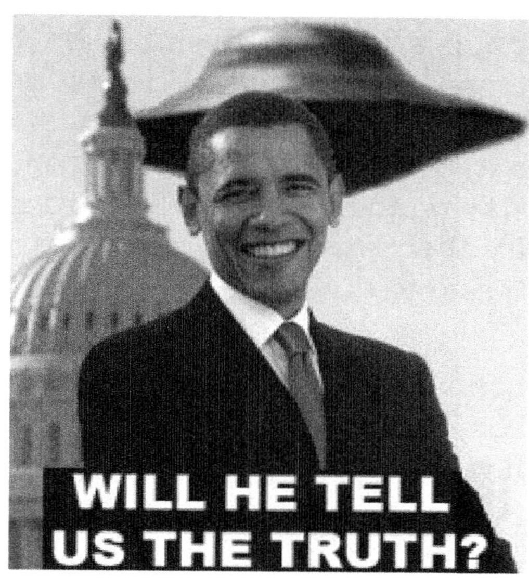
WILL HE TELL
US THE TRUTH?

"So I was not surprised that Obama didn't do anything. It's just not his issue. I guess if push comes to shove and there's a crash and he's faced with this issue and has to deal with it, he's a good politician and he may be the guy who can actually walk us through the thing and bring it out without having the thing blow up."

Beyond those circumstances, the normal tendency is to push responsibility onto someone else.

"Put it on somebody else's watch," Cameron said. "This is not something he wants to be involved in. Because that's the end of your presidency. The minute you get involved with this, you're going to take all the fallout. Disclosure has way more bad things going for it than it does good things."

WHAT WOULD DISCLOSURE REALLY BE LIKE?

"I don't think there's any way to do it," Cameron said, "without everything falling apart. It's not exactly 'The War of the Worlds' or the stock market crashing. The problem with politicians, with government, is that they only want things that are predictable. And this is the most unpredictable thing, because once you let it out . . .

"I looked at Jimmy Carter, a guy who's taught Sunday School since he was 18-years-old and always says he's going to tell the truth. He's going to be honest, to be upfront with people. He always seemed to be an honest-type guy. And I said to myself, 'How did they turn this guy?' The guy was into UFOs and he wanted to release it. He gets to be president and suddenly he turns, he becomes one of them. What did they tell him to convince him to be quiet?

"My background at university was political studies, and I studied Soviet politics and the Kremlin. It's the same sort of thing. You've got to see how these people think and what their thought processes are on this whole matter, rather than taking the utopian view that it would be good to get this released and get free energy and so on. You've got to look at what's motivating them to stay on the sidelines. They're like you and I. They want the best for their kids, for their grandchildren. They're not trying to screw anybody around. They're trying to do the best they can.

"So something has convinced them that this can't be released. They actually believe they're doing the right thing. You start to see that there are some fairly legitimate reasons why these people are absolutely petrified to do it. Once you spill the milk, you can't get it back in the bottle."

Cameron warns that even a partial disclosure of the UFO secret would quickly go spiraling out of control and the president would be faced with questions he simply could not answer. He gave a for instance: "Mr. President, you're constitutionally responsible for the protection of the American people. It's been estimated that millions of people have been abducted by these aliens. What are you doing to stop this?"

"And there's nothing he can do," Cameron said. "Now, if I'm the National Security Advisor to the president, I'd say, 'Mr. President, the longer the time you give us, the more answers we're going to have when you finally have to talk about this. Right now we know about 20 percent of it. If you can drag it out for the next 10 years, we're going to know 40 or 50 percent. We might have the answers. But you can't go out there when we don't have enough of the answers. We're still trying to figure this thing out.'"

Cameron said that he has heard from another source, an eschatologist, or a believer in the End Time prophecies, named Dan Smith. Smith claims that a man named Ronald Pandolfi, who used to head up the "Weird Desk" at the CIA, where he dealt with UFOs and other paranormal concerns, told Smith that there is an employee of the National Security Agency whose job it is to deal with people in the government that have been abducted by aliens. Apparently, that list includes a former member of the Joint Chiefs of Staff and former Vice President Al Gore's two daughters.

"That's a National Security issue," Cameron said, "if somebody is actually getting control of the minds of the people who are running the country. And this is coming from the CIA leaking into the UFO community. So that's the kind of stuff, when we talk about disclosure, that I think is really troubling to government officials."

In the end, the issues surrounding disclosure may all come down to the media suddenly realizing that the UFO phenomenon is something real.

"That's when it gets out of control," Cameron said. "The media is the key to me. They have to start to believe. They have to catch wind that they've been had and realize there's a story that's going to sell some advertising, like a Tiger Woods-type story. Then CNN is going to jump on it 24 hours a day and at that point it's going to roll."

[To read more on the American presidents and their UFO secrecy, visit Grant Cameron's website at: www.presidentialufo.com]

Did President Carter Have A Close Encounter?

[This article first appeared in a 1978 edition of a publication called "UFO Review," edited and published by Timothy Green Beckley.]

Panama City (Special Report to UFO Review) – Experts are stumped over a mysterious object that appeared on a photograph taken of President Carter's military helicopter while he was visiting Panama recently.

"I was watching the President's helicopter take off on the way to International Airport. He was in the country to sign the ratification with officials of Panama. It was an overcast day, but I was standing in what sunlight penetrated the clouds. I was taking photos of the reception party that had welcomed him at Fort Clayton, where I am employed by the U.S. government as part of their Defense Mapping Agency Inter-American Geodetic Survey."

Ms. Linda Arosemena, in an exclusive interview with UFO Review, revealed that she hadn't seen anything at all unusual in the sky on Saturday, June 17, 1978, at 2:20 P.M., the time of President Carter's departure. But, when the film was developed, there, near the helicopter with Carter in it, was a very strange Saturn-shaped object – a definite flying saucer-type craft.

"I can't account for what turned up in the negative," Ms. Arosemena declared, "but I can tell you this – I've never seen anything like it during the 14-odd years I have been working as a professional photographer."

Taken aback by what materialized on her finished print, Ms. Arosemena immediately telephoned the Panama offices of the Federal Aviation Administration and was put in touch with one Mr. Frank Grba, an FAA official who was totally stumped, but had to admit that radar hadn't picked up anything odd at the time. "They were curious, however, and did request that I send them prints. So far, they have not contacted me officially as to what they think the object might be."

Ms. Arosemena also revealed that she sent a print to the President in Washington, "because I thought he would want to see what I photographed." The only response she had gotten to date is a printed "form letter" thanking her for her interest in the President's trip to Panama.

The photo was taken with a Nikon camera equipped with a motor drive, using Kodak TRI-X black and white film, at 1/250 sec., f/16. The negative is exactly the same quality as the rest of the roll and the previous frame taken 10 seconds earlier shows no signs of anything peculiar. Neither the film nor the negative have apparently been tampered with and it is impossible to take a double exposure with this type of camera.

"I'm still not certain what I caught," Ms. Arosemena stated, "but the image is very clear and there have been quite a few UFO sightings in Panama lately!"

According to a front page story in Panama's "Star and Herald" newspaper, the day before, on June 16, at approximately 2:30 P.M., Brenda Reilly was fishing with some friends on the causeway at Fort Amador.

Suddenly her friend Sandra Chandler looked up and asked what the lights in the sky were. They talked about the lights being a plane or helicopter, but realized that they were neither when they saw its shape. Before their other friends could come up the embankment to see it, the object vanished.

"It was spinning, moved forward and then it just disappeared," Brenda said, adding, "It was just about to rain and the sky was overcast."

Brenda drew a picture of it for her mother, Mrs. Velma Reilly. "It had a black inner oval, with a dull gray metal-like outer oval," said the woman. "It looked very much like Linda Arosemena's photograph, except that my daughter made the sketch before this photo was even taken."

UFO activity is on the increase in Panama, though very seldom do the papers carry any information, most reports being passed on by word of mouth.

One report making the rounds is that along the coast, on New Year's Eve, both Americans as well as Panamanians observed a brilliant orange globe which bedazzled and stunned the many eyewitnesses. On another occasion, an employee at the Panama Canal Locks working the late shift was shocked into speechlessness by a glowing sphere that appeared out of nowhere.

"Unfortunately," notes Linda Arosemena, "there is no official agency to report these sightings to." The issue of the "Star and Herald" that carried her photo did ask readers of the paper who might have seen anything "unusual" to step forward and issue a report.

SOME FOLLOW-UP INFORMATION

Tim Beckley says he remembers talking with photographer Linda Arosemena on the phone.

"A lot of people thought I made up the entire incident," Beckley says. "They are always thinking that way. A lot of UFOlogists are backstabbing. They don't want anyone else in the field to get credit for any sort of accomplishment. In any case, the item came to my attention and I spoke to the photographer. She had a credible background and seemed sincere. I remember later someone from the Mutual UFO Network got in touch with me and had a manuscript dealing with this particular incident – with a lot more details. I can't remember what they disclosed to me since so many years have passed. When I requested feedback from MUFON with information on who their representatives in Panama were at the time, I was completely stonewalled."

When Beckley mentioned the photo to Grant Cameron, who has researched the subject of UFO secrecy as it relates to the U.S. Presidency and is interviewed in this book, Cameron was able to find a copy of the photo in the Carter Presidential Library and to make contact with Arosemena, who now lives in Florida, for further verification.

"Grant Cameron is one of the most thorough researchers around," Beckley says. "He really tries to document the truth and not merely make bold and rash statements like some others, who hope that disclosure will come sooner than later to cover their errors or render their misstatements irrelevant."

Meanwhile, Beckley's most basic question remains unanswered.

"Was Carter's helicopter followed by a UFO while he was in Panama in 1978 to ratify our country's treaty with that nation? I don't know, but the photo is in the Carter Library so it must have some status, even though it is filed without any comment."

Did CNN catch a UFO during President Obama's Inauguration?

FORMER CANADIAN DEFENCE MINISTER SAYS UFOs ARE EXTRATERRESTRIAL

By Sean Casteel

Like many highly placed officials in the governments of the world, the Honorable Paul Hellyer had little interest in the subject of UFOs. His political career in Canada left him no time for such a "flight of fancy," his term for interest in flying saucers and their occupants.

Symposium panel discussion. Pictured, left to right: Stanton Friedman, Richard Dolan, Stephen Bassett, and Canadian Defence Minister Paul Hellyer. Photo by: Ethan Eisenberg.

There was a moment, on June 3, 1967, to be exact, when he was still the Minister of National Defence in Canada, when he briefly touched on the subject publicly. He was flown in by helicopter to officially inaugurate an Unidentified Flying Object landing pad in St. Paul, Alberta. The town had built the landing pad as its Canadian Centennial Celebration project and as a symbol of keeping space free from human warfare. The sign beside the pad reads:

"The area under the World's First UFO Landing Pad was designated international by the town of St. Paul as a symbol of our faith that mankind will maintain the outer universe free from national wars and strife. That future travel in space will be safe for all intergalactic beings, all visitors from Earth or otherwise are welcome to this territory and to the Town of St. Paul."

That sentiment suited Hellyer just fine. Throughout his life, Hellyer had opposed the weaponization of space and is known to support the Space Preservation Treaty to ban space weapons.

Hellyer thought the landing pad was an innovative idea from a progressive Canadian community willing to pay for his helicopter ride, but he did not give much thought to UFOs as having serious policy implications. He also acknowledged a private UFO sighting he later had with family and guests, but once again attributed it to a "flight of fancy" with no major impact on his beliefs.

SEEING IS BELIEVING

When Hellyer watched a television special hosted by the late Peter Jennings called "Seeing Is Believing" in February 2005, his beliefs seemed to radically change overnight. The television program prompted him to read a book he had had sitting on his bookshelf for two years, "The Day After Roswell," by Philip Corso. Hellyer was impressed that Corso named real names, people that could be checked and verified independently, as well as events and institutions that existed in the real world.

Hellyer decided to go on his own search for the truth, to confirm whether Corso's book was accurate or a "work of fiction." He spoke to a retired United States Air Force General, who simply said, "Every word is true, and more."

Hellyer then proceeded to press the General about his "and more" statement. Hellyer claims the General told him remarkable things concerning UFOs and the extraterrestrial hypothesis, that aliens had been visiting Earth since at least 1947.

SPEAKING OUT ABOUT UFOs

Being fully convinced now in the reality of the UFO phenomenon, Hellyer agreed to speak at a conference called "Exo-Politics Toronto" about what he called some of the "most profoundly important policy questions that must be addressed."

First, Hellyer declared that the UFO cover-up is "the greatest and most successful cover-up in the history of the world." He confirmed that he and other senior political officials, even at the level of his former post as Minister of Defence, are simply out of the loop when it comes to information concerning UFOs and visiting extraterrestrials. From a democratic perspective, one must therefore be wary about things like the oversight, transparency and accountability of those who do hold that knowledge or are developing technology and other projects concerning extraterrestrials.

WHY CALL ALIENS THE ENEMY?

Second among these profound policy issues is the designation by the United States military of visiting extraterrestrials as an "enemy." Hellyer said this led to the development of "laser and particle guns to the point that they can be used as weapons against the visitors from space." This "targeting" of the aliens caused Hellyer deep concern, who asked, "Is it wise to spend so much time and money to build weapons systems to rid the skies of alien visitors? Are they really enemies or merely legitimate explorers from afar?" This is an important point in terms of understanding the relationship between visiting alien civilizations and world peace.

At the time Hellyer was making his speech, then President George W. Bush had recently decided to build a base on the moon. Hellyer believed that this was an activation of a plan, first launched by Philip Corso's mentor, Lt. General Arthur Trudeau, to build a base from which visiting extraterrestrials could be monitored and possibly targeted as they approached Earth. Hellyer again outlined his opposition to the weaponization of space, something the current liberal government in Canada is also opposed to.

ENDING THE COVER-UP

In the final portion of Hellyer's speech, he called for an end to the UFO cover-up. He declared that the "time has come to lift the veil of secrecy" and to have an "informed debate about a problem that doesn't officially exist." We must understand the evidence of the UFO phenomenon in order to fully prepare citizens around the world for the truth of extraterrestrials despite official denial and secrecy by those "in the loop." He called for major global initiatives to achieve that end, and endorsed plans by exo-political researchers like Alfred Webre to prepare for a "Decade of Contact" in which humanity is prepared for the truth about aliens through informed debate and education.

"Paul Hellyer is the first senior politician," writes Exo-Political researcher and author Dr. Michael E. Salla, "to openly come out and declare the truth about the extraterrestrial presence. He is blazing a trail that many other senior politicians are destined to take. It will be wise if the world's senior politicians quickly learn more about this remarkable Canadian statesman and heed his important advice about data on extraterrestrial visitors and 'the profoundly important policy questions that must be addressed.'"

ALIEN TECHNOLOGY AS OUR SALVATION

In February of 2007, a couple of years after his appearance in Toronto, Hellyer again spoke out on the subject of extraterrestrials. According to a website called Canada.com, he stated his belief that advanced alien technology from extraterrestrial civilizations offers the best hope to "save our planet" form the perils of climate change.

Hellyer called for a public disclosure of alien technology obtained during alleged UFO crashes – such as the Roswell Incident – because he believes that an alien species can provide humanity with a viable alternative to fossil fuels. With concern about global warming at an all-time high, and Canadian political parties struggling to "out-green" one another, Hellyer said governments and the military have a responsibility to "come clean on what they know" now more than ever.

"Climate change is the number one problem facing the world today," he said. "I'm not discouraging anyone from being green conscious, but I would like to see what alien technology there might be that could eliminate the burning of fossil fuels within a generation, that could be a way to save our planet."

GETTING FROM THERE TO HERE

Hellyer said that UFO researchers have amassed undeniable evidence that aliens have visited our planet. Due to the distance such spacecraft would have to travel, UFOs must be equipped with some kind of advanced fuel source or propulsion system, he said.

Hellyer suspects that governments throughout the world know a great deal about alien technology, and that that knowledge may be enough to save the planet if applied to our problems quickly enough.

Even the token debunker quoted in the Canada.com article had to begrudgingly agree with Hellyer on one point.

Michael D. Robertis, of the Ontario Skeptics Society for Critical Inquiry, admitted that, while he doubts the reality of extraterrestrials, if aliens had visited Earth, there is no doubt their technical knowledge could benefit humanity.

"To have traveled hundreds of trillions of kilometers," Robertis said, "interstellar visitors would, at a minimum, require a civilization that is thousands – if not millions – of years ahead of our own. One would imagine they went through their own fossil fuel era and that they solved it and didn't go through some kind of pollution holocaust. There is no doubt they would have different solutions, different fuels and different energy sources."

Perhaps the most amazing thing about Paul Hellyer's going public in such firm, unequivocal terms is that it caused barely a ripple in the world at large, even with sympathetic press coverage that did not in any way imply he was "coming unwrapped," to use an expression. While Hellyer's open statements on the reality of UFOs may seem to come close to the fulfillment of Disclosure with a big D, which some of the interviewees in this book refer to as their ultimate goal, even with his impressive credentials and complete sincerity, the whole affair came and went so quietly that one must assume the time for real openness simply had not yet arrived. We can only hope that, if Disclosure happens, it will come at a time when it will still be possible to respond to that knowledge from a perspective of freedom and dignity.

A.J. GEVAERD: MAKING A BIG DENT IN THE WALL OF SECRECY

By Sean Casteel

A.J. Gevaerd's determination in getting the government of Brazil to open its UFO files is a real disclosure success story. Gevaerd was able not only to mobilize an organization of Brazil UFO researchers, he also elicited the kind of response from Brazilian officials that advocates in other parts of the world can only dream about.

GETTING STARTED ON THE PATH

Gevaerd studied chemistry at several universities in Brazil and then taught the subject at several high schools there. In the early 1980s, he left teaching to devote himself entirely to UFOlogy. His interest in UFOs began in his childhood, as is so often the case.

"I used to read everything that came into my hands," Gevaerd said. "By the age of 14 or 15, I did my first lecture. It was for my colleagues in school. Two or three years later, I was already lecturing at symposia in Brazil.

"It was not too long after that," he continued, "that I had the idea of starting the magazine, when I was 21, 22 years old."

The original title of Gevaerd's magazine was "UFOlogy International and National," but it is now called simply "UFO."

"We've been doing it for almost 27 years," he said. "And now our 'UFO Magazine' is the longest living regular UFO magazine on newsstands all over the world."

GEVAERD'S SIGHTING EXPERIENCE AT AREA 51

While Gevaerd downplays his own sighting experiences, he was willing to talk about them nonetheless. He said that in the early 1990s, when he was lecturing at a UFO conference being held at the Showboat Hotel and Casino in Las Vegas, he felt a sudden urge to visit Area 51, also famously located in Nevada. He and his wife were starting to feel a bit of cabin fever.

"We had just had enough of the casino and the conference," he said. "It was a week long, and by Tuesday or Wednesday you just can't stand anymore of the place. So we decided to get some fresh air and we started thinking, 'Why not go to Area 51?'"

Gevaerd and his wife met another couple attending the conference who agreed to make the drive to Area 51. When they reached the fabled Nevada UFO hotspot, they had a pleasant time at the Little A-Le Inn, famous for being the only restaurant in the immediate vicinity. As they were standing by the equally well known black mailbox (which has since become white, Gevaerd says) the group started to see a very bright light between the car and the mountain by Groom Lake Road.

"All of a sudden," Gevaerd recalled, "something happened and everything changed. We started to be so sleepy. We had such a tremendous need to sleep. Something happened to us; I don't know what. We couldn't see."

When they began the drive back to the hotel, the car could only crawl along at 20 to 30 miles an hour. Gevaerd sat in the backseat with his wife and the other couple was in the front seat. Gevaerd offered to drive, but the other man said he could manage.

"But he was almost sleeping," Gevaerd went on. "His wife was asleep, my wife was asleep, and I was almost sleeping as well. That big light was just following the car at some distance. After 40 minutes had passed, the light just went away. It disappeared. And all of a sudden, we became very conscious. We woke up and we could drive faster."

After the group arrived back at the hotel in Las Vegas, Gevaerd remembers that no one talked much about what had happened, a frequently reported aspect of an abduction experience.

"For ten or eleven years, for some reason I didn't discuss the thing with anybody," Gevaerd said. "Not like I was hiding it from someone else. It just didn't come to my attention anymore after it happened until a few years ago when I remembered it and started exploring that experience again. I want to go into hypnotic regression to see if something else happened. I don't think so, but it's a possibility anyway."

Gevaerd had another experience in the late 1990s when he was in a location in Brazil close to his home working with a television film crew. The truck Gevaerd was driving was stuck in the mud. With the film crew pushing from behind, Gevaerd sat in the driver's seat trying to gun the motor and free the truck.

"All of a sudden," he said, "a very bright light just crossed the windshield. From east to west at a regular speed, not very fast and also not slow, at a continuous speed."

Gevaerd says he has also had some frightening "dreams," one of which he tried to explore through hypnotic regression with legendary American abduction researcher Budd Hopkins, to little success.

"He found that I have a memory block," Gevaerd said, "right at the beginning of what I consider a very strange and consistent dream."

Which, while it is rare, does happen from time to time. The subject and the hypnotist simply can't break through whatever method of imposed amnesia the aliens have used to block the memory. But that's still basically okay with Gevaerd.

"I don't take these small experiences into consideration," he said, "when I do my work as a UFO researcher. What I do is investigate cases and do interviews, and I don't bring my personal experiences into my investigations. They don't have an influence on how I think about the UFOs or what I do."

A GROWING WORLDWIDE CONSCIOUSNESS

"In most of the world," Gevaerd said, "there is a growing consciousness about UFOs. It's going on in Brazil and Mexico and Chile and Argentina. I believe that, all over the world, there is a global feeling that something big is about to happen. It's very solid in Brazil, in Mexico, in Chile, and other South American countries, perhaps because of the spirituality of the people.

"All over the world, except for a few places where I have been recently, there is an increasing feeling that UFOs are very real and will bring a change in our way of life. It's something that's going to have a great impact on all of us. Of course, the government and the church are measuring this. The military is measuring this. It's common knowledge; it can be felt.

"If you go outside and talk to someone in the place where I live, compared to the same people you had 10 or 20 years ago, you definitely feel a change in the way people think about the subject."

MAKING A DENT IN THE WALL OF SECRECY

The feeling Gevaerd is talking about is certainly being helped along by his untiring efforts to get the government in his home country of Brazil to come forward with what they know. He told the story this way:

"In 2004," he began, "my co-editor and I had a discussion with a few friends in Rio. We were pressured by people who asked us, 'Why don't you do something about the government secrets? Why don't you do something to make the government go public about UFOs?' We gave some thought to this and had lots of conversations about it. In a week, we started a campaign – 'UFOs: Freedom of Information Now.'"

Prior to the formation of the Freedom of Information Now group, Gevaerd had helped to organize a group called the Brazilian Committee of UFO Researchers. The Committee was formed in 1997, and was able to host a very successful conference that brought over 70 speakers to Brazil from 35 countries. Gevaerd and the others revived the Committee as part of their new campaign with the government.

"We started by issuing a document," he said, "called 'The Brazilian UFO Manifest,' in which we declared to the public and the government what we, the UFO researchers in Brazil, believed about UFOs. To summarize and make it short, we believe we have solid information about five facts. And they are: Of course, UFOs are real. They have an extraterrestrial origin. They are approaching more and more. Their activity is increasing. And if you combine all these facts, then you have the fifth fact, that it is time for action."

Gevaerd published the UFO Manifest in his magazine, which sells between 30 and 50 thousand copies on the newsstands monthly, as well as on his website, which draws about 15 to 20 thousand visitors per day. The websites of his various colleagues were also put to use. After a few months of heavy advertising of the new movement, the group collected 70,000 signatures on a petition, which was used along with the Manifest to approach the Brazilian government.

THE GOVERNMENT'S SURPRISING RESPONSE

By January of 2005, Gevaerd received a call from a spokesperson who was speaking on behalf of the brigadier general who headed the Brazilin Air Force.

"He told me," Gevaerd said, "that the Brazilian Air Force is fully aware of our campaign, considers it legitimate, and wants to talk to us. They invited me to go to Brasilia, to the headquarters of the Brazilian Air Force, with all my team. We were a group of about seven at the time.

"We were very well welcomed at several Brazilian Air Force facilities, including the Integrated Center For Traffic Control and Air Traffic Control and Defense. In both places we were welcomed by the military and briefed. We were taken to see the operations, like radar rooms, situation rooms, archives and everything. At that time, I had the opportunity to present our government with a very thick document, which was the Brazilian UFO Manifest and the 70,000 signatures on our petition."

The visiting group was told that the General Commander of the Brazilian Air Force had ordered all his personnel to open every door to them. The group could see anything they wanted at the locations they were escorted to.

A. J. Gevaerd' Biography:

A. J. Gevaerd, 48, father of three, studied Chemistry in several universities in Brazil. Chemistry was his first passion and he became a teacher of it as young as 14 years old. By that time, he was already pursuing the mysteries involved in the UFO Phenomena and was a devoted investigator of flying saucers sightings and alien contact with humans. He started lecturing about UFOs in 1978. In 1985, when 23 years old, he decided to quit his carrier as a Chemistry teacher to devote full time to his UFO researches.

A. J. is the founder and editor of the *Brazilian UFO Magazine*, the only one existing in his country, for 26 years, and the long-lasting magazine about Ufology in the entire world today. *Brazilian UFO Magazine* has now two companions, *UFO Special* and *UFO Documental*. All the three magazines are monthly and circulate all over Brazil and Portugal in 30,000 issues. A. J. is also de founder and director of the *Brazilian Center for Flying Saucer Research (CBPDV)*, the largest organization in South America, with over 3,300 members.

As he started his activities as a field investigator very soon, A. J. Gevaerd has been engaged in Ufology for over 35 years and investigated over 3,000 cases personally. For the past 26 years, he is the only UFO researcher in Brazil exclusively dedicated to the UFO Phenomenon investigation in a professional manner as the editor of his magazines. He leads a team of over 400 experts in the subject that are members of the *Brazilian UFO Magazine*'s editorial board. As a national and international speaker, A. J. had lectured over 3,000 times in dozens of cities in his country and conducted investigations and lectures in other 50 countries around the world.

In 1983, he was appointed by Dr. J. Allen Hynek to be the representative of the *Center for UFO Studies (CUFOS)* in Brazil. He is presently one of the international directors of the *Annual International UFO Congress*, Laughlin, and Brazilian director for both *Mutual UFO Network (MUFON)* and *Skywatch International*. A. J. is the creator of the campaign *UFOs: Freedom of Information Now* and head of the Brazilian Committee of UFO Researchers, that has recently been received by the Nation's military and examined secret UFO docs by the very first time in Brazil, in the most recent official UFO disclosure in the World. Towards Brazilian Committee of UFO Researchers efforts Brazil has officially disclosed over 4,000 pages of UFO docs.

A. J. Gevaerd has been regularly interviewed by national and foreign radio talk shows, including Whitley Strieber's *Dreamland*, Errol-Bruce Knapp's *Strange Days Indeed*, George Noory and Art Bell's *Coast to Cost*, and Jeff Rense's *Rense Program*. He has also served as consultant to many TV documentaries produced in Brazil, especially by the largest TV network *Globo*, and in several other countries, such as The History Channel's *Brazil's Roswell*.

E-mail addresses:
aj@gevaerd.com
ajgevaerd@gmail.com
editor@ufo.com.br
www.ufo.com.br

Phone numbers:
Cellular +55 (41) 8872-3839
Home +55 (41) 3205-4974
Fax +55 (67) 3341-0245

"At the end of our trip," Gevaerd said, "we were received in a situation room, a top secret place, where secret decisions are made related to National Security and Defense. A very big room. We were briefed by the commander at that time, who said, 'Now you're going to see what you came to see.'"

The group was shown another room with several files on top of a big table, and were allowed to scrutinize all the material contained in the files. Among the cases detailed in the files were several sightings in the Amazon River area and a case called "The Official UFO Night In Brazil," about which more later. The group also received a promise: that the Brazilian Air Force would work along with civilian researchers to investigate future UFO events.

However, the Air Force did not permit the group to photocopy any of the material or photos, and prohibited cameras and pens as well. They were only allowed to lay eyes on the files.

"Okay, that was the first disclosure in Brazil," Gevaerd said, "but not what we wanted. So we decided to wait a little longer until the Brazilian Air Force actually did what it promised, which was to start a committee for UFO research composed of their members, military investigators and also civilians. By December 2007, we were very pissed off because nothing happened. Everything that was promised to us didn't happen."

Gavaerd and his group responded with Phase Two of their campaign, which involved issuing a much thicker document packed with more accumulated evidence of Brazilian military involvement in UFO investigations.

"We got back to our campaign," he said, "and we started making a lot of noise. By August 2008, finally the government started releasing material. We first got a few folders with a few hundred pages from the 1950s, describing how the Air Force in Brazil dealt with the subject, with cases and reports and this kind of stuff. A few months later, we have material released from the 1960s. Then we understood that the government would release their secret documents by decade."

After receiving documents from the 1970s and 80s, the group has accumulated about 5,000 pages of UFO documents and few hundred folders, including drawings of UFOs that resulted from field investigations made by Brazilian Air Forces officers.

"These are drawings of UFOs that have landed," he said, "in full color, including some with occupants outside the spaceships. This is very hot stuff. Among the 5,000 pages we got, there are some treasures."

A file on what Gevaerd calls "The Official UFO Night" is one of those treasures. The night in question took place in May of 1986. Seven jetfighters were scrambled to pursue 21 spheres, each of them a whopping hundred meters in diameter. The enormous objects appeared over most of the inhabited locations in Brazil, forcing the Minister of Defense to go on national television and admit that something had indeed happened.

The Minister acknowledged that 21 objects were seen in the skies of Brazil and that the matter was being thoroughly investigated and a report would be issued within 30 days. The report never saw the light of day. But Gavaerd was able to ascertain that a report had indeed been done that was sent to the highest authorities in the country because he now has a copy of it, written at the beginning of June that fateful year.

"This material is one of the treasures that we have in all these 5,000 pages," he said. "It declares that the objects detected by radar and pursued by jetfighters on that night were solid and under some sort of intelligent control. That was a full admission that the objects were intelligent in origin.

"Now we have a staff of people," he continued, "going over all these pages to classify and organize them. There is lots of material that is mixed up, pages from one document mixed up with pages from another document. Thirty or forty percent of all these pages is a mess and we're trying to put it all in a good format to be consulted by anyone. It is all in the National Archives and on our webpage at UFO.com.br."

SOME OF THE MILITARY GOES PUBLIC

While the Brazilian government still hasn't publicly declared that UFOs are an extraterrestrial reality, Gevaerd has conversed with high ranking military officials who spoke to him frankly and with the understanding that he would not withhold what he was told from the public. Gevaerd spoke to former Minister of Defense Socrates Monteiro, for example, one of the most decorated members of the military in Brazil.

"I got him to speak a lot about UFOs," Gevaerd said. "He even declared he had a sighting. He also said that when the Official UFO Night in Brazil was happening, that the radar detected objects going up to 3,500 kilometers per hour. Amazing, isn't it? He said the documents, and there are many, should be released."

Another general Gevaerd spoke to told him that there are 12,000 kilos of UFO documents, photos, videos and other material stored in various locations throughout Brazil. An order to move all the material to Brasilia was issued but public access to it is still denied.

"See, what we're getting now is lots of stuff," Gevaerd said, "but it's much less than what we expect. I believe that what the government is releasing, not only here but anywhere else in the world, is only a small tip of a big iceberg. You see France, they have released over 100,000 pages of UFO documents, and Great Britain has released about 7,000 documents. So the Peruvian government, the Chilean government, the Uruguayan government, a few other governments in the world, they have come out with some material and released it to the public. Spain, Denmark, Norway, whatever.

"But all these governments are releasing only the small tip of the iceberg, because what is the actual hardcore, top secret information about UFOs is still being kept secret."

One case Gevaerd is not surprised to see missing from the government-released documents is the crash of a UFO that took place on January 20, 1996, in a part of Brazil called Varginha. Although Gevaerd and his team were able to document military involvement in the crash, there is no mention of it in the files.

Gevaerd went on to explain the strategy he and his colleagues used to obtain the government's files.

"We knew that there was no point," he said, "in coming to the government and the military saying, 'We are UFO researchers. We know that you are investigating UFOs and that you have lots of secrets. We want you to release them.' That's not the way to do it. It would never happen.

"So we decided to go under a strategy, which was to select a very few cases to present to the government and ask, 'We want information and all papers and documents resulting from the official investigations by the military of these cases.' Now of course we selected very strong cases in which we had undeniable, unquestionable evidence, including documented evidence of the Brazilian military involvement in them."

There were three cases chosen. One of the events the group sought the files for was called "Operation Saucer," which took place from September through December 1977 in the Amazon River region. Over the span of months, the Brazilian Air Force took over 500 photographs and recorded 16 hours of film footage.

Gevaerd spoke to one of the officers involved in the long period of nighttime surveillance, who told the UFO researcher that over 3,000 pages of reports on the saucer watch had been prepared by the military in addition to the photos and video. Only a fraction of the collected records have been released.

"Out of this 3,000 pages, we now have about 500 pages," Gevaerd said, "and about 200 pictures. We are still missing over 2000 pages and over 300 photos. This is why I tell you that the government is only releasing very small pieces of information. For its own reasons, the government thinks it can't be released."

In spite of his frustration with the Brazilian government's unwillingness to release absolutely everything they have, Gevaerd still boasts that Brazil leads the way in terms of disclosure.

"Brazil was the first country in the world," he said, "to officially admit to the UFOs' existence. Everybody thinks it was France, right? Because France made a public announcement back in 1976, when their Minister of Defense ordered his people to come forward with some photos of UFOs made in French territory. They went on television and said UFOs were for real, most probably not from this planet, and that France is actively investigating the subject.

"But back in 1954, 22 years before that, a colonel in the Brazilian Air Force went to the United States to exchange information about UFOs with the U.S. military. I believe he was ordered not to speak about UFOs publicly in Brazil, but he decided to do otherwise."

When the colonel returned to Brazil, he quickly gathered together selected members of the press, over a hundred selected members of society and carefully chosen members of the military. They met at the Brazilian School of War, a major institution in Brazil, where the colonel declared that Brazil considers the subject of flying saucers a very serious matter. After that, official investigations of the subject began in earnest.

THE AIR FORCE COUGHS UP MORE

In 1969, a joint committee of the Air Force and the Army was started and centered in Sao Paolo. Called the Unidentified Aerial Objects Investigations System, its similarity to Project Blue Book in the United States is obvious. The committee would reach a level of 200 members who employed a fixed routine and protocol for investigating UFO sightings throughout Brazil. Naturally, as members of the military, they had access to anywhere in the country.

"Now among the papers that were released," Gevaerd said, "and we're talking about 5,000 or 6,000 pages, we now have several dozens of reports made by Brazilian Air Force personnel. They investigated for several years, up through the early 1970s. They issued several documents that were kept secret, and before the disclosure, we only had access to a few documents through 'leakage,' files that we have here and there from people who retired and took the files to their homes and eventually decided to give them away to someone.

"We ended up receiving a few hundred pages of documentation that way and now we have over 2,000 from the Brazilian Air Force System of Investigation of Aerial Unidentified Objects. This material is very strong. It contains drawings made by the military of landed UFOs. It shows the modus operandi of the Air Force, how it investigated these objects scientifically."

HOW BRAZIL SEES ITS ALIENS

When asked what kind of aliens turn up in Brazil, Gevaerd said it was mainly the familiar gray type, about three to four feet in height.

"Now, the difference," he said, "between Brazilian cases involving occupants and the United States cases involving occupants is basic. We don't have as many gray cases as you have in the U.S. Beginning in the 1980s, in the U.S., there are many programs and a lot of information. I would say too much pollution about this subject. So when someone has a sighting, an encounter, in the U.S., the tendency of this person is to fill it, his original experience, with what he sees or reads or learns from TV shows and everything. The information gets a little polluted. Sometimes too polluted.

"But it doesn't happen in Brazil or in most countries in South America because we don't have that many programs. We just have a small fraction of your programs being aired here. We don't have so much information available all over like it is in the United States.

"Because of that, and because Brazil is predominately a rural country, there is a vast un-reached audience of people living on farms. So most of the cases that we get, especially in those areas, when these cases reach us, they are very unpolluted. They are very clear. People have a tendency to describe to us precisely what they saw or what they experienced."

There are many cases in Brazil of abductions or encounters with occupants outside the ships, and over the course of many years Gevaerd has investigated and written for his magazine about several dozen.

"I can tell you," he said, "that the people involved in this are very serious and very simple people. They are not people who create stories. They are people who have given us very straight descriptions. But the way they describe the facts to us, they are sometimes too simple. We have to work, through a series of questions and other techniques, to get more information from the witnesses. The scenario is the same or almost the same in Brazil, Bolivia, Argentina, Chile, Peru, Paraguay, and Uruguay.

"Take Argentina for instance. There are areas in Argentina where you can go and see UFOs on a very regular basis, just like in some areas in Brazil. You can talk to some people who live in the mountains. Out of ten, at least nine will give you very interesting descriptions of sightings. Among those, you'll get two or three that are amazing, with multiple witnesses, multiple observations, etc. So this is something."

ALONG THE BANKS OF THE AMAZON

"I specialized in investigating UFO cases in the Amazon area," Gevaerd said. "I go to the Amazon quite a lot. You know how I investigate? I just get to a place, rent a boat, with a boat driver or whatever you want to call it, and spend days upriver. I go to every house by the banks of the river, small villages or areas where there are only two or three houses. Very small places. I go to every one of them. I stop the boat, I go out and I start a conversation with people who live by the banks of the Amazon River. People who don't see people every day. People who don't have TV and rarely have a radio. Very occasionally they go to some larger city.

"I just have a conversation, a simple conversation. At some point, I ask about lights in the sky, strange objects that have come close to the ground. Out of every ten persons that I talk to, at least nine will give me very interesting stories. I have collected so many. I could take the whole night telling you, and they are very precious.

"Now we're not just talking about lights in the sky. We're talking to people who opened the windows because there was a light, and when they looked at it straight on there was a big structured object, a source of very intense light, with some kind of humming sound or something like that. So it's a very rich description. It's a case that has solid information. This is what we get in Brazil.

"If you asked me whether these people have been suffering from some kind of illusion? Definitely not. We're talking about people who lived their life normally after they had their experience. And when they find someone who's interested in hearing them, like a UFO researcher such as myself and my colleagues, they are very glad to describe what they saw."

Gevaerd said there are many interested parties in the U.S., Europe and Australia who want to come to Brazil and see with their own eyes what is happening there. But travel is difficult to arrange, and a trip to the Amazon requires time on a small plane plus renting a boat as there are few serviceable roads in the area.

WHAT THE ALIENS ARE ALL ABOUT

"I always say this about the aliens," Gevaerd said. "For me, that is what I believe to be one of the most interesting things about this phenomenon. And most people take it for granted. Have you ever noticed that 99 percent of the cases in which someone saw an alien, this creature was a humanlike creature? It had two arms, two legs, a body, a neck, a head on top of the neck, two eyes, two ears, a mouth and a nose.

"Now, if they really came from so many planets, which had so many different evolutionary processes, how come they're all similar to each other and similar to us? For me, the big reason is that all these space people and us, we are all part of the same humanity. That is to say, humanity is not confined to the planet Earth but it's spread all over. We are all evolving.

"And what we are doing now is precisely what they're doing. What are they doing? They're visiting other planets. Exactly what we are doing. We are sending probes to almost every body in the solar system. We are sending probes that have landed on the moon and we also put a man on the moon. We've landed probes on Venus and Mars and many other places.

"Why? Because it is our nature to go outside, to stretch our limits as far as possible, to see what is outside. However, our present technology only allows us to go to our backyard, which is the neighborhood of Earth. But it's going to change. In 20 years, in 30 years, we will be able to go much faster to much further away places. Precisely what the aliens are doing. Call them cousins or half-brothers. But certainly we have some relationship with them. By coming here, they are doing precisely the same thing that we're doing presently with our technology in the neighborhood of Earth."

SOME FINAL THOUGHTS

"I want to tell you," Gevaerd said, "that we are all very excited about the disclosure in Brazil. We expect our government to release more information any time. And when it happens, we will proceed in exactly the same way. We will get it all over the Internet, for everyone to see. Whatever we think is really important, we'll put it in English and Spanish and it will spread through the world."

At the time of this interview, Gevaerd was being bombarded with invitations to lecture and media requests for interviews.

"After disclosure," he said brightly, "things have been upside down. Thank God!"

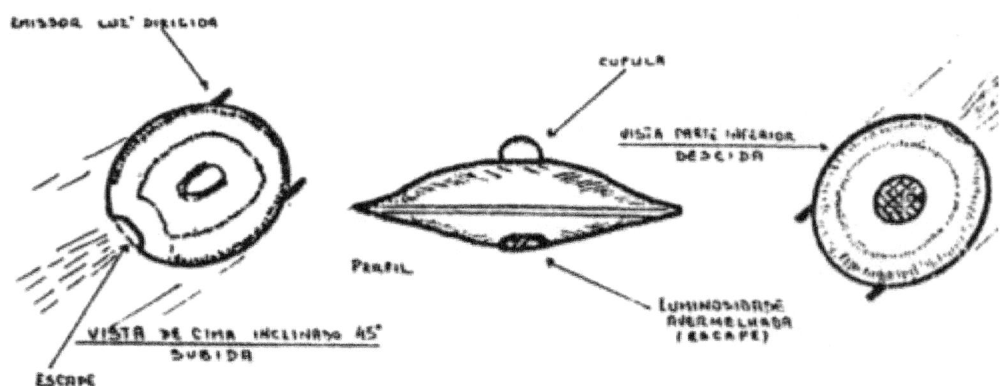

LOCAL: COLARES - PA
LAT. 00°52'40"S - LONG. 048°31' 00" W
DATA : 06 NOV 77 - HORA : 19:00H.
COND. METEOROLOGICAS : NIL. CÉU CLARO
DESCRIÇÃO
DIÂMETRO: 1.5CM. PERFIL: OVAL C/CÚPULA TRANSPARENTE NA PARTE SUPERIOR
(TESTEMUNHA JULGOU SER DEPÓSITO DE GÁS). DOIS TUBOS SEPARADOS ENTRE SI
POR 0.80M (MEIA BRAÇA). EMITINDO LUZ DIRIGIDA NAS CORES VERDE E VERMELHA.
COR DO OBJETO: CINZA CLARO (QUASE BRANCO) COM REFLEXO LUMINOSO EM
TODA A ESTRUTURA. CIRCULO AVERMELHADO NA PARTE INFERIOR. (BRASEIRO)
DISTÂNCIA ESTIMADA 500M.
DESENHO (ADAPTADO) AO ORIGINAL

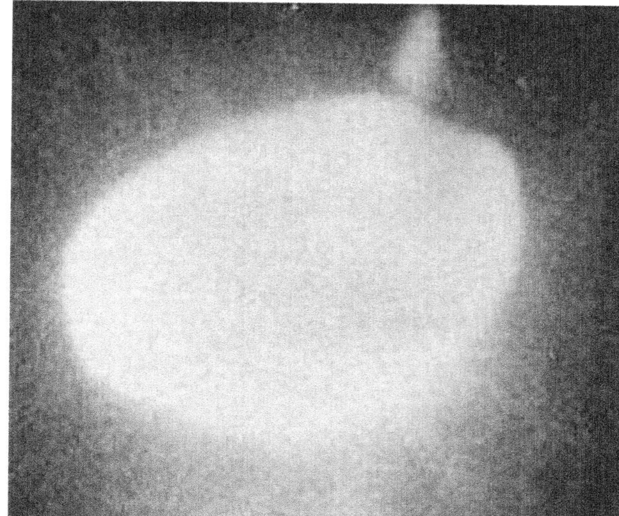

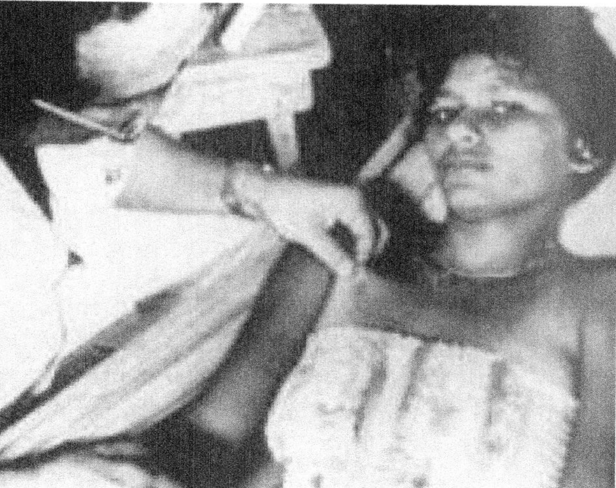

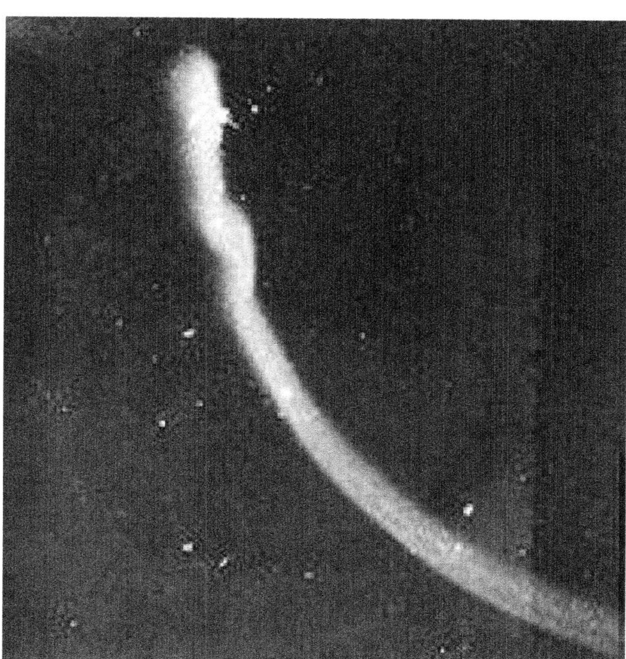

Brazilian Nationals Injured In Unprovoked UFO Attacks

In 1977 the Brazilian island of Colares and the area of the Amazon delta were visited by flying objects of an unknown nature. Nearly all kinds of UFOs were seen, some big, some small, saucer-shaped, cigar-shaped, barrel-shaped, luminous or not. They arrived generally from the North every day, from the sky and also sometimes from underwater, and it lasted for months. Regularly, some Island inhabitants were targeted by the objects beaming strange lights at them and many were badly hurt. The Air Force came, investigated, saw, reported. The weird rays hurt 35 people, and civilians fled from entire villages. You never heard this before? Well read ahead, then.

AJ has long published the very popular Brazilian **UFO Magazine.**

THE ROCKEFELLER UFO REPORT CONTENTS

ANTONIO HUNEEUS: MEETING A GENERAL AND WORKING WITH A GIANT

By Sean Casteel

Antonio Huneeus is a longtime veteran investigator and writer, laboring in the UFO field both in the United States and throughout the world. His international reputation has opened many doors for him as a journalist, including a private meeting with a Chilean general who talked frankly about the subject of an alien presence in his country.

ONE THING LEADS TO ANOTHER

The trail that led to Huneeus' meeting with the Chilean general began in 1997, when Huneeus was attending a UFO conference being held at the University of Santiago. Huneeus had heard of a psychiatrist who conducted UFO abduction research in Chile, a man named Mario Dussuel. The psychiatrist was a friend of the retired Commander-In-Chief of the Chilean Air Force, one General Ramon Vega.

The psychiatrist set up a meeting between Huneeus and Vega, held at the general's office in downtown Santiago.

"He had a relatively small office," Huneeus said. "He was no longer the commander of the air force, but obviously he was still very well connected."

Huneeus presented General Vega with a copy of the "UFO Briefing Document," which will be discussed further later in this chapter.

"So we had a very cordial meeting," Huneeus said. "Now, normally, when you're meeting people like this, you have to make a case for UFOs, you know, to try to convince them that the subject is worthy of study, that it's a serious matter. With General Vega, that wasn't necessary at all, because he was already totally convinced that UFOs are real, based on some experiences he had had. He had a sighting as a pilot, he told us. And I guess also based on reports that he had received from Chilean Air Force pilots or whatever material he had seen. So he was totally convinced that UFOs are real."

A WELL-TIMED PHOTO OPPORTUNITY

The timing for presenting the briefing document was excellent, Huneeus said, because General Vega was then working with Gustavo Rodriguez, an official of the Chile Civil Aviation Agency, to make a case for the Chilean government to create an official agency to investigate UFOs.

"They were putting together a number of documents," Huneeus said, "that would support their case, so our briefing document was added to that material. And sure enough, within a few months, the Chilean government did announce that they had created an official agency, called CEFFA, which is an acronym for like Committee for the Study of Aerial Anomalous Phenomena. It is attached to the Civil Aviation Agency of the government of Chile, which is also attached to the Air Force.

"So that basically was the story," Huneeus continued, "the background of that photograph, in which you see me and the general. The general has the book open, the briefing document, and he's kind of glancing at it."

A DISCLOSURE DISAPPOINTMENT

The story of the briefing document itself is a fascinating one. It began with the financial help of one of North America's richest patrons, Laurence Rockefeller.

"Laurence Rockefeller was the son of the original John D. Rockefeller," Huneeus explained, "one of the original five sons. He passed away a few years ago, but he was well-known to be interested in UFOs and the paranormal, parapsychology, a number of these things. Since at least the 1980s, he had already been involved in funding some of this kind of research. He was sponsoring an outfit called The Human Potential Foundation, which was led by Dr. Scott Jones and located in the northern Viriginia/Washington DC area."

In the early 1990s, Rockefeller, along with his attorney Henry Diamond and Dr. Jones, made a lobbying effort with the Science Advisor of the White House during the Clinton administration, a scientist named Paul Gibbons.

"Basically," Huneeus said, "it was an attempt to get the Clinton Administration to put pressure on the Air Force to make a release on Roswell. There are several documents and letters and so on between the White House and Rockefeller's office about this, and there were some meetings that took place as well. There is a photo released by the Clinton Library which shows Laurence Rockefeller shaking hands with the president."

Unfortunately, Huneeus said, the whole effort was completely defused when the Air Force released the Mogul report. Partially in response to the pressure applied by New Mexico Congressman Steven Schiff, the Air Force felt compelled to make a public statement.

"So they basically came up with those stupid reports," Huneeus said. "The first one, the big one, claimed that yes, there had been a cover-up, but the cover-up was due to Project Mogul, which was a top secret balloon to detect the Russians' detonation of their first atomic bomb. Then they did a second report, which was far worse, the one about the dummies, 'Roswell Case Closed.' So that was the end of the first Rockefeller Initiative, since basically that didn't come to anything. There was a release, but it was not the release that Rockefeller or the UFO community was expecting."

Antonio Huneeus with General (Ret.) Ramon Vega, former Commander-in-Chief of the Chilean Air Force, at his office in Santiago in 1997. Gen. Vega, who was then a Senator, is holding a copy of the Laurance Rockefeller-funded UFO Briefing Document, co-written by Antonio Huneeus. This report helped Vega to convince the Chilean authorities to launch an official UFO investigation called CEFAA (Committee for the Study of Anomalous Aerial Phenomena) attached to Chile's Civil Aviation agency.

SHIFTING GEARS AND MOVING FORWARD

"So then gears were shifted," Huneeus said. "Up until that point, most of Rockefeller's UFO Initiative had been done through Scott Jones and The Human Potential Foundation. Now he shifted instead to Marie Galbraith."

Marie Galbraith was the wife of a former ambassador to France during the Reagan years, Evan Galbraith. Evan was the cousin of John Kenneth Galbraith, the Nobel Prize winning economist who was also an ambassador to India under John Kennedy.

"So these are very influential people," Huneeus said. "Marie Galbraith was fascinated with the UFO subject, and she convinced Rockefeller to fund a different project and create a UFO briefing document that could be sent to VIPs and given to people, like the one I gave in Chile, to General Vega. That's how 'The UFO Briefing Document' came to be."

Huneeus was asked at the outset to participate in the project but was unable to do so because of other commitments in Japan. He promised to help out once his deadlines there were met.

UFO researcher Don Berliner wrote the original draft of the briefing document, and Rockefeller and Galbraith were pleased with the general format. But it was obvious that the document needed far more foreign material. Since Berliner could not read French, Spanish or Portuguese, he was able to base foreign case reports only on secondhand versions, accounts published in places like "The MUFON UFO Journal."

When the decision was made to write about the Belgium UFO Wave for the briefing document, it needed someone who could read French in order to utilize the original reports. At this point, Huneeus, who reads French, had fulfilled his commitments in Japan and was able to step in and assist with the briefing document.

"I made a number of recommendations," he said, "which were all approved. We expanded the document considerably; we rewrote some sections; we added some new case histories. This eventually became known as 'The UFO Briefing Document: The Best Available Evidence,' which was finished in December of 1995 and released in early 1996. It was sent to a number of senators, congressmen, and various people. Unfortunately, there was no coordinated lobbying effort so the report was just kind of given ad hoc to people. There was no real follow-up."

The briefing document was eventually published by Dell Publishing with the help of abductee and author Whitley Strieber. Rockefeller would go on to fund other projects before his death, including some early support for Steven Greer's Disclosure Foundation.

"Undoubtedly," Huneeus said, "Rockefeller was very consistent and he kept funding different things to see what would work. But the whole story still has not been told. Nobody has put all these elements together."

A WALK DOWN A WOODED PATH

Huneeus also talked about a story that was featured in the premiere issue of "Open Minds," the magazine for which he had just begun to work as managing editor.

"This was one of our biggest stories," he said. "There were these photos that were released, taken when Hillary Clinton visited the J.Y. Ranch that Laurence Rockefeller owned near the Grand Tetons in Wyoming. In the photos, you see Mr. Rockefeller with, at that time, the First Lady, now Secretary of State, walking on a wooded path. You can see that she is holding a book, but the book is on the back cover and it's upside down. So everyone was trying to find out, 'What is this book?'"

Initially the only available photos were too small and at too low a resolution. The Clinton Library subsequently released a much larger photo at a higher resolution, which revealed the book in Hillary Clinton's hand to be "Are We Alone? Philosophical Implications of the Discovery of Extraterrestrial Life" by Paul Davies.

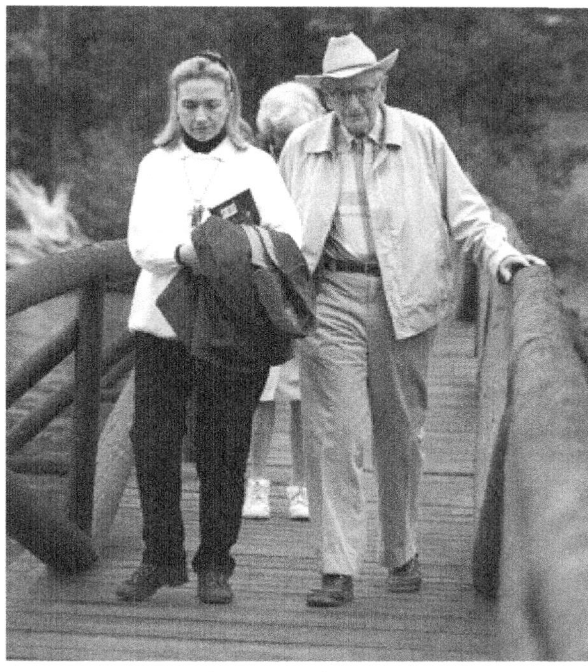

Secretary of State Hillary Clinton and Lawrence Rockefeller take a brisk while they talk about UFOs and the Rockefeller Initiative which Antonio Huneeus worked on.

"At the time," Huneeus said, "it was a famous bestseller. Our guess, and this is only a guess, because Hillary is probably not going to be talking about this, unless she really gets cornered, and of course Rockefeller is dead. But it makes sense that what happened is that Laurence Rockefeller gave her the book.

"It would have been an ideal book to give her because, first of all, it's written by Paul Davies, who is totally a mainstream scientist. It's also a philosophical book, so it's not a 'controversial' book. But it is still about the philosophical implications of the discovery of alien life.

"So that kind of pins it down. That proves what we always suspected, that when Hillary visited Rockefeller, they did discuss the subject of UFOs. But since neither of them was talking publicly – probably Rockefeller didn't want to embarrass the First Lady, so he kept quiet. She of course didn't want to talk about it publicly or create waves politically, so we couldn't prove it one hundred percent. But now that we see the pictures of her carrying that book, then it's obvious that, at least in some respects – casually, if nothing else – the subject was discussed."

World roving journalist and UFO researcher Antonio Huneeus sits down for a chat with Col Robert Friend former head of Project Blue Book.

Nick Pope undertook a cold case review of the Rendlesham Forest incident in 1994, while working on the MoD's UFO project. He has written about the case extensively in the media and discussed it on numerous TV shows.

In the early hours of 26 December 1980, military personnel at the twin bases saw strange lights in the forest. Thinking an aircraft might have crashed, they went out to investigate. What they found was a small triangular-shaped craft that had landed in a clearing in Rendlesham Forest. Nearby farm animals were going into a frenzy. One of the security police officers, Jim Penniston, got close enough to touch the side of the object. He and another of the airmen present, John Burroughs, attached sketches of the craft to their official USAF witness statements. One of these sketches details strange symbols Penniston saw on the craft's hull, which he likened to Egyptian hieroglyphs.

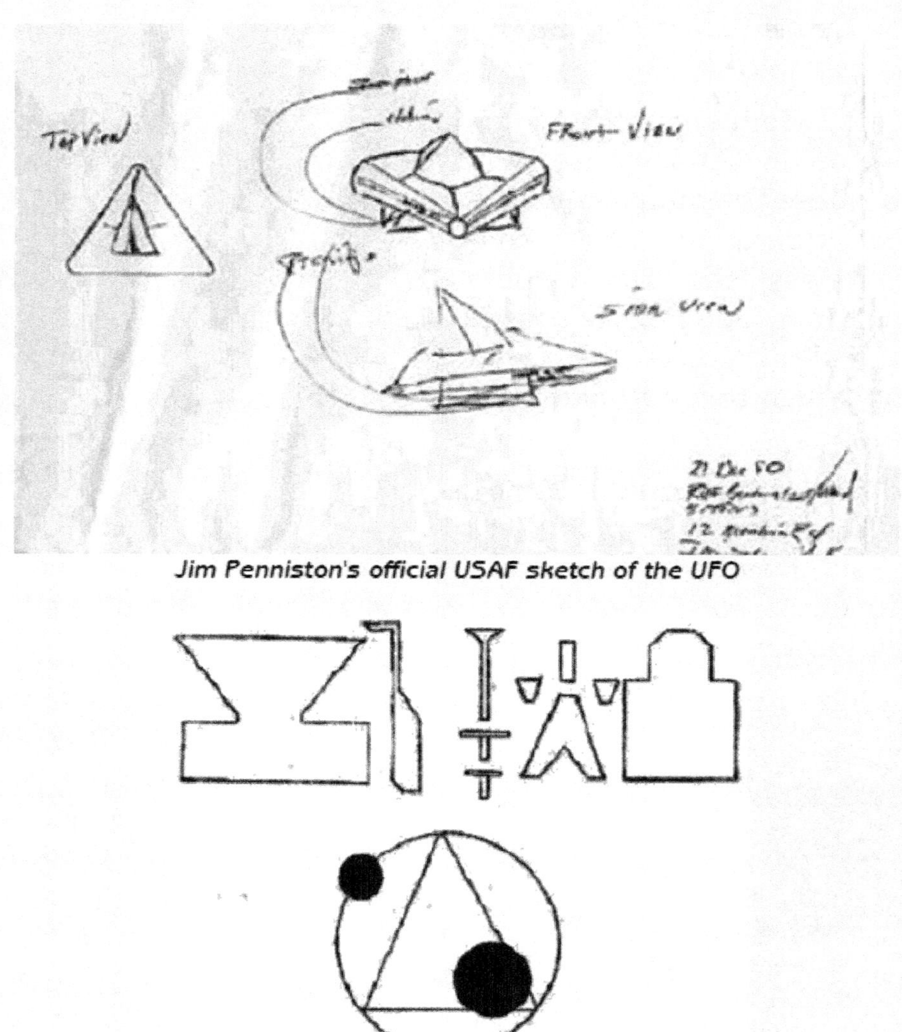

Jim Penniston's official USAF sketch of the UFO

Jim Penniston's official USAF sketch of the symbols

NICK POPE: THE QUIET BRIT AND THE PERFECT STORM

By Sean Casteel

Nick Pope had the honor of working for the British Ministry of Defence for 21 years and is known worldwide for the quiet dignity with which he headed the UFO post there. The obvious first question is of course how he came to that position.

Nick Pope

"I was a civilian employee," Pope said, "so I was never actually in the military. But I obviously worked very closely with military people for most of my career. Between 1991 and 1994, I was posted to an area where my duties included responsibility for the UFO phenomenon, both in terms of policy and investigation – investigating the sightings that were reported to us. We received about 200 to 300 reports a year.

"Now, I had no previous knowledge or interest in this subject," Pope continued. "And indeed I was slightly wary that this would not be perhaps entirely beneficial to my career. I thought it might look a little quirky on my resume. But I soon changed my mind about that and realized that it was an interesting and important subject."

Pope said he had effectively been "headhunted" into the UFO job. His previous assignment had been with the Air Force Operations Room, in the Joint Operations Center during the first Gulf War.

"I was basically a briefer and a watch keeper," he said. "And the person that had the vacancy for the UFO job was my immediate boss down there, so I impressed him with my work during the first Gulf War and he then offered me the UFO job. I did that for three years and then I got promoted, so there was nothing sinister about my being moved. Even if I'd not been promoted, three years was a fairly average posting, so I would probably have moved on anyway."

Pope next worked for the MoD in a couple of different jobs, resigning in 2006.

"I just decided," he said, "that, having done 21 years, I would resign and go and do something else while I was still young enough to do so. So that's basically the story of how I got the job and what happened afterwards."

THE RELEASE OF UFO FILES BY THE U.K.

Should the release of the U.K. UFO files be considered something important to rank-and-file UFOlogists? Or do the cynics who think it's another whitewash have the right idea?

"First of all," Pope replied, "I would say that in general terms the entire release program is hugely significant. It's what I call 'disclosure with a small d.' I know a lot of people in the UFO community talk about disclosure and they tend to spell it with a big D. They imagine some scenario with the president going on television and the hangar doors of some military establishment swinging open and some great revelation of an alien spacecraft. This is not what is in these UFO files. There is no spaceship-in-the-hangar smoking gun.

"That said," he continued, "there are plenty of interesting cases which were not explained at the time. Some interesting sightings from police officers and military personnel, UFOs tracked on radar, those sorts of things. Near-misses between UFOs and commercial aircraft. So this is disclosure with a little d."

Which means one should not look askance at what is there.

"It's the real deal," Pope enthused. "There are literally tens of thousands of pages and this is a government-sponsored release program. So, unlike a lot of documents doing the rounds, there's no dispute over the authenticity of this material. So the release program in its entirety is important."

The U.K. release program followed on the heels of a similar release of files by the French in 2007, a precedent that Pope says the U.K. would have had a difficult time ignoring.

"But the main reason," Pope said, "was that the Ministry of Defence was receiving more Freedom of Information Act requests on UFOs than on any other subject. Literally hundreds of people were bombarding the department with these requests, and they decided that proactively releasing the material to the National Archives would then enable them to respond to virtually any future FOIA request with a one-sentence reply saying that all the material is now available at the National Archives."

The MoD had been releasing the files in chronological batches, and as this book was being written, the fifth and most recent batch of U.K. of material had been released on February 18, 2010 and consisted of 24 files and over 6,000 pages of documentation.

"There were some interesting cases in there," Pope said. "One, which had attracted some media attention at the time, took place on January 6, 1995, and involved a near-miss between a Boeing 737 and a UFO near Manchester Airport. That was an interesting case. There was also an interesting case from February 1999 where a senior air traffic controller tracked a huge target traveling at phenomenal speed on the radar. So the release program continues, and it's good news. I welcome this."

SHOOT-DOWN ORDERS

Another case, released along with the second batch of U.K. files, is consistently mentioned as important, not only by Pope but by others as well.

"This was the case of Milton Torres," Pope said, "a United States Air Force pilot who, in 1957, was based in the United Kingdom. His story is that he was scrambled in response to an uncorrelated target being tracked on radar. He then picked up this thing, which was huge, on his airborne radar and he received an order to shoot it down. He was flying an F-86 Saber, I think, which had 24 air-to-air rockets. He came very close to a position where he would have been in range to do that, but the object, whatever it was – and which he never saw visually, by the way, this was entirely by radar – but from a very slow speed, indeed a virtual hover, it moved away at a speed of about Mach 10 when he tried to get into a firing position. So that's a fascinating case."

There have also been shoot-down orders issued in other UFO encounters, Pope said, in Iran in 1976 and Peru in 1980, adding that, "These shoot-down cases are quite disturbing and interesting."

THE U.K. IS NOT SO UNIQUE

Pope replied to a question as to whether the U.K. is unique in its openness about the UFO phenomenon in the negative.

"I wouldn't say so," he answered. "I would say that in any modern, Western, democratic society where there's a Freedom of Information Act and a relatively free press – we are now seeing either the release of government UFO files or certainly pressure that may well lead to that. France has released its material, Britain is in the middle of a three-year program to do that, lots of documents have come out from countries like Brazil, from Italy, material has come out from Norway and Denmark. So it's almost like a line of dominoes falling. The more countries do this, the more it puts pressure on those that have not to do so."

The semantic conflict continues as well.

"I suppose it comes back to the question," Pope continued, "of what 'disclosure' means to people. Because it prompts the question, 'What do you think there is to disclose?' Now, if people genuinely believe that some governments are aware of an extraterrestrial presence, and are covering it up, then for any number of reasons disclosure may be difficult for them. If, however, you're dealing with a country like the U.K., where – certainly to the best of my knowledge – we can't have that knowledge, then the bottom line is that we didn't know what UFOs were and so it's relatively easy for us to open our files. I guess it depends on who knows what."

The U.K. was following the lead of the U.S. in a great many things.

"The U.K.'s policies were certainly modeled on the U.S. position," Pope agreed, "and indeed the job that I was doing in the early 1990s, in terms of the methodology of investigation, the terms of reference with which I was operating, were very similar to Project Blue Book. Indeed, in the early 1950s, there was certainly some liaison between the British and the Americans as we began our first investigations into this phenomenon and set up our projects. I suppose one could say, as a more general observation, that Britain usually falls in line with American foreign and defense policy. We use the phrase 'the special relationship.'

"I think critics say that it does amount to Britain slavishly following what America does. Whether that's true in relation to the UFO phenomenon, I'm not so sure. Of course America's public position is that they're not in the game at all now. For a number of reasons, I suspect that actually, clearly, if a pilot sees a UFO and something is tracked on radar, someone somewhere in the U.S. naturally will be looking at that because it's a defense, national security and air safety issue.

"But whether there is some great secret program going on and whether Britain has been roped in, I'm frankly more skeptical. I didn't know. There was very little liaison between the U.K. and the U.S. on this issue. Certainly when I was doing the UFO job, the Americans maintained with the MoD the same line as they maintain in public, that 'We're not in this game anymore.'"

WHERE EVIDENCE BECOMES UNDENIABLE PROOF

I asked Pope what would be required to literally force official disclosure of an alien presence. When faced with the same "push-comes-to-shove" question as the other interviewees in this book, Pope gave a thoughtful answer.

"In terms of where evidence becomes undeniable proof," he said, "I suppose, yes, [it would require] the archetypal landing on the White House lawn or the verification by the mainstream scientific community or some artifact that was unquestionably extraterrestrial in origin. A determination of that, of course, might be quite complex, because it might be difficult to be sure that that it was genuinely extraterrestrial as opposed to, say, some deep black program that had thrown up some quantum leap discovery. But isotopic analysis of the material, for example, would be a part of that."

There is another possibility for official disclosure that Pope approached somewhat more cautiously.

"The other strand of all this," he said, "and I know this is not popular with many in the UFO community, but it's the Search For Extraterrestrial Intelligence, SETI. The idea is that at any time it may be that SETI announces that they have picked up a signal, and that, in terms of verification, would be comparatively easy. You couldn't fake the science behind that.

"That's something that might happen any day. Certainly, with the planned construction of the Square Kilometer Array, which in terms of its power and sensitivity is going to be a quantum leap ahead of anything we've got now, there are some exciting times ahead. It may well be that the SETI community beats the UFO community to the punch on that."

HYSTERIA IS NOT INEVITABLE

Would public knowledge of the UFO reality really cause everything to fall apart?

"No, it wouldn't," Pope replied. "There is no real evidence that that's the case. I know a lot of people cite the Orson Welles 'War of the Worlds' broadcast as being proof that there would be panic in the streets. I think there are two points there. Firstly, the reaction to that broadcast is disputed and from my understanding was not quite as widespread in terms of the panic and the belief that that was real as some people will tell you.

"The other point is that of course that was a different age. We're in the multimedia age now of 24/7 news coverage, and, through realistic science fiction films with tremendous special effects, we're almost anesthetized to the idea. Certainly when you talk to people like Albert Harrison at the University of California in Davis, who's done some research into this from a scientific point of view – he's a social scientist – and his suggestion is that actually there wouldn't be panic in the streets. There would be a sort of, 'Well, I always knew it was something like that.' That kind of reaction."

There are many factors to consider, however.

"Picking up a signal at a distance is one thing," Pope cautioned. "Microbial life on Mars is another. A 'War of the Worlds'-type invasion – yes, I guess if we faced that, you probably would have panic in the streets. But a simple announcement that we're not alone, no, not at all. Indeed, there's quite a good precedent to this, which people tend to forget. In 1996 NASA announced that as far as they were concerned, they'd found fossilized evidence of microbial life on Mars. And what happened? Yes, it was front page news for a day or two. David Bowie's song 'Life On Mars' got a lot of radio play. But the world moved on. So no panic in the streets unless we really do face an alien invasion."

ELDERLY STATESMEN OF UFOs

After that interesting conjecture about the future, the conversation turned to some of the elderly statesmen of UFOs in the United Kingdom. Perhaps the best known of these is the late Brinsley Le Peur Trench, the Earl of Clancarty and a member of House of Lords, who ran a kind of in-house UFO club to debate and inform one another on the UFO phenomenon. Pope said he never had the privilege of meeting Lord Trench.

"But I met some of the other people, shall we say, of that era," Pope said, "and certainly other people who were involved in that debate in some capacity. I used to brief, for example, Lord Hill Norton and knew him reasonably well. Of course, he was a tireless campaigner on the subject and raised it in our Parliament on numerous occasions. He was extremely outspoken on this. He believed not only in the extraterrestrial presence but also in a governmental cover-up. And yes, he was an extraordinary character. One of the great heroes of this subject. Even though we didn't necessarily agree on several things, when the history of UFOlogy is written up, the definitive history, I think when you look as it were at the Hall of Fame, Lord Hill Norton's name will be right up there."

The 8th Earl of Clancarty, Brinsley Le Poer Trench was among the first wave of individuals in UK to demand Disclosure of Her Majesty's government.

Pope also made reference to one Sir Peter Horsley as another example.

"He was a Royal Equerry [Author's Note: An "Equerry" is an officer who is an attendant to a member of a royal family.] and a very senior Air Force Officer," Pope said. "It's in his autobiography, 'Sounds From Another Room.' He spoke about Royal interest in this subject, although he was fairly discreet about it I think. Famously, he claimed that he met some individual who he said seemed to know all sorts of things that he could never have known. He said he formed the impression that this individual was from somewhere else. So that was an extraordinary story from another senior establishment figure."

Still another name was put forth by Pope.

"Gordon Creighton is another figure of course," Pope went on. "A former British diplomat who went on to found 'Flying Saucer Review,' the magazine, and was heavily involved in that. These are people who were interested in the UFO phenomenon. Of course it is fairly strongly rumored that certain members of the Royal Family are extremely interested in this issue. I think that's a question where I'm not going to go into details because as a former government employee it's not particularly appropriate for me to talk about that. But there is a lot of material on the Internet about that and it's pretty accurate."

Score one for the Internet bloggers! It is rare to get that kind of semiofficial backing from someone with Nick Pope's credibility in the field. It makes one wonder what other genuine though "secret" information may be on the web hiding in plain sight?

ARE SECRET HIGH LEVEL MEETINGS BEING HELD?

"I've heard, of course, and seen in the literature and on the Net," Pope said, "these rumors about U.N. meetings. And one hears from certain people, like Steve Greer and Steve Bassett, about certain G-7 countries that may or may not be moving forward on this. But I have no knowledge of that. But of course I've been out of government service now for three and a half years and obviously I no longer have an active security clearance and I no longer have 'need to know.' So I wouldn't expect, even if there was such a thing, and I don't know if there is, I wouldn't expect to be briefed on it."

Positioning themselves in front of the United Nations building in NYC and unraveling a custom made Global UFO Flag they hoped to present to the world body (circa 1978), the late Major Colman Von Keviczky (Hungarian Army) and publicist/author Michael Luckman acknowledge a trend toward international Disclosure early on.

A COMPLEX ANSWER TO A COMPLEX QUESTION

What I thought was a relatively simple question, did Pope feel the nature of the UFO phenomenon had changed over the years, turned out to elicit a goldmine of fascinating reasoning and speculation.

"That's a very complex question," he began, "because I think, for a start, that it's difficult to get an overview of the phenomenon. Because what we're actually seeing is the phenomenon but through the filters of the media and the researchers. In other words, we're really only seeing the cases that people are writing about or the material that one has come across personally. So it's very difficult to get an overview because we're getting such a limited glimpse, as it were.

"The other thing," he continued, "is that society itself is changing in terms of its attitude, in terms of things like technology. Just to give one practical example, when I was doing the UFO job, I was lucky if one report in a hundred came with photographs and film. Now, because of the prevalence of cell phones with the capability to take photographs and video, a staggeringly high proportion of UFO sightings are now backed up with imagery. So there has been a fundamental change there."

Another approach to the question involved the frequency with which sightings of triangle-shaped UFOs have been reported over the last couple of decades.

"Have we really moved from saucer shapes through cigar shapes to triangular and delta shapes? On the face of it, the answer to that question might be yes. But I think sometimes we self-select, and because we perceive that the really good cases these days are triangular-shaped craft, if we are picking a case to write about, say in a newspaper article, we might pick that. So it can give what may be a misrepresentation of what's actually going on if you looked at the whole thing. Now, you could say that the whole way that we moved from just flying saucers with no occupants through the contactee era into the abduction era, now that's a change. But is it a change in the phenomenon? Or is it a societal change? Or is it both? I don't know."

Pope also acknowledged that the frequent sightings of triangular UFOs may be a new form of mere earthly technology.

"I think it's taken as given," he said, "that at any time there will be aerospace technology being operated that you won't see at the major air shows or in the media for ten or fifteen years. So it's quite possible that some triangular-shaped UFOs are effectively next generation aircraft or space vehicles. An obvious example, the F-117 and the B-2 were clearly flying for many years before they were publicly acknowledged. One can only imagine what a pilot who happened to get close to one of these things would have thought – and what he would have reported.

"That may explain some sightings, but my gut feeling is that it doesn't explain all of them. One of the points to bear in mind is that certainly if one's looking at things like secret prototype aircraft or drones, these things are almost exclusively test-flown in very restricted, isolated military areas where you wouldn't normally expect members of the public to see them. Particularly when you get reports of these sorts of things in urban areas or semi-urban areas, I'm less inclined to think it's some black project."

POPE'S FAVORITE CASE: A PERFECT STORM

This question was an easy one and brought an immediate and sure response.

"Britain's best known UFO case," Pope said, "the Bentwaters Incident. I would probably say that's one of the most compelling cases that I've come across. And I say that because it's almost like a perfect storm in that it's the coming together of everything you could really ask for in a UFO case if you were scoring it high in terms of credibility and importance.

"Firstly, it wasn't an isolated incident. It happened on at least two, maybe three nights. Secondly, there were numerous witnesses. Thirdly, many of those witnesses were military officers in law enforcement and security. Additionally, there was some physical evidence in terms of damage to trees, marks on the ground where the thing was alleged to have landed on the first night of activity. And of course the radiation levels that were taken at the landing site.

"Now there is some dispute about the importance of the radiation levels. People have questioned the accuracy of the readings that were taken and questioned the propriety of the equipment, whether it was appropriate to the task. To me, that's fine. Obviously, one can only work with the data that you have, not the data you'd like to have. So when the MoD assessed those radiation levels, they could only assess the information they were given. So for all those reasons, I think Rendlesham is compelling."

One advantage Bentwaters/Rendlesham has over the better known case of Roswell is simply that most of the people involved in the latter have now passed on.

"When people go looking for information on Roswell now," Pope said, "generally they're looking at second and third-hand accounts. Little if any contemporary paperwork is available. Then, looking at Bentwaters, we're in the fortunate situation of having a case where many of the witnesses, their names are known, they're on the record, they're still alive and contactable. That's important and it gives Bentwaters an advantage over even Roswell.

"The other point about this is that there is a paper trail. The Ministry of Defence's file on this is now in the public domain under the Freedom of Information Act. The USAF statements that General Halt took from five of the people most directly involved on the first night, including sketches, that's now in the public domain. So everything has come together to make this case compelling."

MEETING WITH THE ROYAL SOCIETY

In the months preceding the writing of this book, in early 2010, the Royal Society held a two-day discussion meeting in London. Pope was there for both days of the event and came away impressed with how the tide was turning in terms of UFOlogy.

"Now arguably," Pope said, "the Royal Society is possibly the world's most prestigious scientific organization. The title of this discussion meeting was 'The Detection of Extraterrestrial Life and the Consequences for Science and Society.' They were very careful to stress that it wasn't a UFO conference. This was a coming together of scientists from a number of different disciplines. There were astronomers, physicists, chemists. But there were also social scientists, anthropologists, theologians.

"And yes, we got into a lot of fairly technical discussions about amino acids and interstellar gas clouds and things like that. But we did get into more speculative discussions about the societal consequences of discovering alien life. And not just microbes – civilizations, too.

"What was interesting about this was firstly the fact that the Royal Society was comfortable putting on an event like that at all. But secondly the fact that – as I mentioned they were careful to stress that it wasn't a UFO conference – outside of the formal sessions, during the breaks, over coffee and biscuits, many people, including some of the speakers, were prepared to be rather more open to the idea of UFOs and visitation than perhaps they would say in public. I think that's a really interesting point."

Pope feels that the media is also beginning to come around.

"I think the release of the British government's UFO files," he said, "has played a huge part in this. The fact that the Royal Society could hold such a conference is in part because society's attitude has changed and evolved on this. The mainstream media is now more prepared to look with a little less of the giggle factor about little green men, though that does still happen. But a little less of that than was previously the case.

"I have seen more mainstream media coverage on this subject recently, and I've seen more serious coverage, in terms of just playing it as a straight news story as opposed to a silly story. I say this as somebody who has written an op-ed piece on this for 'The New York Times' and has appeared on shows like 'Good Morning, America' and 'Geraldo,' shows like that. So I think that all that ties in with this idea that people's views on this are evolving and this is no longer a subject to be treated with ridicule."

If Pope is correct in that assessment, it can only mean good things for the future of disclosure, whether you spell it with a big D or a small one.

Cartoon from Focus (MOD magazine).

Drawn to complement Nick Pope's March 2006 article on the Rendlesham Forest UFO incident. Note the symbols on the side of the alien spacecraft, which are taken from one of the United States Air Force witness statements.

The Real X-Files

by Nick Pope

I've worked for the Ministry of Defence for nearly fifteen years now, and have had a variety of fascinating posts. But by far and away the most amazing was my tour of duty in a division called Secretariat(Air Staff)2a, where for three years my responsibilities included researching and investigating the UFO phenomenon.

I should say first of all that the Ministry's interest in UFOs has more to do with the Russians than the Martians: it stemmed not from any corporate belief in extraterrestrials, but from the understandable desire to know about any object that had penetrated the UK's Air Defence Region. But in keeping an eye out for the Soviet aircraft that routinely probed at our air defences during the Cold War, it soon became clear that there were other more exotic craft operating in British airspace. For at least the last fifty years there has been a steady stream of UFO reports sent to the MOD, some from military sources and some from members of the public. So what's going on?

Each the year the MOD receives two or three hundred UFO reports, although some years are busier than others (there were 750 reports in 1978, 600 in 1981 and 609 in 1996). My job was to investigate these reports in an attempt to see whether there was evidence of any threat to the UK. After careful investigation I managed to find explanations for around ninety percent of sightings, which turned out to be misidentifications of ordinary objects or phenomena. The common culprits included aircraft lights, satellites, meteors and airships. But there was a hard core of sightings that simply couldn't be explained in conventional terms, where trained observers such as police officers and pilots saw unidentified craft performing speeds and manoeuvres way beyond our own capabilities.

The MOD has over two hundred files packed full of information about UFOs. Of these, I believe that around twenty have been made available at the Public Record Office in Kew, where their release is governed by the terms of the Public Record Acts - which generally allow information to be released when it's more than thirty years old. I'm well aware that ufologists have been very excited about the prospect of a UK Freedom of Information Act and have been planning to blitz the MOD with requests for UFO data. This is precisely what happened in America, where the casefiles of the United States Air Force study into UFOs (Project Blue Book) were made public. I had access to all the MOD's UFO files, and can tell people that if and when this information is made public, there is some very exciting information that will be made available. So what can people expect to find?

Over the years, the MOD has been involved in a wide variety of sensational UFO cases which defy any conventional explanation. One of the earliest took place in August 1956 when a UFO was tracked on radar systems at RAF Bentwaters and RAF Lakenheath. Two RAF jets were scrambled in an attempt to intercept the mystery craft, and a game of cat and mouse ensued as the pilots attempted to lock-on to the target. But the UFO was too quick and too agile, and managed to elude the pilots, who eventually ran low on fuel and were forced to return to base.

Britain's most sensational UFO case occurred in December 1980 in Rendlesham Forest, between RAF Bentwaters and RAF Woodbridge. UFO activity was witnessed over a series of nights, and on one occasion a military guard patrol encountered a landed UFO. The Deputy Base Commander, Lt Col Charles Halt, submitted an official report to the MOD, describing the UFO as "metallic in appearance and triangular in shape". Radiation readings were subsequently taken from the landing site, and were found to peak in the three indentations where the craft had touched down in a clearing.

In November 1990 a number of RAF Tornado jets were overtaken by a UFO whilst flying over the North Sea, and this is just one of several aerial encounters on file. The most disturbing of these relate to a series of terrifying near-misses between UFOs are civil aircraft. There were two such cases from 1991, both involving incidents over Kent, and another from 1995, involving a Boeing 737. The pilots encountered what they described as a brightly lit UFO while on their approach to Manchester airport, and believed that it had passed only yards from their aircraft. This incident was investigated by the Civil Aviation Authority, but no explanation was ever found.

One of the most sensational cases I ever investigated related to an incident that occurred in the early hours of March 31, 1993. There had been a wave of UFO sightings that night, culminating in the direct overflight of two military bases, RAF Cosford and RAF Shawbury.

The UFO was described to me by one of the military witnesses as being a vast, triangular craft only marginally smaller than a jumbo jet. It flew slowly over the base at a height of around 200 feet, firing a narrow beam of light at the ground, before flying off at high speed.

These then, are the sorts of incidents to be found in the MOD's UFO files: visual sightings correlated by radar; incidents where military jets have been scrambled; near-misses with civil airliners and reports of landings. Some of these incidents were classified secret at the time.

The files contain various other material of interest to researchers, and because of the perceived link with UFOs, contain some reports of alien abductions, crop circles and animal mutilations. Perhaps it's no surprise that as I got drawn into such mysteries I found myself dubbed "The Real Fox Mulder"!

So will the release of official files end speculation that the Government has been covering up the truth about UFOs? This is unlikely. The release of official files in America simply fuelled interest in the subject, and led to accusations that other more highly classified papers were still being withheld. The US Government's denial was not helped by the claims of a former US Army Colonel, Philip Corso, who claimed that the so-called Roswell incident from 1947 really did involve the crash of a UFO. He claimed that he'd seen the bodies, and that his job at the Pentagon involved him in finding ways to use the technological secrets gleaned from the debris of the craft. Corso died of a heart attack shortly after going public with these claims, so took the secrets to his grave. Conspiracy theorists love this sort of thing, and are unlikely to be satisfied by any release of papers that doesn't support their own bizarre theories about cover-ups and sinister conspiracies. There isn't a cover-up in the UK, although a letter sent from the MOD to the American Government in 1965 admits that MOD policy "is to play down the subject of UFOs".

My three years of official research and investigation into the UFO phenomenon changed my life for ever. I'd come into the job as a sceptic, but on the basis of the cases I'd looked at, and what I'd discovered in the files, I came to believe that some UFOs might well be extraterrestrial. If these files are now to be made public, I think people are in for a big surprise, and I believe that like me, people will come to see that this is a serious subject which raises very important defence and national security issues. As far as these files are concerned ... the truth is in there!

Nick Pope with actor David Duchovny and TV presenter Franky Ma at the UK premiere of The X-Files - I Want to Believe.

CROP CIRCLES: AN OFFICIAL HISTORY

By Nick Pope

Millions of words have been written about the crop circle phenomenon. Several books have been written on the mystery, together with countless newspaper and magazine features. Numerous Internet sites are devoted to the subject. Various theories about crop circles exist, attributing them to such causes as extraterrestrials, Earth energies, wind vortices or hoaxers. This world exclusive article will deal with only one aspect of the mystery, namely official involvement in the phenomenon. Several allegations have been made concerning interest on the part of the Ministry of Defence and the military, but is there any truth to such claims? Have the Government been involved? Is there any official interest? This article sets the record straight and lifts the lid on one of the MOD's most bizarre X-Files.

Army Helicopters

The military and MOD's first involvement with the crop circle mystery was in 1985. A farmer had found a spectacular quintuplet formation on his land and telephoned the Army Air Corps base at Middle Wallop to ask what they were up to, it having been suggested that the pattern might have been formed by the downwash from a helicopter's rotor blades. The Army does a lot of flying training in the area, some of which involves practicing landings. To do this, permission is needed from landowners, making it important to stay on good terms with local farmers. Noise from military aircraft leads to many complaints each year, so it is important for the military to stay on good terms not just with farmers, but with the public more generally. With this in mind, the Army moved quickly to deal with the suggestion that the crop circle in question had been formed by a low flying helicopter.

Copyright Colin Andrews

The matter was investigated by Lieutenant Colonel Edgecombe, who flew over the formation and took photographs. He then attended a public meeting and was able to give a categorical assurance that the downwash from a helicopter's rotor blades could not create symmetrical and well-defined formations of the type being seen. He also pointed out that the Army would not in any case damage farmers' crops in this way. Finally, he told the meeting that he had forwarded a report of his investigation to the Ministry of Defence, together with the photographs. This report went to Secretariat(Air Staff), who did little more than acknowledge it and thank Edgecombe for his hard work.

This incident was to have unforeseen consequences for the MOD. The Army's prompt and very public actions had been noted by certain crop circle investigators, who took it as a sign that the military were interested in the phenomenon *per se*. It was also noted that the report had been sent to Sec(AS), which also handled UFO reports. This confirmed in some researchers' minds a link between the two phenomena, when in fact there were many conflicting theories about crop circles.

Questions In Parliament

The issue of crop circles has been raised in Parliament four times, by means of written Parliamentary Questions. The questions and answers were printed in *Hansard* (The formal, published record of Parliamentary proceedings) and are worth quoting in full:

Cereal Fields (Hansard, 11 July 1989):

Mr Teddy Taylor: *To ask the Minister of Agriculture, Fisheries and Food how many reports he has received of the flattening of circular areas in cereal fields in the south-west and other areas of England respectively; and if he will make a statement.*

Mr Ryder: *The flattening of circular areas in cereal fields is a phenomenon known to occur from time to time. It is confined to winter cereal crops and is more prevalent in dry seasons, but we have no arrangements for recording such occurrences and therefore cannot comment on their frequency.*

Cereal Fields (Hansard, 11 July 1989):

Mr Teddy Taylor: *To ask the Secretary of State for Defence what progress has been made in the inquiries initiated by Army helicopters based in the south-west in investigating the origin of flattened circular areas of wheat; and if he will make a statement.*

Mr Neubert: *The Ministry of Defence is not conducting any inquiries into the origins of flattened circular areas of crops. However, we are satisfied that they are not caused by service helicopter activity.*

Cornfield Circles (Hansard, 26 July 1989) :

Mr Colvin: *To ask the Secretary of State for the Home Department if he will call for a report from the chief constables of Hampshire and Wiltshire on their investigations into the cornfield circles in Hampshire and Wiltshire; what is the estimated cost of these investigations; and if he will make a statement.*

Mr Hurd: *I understand from the chief constables of Hampshire and Wiltshire that there have been no investigations into the cornfield circles by their officers.*

Cornfield Circles (Hansard, 17 October 1989):

Mr Colvin: *To ask the Secretary of State for Defence whether any official assistance has been given by service personnel to civilians investigating the origin of cornfield circles in Hampshire and Wiltshire; and if he will make a statement.*

Mr Archie Hamilton: *I am not aware of any official assistance having been given by service personnel to civilians investigating the origin of crop circles.*

These questions were inspired by researchers Paul Fuller and Jenny Randles, who had contacted their MPs and asked them to raise the matter. The answers would have been drafted by officials within the respective government departments. In the case of the two questions answered by Defence Ministers, this meant that civil servants in Sec(AS) had drafted the responses.

While MOD was careful not to take any position on what might cause the circles, the Ministry of Agriculture, Fisheries and Food (MAFF) was prepared to speculate, probably because they had been put on the defensive by statements from crop circle researcher Colin Andrews, who had suggested that molecular changes in crops within circle formations might have health implications, if the crops then got into the food chain. Environment Secretary Nicholas Ridley had previously dismissed such an idea and stated that the circles were probably caused by wind. In responding to letters from MPs writing on behalf of their constituents, MAFF Minister Richard Ryder suggested that the circles were " ... most likely to result from a combination of wind and local soil fertility conditions in cereals which are prone to lodging". The issue of contaminated crops was therefore unlikely to apply. This response seems to have been influenced by the theories of meteorologist and crop circle researcher Dr Terence Meaden, and so far as I am aware MAFF's view was offered without any consultation with the MOD.

Another politician who made a public comment was Dennis Healey. In a February 1990 television interview he said that he thought a government inquiry into the subject was unnecessary, and stated that although he believed the matter was unresolved, he thought that crop circles were a natural phenomenon. Healey had previously been involved in the debate over crop circles when he photographed a formation at Alfriston in East Sussex, in 1984. The Daily Mail subsequently ran a story on this.

Military Aircraft Activity

Military aircraft (Mostly helicopters, but also C-130 Hercules aircraft based at RAF Lyneham) have been seen and occasionally filmed flying over crop circles. This has fuelled rumours that the MOD is actively monitoring the phenomenon, but there are two rather more mundane explanations for this activity.

The first is that military aircrew are just as likely as anyone else to be intrigued about the phenomenon. Accordingly, some will plan their routine flying training sorties to overfly any formations about which they have heard. Some aircrew will take photographs, and pictures of crop circles adorn the walls of many a crewroom at various military bases. With the above in mind, pages 73 and 82 of Circular Evidence [Bloomsbury Publishing Ltd, 1989] by Pat Delgado and Colin Andrews, show an Army Gazelle helicopter hovering over a formation that appeared at Westbury in 1987. The photograph on pages 74 and 75 was taken by aircrew on this helicopter.

The second reason for such overflights is that once the location of a large crop circle is known, it can be a useful navigational marker (Like any other prominent feature visible from the air) that can be used to verify position during a flying training sortie.

In The Firing Line

My involvement with the crop circle mystery started on 29 July 1991, when I started my tour of duty in Sec(AS)2a. My job included responsibility for investigating UFO sightings, with a view to satisfying the MOD that nothing reported was indicative of any threat to the defence of the United Kingdom. There was no formal remit to investigate crop circles, but as had been the case with Lieutenant Colonel Edgecombe's report six years previously, anything out of the ordinary (Especially if it was perceived as being connected to the UFO phenomenon) was always sent to Sec(AS). Therefore my three year tour of duty saw me researching and investigating not just UFOs, but alien abductions, animal mutilations and crop circles.

I could not have joined at a more interesting time, so far as the crop circle mystery was concerned, and I was soon in the thick of things. News had just broken concerning a spectacular pictogram at Barbury Castle in Wiltshire, and the very day after I joined Sec(AS) another large formation (The first 'Dolphin' pictogram) was reported in a field near the Wiltshire village of Lockeridge. Then on 13 August a spectacular pictogram was found in a field in Ickleton in Cambridgeshire. Dubbed "The Mandlebrot Set", after the computer fractal that featured in chaos mathematics, it was pictured in many national newspapers.

I was quizzed by several crop circle researchers, who asked for details of what the MOD knew about the phenomenon. Some demanded that we take action to investigate matters, while others clearly thought we knew all about it, and were covering up. New theories and allegations abounded and I was often on the defensive. I had to refute the bizarre idea that the formations were caused by the testing of space-based laser or directed-energy weapons, and dispel suggestions that media coverage of the issue had been stifled by use of D-Notices. I had to deny that the 22 October 1987 crash of a Harrier aircraft was caused by energies associated with crop circles, and that these energies had caused the spontaneous firing of the pilot's ejector seat, leading to the man's death (The body was found in Wiltshire, not far from where some crop circles had appeared in the Summer). I also had to deny allegations that The Queen and Margaret Thatcher had expressed interest in the phenomenon and that various high-level meetings were taking place to consider the subject.

On 9 September 1991 the storm broke. Today newspaper ran a front page story concerning Doug Bower and Dave Chorley's hoaxing activities, and much of the rest of the media followed the story. Then on 27 October, Channel 4's Equinox programme examined the phenomenon, with the emphasis again on hoaxing. Some researchers suggested that the MOD had a hand in all this, as part of a strategy to discredit both the phenomenon and the researchers. This was not the case, but the allegations refused to go away.

None of this is to say that my relationship with researchers was universally difficult. I had an 'open-door' policy, and most discussions I had with researchers were friendly and constructive. The late Ralph Noyes was in regular touch. He had retired from the MOD in 1977, having reached the rank of Under Secretary of State, and had been a former Head of Defence Secretariat 8 - the division that later evolved into Sec(AS). When someone with such a background raised the issue it was difficult to dismiss the phenomenon out of hand, or refuse to comment. I undertook to keep a watching brief on matters. I opened a file on the subject, followed developments through the media and the specialist magazines, and visited a few formations in a private capacity, in my own time.

Brainstorming

I would have liked to have done more. During the course of my tour of duty in Sec(AS) I had numerous discussions with specialist staffs, at which various plans were discussed. The military often practice surveillance, and it might have been possible to schedule an exercise in areas where formations had appeared in previous years, to see if we could see and record the creation of a crop circle. Chemical analysis of plants from within crop circles might have been undertaken, and the results compared with control samples from outside the formations. Such work was supposedly being done by civilian researchers, but might usefully have been carried out officially. Such discussions seldom came to anything, because of constraints on time and resources. Furthermore, initiatives along the lines of those discussed here might have become public knowledge, implying a level of official interest greater than was in fact the case.

In July 1992 I did manage to acquire a soil sample that had come from within a strange ground marking that had appeared on private land, and sent it for analysis, via specialist staffs. But before the analysis was undertaken, I discovered that the pattern on the ground had a mundane explanation. The investigation was duly halted.

I continued to keep a watching brief on the phenomenon, as I had promised, but towards the latter part of my tour of duty, interest in crop circles seemed to be declining. Formations were still appearing, and if anything the pictograms were becoming more spectacular, but the bubble had burst. Public and media interest was never again to reach the level that had been seen in 1990 and 1991. For my own part, my work was largely reactive, and because I was now receiving ever increasing numbers of fascinating UFO and alien abduction reports, I found that I had less time for crop circles.

The Current Position

It would not be appropriate for me to comment in detail on the current position. I understand, however, that the file I opened on crop circles has now been closed, and that the subject is no longer under any form of official consideration. This summer's formations may revive public and media interest. Whether this means that the MOD will again find itself on the receiving end of enquiries from researchers, the press and even MPs remains to be seen.

Conclusion

I hope that this article has clarified the position concerning official involvement in the crop circle mystery. While there certainly has been interest and involvement over the years, this has often been misinterpreted, perhaps deliberately or perhaps not. As individuals, military and MOD personnel can be as intrigued by crop circles as anybody else, but where such interest has been expressed it has been mistakenly interpreted as implying greater corporate involvement than is actually the case.

I am aware that the crop circle phenomenon gives rise to passions which are as strong - if not stronger - as those aroused by the UFO phenomenon. With this in mind, I hope that this article is not seen as trying to debunk the crop circle mystery, because while I am convinced that most pictograms are man-made, I do not entirely rule out other more exotic possibilities. The watching brief that I kept during my time in Sec(AS) continues, albeit now in a private capacity.

2009 Update

In 2009, author and researcher Colin Andrews publicly suggested that this article was part of an MoD attempt to "rewrite history". This was the central theme of his book Government Circles, which highlighted new evidence suggesting greater official interest in crop circles than had previously been acknowledged. I wrote this article at a time when I was still working for the MoD and it's no secret that the MoD has downplayed its interest and involvement in the crop circle issue, in the same way that it has with the UFO phenomenon. This has been the policy for many years and clearly I had to play my part in this when I worked for the government. That said, some of the issues Colin highlights have arisen because the line between official and private interest - even within government, the military and the intelligence agencies - can be blurred. There are particular sensitivities and political difficulties when members of the Royal Family are involved.

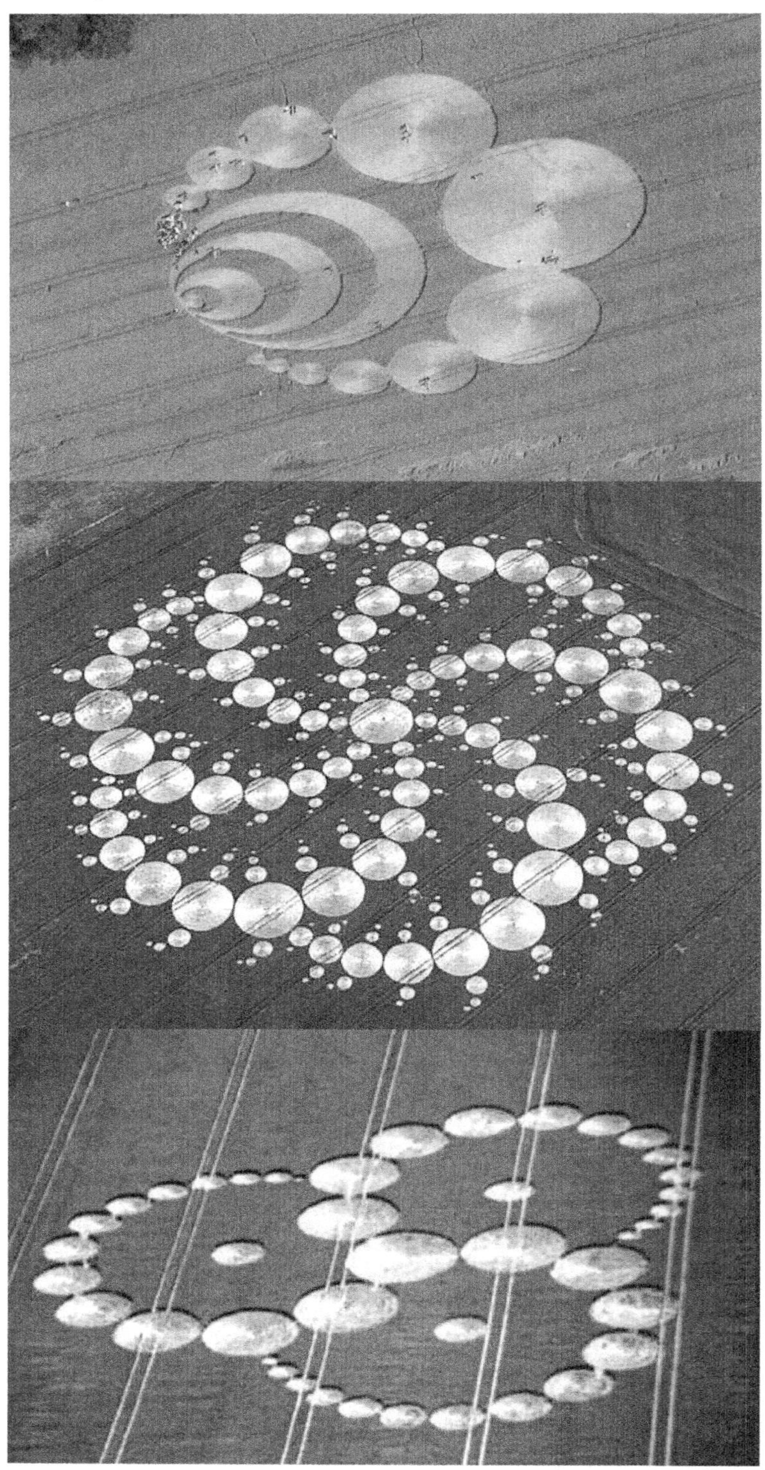

JOHN GREENEWALD: NORAD AND UFOS

By Sean Casteel

John Greenewald is a soldier deep in the trenches of UFO Disclosure. He began his battle in 1996, at the age of fifteen, and quickly earned a reputation as a "UFO prodigy," a kid who could play with the grownups and still hold his own. Greenewald operates a website called "The Black Vault," which makes over half a million pages of formerly classified documents available for download. While he cautions that none of the documents make the flat statement that extraterrestrials are for real, Greenewald says one can still approach the various files as pieces of a puzzle that can be assembled and combined to yield the occasional truth from behind the government's smokescreen. Greenewald delivers a sobering assessment of the state of disclosure today while at the same time declaring that the truest form of disclosure is what we decide within ourselves is the ultimate reality of the UFO phenomenon.

* * * *

Black Vault webmaster John Greenwald and internet radio show host Jerry Pippin discuss the latest in Disclosure.

Q. Can we start with some biographical background? You were quite young when you started The Black Vault website. Please talk about how and why you became interested in UFOs in general and classified documents in particular?

Greenewald: I started The Black Vault when I was fifteen years old. I was struck by curiosity on the UFO topic. I had never seen anything, never had any experiences or any dreams or unexplained events in my life. I literally was just curious. I wish I had a more exciting story. So I, like any curious kid, started surfing the Internet. I'd used the Internet for many years prior. And I came across a lot of the generic UFO stories. Now this was back in 1996. So obviously the Internet was big, but it wasn't as big as it is now. But you would still find hundreds and hundreds of thousands of pages on UFOs. And what I found as a fifteen-year-old was that a lot of the stories would contradict each other, and I had no idea what was real and not real. I one day came across an article that was written about a four-page government document. It outlined what is infamously known in Ufology as the 1976 Iran incident. I read this and it claimed that it was a government document that came from the Defense Intelligence Agency, and that if I didn't believe its authenticity then I could get the document myself.

Now obviously reading all these UFO stories – and I was just doing this as a hobby on my free time. I obviously wasn't thinking that I would become an investigator, nor did I really want to. I mean, it wasn't that I was trying to stay away from it. But I was fifteen. I never really thought I'd started a life's pursuit of trying to discover the truth.

So when I read this line that said I could verify this document, it said to use a tool called the Freedom of Information Act. I really did not know what that was. I'd never heard of it before. I just thought okay, what is this? So I read a little bit more and they said what you have to do is file what's called a Freedom of Information Act request to the Defense Intelligence Agency and you should get the document in return. Well, I didn't believe it, because when you read this four-page document, it really did read like an "X-Files" episode. A UFO shows up over a major city. It acts in essence like a mother ship, where multiple UFOs were coming out of this thing. One of them landed on Earth. It's one of those bizarre stories that you would never think that the U.S. government would admit to. Even though it happened in another country, this was official U.S. government intelligence, military intelligence. So I did. I filed the request to see if I would actually get this thing, never imagining that I actually would.

Filed the request. Sent it off. They pretty much said copy and paste their form letter, which I did. Again, I didn't really know what the Freedom of Information Act was. And to my surprise, it literally only took about two and a half to three weeks, and it popped up in my mailbox, an official letter from the

Defense Intelligence Agency with a four-page document intact. It read line by line exactly what I had read on the Internet. And it was true. So I realized, wow, this is amazing! There must be more to the U.S. government's connection to UFOs out there. There must be more evidence of that connection out there. So I logged back on and I'm searching the Internet, and I really didn't find any information. There were a lot of references to this four-page government document, and a few very brief mentions of other government documents that exist, that talk about UFOs. But I really never found the actual documents, and I needed to see those to believe the stories. So that's kind of how it started. I then realized that, okay, if I'm looking for a site like this, then there must be others. There must be other researchers, investigators or just curious minds like myself that would want access to these documents.

So I started teaching myself, okay, well, if the Freedom of Information Act letter is worded this way, maybe I can change the wording to get these types of documents. So I started teaching myself how to use it and sending off letters. I started with the Defense Intelligence Agency, obviously, because I knew that agency worked. I was learning more and more and I realized that every federal government agency and military agency would have to respond to me. So those four pages really kind of launched this endeavor for me to find everything out there. And I tackled each agency one by one. I was sending out FOIA requests literally 25 to 30 at a time. And I was getting documents in return. So I created that website that I was looking for that really didn't exist. When I originally started The Black Vault, I literally took these documents and typed them in word by word, because I didn't have a scanner. I couldn't afford one. If memory serves me well, because this is going back well over a decade, I think I got up to about 800 or 900 pages of UFO material that I'd hand-typed in before I finally said to myself, okay, I've got to raise money for a scanner. And the story continues. Obviously I was able to get money for a scanner and just built The Black Vault the way I wanted it to be, what I was looking for. I just modeled it after what I wanted.

It has morphed into a fairly large community today. Here we are about 14 years later and there are literally tens of thousands of people that come every day or every couple of days that download these documents by the thousands. It's amazing to build something that I was looking for that I knew people were wanting. It just didn't exist. And that's how it started. That's where we've come from.

Q. Let's talk about The Black Vault the way it is today. Approximately how many pages of formerly classified files are there?

Greenewald: I have more than 550,000 pages scanned in right now that you can download.

Q. Among the many, many files you have there, what are some of the most dramatically revealing? Do you have any files where the government may have unwittingly released something really valuable in terms of UFOs?

Greenewald: It's tough to gauge whether or not they've released anything they shouldn't have. I say that because you're not going to find a government document that says extraterrestrials exist. Not any that are officially acknowledged. We all are familiar with the MJ-12 documents, where obviously the story goes much deeper, where yes, extraterrestrials are verified in these documents. The problem is they're not officially acknowledged, meaning that according to the U.S. government they're not real. When you talk about the officially released ones, you're not going to find black and white "extraterrestrials exist." You've got to put all these documents together like a puzzle. I've had a lot of stories happen along the way. One of them that comes to mind is I received an email from somebody who wanted to quote unquote "leak" information to me and told me to ask about a "Project Tobacco." I get these letters every day, so I didn't really think much of it. But I filed a request to the U.S. Air Force, their headquarters in the Pentagon, for all information on Project Tobacco. Now, the way the government works, if something doesn't exist, they're going to tell you. They're just going to say, "We have no records on it." I never said Project Tobacco was on UFOs. I had filed countless requests for information other than UFOs, so there is really no reason for them to assume that I was requesting UFO information.

I requested these documents on Tobacco, and they responded to me by saying one of their generic UFO responses, which was, "This office is not a repository for UFO information" and that you have to go get all the UFO documents in the National Archives. Now, again, I had never said that Tobacco had anything to do with UFOs or extraterrestrials or anything of the sort. That's not a big earth shattering story or a big revelation, and I get that. I think what happened was – was it an inadvertent admission that there are projects that we don't know about connected to UFOs? Because anybody can Google search Project Blue Book and Project Sign and Project Grudge and you're going to get tens of thousands of references to that government project that are officially acknowledged. Search for Project Tobacco and you're not going to find anything. The only thing you'll find is a link to an article I wrote eleven years ago about it, about was this an accidental admission. I asked the Pentagon about it and they said that they just assumed that it was UFO-related because it was me.

More specifically, though, are there documents that really make you go wow? I think, again, you put these things together like a puzzle. I always bring up the official U.S. Air Force Manual, that specifically references UFOs and how to report them, and that's currently on the books, meaning they are actively collecting UFO reports. Unidentified Flying Objects, whatever that definition is to them, they are filing those reports and sending those reports to the NORAD installation. Now that's not a very exciting story, but when you put it together, when you put it into the puzzle mix – they are so adamant about saying that they are not interested in UFOs. They go overboard on saying, "We don't touch these things. We don't care about UFOs. We did our study and we found out nothing."

They said it ended in 1969, and that's really the basis of a lot of the lectures that I give. Their public statements are that in 1969, all UFO investigations stopped. They didn't care about it anymore. They didn't want to hear about it. And what I was finding out from other military and government agencies was that that statement isn't true. There are thousands of documents on UFOs after the official quote unquote "cutoff date" that the military stopped investigating. They even say no other government agency, for that matter, takes an interest. And yet what I was able to find five years ago is an official U.S. Air Force manual that makes reference to UFOs, which is currently on the books. It's Air Force Manual 10-206. Anybody can look it up, and sure enough, it's in there. And there's really no reason for it to be in there if you take their public statements as gospel and the truth. They shouldn't care about any type of UFO sighting. And yet our commercial aviation pilots are seeing them and obviously our military pilots are seeing them.

So I kind of followed the paper trail, and now it's black and white that they're taking UFO reports from their own military personnel and commercial aviation pilots. And they send them to one location, which is the NORAD installation. So I filed an FOIA request to NORAD for what is called CIRVIS reports. And that acronym stands for Communication Instructions for Reporting Vital Intelligence Sightings. Now UFOs are not the only things that are reported in this. When they see an unidentified military aircraft or for Navy personnel, when they see unidentified boats or submarines – all those are intelligence sightings that are funneled through this one particular manual. But again, what are these quote unquote "UFOs"? So when I filed a request to NORAD to see if I could get my hands on these documents, they wrote me a letter and said that because they're a bi-national command, meaning under the command of not only the U.S. but also the Canadian military and government, they aren't subject to the Freedom of Information Act. So U.S. law doesn't apply.

To me, that's pretty fascinating, that finally you find a connection to present day UFO research or investigation or reporting, however you want to say it. The one place that the reports end up is not subject to the Freedom of Information Act. So it's kind of one of those convenient things for them to send it there because then all of a sudden they just pretty much go into the government abyss and they'll never see the light of day. Now NORAD said in the end of the letter that they in good faith searched for documents responsive to my request and they found nothing. They said that there are no CIRVIS reports at their location, which has to be a lie. This thing has been on the books for years. And so there's not a single report there? Very, very unlikely.

But that's it. I can't knock on their door and say, "C'mon, search again." Or "Hey, c'mon, you're lying." You have to play their game by their rules, unfortunately. So what I didn't realize, and it took me about a year to have it dawn on me, is that maybe, since it is a bi-national command, that the Canadian government would have their equivalent to the Freedom of Information Act and maybe I can access the records from the backdoor, so to speak. I picked up the telephone and called the Department of National Defence in Canada. I didn't introduce myself or tell them what I was calling about, meaning UFO records. I said, "Good morning, sir. I just had a quick question for you. Can an American citizen request records under your Access To Information Act?" And he said, "Well, I guess if the records have been released, I don't see why not." So it was kind of like I was taking his opinion versus official regulations regarding can an outside citizen from the U.S. or say England request information. It wasn't like an official wording; it was more like his opinion. "Well, yeah, I guess so." Which I thought was a little bizarre.

I said, "Okay, let me tell you what I'm looking for. Maybe you can help me out." Obviously I don't know the Canadian government very well and all their backdoors. I mean, I've been doing research with the U.S. government for 14 years and still can't figure them out. So I said, "I'm looking for these reports. They're called CIRVIS reports. It stands for Communication Intelligence . . ." And he interrupted me before I could finish the definition of the acronym, and he said, "Oh, yeah, I have those right here." And I thought to myself, okay, number one, why would he even tell me that? And number two, why would he have them on his desk within arm's reach? The Department of National Defence is huge. They have a lot of things to deal with. So all of a sudden they have these CIRVIS reports within arm's reach. I'm thinking, okay, this has to be pretty good.

So I didn't want to get too inquisitive, since I wanted to get my hands on the documents, and I said, "Really? How much do you think it would take to send those out? Have they been released?" He said, "Yeah, they've been released. Do you have a VISA card?" And I'm thinking, oh, my God, I'm going to be charged $3,000 for boxes worth of documents. I asked him, "How many are there?" He said about a hundred pages. So I'm wondering how much is he going to charge me? He charged me like $3 on a VISA card. It was the best $3 I've ever spent, because he photocopied them and sent them to me. They popped up in my mailbox and I opened them up. And sure enough, they're all CIRVIS reports and they're all on UFOs. There was even a crop circle report in there, if you can believe it. The proof that comes with these documents is that NORAD was lying. By Canadian law as well, these documents have to be sent to the NORAD installation. Even though the Department of National Defence had them, they have to be channeled through the NORAD installation. So it was proof of a blatant lie and cover-up by the U.S. side of NORAD, saying, "Hey, we don't care about these things. No one does. We stopped our investigation." And in reality, there are a hundred pages that showed up in my mailbox. Well, the end of the conversation with the guy, I said thank you very much. And he said, "Oh, by the way, you may want to know that's not all of them." And I said, "Really? What do you suggest? Do you have more?" And he said, "I don't have them. They're over at Archives." He gave me the number. And I said, "Do you know how many are over there?" And he said, "At least three or four boxes worth of reports." And the dates of the reports – and this was around 2005, I think it was – the majority of the reports were from 2001 and 2002. So it was this full circle of not only am I proving the lie from the U.S. government and military, not only am I proving that they're still interested in the UFO phenomenon, but they are collecting the reports and obviously doing something with them. The U.S. government doesn't collect intelligence just to put it into a drawer. We like to make fun of them and say that, but that's not true. They really, genuinely have an interest in this. What that interest is we don't know. I don't want to be too drawn out with the stories, but you can see this gets very complex. You're dealing with multiple agencies and, in some cases, agencies in different countries, to prove just one little thing. And that's how hard it is when you research UFOs.

Q. What do you think might be a likely scenario that would push the government over the edge and make them come clean about what they know? Is there any scenario that might demand they release their UFO files at some future date?

Greenewald: I think one of the only scenarios – and I don't believe that this scenario will ever take place – is really that undeniable first contact, which is what the scientific community would call that. That undeniable first contact, whether it be by radio wave or whether it be they land in the middle of a major city or they show up in our skies – all scenarios that I personally believe are not going to happen, at least not any time soon. I think that's the only situation where the government is finally going to say, okay, here's the information. Or at least officially acknowledge that they exist. I think that what has happened in the last 60 years, especially since this cover-up really in essence began, is that the government really doesn't have to do anything anymore. They don't have to do any active cover-up, even though they keep sticking their foot in their mouth every five to ten years with a new explanation for Roswell that doesn't make sense.

They can just sit back and let this topic morph itself into a Hollywood blockbuster movie and then people go, "Oh, UFOs aren't real. That's something that Hollywood dreamed up." Even though that's not necessarily true. But that's what our society believes – if they see it on television or if they see it in the movies, it's not real. The reason that is is because it's so sensationalized in the entertainment media that people are just not going to look in this direction for the truth. They're not going to think that UFOs may be in our skies and of an extraterrestrial origin. I just think that the vast majority of society, they either look down or straight forward but they never look up. They never really think about what could be out there. And that's really too bad. So the bottom line is I don't think the government has to do anything. I think they won in the respect that they've covered this up and created such a smokescreen to what the truth could be or what the truth really is that now they can sit back and let the UFO community fight it out. If the UFO community itself can't agree, it's not like you've got this armada of people who have all come together with one solid, viable conclusion and the government is going head to head with that group of people – that's not the case. The UFO community, while I love very dearly many of the people in it, many of them don't agree. I don't necessarily agree with a lot of people I call very close personal friends, that I've been friends and colleagues with for a decade. But I don't believe in what they say or their conclusions because we all think differently, we all obviously see different research, we all need different levels of proof. And so you get all these different conclusions, all these contradicting conclusions. So why does the government have to do anything? The UFO community is just going to duke it out for decades to come. And on a positive note with that, I think that's the fun of this community, if you can do it respectfully. I can sit down and have a conversation with someone like Stanton Freidman, who I adore immensely. I think he's a phenomenal investigator and researcher, and he makes me think. Do I agree with everything he's concluded? No. Does he agree with me? I can't speak for him, but probably not.

And that's okay. He and I can sit down and have a conversation. But there are others who can't sit down. It's either their way or the highway. And I think that that really enforces the government's win, that they don't have to do anything. They don't have to officially acknowledge or disclose anything. So unfortunately, I don't mean to be a pessimist about the whole thing, but I think it's up to us, one by one, individually to really figure out what that truth is. Another thing that I talk about when I lecture to audiences, one of the top questions is, Will disclosure happen? And I say, you know, disclosure is going to happen on a case-by-case basis within yourselves. We have to make it happen for us. If we believe it, great. That's the disclosure. We don't need an official acknowledgment. We're all intelligent enough to create our own opinion and our own conclusions. Unfortunately, at this point, I think we can't draw a solid, viable conclusion, which is not going to make the government have to even think about disclosing anything.

Q. So you don't think it's possible to have "Disclosure With Honor," where the government simply discloses what they know without some kind of apocalyptic landing or something? You don't think something like that could ever happen?

Greenwald: Yeah. And again, I don't mean to be a pessimist about the whole thing. I think the optimistic way of looking at it is that it's up to us to figure it out for ourselves. And until that day happens when one of them lands on our lawn, it's really up to us to figure out, okay, scientifically, is this viable? Absolutely. I think absolutely that, in a scientific way of looking at this, yeah, it's absolutely possible. Then the question is, have they come here? And then you answer that. It's a step process. You can't introduce someone to the UFO topic and make them believe in it – if they've never seen anything before – by telling them about an abduction. You're going from zero to 90 in the snap of a finger. You can't do that. It's a step process for each and every one of us. Maybe there are some people that can handle something like that. But to me that's the step process to a disclosure. Disclosure, yeah, everybody wants to think that the government is going to come clean – they don't have to. We are intelligent enough to figure it out. And until we come up with one of those conclusions, unfortunately I just don't think the government's going to do it.

The Black Vault where over 50,000 Freedom Of Information documents can be found.

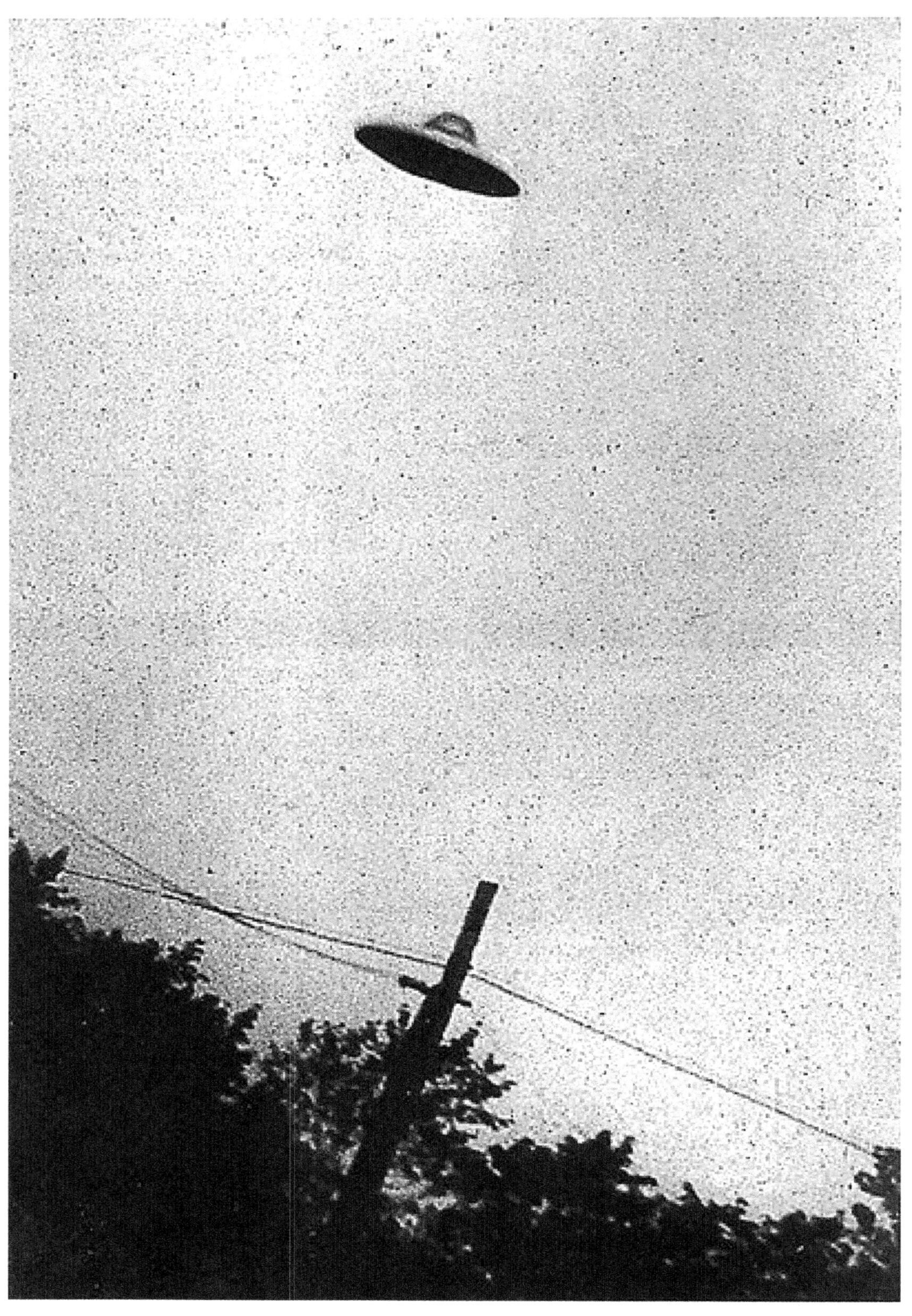

DISCLOSURE: WHAT'S ALREADY THERE?

By John Weigle

The truth may be out there, but it's not easy to find.

That became quite clear to me when Sean Casteel asked if I'd be willing to help with this book by finding declassified UFO reports on the Web that would add some spice and show that good sightings had been, for some time, kept secret from those who were paying the governments to determine what was flitting around the skies in ways that, as far as we know, human beings cannot. Knowing that several countries had declassified thousands of pages and put them on the World Wide Web, I agreed to see what I could find. It turned out to be a case of looking for the proverbial needle in the haystack and not even being sure that I was in the right haystack.

The Internet is a wondrous place, but it's also a place where anyone can put up anything and call it fact, even if it's no more than the ranting of a loon. "They couldn't print it if it wasn't true" used to be said of people who wrote articles for newspapers and magazines or who wrote books. The only problem with that saying is that it's not true – and it's even less true on the Internet, where there are few editors who make any attempt to fact-check postings. That's why my hope was that we would find government documents on government sites, rather than purported government documents mailed to a blogger in a plain brown envelope and posted on one of the Web's thousands of UFO sites.

The U.S. sites are easy to find, although there is little new on them because the government closed Project Blue Book in December 1969, saying, as it had many times before:

"No UFO reported, investigated and evaluated by the Air Force has ever given any indication of threat to our national security.

"There has been no evidence submitted to or discovered by the Air Force that sightings categorized as 'unidentified' represent technological developments or principles beyond the range of present-day scientific knowledge.

"There has been no evidence indicating that sightings categorized as 'unidentified' are extraterrestrial vehicles."

The Air Force said it had investigated 12,616 sightings, but only 701 remained unexplained.

Writing about U.S. documents made available through Freedom of Information Act requests, Mark Rodegheir, director of the J. Allen Hynek Center for UFO studies in the spring 1998 issue of The International UFO Reporter said, "These documents do not contain a smoking gun to prove that the U.S. government has a secret UFO project. They did show that many agencies had an ongoing interest in the UFO phenomenon that was often independent of the Air Force's UFO project, and that the interest continued after it ended."

(The full article is available at http://www.cufos.org/UFO_Documents_internet.html.)

We can dispute the Air Force conclusions, and those of other governments, but as Rodeghier and others have noted, none of the reports released by any country have provided the "smoking gun" that everyone interested in UFOs has hoped for. No document that can be definitively confirmed as valid declares the existence of extraterrestrial visitors (or supports any of the many other proposed explanations, other than natural phenomenon). The Majestic 12 documents, if their validity were proven beyond doubt, would fill the bill. But, at best, the UFO community is split on the validity of the documents, with some claiming they're outright hoaxes, some saying they're disinformation from U.S. intelligence agencies, and some arguing that at least a few of the documents, especially the so-called Eisenhower briefing document, are valid, while others are not. The government disavows all the documents, and the best that can be said for them is that some might be real, but none have been proven to be so. For opposing views, see the Web site Majestic Documents, Evidence That We are Not Alone, at http://www.majesticdocuments.com.)

The primary fear about documents from unofficial Web sites is that they're forgeries. With today's scanners, photocopiers and computers, almost anyone who wants to could do some research and prepare documents that, at least on a computer screen, look quite valid. Sometimes, however, documents are – or were – available from governments only in hard copies at selected offices, rather than on the Internet. In those cases, there are some trusted sites that have posted information received under Freedom of Information Act requests in the United State. The best example is John Greenwald's The Black Vault at http://community.theblackvault.com.

Even unquestioned official documents, however, can have a number of problems:

MISTAKES AND OMISSIONS IN THE ORIGINAL DOCUMENT: There are no guarantees that the person who prepared the document got everything right. Names, if they haven't been redacted to protect witnesses, might be misspelled, numbers can be transposed, statements can be misunderstood, and important information might not be included because no one thought to ask about it.

REDACTIONS: Most UFO reports posted by governments have names and addresses of witnesses and other information that could identify them blacked out to protect their privacy. While understandable, this makes it difficult to track down additional information on sightings that have not been generally reported. Documents posted by intelligence agencies also black out information concerning sources and other information about how the material was gathered so that governments being spied on can't easily determine the sources.

The Guardian of England reported in a Feb. 21, 2010, article on the release of more UFO documents by the Ministry of Defence:

"The newly released memo to ministers and defence chiefs, dated September 2007, discusses how to handle making the information public.

"It notes: 'The majority of the files are of low security classification, but include references to air defence matters, defence technology, relations with foreign powers and occasional uncomplimentary comments by staff or police officers about members of the public, which will need to be withheld in accordance with FoI principles.'

"The document continues: 'The MoD is aware of no clear evidence to prove or disprove the existence of aliens, and consequently the files are considerably less exciting than the "industry" surrounding the UFO phenomena would like to believe.' "

LEGIBILITY: Some documents are difficult, if not impossible, to read. This notice included with many documents from the Australian National Archives points out the problem: "This page is reproduced from a badly faded or illegible source. Scanning this item at a higher resolution will not improve its legibility."

There are many reasons for legibility problems:

(1) The original document is a carbon copy. Remember that in the early days of UFOs, documents were handwritten or typewritten. Copies were made by inserting carbon paper between sheets of blank paper. Each copy beyond the original got lighter and lighter, with how light depended on the typewriter and the typist. When such documents are photocopied, quality is further degraded, and every time a copy of a copy is made, the document becomes more difficult to read. And, of course, even the first copy might have been light because of an old typewriter ribbon.

(2) Thermal records – such as the receipts from automatic teller machines – fade quickly, becoming illegible or, sometimes, simply disappearing. Photo copies also fade over time.

(3) The original copy was handwritten and the handwriting is poor or was written with a hard pencil which does not reproduce well.

LANGUAGE / TRANSLATIONS: Documents from foreign governments, naturally, are usually not in English, requiring that the reader be multilingual or know someone who is, in which case problems with interpretation can arise. Word-for-word translations by someone not familiar with a language's idioms can have entirely different meanings than those prepared by those more familiar with the language and how it spoken and written. Internet translation tools can help here, but they cannot read photographic copies of documents.

THE EVER-CHANGING WEB: Web links disappear as owners of domains let them expire or, more likely with government sites, webmasters rearrange and rename pages, breaking all earlier links.

ARGUMENTS FOR AND AGAINST DISCLOSURE

Spanish researcher Vicente-Juan Ballester Olmos has written a report on "State-of-the-Art in UFO Disclosure Worldwide," which includes 14 pages of the types of material released, as of December 2009, by the United States, Brazil, Australia, Argentina (pending), Canada, Sweden, New Zealand, France, Spain, Italy, Uruguay, Soviet Union/Russia, United Kingdom, Chile, Norway, Belgium, Portugal, Switzerland, Philippines, Peru (pending), Mexico (pending), Ecuador, Ireland, Rumania, Denmark, Greece and Finland. Some nations are listed as having released details of a single sighting, while others have released many documents. The vast majority of the material was released by the United States.

He notes that many researchers doubt that any country, especially the United States, has released everything. Researchers also question the reasons given for redacting some information from declassified documents. "It seems evident that in most countries the release of UFO documents is linked to lobbying by the media or UFO organizations," he adds. "In other cases, it simply runs parallel to the routing declassification of government archives."

His full report is available at http://www.anomalia.org/disclosure2.pdf

PROS AND CONS OF DISCLOSURE

There are many reasons that most UFO information should be released.

If any of the explanations for UFOs beyond misinterpretation of natural phenomena – extraterrestrials, time travelers, angels, devils or inhabitants of an inner Earth, for example – could be substantiated, it would be among the biggest, if not the biggest, event of all time. The people who have paid to find that information deserve to know what they have bought.

Unfortunately, if any of those explanations is correct, they also provide some of the best reasons that governments might use to decide to withhold information. Consider what could happen to the stock market if ET's had the secret to free energy. Consider what would happen to the world's religions if we learned that our prophets were aliens. Consider what would happen to the defense industry if governments announced that someone or something had complete access to the skies over every nation, could conduct medical exams on animals and abduct human beings, and nothing could be done about it.

Governments would have had perfectly valid reasons to keep secrets when the modern UFOs first came to public attention in 1947. The hot war was barely over, and the Cold War was under way. If the Soviet Union was testing weapons over the United States, there was good reason to keep the information from the public, just as information about Japanese balloon attacks during World War II was covered up. If the governments had proof that extraterrestrials were flitting around the skies, there could have been even better reasons, even if releasing the information might have united the world against what it considered a common enemy from elsewhere.

The longer that information is withheld, the more difficult it becomes for a government to release it, even if the original reasons for classification were completely valid. What president, for instance, would be willing to stand before Congress and say, "Since 1947, we have known that extraterrestrials / time travelers / angels / demons / underground races have been flying about our skies. We have been unable to prevent their activities and, essentially, have been and continue to be at their mercy. (Or, We have made contact with them and agreed to their request to periodically take and examine – or kill, in the case of some animals – in exchange for peace / technology / whatever.) We are now ready to announce this to the general public on the grounds that..."

It's not a likely scenario.

Whatever the reasons were for withholding data, and no matter how valid they were at the time, however, there are still reasons to release it today.

Vicente-Juan Ballester Olmos offers four:

"(1) UFO phenomena represent no threat to national security; therefore it is not a military concern.

"(2) UFO investigation must be left exclusively to science, by methodology, approach and instrumentation.

"(3) To withhold information is hardly compatible with a democratic policy.

"(4) Many countries in the world, both large and small, have already made public their UFO records."

Richard F. Haines, chief scientist of the National Aviation Reporting Center on Anomalous Phenomena, suggests another serious reason: public safety. In an Oct. 15, 2000 paper, "Aviation Safety in America – A Previously Neglected Factor," he writes:

"Three kinds of reported UAP [unidentified aerial phenomena] dynamic behavior and reported consequences are addressed, each of which can affect air safety: (1) near-miss and other high speed maneuvers conducted by the UAP near the aircraft, (2) transient and permanent electromagnetic effects onboard the aircraft that affect navigation, guidance and flight control systems, and (3) close encounter flight performance by the UAP that produces cockpit distractions which inhibit the flight crew from flying the airplane in a safe manner."

He continues:

"I conclude that: (1) In order to avoid collisions with UAP some pilots have made control inputs that have resulted in passenger and fight crew injury. (2) Based upon a thorough review of pilot reports of UAP over the conterminous United States between 1950 and 2000 it is concluded that an immediate physical threat to aviation safety due to collision does not exist because of the reported high degree of maneuverability shown by the UAP. However, (a) should pilots make the wrong control input in the wrong time during an extremely close encounter the possibility of a mid-air collision with a UAP still exists, and (b) if pilots rely upon their instruments when anomalous electromagnetic effects are causing them to malfunction the possibility of an incident or accident exists. (3) Documented UAP phenomena have been either ridiculed or instructed not to report their sightings publicly. (4) Responsible world aviation officials should take UAP phenomena seriously and issue clear procedures for reporting them without fearing ridicule, reprimand or other career impairment and in a manner that will support scientific research, (5) Airlines should implement instructional courses that teach pilots about optimal control procedures to carry out when flying near UAP and also what data to try to collect about them, if possible, and (5) A central clearing house should be identified to receive UAP reports (e.g., ASRS; Global Aviation Information Network (GAIN). This unclassified clearinghouse should collect, analyze, and report UAP sightings for the continuing benefit of aviation safety as well as scientific curiosity. Whatever UAP are they can pose a hazard to aviation safety and should be dealt with appropriately and without bias."

The full report is at http://www.narcap.org/reports/001/narcap.TR1.AvSafety.pdf.

DISCLOSURE AND WAR

Even before fears for aviation safety, at least two organizations – one government and one private – suggested that UFOs could cause an accidental war or be used by the Soviet Union to frighten the United States government.

In 1953, the Central Intelligence agency created what was called the Robertson Panel (after its chairman, Dr. H.P. Robertson) to study UFOs. It said, among other things:

"The Panel took cognizance of the existence of such groups as the 'Civilian Flying Saucer Investigators' (Los Angeles) and the 'Aerial Phenomena Research Organization (Wisconsin). It was believed that such organizations should be watched because of their potentially great influence on mass thinking if widespread sightings should occur. The apparent irresponsibility and the possible use of such groups for subversive purposes should be kept in mind."

And, after concluding there was no evidence that UFOs were a threat to national security or devices of foreign powers, the panel said:

"3. The Panel further concludes:

"a. That the continued emphasis on the reporting of these phenomena does, in these parlous times, result in a threat to the orderly functioning of the protective organs of the body politic.

"We cite as examples the clogging of channels of communication by irrelevant reports, the danger of being led by continued false alarms to ignore real indications of hostile action, and the cultivation of a morbid national psychology in which skillful hostile propaganda could induce hysterical behavior and harmful distrust of duly constituted authority.

"4. In order most effectively to strengthen the national facilities for the timely recognition and the appropriate handling of true indications of hostile action, and to minimize the concomitant dangers alluded to above, the Panel recommends:

"a. That the national security agencies take immediate steps to strip the Unidentified Flying Objects of the special status they have been given and the aura of mystery they have unfortunately acquired.

"b. That the national security agencies institute policies on intelligence, training and public education designed to prepare the material defense and the morale of the country to recognize most promptly and to react most effectively to true indications of hostile intent or action."

The National Investigations Committee on Aerial Phenomenon, a highly respected civilian group that investigated UFOs, made a similar argument to Congress in 1960.

"There is a serious and growing danger that UFOs may be mistaken for Soviet missiles or jets, accidentally setting off war," NICAP Director Donald E. Keyhoe, a retired Marine Corps major, wrote on June 21, 1960. "Several Air Defense scrambles and alerts already have occurred when defense radarmen mistook UFO formations for possible enemy machines. NICAP agree with this sober warning by General L. M. Chassin, NATO Co-ordinator [sic] of Allied Air Services."

"'It is of first importance to confirm these objects ... the business of governments to take hand, if only to avoid the danger of global tragedy. If we persist in refusing to recognize the existence of these UFO we will end up, one fine day, by mistaking them for the guided missiles of an enemy – and the worst will be upon us.' ...

"There is an increasing danger – as the NICAP Board has warned the AF – that Russia could exploit the muddled UFO situation at any time. If successful, this trick would greatly increase tension in the U.S. and allied countries. It could be planned to upset the 1960 political campaigns, or at any desired time to increase fear of USSR attack power."

The major argument against disclosure seems to have come from John Lear several years ago. Some consider Lear in the fringe of ufology, while others believe he has found the true story. His argument was posted at http://www.world-mysteries.com/doug_ufo2.htm by Doug Yurchey. Lear presented the argument, among other places, on a Coast to Coast AM radio show with Art Bell.

Lear says the U.S. recovered several UFOs in the 1930s and early 1940s and finally recovered two live aliens at Roswell, one of whom died soon after and one of whom lived until 1956. We learned that 18 alien species are visiting Earth and that we're "the experimental product, if you will, of an alien race who we never met and we don't know who they are." Some of the species are good, some are evil, and some are indifferent. What we call Grays are cybernetic organisms. The aliens refer to us as containers, and we don't know what the experiment is, although we know we were corrected about 65 times.

"Since 1938, we've lost over 200 aircraft due to UFO hostilities and thousands of soldiers in all kinds of actions with aliens. Since that time, several hundred thousand civilians have disappeared with no trace. Several thousand of those were eliminated (killed) by us because of their chance encounters with the aliens which we could ill afford to have publicized," he says.

Like cattle, human beings have been mutilated while still alive and conscious, he continues. We had made a deal to allow a small number of abductions in exchange for technology but "got something less than the technology we bargained for and found the abductions exceeded by a million fold than what we had naively agreed to."

President Eisenhower supposedly met with a representative of another species in 1954 at Muroc Test Center and rejected a deal to get rid of the Grays.

"At this point, it became apparent to all involved that there was no such thing as God, at least how the public perceives God. Certainly some form of computer recorder stores information and an occasional miracle is displayed by the aliens to influence a religious event. This so unnerved Eisenhower that he had 'In God We Trust' put on paper money and coins and put it in the Pledge of Allegiance to reaffirm the public belief in God. Shortly after this, it was determined in meetings between the U.S. and the Russians that the situation was serious enough that a COLD WAR should be manufactured as a ruse to divert attention away from UFOs and towards some other scary threat like the H-Bomb. It was also decided to keep the ruse secret from any elected or appointed officials within both the U.S. and USSR governments. It was decided that the ruse was easier to manage if the top people didn't know about it. ...

"When the bogus Russian threat began to fade, we introduced Vietnam which kept the public occupied for over 10 years. The cover-up and personnel to run the operation began to get bigger and bigger and required more and more money. We were forced to inflate the Defense budget. Then we got into the drug business..."

Lear says President John F. Kennedy was killed because he planned to release what little information he knew about the aliens. "After Kennedy, we never told any President anything. Nixon knew because he was briefed as Vice President in 1952. That's how he knew to take Jackie Gleason to Homestead AFB to see the alien bodies we had in storage there."

Given this kind of cover-up of a continuing invasion, Lear argues, who would be willing to release the truth, especially if we had no weapons to fight the invaders?

WHERE TO FIND THE DOCUMENTS

United States

Air Force:
http://search.dma.mil/search?q=project+blue+book&btnG.x=0&btnG.y=0 &client=AFLI (this is a series of links to search results for Project Blue Book)

http://search.dma.mil/search?q=ufo&site=AFLINK&btnG=Search&entqr=0 &output=xml_no_dtd&sort=date%3AD%3AL%3Ad1&client=AFLINK&btnG.

y=0&btnG.x=0&ud=1&oe=UTF-8&ie=UTF-8&proxystylesheet=AFLINK&site=AFLINK

(This is a series of links to search results for UFO

Central Intelligence Agency: http://www.foia.cia.gov/ufo.asp

Federal Bureau of Investigation: http://foia.fbi.gov/foiaindex/ufo.htm

Library of Congress UFO page: http://www.loc.gov/rr/scitech/tracer-bullets/ufostb.html

National Aeronautics and Space Administration: http://www.nasa.gov/vision/space/travelinginspace/no_ufo.html (an explanation of a single sighting)

National Archives: http://www.archives.gov/foia/ufos.html

National Security Agency: http://www.nsa.gov/public_info/declass/ufo/index.shtml

National Technical Information Service: http://www.ntis.gov/search/index.aspx

This is the search page for the NTIS.

Office of the Secretary of Defense and Joint Staff: http://www.dod.gov/pubs/foi/ufo/

For an unofficial, but comprehensive, review of government secrecy, visit "Declassified Documents

and Other Sources for Secrets," compiled by the Michigan State University Libraries, at http://staff.lib.msu.edu/foxre/declass.html,

Brazil

http://www.ufo.com.br/index.php?arquivo=notComp.php&id=4438 (This is a link to UFO Magazine of Brazil, obviously an unofficial site. It notes that the files are provided at the initiative of Brazilian Committee of Ufologists (CBU).

Canada

http://www.collectionscanada.gc.ca/databases/ufo/index-e.html

Denmark

http://forsvaret.dk/FTK/Nyt%20og%20Presse/Nyhedsarkiv/nyheder/2009/Pages/UFO.aspx (This is the news release on the files, with links to the download sites; the files are large and take a long time to load)

A discussion of the documents that Google can translate can be found at http://www.sufoi.dk/ufo-mail/2009/um09-105.php#01. SUFOI is Skandinavisk UFO Information.

France

http://www.cnes.fr/web/CNES-en/5038-geipan.php

Great Britain

Ministry of Defence UFO pages

Cosford Incident: http://www.mod.uk/DefenceInternet/FreedomOfInformation/PublicationScheme/SearchPublicationScheme/UnidentifiedFlyingObjectsufoCosfordIncident1993.htm:

UFO Reports 1997-2007: http://www.mod.uk/DefenceInternet/FreedomOfInformation/PublicationScheme/SearchPublicationScheme/UfoReportsInTheUk.htm

UFO Reports Feb.-Apr 1993: http://www.mod.uk/NR/rdonlyres/43874D02-7CA6-48C7-BAF7-E47AB8FBFA2A/0/ufo_report_febtoapr93_enc.pdf

Alleged UFO Incident at Felpham, October 4, 2007: http://www.mod.uk/DefenceInternet/FreedomOfInformation/DisclosureLog/SearchDisclosureLog/AllegedUfoIncidentAtFelpham.htm

Alleged UFO Incident at Llanilar, January 1983: http://www.mod.uk/DefenceInternet/FreedomOfInformation/DisclosureLog/SearchDisclosureLog/AllegedUfoIncidentAtLlanilarJanuary1983.htm

News Release, Ministry of Defence Releases Further UFO Files, May 14, 2009:

http://www.mod.uk/DefenceInternet/DefenceNews/DefencePolicyAndBusiness/MinistryOfDefenceReleasesFurtherUfoFiles.htm

National Archives: http://www.nationalarchives.gov.uk/ufos/

NOTE: Great Britain requires a fee to download the documents.

Notes: All URLs for Web sites were valid when this was written in April 2010, and were copied and pasted from a Web browser address bar to avoid typos.

There is some confusion whether this photograph was taken over Maryland or the Edwards Air Force Base in California. But judging by the landscape, it seems that the photo was taken over Maryland. The photo was taken in 1954 and not in 1957, as mentioned in several articles.

GOING ON THE RECORD ABOUT UFOs

Over the years, numerous politicians, astronauts and military personnel have made public statements supporting the reality of the UFO phenomenon. Here is just a sampling of what's been stated on the record, by people whose words carry a significant amount of import.

"I've been convinced for a long time that the flying saucers are real and interplanetary. In other words, we are being watched by beings from outer space."

Albert M. Chop,
Deputy Public Relations Director for NASA and former
U.S. Air Force spokesman for Project Blue Book.

"When the long awaited solution to the UFO problem comes, I believe it will prove to be not merely the next small step in the march of science but a mighty and totally unexpected quantum leap. We had a job to do, whether right or wrong, to keep the public from getting excited."

Dr. J. Allen Hynek,
Director of the U.S. Air Force's Project Blue Book and a scientific
consultant as an astronomer, investigator and analyst.

"Of course it is possible that UFOs really do contain aliens as many people believe, and the government is hushing it up. To my mathematical brain, the numbers alone make thinking about aliens perfectly rational. The real challenge is to work out what aliens might actually be like."

Professor Stephen Hawking,
world renowned scientist.

"Given the millions of Earth-like planets, life elsewhere in the Universe, without a doubt, does exist. In the vastness of the Universe, we are not alone."

Albert Einstein.

"It is my thesis that flying saucers are real and that they are spaceships from another solar system. There is no doubt in my mind that these objects are interplanetary craft of some sort. I and my colleagues are confident that they do not originate in our solar system."

Dr. Herman Oberth,
the father of modern rocketry.

"Extraterrestrial contact is a real phenomenon. The Vatican is receiving much information about extraterrestrials and their contacts with humans from its embassies in various countries, such as Mexico, Chile and Venezuela."

Monsignor Corrado Balducci,
a Vatican theological insider close to the Pope. Balducci is also a member of a Vatican commission looking into extraterrestrial encounters and how to cope with the emerging general realization of contact.

"I am convinced that these objects do exist and that they are not manufactured by any nations on Earth."

Air Chief Marshall Dowding,
Commander-in-chief of the
British Royal Air Force Fighter Command.

"The UFO phenomenon being reported is something real and not visionary or fictitious."

General Nathan Twining,
Chairman Joint Chiefs of Staff, 1955-1958.

"With control of the universe at stake, a crash program is imperative. We produced the A-bomb, under the huge Manhattan Project, in an amazingly short time. The needs, the urgency today, are even greater. The Air Force should end UFO secrecy and give the facts to scientists, the public, to Congress. Once the people realize the truth, they would back, even demand, a crash program for this race we dare not lose."

Major Donald E. Keyhoe, USMC, Director of the National Investigations Committee on Aerial Phenomena.

"Unknown objects are operating under intelligent control. It is imperative that we learn where UFOs come from and what their purpose is. I can tell you, behind the scenes, high-ranking military officers are soberly concerned about UFOs."

Admiral Roscoe Hillenkoetter, former Director of the Central Intelligence Agency.

"I can assure you that flying saucers, given that they exist, are not constructed by any power on Earth."

President Harry S Truman.

"The U.S. Air Force assures me that UFOs pose no threat to National Security."

President John F. Kennedy

"I certainly believe in aliens in space, and that they are indeed visiting our planet. They may not look like us, but I have very strong feelings that they have advanced beyond our mental capabilities. Flying saucers – Unidentified Flying Objects – or whatever you call them, are real."

Senator Barry Goldwater.

"I strongly recommend that there be a committee investigation of the UFO phenomenon. I think we owe it to the people to establish credibility regarding UFOs and to produce the greatest possible enlightenment on this subject."

President Gerald Ford,
speaking in 1966 when he was still a Michigan Congressman.

"I don't laugh at people anymore when they say they've seen UFOs. I've seen one myself!"

President Jimmy Carter,
during his presidential campaign.

"I looked out the window and saw this white light. It was zigzagging around. I went up to the pilot and said, 'Have you ever seen anything like that?' He was shocked and he said, 'Nope.' And I said to him, 'Let's follow it.' We followed it for several minutes. It was a bright white light. We followed it to Bakersfield and all of a sudden, to our utter amazement, it went straight up into the heavens. When I got off the plane, I told Nancy all about it."

President Ronald Reagan,
describing his 1974 UFO encounter to a Wall Street Journal reporter.

"I think how quickly our differences worldwide would vanish if we were facing an alien threat from outside this world. And I ask you, does not this threat already exist?"

President Ronald Reagan,
in his 1987 U.N. address.

"The phenomenon of UFOs does exist, and it must be treated seriously."

Mikhail Gorbachev.

"I'm not at liberty to discuss the government's knowledge of UFOs at this time. I am still being personally briefed on the subject!"

President Richard M. Nixon.

"We all know that UFOs are real. All we need to ask is where do they come from and what do they want? All Apollo and Gemini flights were followed, both at a distance and sometimes quite closely, by space vehicles of extraterrestrial origin – flying saucers or UFOs, if you want to call them by that name. Every time it occurred, the astronauts informed Mission Control, who then ordered absolute silence."

Apollo 14 Astronaut
Captain Edgar Mitchell.

"I did see an object; I don't know what it was."

Clare Booth Luce, former ambassador to Italy, who with many others sighted a UFO in Rome.

"The evidence available is convincing enough to arouse a continuous and fervent interest. If it is true that the U.S. Air Force withholds tale-telling facts, then one can only say that this is the most un-psychological and stupid policy one could invent. The public ought to be told the truth."

Dr. Carl G. Jung, famed psychologist, writing to NICAP Director Donald E. Keyhoe.

"Congressional investigations are being held on the problem of UFOs. Most of the material is classified; hearings are never printed."

Representative William H. Ayres of Ohio.

Website Addresses For Interviewees

If you'd like to learn more about the exciting work of the personalities interviewed for this book, visit their websites!

- Stephen Bassett/The Paradigm Research Group
  www.paradigmresearchgroup.org

- Grant Cameron/The Presidents UFO Website
  www.presidentialufo.com

- Nick Pope's Official Website
  www.nickpope.net

- John Greenewald, The Black Vault
  www.theblackvault.com

- Antonio Huneeus, Investigative Reporter
  www.openminds.tv

- **Free Subscription to Conspiracy Journal E-Mail Newsletter**
  www.conspiracyjournal.com

Concludes on following Page >

Credit Card Hotline: 732-602-3407 · PayPal: MrUFO8@hotmail.com

HIDDEN MONASTERY IN THE ANDES HOSTS MAGICAL SUN DISK!

MAGICAL RELIC OF LOST CONTINENT SECRETLY BROUGHT TO PERU BY ELDER RACE OF GIANTS

The Golden Sun Disc of MU was not made of ordinary gold, but was transmuted gold, and unusual in its qualities in that it was a translucent metal similar, evidently, to the 'metal you can almost look through' of the UFOs.

Held by ropes of pure gold in a shrine in the greatest Temple of the Divine Light of the Motherland of MU, the gigantic Golden Disc of the Sun was placed on an altar, which was a pillar carved out of solid stone, there blazed the eternal white Light of the crystalline Maxin Flame, the Divine Limitless Light of Creation. About 30,000 BC the Maxin Light went out because of the evil of some of the priest-scientists of Mu. The Sun Disc remained in its shrine, however, until the time of the final destruction and submergence of 10-12,000 BC. The Disc eventually found its way to Lake Titicaca and was placed in a subterranean temple of the Monastery of the Brotherhood of the Seven Rays. Here it was used not only by the students of life daily, but also by the Masters and Saints from the Mystery Schools throughout the world so that they might be teleported back and forth to sit in Council or to participate in some Transmission Ceremony.

EXISTENCE OF SUN DISC SOON TO BE REVEALED TO BRING GREAT BENEFITS TO THE WORLD!

When the spiritually advanced race of giants came to Peru they placed the Disc of the Sun in a specially constructed Garden of Gold where it will remain until the day "when man is spiritually ready" to receive it and use it once again. On that day the Golden Disc will be taken out of its subterranean chamber and placed high above the Monastery of the Brotherhood. For many miles the pilgrims of the New Dawn will see it once again reflecting the glorious rays of the Sun. Coming from it will be an undeniable tone of purest harmony that will bring many followers of light up the foot-worn path to the ancient gate of the Brotherhood of the Seven Rays and they shall enter the Valley of the Blue Moon for fellowship.

This book details the extraordinary adventures of Brother Phillip in this lofty ashram high above the world, out of sight of prying eyes who would like to capture the Sun Disc for less than benevolent purposes, as good versus evil in these End Days.

EXTRA BONUS MATERIAL. An Appendix has been added to the original work by Brother Phillips updating his material with several recent articles contributed by those who acknowledge the existence of MU and its connection with the Andes.

Add a copy of **SECRET OF THE ANDES** by Brother Phillip to your personal literary collection today—**$20.00 + $5 S/H:**

INNER LIGHT · Box 753 · New Brunswick, NJ 08903
Credit Card Hotline: 732-602-3407 · PayPal: MrUFO8@hotmail.com

IF YOU HAVEN'T ORDERED RECENTLY - PLEASE DO SO TO REMAIN ON OUR MAILING LIST! OURS IS A VITAL SERVICE. . .KEEP INFORMED OF THE TRUTH!

CONTINUED ON NEXT PAGE >

SUBTERRANEAN WORLDS INSIDE EARTH by Timothy Green Beckley

Is the earth hollow? Is our planet honeycombed with caverns inhabited with a mysterious race? Are there civilizations of super beings living beneath the surface? Here are strange and unexplainable legends of the "Wee People," the Dero, and long-haired Atlantean giants! ISBN: 0-938294-22-1 • $14.95

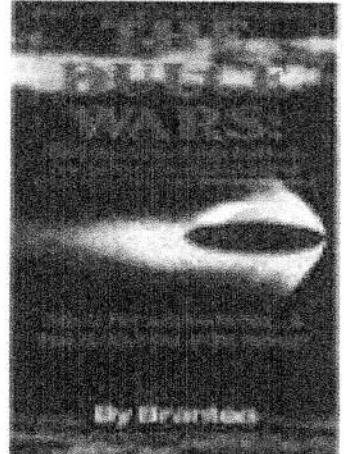

THE DULCE WARS: UNDERGROUND ALIEN BASES AND THE BATTLE FOR PLANET EARTH by Branton

In the corner of a small town in America's Southwest, something very strange is going on! An alien Fifth Column is already active on Earth and may be preparing for global conquest. Dulce, New Mexico is the epicenter of cattle mutilations; energy grids; secret societies; underground anomalies; conspiracies between townfolk and "outsiders;" unexplained legends; lost civilizations, as well as abductions and missing time. ISBN: 1-892062-12-7 • $17.50

UFOS, PROPHECY AND THE END OF TIME by Sean Casteel

Is this mankind's final wakeup call? Explores Terrorism in America! Violence Overseas! War In The Middle East! Natural Disasters Worldwide! Man versus Nature! Religious Jihad, and unholy perversion in the Church. But, perhaps most important, almost ignored, is the worldwide appearance of UFOs and the abduction of humans by what may well be the "gods of old." This volume draws from Biblical prophecy and reliable UFOlogical sources and represents a divine revelation from The Heavenly Ones On High. ISBN 1-892062-35-6 • $16.95

THE LONG LOST BOOKS OF T. LOBSANG RAMPA FEATURING: MY VISIT TO AGHARTA by T. Lobsang Rampa—For decades Rampa's books brought great enlightenment, comfort and joy to millions who have repeatedly clambered for more of his enchanting narratives, despite the fact that he has been deceased for more than a decade. Recently a "lost" manuscript was discovered detailing Rampa's journey to Agharta, the sacred underground land in the hollow earth. This previously unknown land is populated by enlightened masters of great wisdom. Also in this book are excerpts from some of previously unavailable works. Topics include: Death and Life on the "Other Side;" Other Dimensions; Astral Projection; Contact With The Space Brothers. ISBN: 1-89206-34-5 • $19.95

MJ-12 AND THE RIDDLE OF HANGAR 18: THE NEW EVIDENCE by Timothy Green Beckley with Sean Casteel—Stored away in a secret underground hangar are the remains of the UFO that crashed at Roswell. According to the author, the last eight presidents have been in on the ultimate deception...a "Cosmic Watergate!" Over 60 cases of crashed UFOs are documented, offering proof of the existence of MJ-12 and the Interplanetary Phenomenon Unit involved in the recovery of crashed UFOs and their occupants. ISBN: 1-892062-53-4 • $24.95

NEW MAGICK HANDBOOK: SIMPLE SPELLS FOR A COMPLEX WORLD by Dragonstar—Utilize everyday items to promote success: candles, crystals, herbs, gemstones, pendulum, charms, incantations and other proven methods of empowerment. The author is a mystic and occult adept who learned the science of alchemy and other universal laws. Here are spells and rituals to promote good health; encourage love; succeed in business; rid yourself of unwanted relationship and MORE!

ISBN: 1-892062-19-4 • $14.95

A NEW BOOK OF REVELATIONS as Channeled through Tuella—This work corrects many of the misconceptions and inaccurate translations of the Old and New Testaments and lays the foundation for a New Book of Revelations as transcribed from the highest spiritual powers of the Universe. Shocking revelations include: The true meaning of 666; The special significance of the 13th Vortex; How the Primary Channel for this work was able to thwart the forces of darkness and facilitate the departure of the "Fallen Ones;" How God's rebellious son Jehovahn inserted distortions into the original Biblical Scriptures to create disharmony; How a legion of Angels will protect you personally during a global war. Tuella's other works include: Project World Evacuation and Ashtar, A Tribute.

ISBN: 0-938-294-85-7 • $14.00

Global Communications, Box 753, New Brunswick, NJ 08903
Credit Card Orders 732 602-3407 MRUFO8@hotmail.com

Printed in Great Britain
by Amazon

55047103R00165